"I've spent considerable time worrying about your best interests, Genny,"

Odessa drawled. "My conclusion—should you wish to hear it—is that we make a detour to New York first."

"You," Genny shot back, "are not worried about my best interests, Odessa Gold, so don't pretend otherwise."

"Hey, Angel, didn't I say that Genny should have a decent wardrobe before she tries to find some wealthy old coot to marry her?"

"I wouldn't touch that one with asbestos gloves, Odessa," Angel answered.

With her eyes raised to heaven, Genny ground her teeth.

Odessa's smirk was guileless. "Genny, Genny, Genny." He shook his head woefully. "If you want to attract a husband, you're definitely going to have to buy new clothes, show a bit of shoulder. You know, a little more . . ." He outlined a woman's figure with his hands. "Old men . . ."

Genny wanted to scream at him. She wanted to slap his sanctimonious face!

"Forgive me. I should have said 'gentlemen of a more genteel age.' Whatever, they tend to require a bit more stimulation. . . ."

Dear Reader,

Welcome to the world of Harlequin Historicals. This month, we bring you another tale from the faraway islands of Hawaii with Donna Anders's *Ketti*, the story of the daughter of Mari and Adam from the author's April release, *Mari*.

For those of you who have long enjoyed her contemporaries, we are pleased to have *Odessa Gold*, Linda Shaw's first Harlequin Historical. Don't miss this delightful tale of honor and betrayal set against the backdrop of turn-of-the-century high society in Saratoga Springs and New York City.

Private Paradise by popular author Lucy Elliot and Jennifer West's first historical romance, *Passion's Legacy*, complete the roster. To start your summer reading off right, look for all four Harlequin Historicals at your local bookstore.

From all of us at Harlequin Historicals, our best wishes for a relaxing and enjoyable summer.

Yours,

Tracy Farrell
Senior Editor

Odessa Gold

Linda Shaw

Harlequin Books

TORONTO • NEW YORK • LONDON
AMSTERDAM • PARIS • SYDNEY • HAMBURG
STOCKHOLM • ATHENS • TOKYO • MILAN

Harlequin Historicals first edition June 1991

ISBN 0-373-28680-5

ODESSA GOLD

LINDA SHAW

saw years of hard work come to fruition during the 1980s with the publication of numerous contemporary and historical novels. A decade of writing is now behind her, and she shows no signs of slowing down. She lives with her husband in Keene, Texas, where she surrounds herself with her children and three young grandchildren.

To Betty Hopmann,
who has an eagle's eye for typos
and
to Shelley Webb, my daughter,
whose taste I value deeply.

Chapter One

Wyoming, 1897

The Wyoming State Prison, old-timers liked to say, was Hell's angry fist shaking at heaven.

Sweltering beneath a ferocious July sun, Governor Nathan Hodges waited outside its forbidding stone walls and agreed completely. Waiting was one of Hodges's two pet peeves. The other was his wife, but Beatrice was in Cheyenne, cool, elegant and inebriated in the governor's mansion.

Hodges, meanwhile, was blotting sweat from his meticulously fringed scalp and wiping the lenses of his rimless spectacles while he cursed the man who had caused this hasty trip from the capitol. Beside the luxurious lacquered coach, eight mounted outriders were shifting restlessly in their creaking saddles. This was sagebrush country. Here, it grew as high as a man was tall, but the ground around the prison was devoid of anything more than scrawny thistle, packed hard from the constant traffic required to keep law and order in the West.

Hodges replaced his spectacles and ran his fingers absently behind his ears. High atop a pole at the prison gates, a flag was snapping and whipping in the hot wind. The only thing that relieved the scene of despair were the mountains thrusting in the distance—eternal, serene, promising wide blue-green rivers and rampant evergreens.

Hodges looked at his watch for the dozenth time. Half-past noon. *That bastard Potanski. He enjoys making me wait.*

A guard bent low in his saddle to peer inside the coach, sending the stench of dust filtering through the window. "You want I should go make inquiries, Your Honor?"

"No, no." Snapping the watch closed, Hodges mopped his neck with a silk handkerchief monogrammed by his sainted mother. "It's better out here than inside with those savages. Potanski knows I'm here molding like a musk-melon."

If Hodges could have found anyone to run the prison half as well as Potanski, he would have replaced the warden years ago. But a special breed was needed to deal with cold-blooded criminals, so Hodges learned to live with Potanski, and Potanski continued to vote for Hodges's opponents.

"He's here, sir," one of the guards informed him as a flurry occurred at the prison gates.

Hodges made sure his bow tie was properly straight and then sucked in his breath to button his waistcoat over his prim little paunch. He picked up his Panama hat, the headgear that fashion-conscious men in the East were wearing this season, and settled it on his balding head.

The driver climbed down from his perch and opened the carriage door. A step swung out, and Hodges placed a small Cordovan shoe upon it as he snapped his fingers.

Two guards dismounted. They knew the drill and closed ranks. They gave the cylinders of their Smith and Wessons a whirring spin and speared them into their holsters, then swaggered toward the wooden gates with a chorus of spitting tobacco and clanking spurs.

The open gates afforded only a narrow glimpse of the misery inside, as two prison guards emerged to stand at attention like bookends. Warden Potanski and a tall, work-hardened inmate stepped between them and out through the gates.

The prisoner was a head taller than Potanski and two heads taller than the governor. A wilted, flat-crowned hat splotched with sweat stains threw much of his face into shadow. His mouth was half-hidden by a coffee-colored mustache, and his jaw was partially concealed by a stubble of several days' growth. He was only thirty-three, but he looked forty-three.

Hodges sighed. When the prisoner squinted, his lips drew back from teeth that were large and strong and white. His brown suit was a decade out of fashion and hung on him like a sack. With his weight shunted to one hip, he gave the impression of nonchalance, but there was something about him that gave a person pause.

Ten years in this place, Hodges thought with a grudging flicker of admiration, and you still aren't broken.

The man gave no evidence of hearing a word Potanski was saying. When the warden finished, he inclined his head to Hodges as if to say, You wanted 'im, you got 'im. Then Potanski snapped a salute, turned on his heel and disappeared back through the opening in the gates.

Hodges could feel the sun burning his scalp through his hat. "Don't do anything unless I tell you to," he instructed his guards as they approached the prisoner, their movements kicking up a storm of dust. "And for pity's sake, give me space, McPherson."

McPherson was a gangly ex-cattle drover with the best aim in the county and a quick temper to match. His fingers opened and shut above his handgun.

"Wouldn't trust 'im, if it was me, sir," he advised. "Man's a killer."

"Yes, well, he won't try anything here."

"Wouldn't bet on it."

Hodges was near enough to see the deep lines scoring the man's face and the wicked scar that jagged from his right cheekbone to his mustache.

"Easy now." He held out his hand to stop his men. "Don't get trigger-happy."

"Governor," the prisoner raised a voice embroidered with mockery, "how flattering of you to come."

"This isn't a social visit," Hodges returned.

"Then you must be gearing up for another four years at the mansion."

Hodges flinched before the man's gunpowder-gray eyes. Shrugging, the prisoner took several steps toward the mountains. He shifted his weight, as if impatient to be on his way.

"It didn't need to be this way, you know," Hodges reminded him.

"I did what I had to do."

"I'm just saying, you could've been released much sooner. I want you to understand that."

"Consider it understood. Is that all you came to say, Governor?"

A rutted road snaked across the plain and then split, one end angling toward Laramie, the other to Cheyenne. The man hooked his thumbs in the back pockets of his trousers and pondered the road.

"Dammit!" shouted Hodges.

The convict swung around, and the bitterness between them was suddenly as sharp as a bath of acid. Hodges could feel the man's scorn, and he shot his guards a nervous warning.

"Why don't you say what you came to say, Governor?" the man said at last, though his gaze became fixed on the prison, as if he wanted to make one final commitment to memory before leaving. "It would save a great deal of time all the way around."

Hodges blotted his forehead. He was sweating like a pig. "You're right, of course," he wheezed. "But you refused to respond to my letters. You've refused to see me when I've come here, at no small convenience, I might add. Do you think I can afford to waste time on you? This is the last time I'll ask. Bring charges against McFee and Platt.

You're out of here now. You can disappear. They won't be able to find you."

"You came for *that*?" The man's smile reached the corners of his mouth in a malicious curl. "You just wasted yourself a trip to hell, Governor."

"You're tying my hands!" How dare this scum of society use such a tone with him? "Can't you see that, you fool? You're crippling me! They're guilty. You're impeding justice. You *have* to press charges!"

In three steps, the convict was towering over Hodges, his feet planted well apart and the lines in his face threatening. The guards closed in, and Hodges, his heart beating in a fearful cadence, threw out both hands to waylay them.

"Keep back!"

"I don't have to do anything on God's earth except die," the man snarled. "And if you think I care about that—" he stabbed a finger at Hodges's wilting shirt front "—*you're* the fool."

"You mongrel dog!" McPherson yelled and spat into the dust. "You can't talk to the governor of Wyoming like that!"

McPherson whipped his .45 from its holster and darted from behind Hodges. Lunging toward the prisoner and shoving the barrel into his ribs, he was thrown off guard when the man grinned and held up both hands in a placid surrender.

"Easy, easy," he soothed. "No need to get all riled. We're reasonable men here. Everything can be negotiated."

McPherson swaggered with a lusty bravado and hitched at his pants with a this-is-how-you-handle-white-trash look. "That's more like it."

Before the words were finished, the convict whirled. With a blur of dexterity, he deflected the .45 with the side of his hand. The next thing McPherson knew he was being grabbed from behind and his throat pinioned in a headlock that threatened to crush his windpipe. Gagging, he felt the barrel of the .45 jab into his right ear.

"You were saying, my friend?" the prisoner grated between bared teeth. "Do you know, I could snap your neck without even working up a sweat. Or I could shoot you in your ear. Might have a chance that way. Doesn't always kill you right off, you know. You could live for hours."

McPherson's whimper was a plea for mercy, and Hodges hurried desperately toward them.

"No! No, please," he begged the prisoner. "There's no need for this. Please, it was my fault. Let him go, let him go."

The man's gray eyes glittered as he confronted the governor. Wolf's eyes, Hodges thought with a shiver.

With a stab of the gun barrel that made McPherson howl, the man thrust him away. McPherson bent over and cupped his ear with his hand, rocking with pain.

"All right," Hodges conceded shakily, and removed his silk handkerchief to wipe away the sweat streaming into his eyes. "We'll let the matter rest. Everything is fine, just fine. You don't have to press charges against anyone."

"Why, thank you, Governor." The ex-convict's snort of disdain was as insulting as his move had been unpredictable. He sent McPherson's .45 spinning into the sunshine like a child's Fourth of July rocket, and none of the guards dared make a move to retrieve it when it struck the ground a short distance away.

Hodges regretted having come to the prison at all. This man could not be reasoned with; he could not be flattered. How did one deal with someone who refused to be flattered?

"I misread you," he confessed. "I thought you cared about justice. You killed a man, and you claimed it was because no one would bring him to justice. Now I'm trying to bring the other two men to trial, and you won't help."

Shrugging, the man insolently turned his back. "Let it alone, Governor. Go back to your safe pretty mansion and drink wine from your crystal goblets with your beautiful wife. Let the dark forces of the world take care of their own."

"So, you intend to take the law into your own hands?" he bawled as the ex-convict began walking way. "Again?"

The man gave no indication of having heard him. The sun splintered hotly upon his back, and his shadow danced jaggedly alongside as his shabby boots kicked up tiny thunderheads of dust. He walked with the loose-jointed disinterest of a man who has faced his own mortality and no longer gives a damn.

Hodges wished he had a reason to throw the man back into prison for another ten years.

"Things have changed since you went inside!" he bellowed, smelling his own failure. "Your enemies have grown powerful. D'you think you're going to waltz back into life and pick up where you left it? You got stripes on your skin, mister! You're going to wish you had a friend! Are you listening to me?"

The man kept on walking until he was swallowed up by the purple sagebrush that weaved serenely in the wind.

Nathan Hodges returned to his carriage in disgust. "And you'd damn sure better guard your back," he muttered vindictively. "That's all I've got to say."

The driver, melting in his livery, peered into the carriage. "Your Honor?"

"What are you waiting for?" Hodges snapped as he unbuttoned his soggy jacket and peeled it off. "Let's get out of here. Wait! McPherson, come here."

The driver stayed the reins. McPherson, burning with murderous rage, guided his horse to the window of the coach and peered in, his ear bruised purple and swollen.

"Send one of the guards to follow that man," Hodges directed. "I want to know everywhere he goes and who he sees. And you, ride on ahead to town. Send a telegram to McFee about his release."

"In your name, sir?" McPherson was confused.

"Use a fictitious name, any name. McFee'll know where the wire comes from, in any case."

"Yessir."

Hodges climbed into the luxurious interior of the carriage. He wanted the arrest of C. E. McFee and Manville Platt so badly his bones hurt. He wanted to reopen the case and break it wide from coast to coast. With the coverage, his third term would be guaranteed. Perhaps the beginning of the dream he hadn't shared with anyone yet, not even with Imogene: the White House.

Well, there was more than one way to get what he wanted. Politics, like God, worked in mysterious ways. Meanwhile, there was work to be done, and he wanted out of this blasted heat!

He sagged against the seat as the heavy coach with its high-stepping thoroughbreds jostled down the rough road, returning him to Cheyenne and the mansion and Beatrice and his sainted mother and the beautiful crystal goblets.

Chapter Two

Genevieve Carlyle sat brooding about her virginity and other equally pressing matters. All afternoon the train had been whizzing across the state at an exciting twenty-five miles an hour. It had streaked from Cheyenne down through the southeastern corner of Wyoming—an arid, forbidding place so devoid of vegetation that vultures wheeled and tilted overhead and ravenous hawks scanned miles in search of some delicacy, perhaps a snake or unfortunate prairie dog.

Four riders crested the sandstone ledge and paused there, silhouetted against the sky with their dusters spread across the rumps of their horses and rifles nested in their saddle scabbards. Their hats were pushed back on their heads as they gazed down at the puffing train. Framed by the window with the sun exploding at their backs, they looked for all the world like a painting by Remington.

Genny dismissed them with a shrug as the coach jostled on. Cattlemen, probably. Out harassing some poor sheepmen. Or vice versa. The range wars weren't her problem at the moment. Old-maid-schoolmarm jokes were her problem. And hunger. Especially hunger.

After she reached St. Louis, the problem of hunger would be solved, at least. Both problems, actually; she would be Mrs. Adam Worthington, the mystery of her virginity would be ended and life would be better. In St. Louis, she wouldn't teach school for months on end without being paid, and the winters didn't kill people. When she went to sleep, her belly wouldn't gnaw because she'd slipped most of her food onto the plate of an unsuspecting Jessamine.

Months before, Adam had gone ahead to prepare the way—to mend a few fences, he had said, and she'd surmised a history of bad feelings with his father, who was a successful physician in St. Louis. It was ironic—Adam, cowpoking around Wyoming, starving when he could be living in a city where one could buy a newspaper every day and fresh fruit and tickets to the ballet.

"Where are we now, Geneena?" Jessamine MacGowan asked as the locomotive belched a great cloud of soot and stench into the defeated July sky.

Seventy-two years had creped Jessamine's skin and turned her thin hands the color of parchment. Jessamine MacGowan was her dearest friend in the world, the mother she had never truly had. She was reed-thin and always smelled of lavender. Genny adored her.

"We're ten miles farther from Cheyenne than we were the last time you asked," Genny teased fondly. "And ten miles closer to St. Louis."

Jessamine's fingers probed behind her ears for her spectacles, the lenses of which were small and round and black. As if she could actually see through them, she pulled them off and blew her breath and wiped them with the hem of her best calico dress.

"Ten miles closer to Denver, Geneena," she corrected politely.

Genny laughed. "Yes, Jessamine, ten miles closer to Denver. And ten miles closer to Kansas City and ten miles closer to St. Louis. Why don't you take my seat on this side, where I'm all to myself? You can lie down and take a nap. When you wake up, we can share the sandwich."

"Oh, no dear. I wouldn't dream of it." Another passenger dozed on the seat, next to Jessamine, and she'd been meticulously diligent lest she take up more than her fair share of space.

She whispered, too, so as not to disturb the man's sleep. "You eat the sandwich. I insist. You must keep up your strength, Geneena. I'm perfectly fine where I am, perfectly fine." She smoothed her skirt. "And I'm not hungry at all. I couldn't eat a bite, not a single bite."

As if to prove her point, the woman felt about for her knitting, a half-finished green sock. Knitting was the only thing Jessamine could do now that her eyesight had failed, and even that was laborious, for she was constantly dropping stitches. With her spine as straight as one of her needles, she fervently began to knit and purl.

Genny opened the bag at her feet and peered longingly at the sandwich wrapped in heavy paper, but snapped it shut before she could weaken. "You're paying your way, Jessamine. And more."

"Tsk, tsk. My few pennies don't begin to cover the cost of expenses."

"Will you stop keeping score?"

"And I don't intend to intrude upon your and Adam's plans, believe me. I've always said, young people need to be with folks their own age. You mustn't feel as if you have to arrange your life around me, Geneena. I would be most unhappy if you did."

Sometimes Jessamine's self-sufficiency had its exhausting aspects. "I'm not listening to any more of this talk, Jessamine. Now, come over here and lie down. You're the one who's going to need strength to get through the next few days."

"I can doze perfectly fine right here, dear."

So saying, Jessamine dropped her knitting to her lap and dropped her silvery head to her chest.

Genny pinched the bridge of her nose with a weary groan. "I swear, Jessamine MacGowan, you'll make me old before my time. Soon this red hair of mine will be gray as a rat's."

The old woman tucked a smile into her staid ruched collar. "Gray is your best color, Geneena."

Laughing softly, Genny leaned back and slid a speculative look at the man sprawled so negligently in the seat beside Jessamine. He'd been sleeping when they boarded at Cheyenne. With his wilted hat pulled low, all one could see of his face was a mustache, the beginning scythe of a beard and a disorderly shock of chocolate-colored hair. She and Jessamine had been obliged to literally pick up their skirts and climb over the man's legs. After all their shifting and whispering and settling in, he'd done nothing more than mumble in his sleep and sprawl even lower on the seat.

Now his legs were extending rudely into her own meager foot space. She considered giving him a kick to nudge him onto his own side. Accidentally, of course. But to annoy a stranger whose eyes she hadn't looked into was too much like stuffing one's hand into a dark hole in the ground.

A hail of cinders rained back into the coach, and she brushed them from her skirt, continuing to resent the man's boots—too paper-thin, disgustingly run-down at the heels and mended in the wrong places to be a cowboy's. His suit, brown and surprisingly well-tailored if out of date, hung on his frame as if he hadn't eaten in months.

He shifted onto his side and mumbled something beneath his hat. Genny drew back with a start, then glanced around warily to see if anyone was watching.

Most of the passengers in the coach were dozing, though one elderly couple had spread napkins upon their laps and were happily peeling boiled eggs. At the opposite end of the car, a mother was crooning to a fretting baby.

Sucking pensively on her lip, Genny placed the toe of her shoe against the man's boot, gave a vigorous shove and bobbed briskly around to stare out the window, a picture of innocence.

The man snorted and at that moment Genny saw the four horsemen nosing their mounts down the side of the sandstone ledge toward the railroad tracks. She leaned sharply forward, bumping the window. Surely they weren't intending to intercept the train!

None of the other passengers appeared concerned. The riders kept coming, much faster now, their horses' heads thrusting with a steady sinister rhythm like the clatter of the iron wheels upon the rails. They signaled each other with gloved hands, and the horses, their great chests lathered and their foam-flecked mouths chewing at the bits, thundered nearer and nearer. Now they looked less like a Remington painting and more like the horsemen of the Apocalypse.

Genny touched her throat in dismay. Maybe they weren't ranchers at all. Maybe they were Jesse James and his notorious gang of thieves.

Nonsense! She should have been a writer! Nevertheless, she made sure her reticule was tucked safely between her and the side of the seat, and wasn't it fortunate that her small savings had gone on to St. Louis with Adam?

Anyway, even if the men were the most notorious thieves alive, one look at her and they would know she possessed little beyond the clothes on her back—an exhausted, brown linen skirt and a cream-colored shirt the collar and cuffs of which had been turned so many times, the only thing holding them together was starch. Her sole finery was a scrap of grosgrain ribbon at her collar. Her hat, brown straw the color of her skirt, lacked a bow or even a silk flower. Her fizzing red curls were forced into a net that was barely in one piece, and she didn't even own a pair of decent gloves.

Jessamine, blessedly, had finally succumbed to sleep, and her head lolled peacefully to one side. Genny had to smile at the boots peeping traitorously beneath the hem of the older woman's skirt. When Betty Parson's husband had died the previous spring, Betty had given Jessamine her husband's almost new boots. Jessamine had been torn between fashion and a bitterly frozen Wyoming ground. Fortunately, Dwight had possessed a small foot.

"Look," a man's voice exclaimed at the opposite end of the car.

"Well, I never . . ."

Genny peered down the center aisle. A florid-faced man with atrociously unbecoming muttonchop whiskers was weaving between the seats like a tipsy sailor. "Who do you suppose they are, Fiona?"

He stabbed at the window with the tip of his walking stick. A woman, obviously Fiona, laid her hand on her formidable bosom. "Why, I'm sure I wouldn't have an idea in the world, Papa."

Another woman chimed in with, "I do believe they intend to stop this train. Amos, could those men be brigands? Merciful heavens!" Her voice raised to an alarmed shriek. "We're going to be robbed, Amos!"

"Turkey feathers," was Amos's opinion.

"Aw, heck, ma'am," another man pleasantly scoffed. "Pardon the language, but robbin' and murderin' only happens in one o' them dime nov-ils. Somebody's got theirselves a burr under their tail, that's all. More'n likely they have t'git a message to Pres'dent Cleveland real quicklike."

"What do you think those telegraph lines are for, sir?" Amos's wife snapped peevishly. "If not for messages to President Cleveland?"

The aisle was abruptly jammed with passengers. Women fought their troublesome skirts and bustles as they stopped to squint out the windows into the blinding sunset, and men tugged at their waistcoats and mouthed that the country was going to the dogs when honest people couldn't travel in peace. The fretting baby began to wail.

"Maybe the engineer will throw on the coal and outrun the varmits."

"I got a Colt in me grip. Ya think I should get it?"

"We ain't got nothin' to worry about, folks. We'll just set, tight as ticks."

"Amos, why did you bring me out here to this godforsaken country? Indians and train robbers. That's all there is out here. I should've stayed in my father's house, that's what I should have done."

"Perhaps you should have."

Genny shot a concerned look at the man beside Jessamine. How could he sleep through this bedlam? Even Jessamine's head had popped up, and she was reaching out with the vague swimming motion of the unsighted.

"What's happening, Geneena? What's going on?"

"Some men have ridden down off the range," Genny told her. "Everyone's wondering if the train will stop."

"Will it?"

"I haven't the faintest idea."

The riders were out of sight now, and the engine's whistle continued to shrill as the smokestack spewed soot and cinders into the cars. People returned to their seats, but apprehensive whispers passed back and forth and heads jerked round at the slightest sound.

Genny considered the four dollars tied in the handkerchief inside her reticule, the sum total of her money that hadn't gone with Adam. If the men did stop the train, she, along with Fiona and Amos's wife, would be forced to hand over her bag. She'd be switched if thieves would take her last dollars that she'd gone hungry to save!

Wedging herself into the cramped space between Jessamine's feet and the man's dubious boots, she removed the handkerchief and plucked impatiently at the knot.

"Jessamine?" she whispered, turning back the hem of the woman's skirt.

"Oh!"

"Don't be frightened. Stick out your foot."

"My foot?"

"Just do it, please."

Not understanding, Jessamine nonetheless inched a boot forward, and Genny deftly untied the lace. Sliding a furtive look at the man—he was undoubtedly as deaf as Jessamine was blind!—she slipped four bills from her handkerchief and poked two against the sole of Jessamine's boot. Feeling as if *she* were the criminal, she repeated the procedure with the other boot and then retied the laces. That done, she swiveled and was in the process of rising half up, half down, when she abruptly found herself confronted by a pair of the most riveting gun-metal gray eyes she'd ever seen.

A heartbeat snagged in her throat, and her knees began to quiver as she laid her hand upon her collar.

"It's still there," he drawled in a deep voice that registered somewhere between that of a scholar and a bootleg-whiskey runner. "You're safe. Temporarily, at least."

His lips twitched in the merest hint of a smile beneath his mustache, and a scar crinkled the right side of his face from his cheek to his lip—not a thin white line but an uneven rivulet that appeared to have a violent history.

Flushing, Genny gathered her skirt in her hands and stood straight. A bootleg-whiskey runner. Definitely.

"I beg your pardon," she said and threw up the barrier that announced to the world that there were, after all, lines that must not be crossed. "I assumed you were sleeping."

"Assumptions can be a dangerous business." He touched the brim of his hat with an insolent fingertip. "Ma'am."

Did that mean he hadn't been sleeping? That all that time he'd been listening and watching? Good Lord, she'd kicked the man!

Genny dipped her head and mumbled, "Not particularly polite, if you ask me."

His chuckle was lost in the abrupt shrill of the engine's whistle. "I'm not a particularly polite man."

"Then you must be from Laramie," she snapped, dismissing him with her that-explains-everything tone. "Excuse me, please."

With as much regal bearing as was possible under the circumstances, she turned to take her seat. At that precise moment, unfortunately, the engineer chose to respond to the commands of the four riders outside. The steel brakes bit savagely into steel, and with a sound like a thousand demons in torment, the coupled cars bucked and jerked and began to skid to a stop.

Satchels and bags flew from the open racks overhead and slid down the aisle. Passengers were hurled against the seats in front of them. Gas lamps jangled on their mounts. Genny, arms waving like a windmill, was catapulted against the man before her with a force that knocked the breath from them both.

"Oh!" she gasped as her head cracked his chin and her hat was knocked, helter-skelter, into the aisle.

The man gave a muffled grunt of surprise. Genny's eyes flew open to find her nose blunted painfully against a jaw that smelled amazingly like lye soap—sharply clean. She was plastered upon him in an appalling fashion, she realized, with her hands jammed embarrassingly against his ribs and her breasts flattened to his chest and one of his knees jammed between her own in a place that not even *she* knew too much about!

The train's stop seemed to go on forever. Genny found herself abruptly planted back in her own seat as the man lunged forward and caught Jessamine just as she was being bounced toward the window glass. "Easy now, ma'am," he comforted.

Jessamine's skirt had become twisted high on her legs, and for all his questionable manners, the man twitched the garment back into place. "No harm done, Miss Jessamine."

So he had been awake the whole time, the crafty villain! He knew Jessamine's name and that she was blind. Then he had to know...what? What had she said? What could he have learned about her?

The train came to a final, shuddering stop, and the shock drifted over the car like the dust that was silting down from the luggage racks and ceilings and making passengers sputter and cough.

Slowly, people inched up to peer at one another. From far ahead came the wheeze and hiss of the steam engine's idling, the sound of men shouting. The mother attempted to shush her frightened baby. Others began to laugh nervously.

"Are you all right?" the man asked Genny.

No, she was not all right! Couldn't he see that she was about to faint because she was so un-right?

"Yes, thank you," she said, and sagged weakly back in her seat.

"Like I always say," Amos's wife was declaring with an injured sniff, "if it's not one thing, it's another."

"Would you get off my foot?" Amos said.

Suddenly Genny realized her head was bare. "My hat!" she gasped, lunging to retrieve her headgear.

"Allow me."

Quickly, for now they possessed a history, however brief and distasteful, the man scooped her hat from the floor and leaned back in his seat, cupping the poor headgear in his palms as if it were a wild creature whose life had been crushed from its little body.

"Perhaps artificial respiration would help," he mused and rubbed it against his mustache in an intimacy that sent Genny's senses toddling.

"It's quite all right, thank you," she said and quickly snatched it from his fingers, adding with a dryness that was not her usual reserve, "It never was alive."

His laughter was amazingly rich as it rang out—satisfying, like the coolness of shade on a hot day.

Jessamine was attempting to ascertain the damage done to her person, patting her head and her skirt, then searching for her knitting. "Why, I do believe I dozed off."

Genny thrust the yarn and needles into the woman's lap. "The train's stopped," she said unnecessarily and wished the man would stop staring.

"Cattle on the tracks," Jessamine said.

"I don't think so." Genny groped through her curls for pins. With a few deft twists of her wrist, she coiled her hair into a shank and captured it with the fraying net. After tying the ribbon and anchoring it with pins, she clapped her damaged hat back onto her head and held it in place with one hand while she searched for her hat pin with the other.

"What's the matter?" Jessamine asked, her intuition uncannily accurate.

"I've lost—"

"This?"

From beneath his thigh, the man withdrew five inches of hat pin that glittered with as much deadly potential as his grin.

"Oh, dear," Genny said with genuine concern. "You're not hurt, are you?"

"From this little thing?" He grinned. "No."

He thrust and parried briefly with the pin before proffering it, and Genny realized she was smiling. Exactly how many seconds she sat like that, foolishly besotted, she wasn't sure, but his smile ceased abruptly, and a shutter slammed shut over his face.

Without warning, something inside Genny shifted and realigned so that she was put together in a different way. Confused, she looked around at the sound of spurs jangling outside the car and boots clamoring up the steps and stomping briefly upon the platform.

Talk inside the car hushed. Everyone waited as if for a trap door to open. Genny glanced at the man, but his face was closed.

Well, he had his troubles, and she had her own. She considered her ringless hand. It had been at her insistence that Adam had not bought her an engagement ring. Times were too hard. Now she was glad, and she made certain that her reticule was still tucked under the folds of her skirt.

The door burst open and crashed back on its hinges. Two dust-coated men stepped into the car, the men Genny had seen on horseback. The stink of their mounts accompanied them, and in the crooks of their arms were rifles.

One positioned himself at the door and the second moved deeper into the car, then stopped, anchoring his boots to the floor.

His jacket was pulled aside so that his handgun was clearly visible. A badge gleamed from his leather vest.

"Genevieve?" Jessamine whispered fearfully.

When Jessamine used Genny's full name, she was desperate.

"Why, they're lawmen!" Genny exclaimed with a gasp of relief.

Presently the other passengers began to relax, too, pretending to their neighbors that they hadn't really been worried. The law. Why, they'd suspected it all along. Everyone would be all right now.

As Genny's own spirits brightened, she turned to see the man.

Sweat had broken out on his forehead, and a muscle was knotting in his cheek. His tension made his skin appear stretched too tightly over his bones. His whole body was strained to its limits—steel-hard, as capable of destruction, Genny thought, as the cocked trigger of a gun.

"Ladies and gentlemen," one of the lawmen announced as he waited for the stir to settle, "please be calm and remain in your seats. Leave your hands in plain sight. We regret the inconvenience and kindly request your cooperation. This will take only a moment of your time."

"What's going on, Deputy?" a man asked.

"Yes, we have the right to know."

"You there, ma'am," the deputy said, ignoring the questions, "would you keep the boy in his seat, please?"

"Genevieve?" Jessamine whispered, her arm sweeping out in a futile arc.

The man moved with the quick flash of a predator. Or was it quarry? Slipping into the seat beside Genny, his arm suddenly curving about her back so that he was surrounding her with a power she could only guess at, he speared his fingers into her hair and held her prisoner as certainly as if he had placed a blade at her throat.

Trembling gusted through Genny. She tried to lean away but could not move. "Sir!"

"Genevieve." His whisper fanned her cheek. "Genny..."

Genny's pulse lurched wildly. "Sir, I..."

His lips grazed the curls framing her ear—the merest facsimile of a kiss—and as the brim of his hat isolated them, the tremble of his whisper was as potent as a seduction. He touched her jaw with his fingertip, and Genny was immobilized by the roughness of it. Who was he? What was he doing? What was *she* doing?

"My name is Gold." His whisper was fraught with desperation. "Odessa Gold. I want you, I *need* you, Genny, to be my wife. For the next ten minutes, would you be my wife?"

Chapter Three

His name was not Odessa Gold.

Thirty-three years before, in Albany, New York, Felicia Stuart Goldman had borne her first and only son of five children—a bouncing, laughing boy who proved to have inherited the good Goldman character along with the striking Stuart beauty and artistic bent. The boy was named Andrew Stuart Goldman.

The Goldman children were given an upbringing typical of a privileged mercantile family. Excellent marriages were arranged for the daughters, and they received a healthy slice of the Goldman fortune as it rolled out of the mills, but Andrew was the one expected to carry on the family business and traditions.

As the girls were born, Felicia added to her burgeoning staff, and they, the servants, tended to all the little feminine needs. But Andrew's rearing Felicia attended to personally. She spared nothing. When Andrew was four, she whisked him off to Europe for the first time—nothing but the best for her darling.

The Goldman home was a sprawling Georgian house set on the bank of the Hudson River. There, Andrew basked in the attention of his mother. He especially liked the long morning walks in her garden where he would sit on the flagstones and sketch while Felicia did her needlepoint and spun dreams about his future.

Early on, Albany mothers with daughters to marry off went to extravagant lengths to cultivate the favor of Felicia and Morgan Goldman. One of them was Portia Houseman, who fancied her daughter, Anne, as Andrew's perfect match.

Anne Houseman was descended from a line of respected scholars. Her father, Samuel, had inherited the famous Houseman Press that had printed some of Benjamin Franklin's early works. As the Goldman millions had been created from the manufacture of paper and the Houseman millions from publishing, it seemed only fitting when Anne and Andrew married.

Soon afterward, Andrew, who possessed a good working knowledge of the paper business and had achieved a moderate amount of respect as a fledgling artist, received a handsome advance from his publisher father-in-law to undertake an illustrated history of the American West.

It was the chance of a lifetime! At the tender age of twenty-three, Andrew took his new bride and six brass-bound trunks on a combination honeymoon and business trip.

For eight months the newlyweds traveled. Anne soon became pregnant, but since she was one of the new, free-thinking young women, she refused to stop traveling and go into seclusion. Besides, she was doing much of Andrew's writing.

Andrew's portfolio began to bulge with paintings and sketches. Appalled by the plight of the American Indian, he made friends with the Crow and Navajo tribes, and he and Anne lived, for a time, almost in the wilds.

It was as they were en route to Santa Fe that their train was held up by brigands—three blood-chilling men with bandannas tied over their faces, each carrying a Sharps rifle and clattering through the cars with noisy spurs and shouting commands.

But from the beginning the robbery was bungled. To the credit of an alert railroad crew, the thieves suddenly found themselves outnumbered and outmaneuvered. In an attempt to ensure their escape, the men grabbed a hostage—the woman nearest them, Anne Houseman, who was now heavy with child. They dragged her, fighting and screaming, through the coach to the door.

In a raging, half-blind desperation, Andrew attacked the thieves bare-handed, for he didn't possess a weapon. He flung himself headlong at the bandits, fighting like a wild man, but he was no match for the three of them, and one clubbed him with the stock of his rifle, splitting his cheek and creating a scar he would carry the rest of his life. In Andrew's crazed struggle, however, he clawed the bandanna from one of the men's faces.

Later, when the posse found Anne, Andrew didn't believe the thieves had actually intended to kill his wife and baby. Anne simply became too burdensome to their escape, and they left her in the wilds where the infant, a son, came too soon and caused them both to die in a dark pool of blood.

Kneeling beside them, numb with an emotion he had never before known in his gentle life, Andrew shuddered and clenched his hands. He raised his fists high above his head and brought them to the earth with a force that jarred his bones. Again and again he beat the ground, roaring with an animal sound of eternal pain. Not until his hands were bruised and bleeding did he cease, and then he sank, weeping, to the ground into which had seeped the blood of his wife and son.

Filled with grief and anger and self-blame, Andrew became consumed by the need for revenge. He would not rest until he'd done to the men what they had done to his family.

Devastated, Samuel Houseman had come to Santa Fe to take his daughter's body back to Albany for burial, but his son-in-law refused to return to New York with him. Andrew gathered up the boxes of paintings and text and shipped them back with Samuel, but he remained in Santa Fe where he slowly began to change. His handsome face grew hard and drawn with bitterness. He bought a handgun and a rifle and learned to use both with murderous skill. His reflexes became quick and lethal. He did not communicate with anyone. He placed the letters that came from his mother in a saddlebag, unanswered.

Through a devastating winter Andrew traveled on horseback, searching every town and settlement for the three men. He talked with sheriffs and deputies and federal marshalls who were sympathetic but warned him to let them do their jobs. He talked to innkeepers and ticket masters and merchants and newspapermen. Over and over he sketched the three men until even the slightest details were branded in his mind. With an artist's penchant for seeing a face from the inside out, he knew things only an artist's eye could see: that one man's face, the one he had seen, was gaunt, a vulture's beak for a nose and a rosebud mouth; that the second belonged to a bulldoglike man, his blue eyes widely spaced and silver brows winging to sharp peaks; that the third face was narrow with a hairline forming a chevron from the sideburns to the top of the scalp. His tricolored hair might have passed unnoticed by an ordinary man but to an artist, the combination was extraordinary—red, yellow and brown, and a part of that beginning to gray. To Andrew, the men's faces were as individually unique as fingerprints, and when he found them, the justice he enacted would show no mercy.

Nine months after Anne was buried, Andrew rode into Fort Laramie, Wyoming—a purgatory where, it was said, all gamblers, gunmen and drovers eventually wound up on their way to hell.

Andrew looked no different from the worst of them. His artist's hands were no longer smooth, and his hat was pulled low over his scarred face, his holster holding a Colt tied about his right thigh and a Winchester tucked into his saddle scabbard. His trousers and jacket were stiff with dust, and he hadn't changed his shirt in three days.

Dismounting, he tied his big bay to a hitching post and swatted dust from his pants with his hat. With a deftness that was now automatic, he removed his Winchester and tossed his saddlebags over one shoulder.

"I'll take a room," he told the clerk of the Sweet Charity Hotel.

Checkers Peabody had inherited his name because every other tooth was missing. He had been an employee of Sweet Charity since the day the doors had opened. He knew everybody, and everybody knew him.

"Ah, there be no firearms allowed in the rooms, mister," he lisped when the tall, wind-bitten man placed money upon the counter.

"Is that a fact?"

The man's hard gray eyes made Checkers wince.

"Y-yes, sir. But yore welcome to check yer guns at the desk. When you go out, stop by an' I'll be right obliged t'hand 'em back." Checkers peered cautiously over the desk at the man's boots. "I expect you'll be goin' out."

"I expect so."

Andrew unbuckled his gun belt and laid the Colt and holster upon the counter. To that, he added the Winchester. While Checkers put them into a special rack behind the desk, he asked, "Where could I get someone to take care of my horse?"

"I can see t'that, mister. I'll git somebody directly."

Checkers whipped the registration book around on the counter, and Andrew ran a finger down the list of paying guests, though he didn't expect to recognize any of the names. Dipping the pen into an inkwell and preparing to write his own name, he glimpsed his reflection in the gilt-trimmed mirror over Checkers's head.

Andrew was shocked at the stranger who stared back. The wide mouth that his mother had laughingly teased was as beautiful as a woman's was twisted and thinned. His hair was as shaggy as an animal's. Sweet God in heaven, what would Felicia think if she could see him now?

He was suddenly ashamed of what he'd become, and he held the pen poised above the book. When he finally touched it to paper, he did not write Andrew Goldman but Odessa Gold.

Extending a room key, Checkers said, "Thankee, Mister Gold."

Andrew walked to the stairs, then hesitated and retraced his steps. "Checkers?"

"Yep?"

Reaching into an inside pocket of his jacket, Andrew drew out a finger-stained drawing of the man whose bandanna he had snatched away. He spread the sketch on the desk.

"Ever seen this man?" he asked, pointing.

Checkers obliged by removing a pair of spectacles from his pocket and laboriously fitting them around his ears. He picked up the drawing and held it to the light, then laid it to the desk and pushed it toward Andrew.

A sharp breath whistled through the spaces in his teeth. "I reckon so, Mr. Gold," he lisped. "This here man is Laramie's deputy marshall, Eli Wright."

When Genny Carlyle found herself drawn shockingly into the embrace of Odessa Gold, while the train wheezed upon the tracks and badges glinted upon the lawmen's chests, the truth went through her like a shaft.

"You!" she gasped and twisted within the circle of his arm to rake him with horrified eyes. "*You're* the one they want! You're the reason they stopped this train!"

His arm tightened ever so slightly about her shoulders, but the rest of his body didn't move at all at her accusation. A casual observer would have seen nothing amiss, thinking them an ordinary married couple whose heads were bent to one another as they conversed.

You've done something terrible, Genny thought as the blood left her face and her skin went cold and stiff. You're in trouble, and you want me to help you. You look at me and make me want to trust you, even to lay my head on your shoulder, but you're a bad man. I will not be lured into your trap.

Odessa was not a man who mistreated his women—when he'd had them, that is. Genny Carlyle was the first woman he had been close to since Anne's death, and now she was unwittingly the crux upon which his freedom pivoted, possibly his life. He didn't enjoy placing her in this position.

She was, as far as he could tell, amazingly unspoiled and self-sufficient, as different from the women of his past as he was from the man he once had been. The last thing he wanted to do was frighten her, yet her lips had lost their rosy pinkness. They were trembling, and her remarkable skin was so white, the freckles on her nose stood out in bold relief.

"What have you done?" she demanded as the deputy marshalls clanked down the aisle.

"There's no time to explain," Odessa said through a smile, his head still angled so that the brim of his hat gave them privacy. "Please don't betray me, Genny. Trust me, if you can."

Though he had no evidence that the lawmen had been sent by his enemies, C. E. McFee and Manville Platt, Odessa's intuition was honed to a glittering edge, and he guessed they were. What did McFee think he would do, for heaven's sake? Talk? Tell the authorities that he and Platt were the other two men? For ten years he'd rotted in prison and hadn't talked, so why should he now? It didn't make sense.

The words *aiding and abetting* had flown to Genny's mind at his words. And *guilt by association*. The deputies were pausing to inspect every face and weigh every expression in the scales of their justice. Soon they would be examining her face, and guilt would be plastered on it.

Odessa Gold released her shoulder and slid the back of his hand along the side of her neck. They could have been anyone, or no one.

"What's your destination, sir?" a deputy asked of the man two seats behind.

"I'll be going on to Kansas City," the man said. "My wife has people in Kansas City."

"Yes, sir. And you, ma'am?"

"Amos and I are going to Denver to see my father. He's quite ill. My father is an important man. He owns a newspaper."

"Thank you, ma'am."

Do something outrageous! Genny told herself. *Do anything! Be a heroine!*

Odessa Gold was slouched beside her, an ankle balanced on his knee and his hat on top of it, sprawling as if he hadn't a care in the world and had only the most idle curiosity about the lawmen.

His fingers toyed with the linen of her skirt and casually pressed a crease in it with his nail. "Don't be so nervous, Genny," he murmured under his breath. "Turn a little. Smile at me and talk. Say something. Tell me your last name."

This wasn't happening, Genny thought. She was an old-maid schoolmarm. She taught children how to read. She didn't sit with men and let them put their hands on her!

"Carlyle," she murmured, then added, "I don't know what else to say." She trembled, hardly moving her lips at all as her eyes glazed over in fear.

His knuckle stroked the bones of her knees, and a thrill shot to the soles of her feet. "Tell me about Cheyenne, darling. Tell me about your mother. Smile. How do you know Jessamine? Is four dollars truly all the money you have in the world?"

As if she had said something amusing, he laughed softly—a wonderful, infectious laugh, yet she could feel the animal danger in him. He was like a leopard she had once seen in an iron cage as it crouched in its corner and watched men approach with prods, which they would jab through the bars until he screamed with rage and slashed at them with unsheathed claws.

"They'll know I'm lying," she whispered, trembling.

"Talk to *me*, pretty Genevieve, not to them. Forget everything else in the world, but my eyes. Look at me, Genny Carlyle."

Her eyes were drawn to him until she was pinned by the magnetic power of his gaze. It held her and moved slowly and thoroughly over her face. The scar on his cheek crinkled when he smiled.

"Do you have any idea how pretty you are?" he said with an amazed earnestness that seemed, for a moment, real, as if he had forgotten where they were.

Genny was appalled by her impulse to reach up and smooth the chiseled groove from between his brows, to brush back a strand of brown hair that had fallen across his forehead.

"I'm not pretty," she countered with an equal earnestness. "And I resent very much your attempt to flatter me. If you want something, ask. But don't flatter me."

A gray spark twinkled briefly in his eyes. "They don't have mirrors in Cheyenne?"

Spurs jangled close by, and Genny could smell the stench of horses. She stiffened.

"Easy does it, darling. The deputy is one seat away." He leaned closer and unexpectedly grazed her cheek with his lips.

His breath was warm and sweet, Genny thought from her daze, but as shallow and nervous as her own.

"Smile, pretty Genny," he pleaded. "Smile for me."

Genny felt as if she were a performer, caught in the violent throes of stage fright, unable to speak or move or faint or die.

"I can't," she squeaked soundlessly.

"Yes, you can."

His hat slid from its precarious perch on his ankle, and when he grabbed it he collided with her legs and begged her pardon and straightened to flash his teeth beneath the bush of his mustache. Genny laughed softly before she thought.

"See?" He straightened her skirt as if he'd been doing it for years. "Everything still operates."

"Geneena?" Jessamine whispered from her place by the window.

"There's nothing to be afraid of, Jessamine," Genny whispered back. *Except this man who is casting a spell on me.*

Odessa clapped his hat onto the back of his head and stretched out his legs in the manner of a man completely at ease. As the deputy moved to question the couple in the seat directly across the aisle, Odessa said, "What did you do in Cheyenne, pretty lady?"

His persistent endearments had a way of opening her up, though she didn't like them and certainly didn't believe they were genuine.

"I taught school. Mr. Gold—"

"Ah." His smile was brilliant. "A noble profession, teaching school. Have you always been a teacher?"

"Before that I worked with a missionary to the Indians. Actually, I did odd jobs for him."

"Also noble."

"Did you rob a bank?" she asked bluntly.

His laughter, when he tipped back his head, was deep and resonant and rich as dark honey. Obliquely, Genny could see the lettering on the badge of the deputy marshall.

"No, no," he said and boldly picked a piece of lint from her lap.

Now was the time to do the right thing. Now was the time to cry out. Odessa Gold wasn't armed. At least, she didn't think he was. She could signal the deputy with a lift of brows. All she had to do was raise her head.

"You there, ma'am," the deputy said to Jessamine. "What's the matter?"

With a sudden shift so that his back was to the deputy, Odessa covered Jessamine's hand with his.

"Jessamine is blind," he said with sharp impatience as he gave the gnarled hand a reassuring pat. "She's frightened by all this."

"Beg your pardon, ma'am." The lawman turned to see where his partner was, and Genny's nerves, when he looked abruptly back to her, snapped like a plucked elastic band. "And you, ma'am, where are you headed for?"

"St. Louis," Genny replied and nervously removed her handkerchief from her bag and wiped her sweating palms.

"This is your husband?"

The lie caught in Genny's throat. As Odessa turned from Jessamine, his knee colliding with hers, Genny glimpsed the undisguised desperation on his face. He was so vulnerable, so without anything to lose, it was as if the jam of a lock had slid into place and they were, in that bizarre moment, irrevocably connected. Had always cared for each other and always would.

"Yes," she said quickly and could not believe what she'd done.

The lawman shifted his weight in order to see Odessa Gold's face better. With an instinctive reaction Genny would question the rest of her days, she took the bottom of her reticule and, pretending an accident, deliberately dumped its contents upon the spurred boots of the deputy marshall. A small vial of lotion rolled on the floor about his feet, joined by three coins, the stub of a pencil and a heart-shaped locket on a chain.

"Oh!" she exclaimed and bent with a flurry to retrieve her belongings.

"Darling!" Odessa exclaimed and dropped his knee into the space between the seats to begin collecting the spilled things. To the deputy he said, "Guns make Genny nervous, I'm afraid. She can't even bear to have one in the house."

The lawman, distracted, shrugged and said as he touched the brim of his hat in apology, "Pardon the inconvenience, ma'am. Enjoy your trip." He moved up the aisle to where his partner stood waiting and called out, "Everything checks out, Earl. Let's get outta here."

Sounds of the passengers' relief filled the car, and Genny was startled by the pressure of Odessa Gold's hand clasping her knee from where he knelt. She looked down and saw written on his face a raw, searching amazement, and gratitude.

At the door, one of the deputies turned and said, "We do thank you kindly, folks."

Their spurs clanked as they moved down the steps and onto the platform. There, they conferred, heads bent in conversation. One looked eastward and gestured broadly, another shook his head. With a shrug of failure, they fixed their boots into the stirrups and swung up into the saddles.

Hardly had they laid the reins to their mounts than the pistons of the steam-snorting engine began to move. Faster and faster the wheels turned until, from the fog banks of her daze, Genny glimpsed thistles and weeds blurring outside the window.

Her life. It was her life that was blurring. Hadn't she always tried to be true? To never cross that line into an existence of lies and deception that led to destruction, the line her parents had crossed? Hadn't she just crossed that line and become Odessa Gold's pawn?

She slumped in her seat and let her head loll weakly. Lifting heavy eyelids, she fixed the wanted man in her sights. He would explain what had happened just now, the reason for it and why he'd been so desperate. Or perhaps he would feed her lies and make her feel better about what she'd done.

But Odessa Gold returned to his seat beside Jessamine without so much as a word. He pulled his hat low, and all she could see was the shadow of his stubble and his hair furled too long over his collar.

He was shutting her out! Jessamine, having taken up her knitting, sat fingering the stitches and counting to herself as if nothing had happened.

Genny sat limply in shock, unable to believe them or herself. Was she losing her mind? She had aided and abetted a criminal! Her entire future could be stained by the impulse of this single act. Was she the only one who found it horrific?

She felt like a fool. She *was* a fool. She was her mother's daughter. She had let a seductive smile and a pair of gray eyes rob her of her virtue.

Dear heaven, what would she tell Adam? *Oh, Adam!* He was waiting for her in St. Louis, trusting her to be the good decent woman he wanted to marry. And she would be. She would be a good, dutiful wife and maybe God would forgive her for this one insane folly. But would she forgive herself?

She turned her face to the window and dismally watched the sun slide behind the sandstone ledge.

Chapter Four

Odessa's downfall was that he believed he could spend 950 miles, nearly three crawling days, watching a woman like Genny Carlyle without forfeit.

In prison he had taught himself—at great cost—not to feel. He had developed that numbness to a fine art until nothing moved him, not happiness nor sadness nor anything in between.

Until Genny Carlyle had knelt to hide her money in Jessamine's boots. It was Genny, with her mane of impertinent hair that contrasted so ludicrously with her solemnity, that reminded him what he had left on the outside. Before he knew her name he was imagining how gracefully her hips would flare from her waist and fill his hands. He was envisioning her softness in his supplicant palms, her breasts like purest cream, surrendering, and her thighs sleek and firm but oh, so tender inside.

His second mistake was failing to find somewhere else to sit.

After the deputies swaggered off the train and Genny shrank against the window as if she would like to disappear through it like Alice into the looking glass, he should have thanked her for helping him and then quietly excused himself and changed cars.

But he hadn't. The miles had passed and night had blanketed the huge, star-slashed sky. He sat pondering C. E. McFee and Manville Platt and wondered how they'd learned about his release so quickly. Who'd informed them? Potanski?

It was always possible, of course, that the deputies hadn't been looking for him at all, but he couldn't swallow that. It made sense. And it was unforgivable to pull Genevieve Carlyle any further into the vortex of his trouble.

So he withdrew into himself and did not speak. Between the brief stops and starts at stations along the way, passengers gradually succumbed to the darkness. Periodically, the conductor would stroll through the cars, announcing an upcoming stop or pausing to chat with a restless passenger.

On and on they rumbled while Genny Carlyle reclined on her seat, hatless, her hair tousled so bewitchingly that he wanted to lift a strand of it to his lips.

She had pulled up her knees and tucked her feet primly beneath her, then arranged her skirt fastidiously so only a modest amount of stockinged feet peeped from under the hem.

He smiled.

As if she had divined his thoughts, her eyes snapped open and focused on him through the shadows.

Odessa raked his teeth across his lip. Keep your own counsel and be silent, you fool. "Thank you for what you did this evening, Miss Carlyle," he said mildly.

Her look bore little sympathy for him, and her tone was cool and detached. "That isn't necessary, Mr. Gold."

Her eyelids dropped. The coach swayed from side to side to the seductive clatter of steel on steel.

What was it about her that was different from other women? Not great beauty, certainly. Though her face was well-formed, it was minus any outstanding features unless one wanted to consider her skin and her freckles, the dash of her chin, perhaps.

But it was a fascinating face—strangely wary, constantly on the verge of a mood change, making it impossible to stop watching her, wondering what would come next. Happiness or sadness, or something in the middle.

She laid her arm across her eyes in a blatant announcement that she wanted to be left alone. The bones of her wrist were smooth and lightly freckled and he wished he could press his lips to the spot where the little pulse was throbbing.

The hair on his nape stiffened as he imagined kissing her, sliding his mouth along the slender column of her throat to the thrust of her breasts that were rising and falling as she breathed.

He said the first thing that came to mind. "You're going to St. Louis?"

His question didn't merit a look. "Yes."

"To be with your family?" he persisted.

"No."

"On holiday?"

"No."

Odessa sighed. "At least you say what you think," he gritted and told himself he had it coming. "For that, we can all be grateful."

Pulling her arm away from her face, she stared hard at him with her cucumber-green eyes. "You don't really want to know what I think, Mr. Gold. Believe me."

Odessa cursed the fates that had failed to make this woman ugly and stupid. He made his smile as nasty as possible. "Miss Carlyle, you would be surprised how little I believe."

He got the distinct impression that something came to her mind to say. Her breath snagged on a sharp spur, but then she let it out in a rush and returned her cheek to the pillow of her arm. "I'm very tired, Mr. Gold."

No more olive branches, Odessa fervently promised. He was glad she hadn't given him the opportunity to explain. By shutting him out, she was doing them both a favor. Once they parted company, this night would cease to be anything more than a misty memory, anyway. Surely he could resist her that long without making a fool of himself.

He stretched his legs beneath her seat and glumly pulled his hat over his face.

"In that case," he said dourly into the crown, "you'd better get some rest. Good night, Miss Carlyle."

Complimenting himself on his good sense, Odessa forced himself to concentrate on the sound of the wheels vibrating beneath the seat. Someone nearby was snoring.

To his dismay, Genny murmured softly, "I've done nothing to be ashamed of, Mr. Gold."

Odessa refused to look at her. Thank God they would reach St. Louis tomorrow.

"If a person's been alive ten minutes," he said bitterly into his hatband, "they've done something to be ashamed of."

By the time the train stopped at the water tower a hundred miles outside St. Louis, everyone on board was desperate for an opportunity to stretch their legs, including Genny.

Jessamine MacGowan sat with her spine as straight as if she were in her church pew at home. "You run along, dear," she told Genny with stately kindness. "Take some fresh air. I'll be better off here in the car than stumbling around on the rocks."

"Jessamine, you know I don't mind helping you off the train."

"I wouldn't hear of it, dear."

The Ozark Mountains were covered with scrub cedar, and great gray boulders lay so closely beneath the thin top soil, they appeared to be bursting through the ground. Smaller rocks cluttered the land like confetti after a party. Passengers gingerly picked their way among them.

Unable to imagine anything less appealing than stumbling around like a dolt in the wake of Genevieve Carlyle, Odessa had stayed in his seat. When Jessamine's ball of yarn dropped and rolled to rest beside his boot, he bent to retrieve it.

"My mother used to knit," he mused as he placed his hat on the seat Genny had vacated. "I don't know... the click of the needles somehow takes me back... to a steamship somewhere. I can see her on the deck, the wind in her hair."

Jessamine smiled politely, and Odessa rose to remove his jacket and fold it neatly over the seat. He shoved his fingers deeply into his hair.

"I perceive you are a well-traveled man, Mr. Gold," Jessamine said.

"I've been a few places." Some of them I couldn't tell you about, though.

"Geneena really shouldn't have brought me, of course. She's young, and I'm such a burden. But it's been such an exciting trip. I enjoy meeting all kinds of people."

Odessa chuckled at the irony. "I expect you've drawn your conclusions about the kind I am, Mrs. MacGowan."

The old woman smiled. "I wasn't exactly born yesterday."

Nor was I, he thought. Through the window he saw Genny strolling through a clearing worn smooth by many stops by many trains. Slim, hatless, her sleeves rolled back and her arms swinging vigorously free, she paused to shade her eyes against the sun and study the storage tank and the windmill that fed it.

She waged a delightful battle with the wind for control of her hair, and her head, thrown back, glistened with the health that came from many hours outdoors. Odessa knew, then, why she held such attraction for him. The other women were mincing their way through the stones, moving like delicate dolls, with their cinched waists and laced ribs and leaning heavily upon the arms of their men.

Genny, on the other hand, was fresh and lithe and took the ground with energy. When the wind tucked her skirt between her legs, the sculpture was of strong, slim legs and firm hips, bones that artistically framed her pelvis and sheltered the femininity nested between her thighs.

Odessa had to force his attention back to the old woman.

"My point was—" Jessamine carefully took a stitch "—that you're a gentleman of considerable breeding, Mr. Gold. Like my dear husband, God rest his soul."

"I regret, madam," he teased her, "that more people aren't of your discerning bent. What did your husband do?"

"He raised cattle. But, alas, he also played the stock market and lost everything in the crash. It killed him, you know. Not immediately, but in time. I, too, used to go abroad on holiday. No more, though. What do you do, Mr. Gold?"

Tension needled Odessa's body as an emotion, long dormant, began to awaken. "I used to paint."

"You're an artist?" She was amazed and deeply impressed.

"*Was* an artist. I haven't painted in many years."

"Oh, you should definitely take it up again, Mr. Gold. The world has too little beauty."

"I, uh, don't quite consider myself an artist anymore."

"Tsk, tsk, that's too bad." The old woman tipped her head in the curious, listening pose of those without sight. "Please forgive my presumption, but might I ask what you look like? Are you fair? Dark? Fat or lean? Rich man or poor?"

Chuckling, Odessa lifted one of Jessamine's hands and placed the palm on his jaw so that she could feel his face. When her fingers curled back, hesitating, he feared he had offended her.

She shyly explained, "You forget, Mr. Gold, I wasn't born blind. I only recently became that way."

"Forgive me. I was too forward."

"Not at all, not at all." Guardedly, she followed the line of his lean jaw with her fingers. "You have a beard. Did I mention that Geneena is teaching me braille? Mr. Braille was blinded at the age of three while cutting leather in his father's shop. Did you know that?"

"No, I didn't."

"He was an excellent organist and cellist, though. The truth is, Mr. Gold, I've never touched a man except for my dear Mr. MacGowan, rest his soul. I haven't had the courage to ask anyone."

He would definitely miss this old woman, Odessa thought, glancing outside again to where Genny was chatting with a short, bewhiskered man. Without a shred of the inhibition she had showed toward him, she was gesturing broadly and animatedly, obviously warmed to her subject, to the intense pleasure of the diminutive man.

Odessa felt obscurely cheated, and said to Jessamine, "Then we'll let this be a secret between the two of us." He chuckled. "An experiment in scientific research."

Slowly, slowly, her fingers traversed his features, inch by inch over the broom of his mustache, awkwardly finding his nose and his eyes. She laughed softly to herself as she discovered the deep crevice etched between his brows. Nodding, as if that groove told her much, she shaped the bone of his cheek and found the scar that traveled down to become lost in his whiskers.

Her lips parted in amazement. "I think I see a man of great character, Mr. Gold," she said and assessed his ears and breadth of forehead. "A high forehead is a sign of great intelligence. You see, I wasn't mistaken."

Odessa didn't have the heart to erect his facade. Instead, he flicked a glance at Genny, now returning with the other passengers to the train. Her skirt was catching on tufts of dried weeds, and she lifted it to reveal worn slippers.

A line of sweat beaded Odessa's brow, and he imagined her running toward him, her hair a streaming sun, her laughter rippling in sweet music.

"I was in prison, Mrs. MacGowan," he said quietly and took the old woman's hands in his, hoping to settle the murk that had kicked up from the bottom of his stagnant heart. "For killing a man. I'd like you to know that. But maybe you've figured it out already."

Jessamine's smile was infinitely tender. "It wasn't very difficult to deduct, my dear man. Is that where you got the scar?"

With an aching sigh, Odessa replaced the knitting in her hands and leaned back in his seat.

"In prison a man can be forced to take a lot of stands— how far he'll allow himself to be pushed around, for one thing. And when he's pushed past that..." He laughed aridly. "The one thing my, er, considerable breeding did not teach me was how to fight."

She found no amusement in that and sat very still, her silvery head bent.

The engine had quenched its thirst now, and the whistle was shrilling a warning for everyone to hurry back on board. The car was filling with laughter and the inevitable gossip and calls to friends and children.

Quickly before Genny could find her seat, Jessamine leaned towards him and said, as if it were a secret, "Please don't think badly of my Geneena, Mr. Gold. Understand that she isn't being rude. She just doesn't know how to accept kindness. She's very special, you know."

Not so special, he wanted to say. Now, Anne...his Anne had been special. She was also a perfect companion. From her birth, Anne had known she would marry a rich man, and in order to preserve a life of luxury, she had learned all the ways of pleasing a husband.

Genevieve Carlyle, on the other hand, was about as pleasing as a tack in the seat of a chair. Which was why she fascinated him so much, he supposed.

He drew his watch from its pocket and pressed a button, and the lid flipped open with a tiny chime.

"Oh!" Jessamine laughed. "A pocket watch."

Odessa smiled as he placed her fingers on the engraved lid. "It's the only link I have left with my past, I'm afraid. If I have a weakness, it would have to be this watch, Mrs. MacGowan. My father gave it to me on my wedding day."

* * *

Nathan Hodges's mansion, known generally in Cheyenne as "Buckingham's palace," had been built by his father Buck Hodges, long before Wyoming was admitted to the Union in 1890.

Most of the dwellings around Cheyenne were sprawling, low-slung ranches built on enormous blocks of land, some fenced, some not, depending on the availability of guns, and manpower to string the wire. Imogene Hodges had fought loudly and long against moving to the West, and to appease his wife, Buck promised her a mansion worthy of the luxury she was accustomed to. He kept this promise, though he failed to mention that he would use Imogene's own money to build the thirty-room monstrosity overlooking Crow Creek while losing his own money to Wyoming winters and other various "divine wraths."

Most of the spectacular aspects of the house had been shipped from the East by train—the marble that lined the hall and formed the now famous stairway where Buck had died of an heart attack and fallen to the bottom; the teakwood in the library, reputed to hold the largest collection of books in the West; the Italian stained glass, the Oriental rugs; the original paintings; the exquisite vases and lamps of gold and silver.

It never occurred to Imogene that her home was the subject of much laughter. She had made an in-depth study of Fifth Avenue society and emulated the icons right down to Caroline Astor's exclusive afternoon teas and soirees. No person of any worth came to Wyoming without being invited to Buckingham's Palace for tea.

Determined that her son would one day redeem the Hodges's prestige and good name, Imogene gave Nathan his inheritance early, and when Nathan came of age and experience, she bought him the governorship. This, on the condition that she be kept on as part of his household until her death.

When Nathan married Beatrice Kemp, war erupted in Buckingham's Palace. Beatrice went promptly into her own wing, Imogene to hers.

Nathan, weary of hearing the complaints, one against the other, made himself an office where he could disappear at a moment's notice. There, he installed his own telegraph terminal and one of the fancy telephone contraptions that was taking the Eastern cities by storm. And a clever private secretary named Lewis Roberts.

By the time Nathan was sworn in as governor, Andrew Goldman's murder trial was something Nathan had only read about in the newspapers. Then Samuel Houseman began camping on his doorstep.

Over a period of years, Nathan had been besieged by countless letters and telegrams from the grief-crazed man, which he ignored for the most part. That was before Houseman had appeared in Cheyenne with lawyers, begging for the state's reintervention in the case.

As was his habit, Nathan consulted Imogene.

"No matter if Andrew Goldman is as innocent as a newborn," Imogene said, "without his testimony, there's nothing you can do."

But then Lewis Roberts had come up with a marvelous idea. Why not use the Goldman case as a public-relations gimmick? Even if Goldman was guilty, Hodges would be seen as a man fighting to the last inch for a man's chance to prove himself innocent.

The idea caught Nathan's fancy. Lewis was given a raise and moved into the house. Which proved to be a stroke of genius because Lewis, besides keeping official business on an even keel, took a fancy to Beatrice.

Dinner at the Buckingham's Palace was a nightly event.

Each day, beneath the supervision of Imogene's clever eye, the table for twenty-four was laid out with the Limoges china and heavy sterling she had brought from Philadelphia. Raines, the butler, who doubtless knew more about the state's goings-on than many of Wyoming's officials, presided in the kitchen, where menus were planned by the month.

The guest list was Nathan's responsibility. For weeks in advance, he saw that each dinner included someone from the clergy, a local merchant and his wife, someone from the educational community, an Indian spokesman, two army officers, a politician and a lawman. Each evening, sick or well, Beatrice was expected to dress in an evening gown and play hostess to her husband's constituents.

Tonight, Raines moved to the governor's elbow, bent solicitously and murmured in an intimate undertone to Hodges, "Two gentlemen to see you, Your Honor. I've put them in the library."

Hodges carefully removed the napkin he had tucked beneath his collar like a baby's bib, blotted his lips meticulously and placed the linen into Raines's hand. Rising, he held up his hands in a benediction.

"My dear guests, forgive me," he said and bent his balding head so that its dome reflected the light from the chandelier. "A matter of extreme importance has called your governor away for a moment." He sent them all a politic smile and extended his arms. "But enjoy, enjoy, one and all. You there, Senator Hathaway, I trust you can keep the ladies entertained with your wit and charm."

Ever susceptible to compliments, the senator flashed his famous smile and struck himself dramatically upon his handsome chest. "I, sir, shall rise to the occasion."

Laughter rippled around the glittering table, and as glasses clicked in the umpteenth toast to the governor's campaign for a third stunning term, Hodges mumbled on his way out of the room, "Then don't forget who's putting the food in your mouths, come election day."

To Raines, he said, "Did they say who they were, Raines?"

"Only that some man named McFee had sent them."

"Ah, yes. Very good." Hodges smiled.

As Beatrice watched her husband leave the room, her head pounded as if it were being struck from behind with a metal mallet. She was sitting next to Dan Hathaway, and she wished wretchedly that she had never tried to talk politics, had never come down to dinner, had never married Nathan Hodges and had never been born.

Her mother-in-law was staring at her with open disgust, and her own most recent faux pas, an inconsequential remark about the Indians' rights to the land upon which the governor's mansion was sitting, would undoubtedly instigate a conference between Imogene and Nathan that would last well into the night.

She could no longer bear to remain at the hypocritical table. She rose unsteadily to her feet and curved her fingers about the stem of her wineglass. Raines, who had returned from escorting the governor from the room, hurried dutifully to her side.

"I wonder if you would excuse me," she said on a shaky breath.

Guests on her end of the table were accepting second helpings from the silver serving dishes that were being passed round. They appeared surprised that she was even present at the table, Beatrice thought, as she added with lame apology, "I seem to have developed a splitting headache."

"Of course, dear," Imogene purred maliciously, touching her lips daintily with a napkin. "You are looking a bit pale. Do go to your room. I'll have Raines bring your dessert on a tray."

After a moment of unsympathetic curiosity, the guests smiled stiffly and returned to their eating.

Before Beatrice was out of the room, Lewis Roberts was at her side. "Let me see you up, Mrs. Hodges," he offered smoothly.

"Yes, Lewis," Imogene called after him. "Do see poor Beatrice to her room."

Beatrice wished she dared toss the glass of Montrachet she carried in Imogene's face. Would it do any good to ask Nathan again for a divorce?

"That's not necessary, Lewis," she said.

"Nonsense." Lewis slipped his arm about Beatrice's waist and drew her to his side, his lips hovering near her ear as she walked unsteadily to the stairs. "We wouldn't want you to fall and bruise that gorgeous body, would we?"

Beatrice didn't have the energy to object as Lewis's hand strayed errantly to her breast as they reached the landing. She really did have a headache, and she was in no mood for his insatiable sexual appetites. But it was easier to take whatever came her way than put up a fight. If she could drink just one more glass of wine, it wouldn't matter so much.

Her maid, Gretchen, was turning down the bed when Beatrice opened the door.

Beatrice moved to the crystal decanter that was kept filled upon her dressing table. She attempted to refill her glass, but she knocked it against the decanter, and it fell to the Brussels rug.

Gretchen was immediately there, blotting and cooing, "No damage done, my lady. Gretchen will clean it. Would you like me to run you a nice hot bath?"

Lewis Roberts skewered the young woman with a look. "Leave us, Gretchen."

"But, sir—"

"Leave us!" Robert smiled evilly. "Unless you'd like to participate."

Gretchen hurried to the door and slipped out, shutting it soundlessly behind her. Later, she would return and help the governor's wife into a tub and bathe her and put her to bed like a child.

Before Beatrice could find another glass, Lewis had unfastened his pants and was pulling her down onto the nearest chair and pushing up her skirt.

"I can never get enough of you," he growled as he freed himself.

Lewis's second greatest vanity—the first was being the silent power behind Nathan Hodges—was his virility. He loved for Beatrice to undress him and tell him how big and potent he was. When she did not, he grew unhappy, and when Lewis was unhappy, he was dangerous.

"Lewis," Beatrice whispered, "I really do have a headache."

"And I know exactly what you need," he said as he forced her knees apart and wrapped her legs about his waist. "Just what you need and what you want, my dear."

Beatrice made no attempt to resist. If she lay very still and accepted, it was over more quickly.

The two deputy marshalls came awkwardly to their feet when Nathan Hodges entered his office and walked immediately to the cabinet where he kept his best spirits.

"Keep your seats, gentlemen," he said expansively. "What're you drinking this evening?"

The lawmen, caked with dust and uncomfortable in the luxury of the teakwood library, sat upon the edges of their seats and awkwardly accepted the crystal goblets Hodges placed in their hands.

Sinking to a leather chair, Hodges lifted his glass in a salute. "You have a report from McFee?"

The men looked warily at each other, and the spokesman said, "Mr. McFee got the telegram, sir, uh, Your Honor. By the time we got over to the depot, the train was gone. We pulled it over outside Cheyenne, but you got yourself some bad information somewhere, Your Honor. Goldman weren't on it."

Placing his glass on the table at his side, Hodges drew his spectacles off his face and removed his handkerchief. He methodically blew his breath on each lens and wiped it clean.

"Goldman's family lives in Albany," he said. "He'll go there. Eventually. Get men at the major terminals between here and there—Denver, Kansas City, St. Louis."

"That'll take some doin', sir. Connections, money."

"Everything takes connections and money. Does McFee want Goldman or not?"

"He wants him, sir."

"Then get on the telegraph. There's no time to waste. You have Goldman's description. Use it. And I'll expect a return of this favor at the proper time. Don't fail to remind McFee of that."

"He isn't likely to forget, Governor."

"Good."

Nathan had half a mind to throw the deputies out of his house, but there was a time to be powerful and a time to be wise. McFee was nibbling at the bait.

"If there's nothing else, gentlemen," Hodges said, "I have guests."

Flushing, the two men rose and clumsily placed their glasses upon the table with a clatter. They stood turning their hats in their hands as Raines appeared with uncanny timeliness at the door and saw them out.

Once he was alone, Nathan removed the telephone earpiece from its hook and gave the crank on the wall-mounted box a twist.

"Yes, Ella Mae," he said when the operator in Cheyenne came nasally on the line. "I want you to ring the boarding house over by the square and get Cyrus McPherson on the line, then call me back."

"Is this official business, Governor?"

"It doesn't matter, Ella Mae. Just do it."

"Right away, sir. Your Governorship."

Once McFee closed in on Goldman, he would have to be ready to move with lightning speed. He wanted to be close enough to catch McFee with blood on his hands.

Chapter Five

Union Station in St. Louis was not an ordinary train shed.

The largest depot in the world, it was a Romanesque masterpiece designed by Theodore C. Link to please the most pampered and discriminating traveler. The last thing Genny wanted to feel when her train inched its way inside was reluctance to be parting company with Odessa Gold.

Jessamine had whispered that Odessa had confessed to having killed a man and had served time in prison. Somehow, Genny's surprise was not that the man had been convicted of murder but that her own mysterious preoccupation with him continued to linger.

Over and over the riddle tumbled about in her mind. She should be delirious to escape and get on with her life as the future Mrs. Adam Worthington, yet a dread of some unnamed emptiness lurked in her thoughts, and she could not shake it.

It took forever to creep into the shed. When the train finally came to a halt, Odessa insisted on helping Jessamine off, and Genny was reduced to stumbling along in their wake like a recalcitrant child. But on the platform steps she paused and stared in wonder.

The shed could have been the den of great, prehistoric steel monsters. Dozens and dozens of trains filled the slips, and the huge cathedral space echoed with a mad cacophony of sounds so that a person had to shout to be heard. Up and down, firemen and brakemen were inspecting boxes, climbing over connectors that were as thick as their bodies. The whole place smelled of coal and wet steel.

Genny hugged herself. Where was Adam? She'd expected him to be standing beside the step with the porter. But Odessa, not Adam, was waiting by the step, his hat pushed back to a cocky angle as he grinned and reached for her hand.

Loath to deal with the electricity that sparked every time they so much as brushed each other, Genny pasted a smile on her face and extended the meagerest tips of her fingers.

Laughing, he grasped her waist with both hands and swung her down with a buccaneer's boldness as if she weighed no more than thistledown. Genny's legs quaked when he put her down, and he tightened the circle of his arm and said loudly against her hair, "One thing about you, Genny. You keep a man humble."

What was that supposed to mean?

She pushed weakly against his waist. "Humility is next to godliness, Mr. Gold."

He winked. "I believe that's cleanliness, my dear."

The engines were deafening. "What?" She cupped her hand about her ear.

Grinning, he leaned closer. "I'm going to miss the deadliness of your aim."

Impertinent man! Genny scanned the platform for her bag and finally spied it a distance away where the porter had placed it. She was properly cool, properly distant. "Thank you for helping us, Mr. Gold. You're very kind."

One side of his mouth curled with self-mockery. "It's been a long time since anyone accused me of kindness."

Unable to endure the honesty of his look and his blatant disregard for propriety, Genny twisted to search for the blind woman. "Jessamine, where are you?"

"I'm here, dear. Where's Adam?"

Where *was* Adam? "He's probably upstairs, looking for us."

Up and down the long tunnellike passage people were streaming—black men with red hats pushing carts loaded with luggage, mothers hurrying children, and fathers quizzing railroad personnel. To Genny, the air was suddenly heavy and oppressive.

With an old-fashioned courtliness that threw her even more off balance, Odessa said goodbye to Jessamine, lifting her gnarled hand in his and kissing it with an affection Genny could see was not feigned. "Miss Jessamine..."

"I do wish you the very best, Mr. Gold," Jessamine said. "And whatever your destination, whatever you do, God go with you, sir."

"And with you, dear lady." He gave her a princely bow.

"All aboard!" a conductor was calling from the steps of the neighboring train.

With his hat in his hands and a grim twist to his mouth, Odessa waited to bid Genny a final farewell.

The foundations of Genny's composure cracked, and she drew about her an aloofness that didn't seem worthy of the days and nights they had spent sitting across from one another or the risk she had run to her peace of mind by compromising her integrity with two U.S. deputy marshalls.

She thrust out her hand in a too hearty generosity. "Please don't worry about us, Mr. Gold. We're being met. Everything will be all right." Her smile covered all contingencies. "And I truly thank you for your kindness to Jessamine. It meant a lot to her, and I—"

"What did it mean to *you*, Genny Carlyle?"

Words tangled on Genny's tongue—silly, stupid words—and tears banked behind her eyes. He was peeling back the layers of her, searching for words she didn't have the courage to say.

"Genny." The velvet in his tone made her flinch.

She plodded doggedly on. "I wish you the best, sir. I honestly hope you work out your troubles."

Though she didn't look, Genny knew that the lines at the sides of his eyes had tightened. His boots were abruptly intruding beneath the hem of her skirt. His breath fell upon her cheek.

"In another time, Genny Carlyle," his voice was raspy and thick, "I would have come after you. I would've come after you until you couldn't take another step."

His virulent maleness was suddenly overpowering. When his hand found her shoulder and drew her closer, her own breath was harsh in her ears. "Mr. Gold—"

Before she realized he would dare, his lips were finding hers in the softest, most audacious suggestion of a kiss she could imagine. She weaved dizzily, and her lips parted of their own volition, but he had already released her and moved away.

She felt herself falling into an abyss of disappointment. Why hadn't Adam been here? This would never have happened.

"Goodbye, Genny Carlyle," he said softly. "When the night is long, think of me."

His parting left a gaping, empty place, and Genny understood the dread she had been feeling all along. She didn't want him to say goodbye.

"Goodbye, Mrs. MacGowan." He touched the brim of his hat. "I hope your party is here soon to meet you."

Jessamine's face was creased in a sweet, trusting smile. "Oh, Adam will be here. Don't you worry. A man wouldn't fail to meet his bride-to-be. He'll be here."

As long as she lived, Genny thought, she would remember the look of confused pain that swept across Odessa Gold's face as he shot her one last betrayed look before spinning hard on his heel and walking away.

"Next? Next? You, sir. Are you next?"

"Yes, sorry." Odessa slapped at the air before his face as if shooing an annoying cloud of gnats. You were a fool. All that time, you were a fool, thinking something was there. Nothing was there, only the husk of what you once had dreamed.

He asked, "When's the next train to Saratoga Springs?"

"Let's see, departure at 7:18, sir. Very good, you have the correct change, I see."

"Will it depart on time?"

"Yes, sir. Ten minutes. It's boarding now, I believe."

"Thanks."

"Oh, sir, don't you want me to stamp that ticket for you?"

"What? Oh, yes, thanks. What gate is that?"

"Gate seven, sir."

"Thanks."

"Oh, your ticket, sir. You forgot your ticket."

Odessa stalked back to the ticket window and snatched his ticket.

"Enjoy your trip, sir," the agent said. "Next? You there. Next?"

From an alcove a distance away, a tall man with blond hair streaming to his shoulders and a perfect, pointed goatee moved toward the line of passengers who waited to purchase fares. Without a qualm, he intruded himself before the man next in line at the window and bending down, fixed the ticket agent with a deadly stare.

"The man who just bought a ticket," he said. "What was his destination?"

The agent stubbornly pursed his mouth. "Ordinarily, we don't give out that information, sir."

"This isn't ordinary. And you will give it, or I'll come around there, and you'll beg to give it to me."

"Saratoga Springs," the agent said as sweat began to pour from his underarms.

"Thank you. I congratulate you on your good judgment. I'll have a ticket, too."

"But I was waiting on that—"

"A ticket, please."

The agent took the man's money, thrust a ticket at him and said with a bitter, sullen expression. "Gate seven. The train leaves in nine minutes. You'd best go there immediately."

Odessa walked quickly across Union Station and paused to draw out his pocket watch and press a lever. He looked around, wondering if he had time to pick up something to eat before boarding—a bag of peanuts, or a sandwich at three times the usual price.

As he panned the huge terminal his eyes came to rest on a bench far away, where Genny and Jessamine Mac-Gowan sat alone.

Anger surged through Odessa that he must now be reminded of feelings he had almost felt. Where was the venerable Adam Whoever-he-was? Well, it was not his affair.

He turned to walk away, but was drawn to look over his shoulder.

Jessamine's box was resting staidly upon her knees, and her hands were folded primly on top of it as if she were posing for a photograph. Beside her, pretty and slim and so lost that he found himself paralyzed with foolish irrational hope, Genny was searching the sea of faces.

She had rebuttoned her cuffs and collar, and her breasts rose and fell in weary frustration. She pushed a strand of hair from her eyes.

The sight of her innocent vulnerability quickened his pulse. If she had shown half the eagerness to find *him*, he damn sure wouldn't be needing a train to reach Saratoga Springs. He would fly there!

Before he could think, he started toward the women, but then a winch tightened about his ankles, shackling him. Genny Carlyle couldn't have been clearer about wanting him out of her life, nor about her eagerness to see her beloved fiancé.

Gripping his bag with the same rebellion he had felt when Nathan Hodges had tried to bend him to his official will, Odessa turned and strode toward gate seven and prepared to descend the steps to the tracks.

One last look revealed Genny having steepled her fingers and brought them beneath her chin, bending to say something to Jessamine.

The noise of trains drifted up through the stairwell. Odessa squinted down at the great, coughing engine that would carry him to a place of new beginning. Steam was swirling from beneath the chassis like the breath of a rousing beast. Firemen in grimy clothes were making their final checks. He removed his hat, shoved his fingers into his hair, shifted his weight and dropped his shoulders in a long, bitter sigh.

"Well, hell!" he growled and retraced his way through the passengers. Before he reached her, as if her thoughts were connected to his by some invisible thread, she turned, her lips parted and a bloom of color spread the length of her throat.

"Mr. Gold!" she exclaimed and stepped eagerly forward, a smile dancing over her face and her eyes twinkling like sunlight upon a green sea.

Odessa's spirits shot to the rafters of the terminal, but apparently she realized almost immediately that she had been too bold, and she touched her lips as if to force the smile back inside.

"I thought you'd be gone by now," she said and turned to the older woman. "Jessamine, it's Mr. Gold."

"Mr. Gold." Jessamine laughed in his general direction. "How kind of you to come."

"He didn't *come*, Jessamine," Genny corrected from the side of her mouth. "He just—"

"Came," Odessa cheerfully supplied and wrapped her with his smile.

Jesus, the sound of her voice was so good! Like returning home. In this light she was incredibly beautiful. How had he not found her beautiful from the beginning?

"I didn't really expect to find you, either, Miss Carlyle," he said, his formality making her blush.

Now, Odessa supposed, he would be barraged with a litany of feminine excuses about the wonderful Adam. But she said with surprising candor, "My fiancé isn't here to meet us, I'm afraid."

"Ah."

With a shake of her head, Jessamine clucked to herself.

"Maybe he's been detained," Odessa suggested happily.

She plucked girlishly at her lip and shrugged. "Adam's always been a stickler for punctuality. I think something terrible must have happened."

"Perhaps he took ill." This thought brought Odessa even greater pleasure.

Her eyes fell to the chain of his pocket watch. "What time is it, Mr. Gold?"

He removed his watch and touched the button that opened it. "A quarter past seven." He pocketed the watch.

Below them, an engine's whistle blasted.

She asked, "Your train?"

"Oh, no," he lied with grace. "My train's been delayed. My time is yours."

As the train for Saratoga Springs backed slowly out of its slip, the tall blond man walked methodically through the cars. He was looking for someone he knew only by description, the man he had watched for all day at the ticket windows.

The passenger cars were filled nearly to capacity. He wanted to make sure he shared the one with the man he was following. Whoever this man was, his whereabouts were wanted badly by some very important people.

Genny's shame was that her gladness upon seeing Odessa Gold had nothing to do with Adam's tardiness or her worry that her fiancé might have been robbed or turned ill or worse.

It was as if, by sharing a kiss with Odessa that hadn't lasted two seconds—if that—they had concocted themselves a past that was more irrevocable, more deeply sexual than anything Adam had ever aroused or would arouse.

That feeling had something to do with the physical things—the power of the bone and muscle and pinions that held him together—but also the dark history of his scar and the white-hot urgency of his survival instincts, his near-pagan ability to slash away the husks and lay bare the roots of her.

But it was more. Whatever Odessa Gold was, he was a man of wholeness. As simple as his needs and desires might be, he wanted all of them. He would never let his woman give less, and he would never give less to his woman. Nothing would go unexplored, for he thought of life as now, today, this moment.

The thought of them in some forbidden embrace was wildly exciting, and Genny dropped her eyes to her hands, which for some reason she couldn't still.

"If you'd like me to," he was offering, "I can make a few inquiries about him."

"About wh-who?" She'd forgotten what they were talking about.

His grin burned a dozen places of her body. "Adam." He gestured futilely. "Your lover."

"Adam Worthington!" she snapped in a pique. "And he is not my lover!"

"Then he's a bigger fool than I gave him credit for."

"That—" his eyes could still infuriate her "—is unforgivable, Mr. Gold. Adam isn't your concern. I will make the inquiries."

"You're right. I'm not concerned at all."

Must he do everything to make her come apart?

Genny yanked the strings of her purse brutally hard. He walked blithely over to drop onto the bench beside Jessamine. His fingers found the buttons on his jacket, freeing them, and he stretched out his legs as if he had all the time in the world.

He tossed his hat aside. "Since Genny's going to be so busy with inquiries, Jessamine," he said in a stage whisper, "I'd consider it a privilege to sit with you."

"Why, thank you, Mr. Gold," she returned with a bright eagerness that made Genny want to pinch her.

"Mr. Gold . . ." Genny warned with exasperation.

Odessa smiled with cherubic innocence. "Yes, Genny, dear?"

Aggh! He could be so, so . . . male!

"No, no, don't bother to thank me." He held up his hand in mock protest. "Go about your business. I'll buy a paper and read it to Jessamine until you return."

Genny thought it would bring her a great deal of pleasure to bury her hands in his thick hair and pull it out by its chocolate-brown roots.

Her gritted smile, which would have incapacitated a lesser man, deflected easily off Odessa's lazy imperviousness.

"I would appreciate that very much, Mr. Gold," she said between her teeth.

Genny hoped, as she stalked away, hugging her purse like a bandage to her breast, that they both enjoyed themselves to death!

The best way to find Adam, Genny decided from the outset, was to go straight to the Union Station dispatcher.

"How could a person go about locating someone in this city?" she asked as he half rose from his desk and promptly plopped down again.

"Do you have an address, ma'am?" he asked, then honked his nose into a handkerchief and peered over the hem with streaming eyes.

"I know approximately where his parents live."

"Darned cold." The dispatcher gingerly dabbed camphor under his reddened nostrils. "If it was me, ma'am, I'd speak with the constable."

"Could you tell me where I might find the constable?"

"Usually in his office. But I'd check with the head waiter at the dining room. The constable has dinner there every night about this time."

"Thank you very much."

"You're welcome. *Achoo!*"

Having passed through the worry stage and now entering the angry stage, Genny fully intended to give Adam a piece of her mind when she found him.

The facilities of the hotel and dining room were part of the Theodore Link's overall design to provide the modern traveler with every luxury under one roof. Rank upon rank of cloth-covered tables had been laid with the finest silver and glass. Black waiters moved about, balancing great trays of food—succulent lobster and broiled, fresh-run salmon.

Genny inquired of the headwaiter as to the whereabouts of the constable, and the man peered down at her over a chest covered with snobbish, starched pleats. If madam would remain here, he pontifically informed, he would have the constable brought to madam.

Constable Hickey was a man of ample girth, with white frizzy whiskers framing a baby-soft face. "You'll be talkin' about the son of Dr. Craig Worthington," he said after she had explained her purpose.

"Do you know the address?"

"Dr. Worthington be on the staff of St. Mary's Hospital. He removed me mother's gallstones, rest her soul." The constable crossed himself, then added quickly, lest she misconstrue his mother's death, "Oh, it weren't the doctor's fault, you understand. She were doin' perfectly fine right along, but she tripped on a rug and fell down a whole flight of stairs." He drew out a handkerchief and dabbed at his eyes. "I miss her sorely."

"I'm very sorry, sir," Genny said. "You do know Dr. Worthington's exact address?"

His brows snapped into a suspicious frown. "You be family?"

"Well, not exactly yet, I'm not." She smiled. "But soon." Despite Odessa Gold.

The constable was reluctant to give her the address, but finally he wrote it laboriously on a piece of paper. Thanking him and wishing him a good evening, Genny considered returning to Odessa and Jessamine and letting them know. But if she did, Odessa might insist on hiring the cab and looking up Craig Worthington himself and she would end up even more indebted to him.

Though she had never done it, she hired a hansom cab and showed the constable's paper to the driver. The address took them high above the Mississippi River into the most affluent section of St. Louis. Fog was rolling in. Boats were hooting their warnings.

The driver stopped before a house so grand that Genny, had she been given the alternative, would have returned to Union Station. He helped her out of the cab, and asking him to wait, she walked to the door. The knocker was brass and echoed through the house. Footsteps approached and presently the heavy door swung back on its hinges.

"Madam," a butler said and peered imperiously down at her as if she were an enemy from a foreign land.

Hating Adam for putting her in this position, Genny explained her purpose.

"The doctor and his wife are in Newport for the summer," the butler haughtily informed. "Miss Amy is having their first grandchild."

Genny felt like a fool. "Actually, it was Adam I wished to find, sir."

The man's face closed as if he'd already shut the door.

"He returned to St. Louis very recently," she added with a growing feeling of anxiety.

"Mister Adam always returns to St. Louis," the butler droned out his weary reply. "He had a quarrel with his father and moved out of the house. Is there anything else I can do for you, miss?"

"Out of the house?" Genny could scarcely speak around her confusion. "But where did he go?"

"Are you a lawyer?"

Her jaw sagged. "No, I'm not a lawyer. I'm a...friend."

"Well—" the man touched his perfect tie "—I suppose it won't do any harm to tell you. Do you know where Hollybrook Street is?"

"I'm sure the driver will."

After the butler gave her the street number, Genny practically ran to the coach and climbed in before the driver could assist her. She shrank back in the seat and sat

shivering as the cab took her across town to an area filled
with row upon row of dingy tenement buildings.

The stench of the docks swirled through the window and
Genny found her handkerchief and covered her mouth.
She feared something terrible was about to happen.

At last, the driver pulled up before a particularly run-
down building. He climbed down to give her a hand out of
the cab.

"Wait for me," she said, and shakily removed one of
her precious dollar bills and pressed it into his palm.

"Please make haste, miss," he said and tucked the bill
into the frayed opening of his pocket. "'Tis not me favorite thing, bein' down here by the docks at night."

Did he think it was her favorite thing?

Adam's flat was three flights up. As she trudged up the
stairs, Genny's anger was giving way to hurt. She had been
a fool to come on this wild-goose chase. If she could only
get her money back from Adam, she would shake the dust
of this episode off her feet and go back to Wyoming. At
least all Wyoming had done was starve her.

When she knocked on the door and waited for the footsteps to grow louder and the bolt to be thrown, she took a
deep breath. *Prepare yourself for the worst. It could just
happen.*

She was not disappointed. A woman answered the door.

Chapter Six

When Genny discovered, at thirteen, where her mother went when she slipped out of the house at night, she made herself a promise: she would never be like Amelia. She would never dream of things she could not have, and her commitments, once made, would be forever.

Raymond Carlyle had been a hardworking man— steady, slow of speech, down-to-earth, a lineman on the Missouri Pacific Railroad, a gentle moose of a man with the sweetness of a boy. For days he would be gone from the leaky three-room house tucked in the sassafras thickets of the Missouri River. When he returned, Genny's chore was to unharness the mule from the wagon and draw water for his bath. After supper, Raymond would doze in his chair and take himself quietly off to bed where he slept the peaceful slumber of a simple, guileless man.

Amelia rarely complained to her husband, but she took more and longer walks. For her nerves, she explained to Genny. As Genny grew older and her own body began to awaken, Amelia assumed a distance that puzzled Genny. There were times when Genny felt alone even when her mother was in the room.

Genny once asked Amelia why her nerves needed so much calming, and Amelia snapped, "It's not a matter for little girls to ask about. Nor to talk about, either, so say no more about it."

One hot June night, Raymond sat on the porch and smoked a hand-rolled cigarette, then, after yawning and stretching, took himself to bed. Soon the rhythm of his snoring filled the house and for the first time Genny saw her father as a cloddish, dull man.

The front screen slapped gently, and Genny rose from her bed and moved through the creaky house. Far away, an owl hooted, and the whippoorwills chanted back and forth across the river.

Genny hugged herself as she saw Amelia moving across the yard in her nightgown, pale as a lunar moth flitting from shadow to shadow. But eagerness was in Amelia's flashing legs. Genny couldn't remember such liveliness in her mother, and an unnamed dread collected in her chest. Skimming out the door and across the porch and down the steps, her own skimpy gown billowing out behind her, she made the crickets hush as she ran.

Amelia kept off the road. For half a mile, Genny followed, and when a man stepped from the darkness and confronted Amelia, Genny wasn't surprised.

Her mother rushed into the man's arms and kissed him. Genny wished desperately that she had not spied, but she was powerless to leave as the man drew Amelia out into the fragrant summer meadow and pulled her gown over her head. Amelia's nakedness was the perfect purity of cream.

Genny didn't entirely understand the sounds that followed. Hideously fascinated, she moved closer and closer until she could see the veins protruding from the man's neck in the moonlight. Her mother lay on the ground, her legs wrapped around the man. Amelia's head was thrown back and her neck arched high.

A small, dusky creature awakened inside Genny then, nibbling painfully at her own budding nipples and curl-nested femininity. In a moment of ghastly clarity, Amelia turned her head and looked straight at Genny. Neither of them said a word, and Amelia brazenly reached up and invited the man's kiss as he plunged violently for his release.

As if the devil himself was chasing her, Genny fled. Neither she nor Amelia spoke about it afterward. Amelia went about her duties in sullen silence, and Genny feared to look at her. Two nights later, when Raymond was asleep, Amelia slipped out of the house and never returned.

Over and over Genny told herself that Amelia had made her own choice, but somehow, she felt she had failed her mother. Driven by some twisted need to do penance, she tried to fill Amelia's shoes. She cared for Raymond as devotedly as a mother would tend a deprived child. For two years Raymond mourned Amelia's desertion until Genny wanted to take him by the shoulders and shake him until his neck snapped.

Eventually Raymond stopped working. He sat in his chair on the porch and drank, first in the evenings, then all day. As the sassafras thicket crowded around the house he sank into the depths of his own heartbreak, and one warm evening as the leaves were turning, Raymond went to sleep in his chair and never woke up.

More than Raymond's body was buried in the ground that year. Genny's body changed and became capable of childbearing, but nothing in her hungered for the touch of a man. Until she was sixteen, she lived with a neighboring spinster. Minerva Carson taught her to read and work sums, gave her lessons in history and Latin and science. Then Minerva married a man and moved away. A traveling preacher told Genny about the Wyoming Territory where he was going to convert the Indians. He offered to send her to school if she would go there and help his ministry.

Genny went and never looked back. There, she finished the equivalent of high school. On Beech Street in Cheyenne, she met Jessamine MacGowan, who owned a modest dress shop.

Adam Worthington was the first man to give Genny a passing thought. Good-looking with a quick, pleasant

tongue, he made her laugh more than she cried. Saying yes
to his proposal of marriage was easy.

"Yes?" the young woman half-hidden behind the tenement door said to Genny.

Genny saw many things at once—the woman's youth,
her prettiness and the blond ringlets piled high upon her
head. A wedding band was on her finger, and her breasts
were full and high.

Behind her, the small flat was starkly furnished, but the
rooms had been tastefully arranged with small feminine
touches, a knitted shawl draped over the back of the ragged sofa, a quilt folded neatly across the foot of the iron-
rail bed, a modest stack of hand-hemmed towels arranged
beside a wash bowl on the vanity.

"I'm sorry," Genny apologized, wanting to turn and
run and pretend she had not come. But she could no more
do that than she could have stopped pursuing her mother.
"I was looking for someone, and I was told that he lived
here. Forgive me for disturbing you."

"Adam?" the woman gasped.

With a feeling that had to be akin to death itself, Genny
started to walk away, but the woman slipped through the
door and caught her sleeve.

"Wait, don't go. Please. My name is Mary Faye
Spender. You're looking for Adam? Please, come in. What
did you say your name was?"

Genny didn't want to be standing in a dark hallway
talking to this woman. She wished she were at Union Station. She wished she were on Beech Street in Cheyenne.

"It's Genny," she said dully. "Genny Carlyle."

"Adam's never mentioned you."

"I'm sure he hasn't."

Mary Faye's laughter was innocent. "But don't hold
that against him." She shrugged prettily. "Adam and I
haven't known each other long. There's a lot I have to
learn."

Thinking that Jessamine wasn't the only one who was blind, Genny allowed herself to be guided into the tiny apartment. She took the proffered chair and sat with her knees pressed dismally together. She watched in silence as Mary Faye lit a gas jet on the stove and placed a kettle on it.

"Will tea be all right?" she asked. "It's really all I have."

"Tea will be lovely."

Mary Faye returned to take another chair. They were sitting as precisely as two bookends, their knees almost touching.

"You'll have to forgive me," Mary Faye said cheerfully. "I'm four months pregnant, and landsakes, I get so winded, sometimes I think I'll just go right into a dead swoon."

Genny closed her eyes in horror. Dear God! "You and Adam are going to have a baby?"

The water began to boil and Mary Faye bounced from her chair. "If you know Adam...Lord, that man can dream. He had this terrible row with his father. Between you and me, the man's as rich as old Gould ever was. Anyway, two weeks ago Adam went up to Saratoga Springs." She lifted her gaze from the tea. "Do you know where Saratoga is? The summer place in New York where all the rich people go?"

"Yes," Genny said as numbness crept from her feet into her legs. "I know the place."

"Well, Adam's going to earn all this money. That's why I haven't really fixed this place up very much. It took everything both of us could scrape together for him to go. That's why I was so rattled when you knocked on the door. It's been a few weeks since I've heard from him and I thought, Oh, no. Something awful's happened."

Genny wondered if she could be forgiven for taking the coward's way out and sneaking off into the night to lick her wounds. But then she thought of the unborn child this woman carried. Poor Mary Faye. She was so trusting. She would wait for Adam until there was nothing left. Then she'd be forced to go to a poorhouse and bear her child who would, in all probability, be adopted out. May God damn Adam Worthington to hell!

"Mary Faye," Genny said tenderly, rising to go to the stove and stop the woman's hands from fussing with the cups and saucers. "Forget the tea. I'm going to tell you something that is going to be painful, but if I were in your shoes, I would want someone to tell me."

The color drained from Mary Faye's face when she turned, and Genny squeezed her eyes tightly shut. *Sweet Jesus, I was very nearly in your shoes.*

After Genny told her the truth, they held each other and wept for the child who had not yet been born. Before Genny left, she swore to Mary Faye that she would come back, that together they would do something. But in the meantime, Mary Faye must find someone who would listen. A minister's wife, perhaps.

Genny was numb as she made her way back to the cab. She felt as if someone had died. But with death a woman could touch the clothes of her beloved and go through personal effects and remember. She could accept because she had seen the body go into the ground. She wanted desperately to bathe. She wanted to throw herself into the Mississippi and scrub herself with sand down to her bones. She wanted to hack away the part of her brain that had trusted Adam. She wanted to die.

But she could not die. Who would take care of Jessamine?

"I am *not* Mary Faye Spender," she whispered angrily to the interior of the cab. "I am *not* Amelia Carlyle, and I'm not Raymond. I am me, Genevieve Carlyle." And, on a bleak sigh, she added, "Whoever *she* is."

She must find a way to rise above her mistakes and rebuild. But how?

"I will never trust another man," she promised herself devoutly. "Not even Odessa Gold." Especially not Odessa Gold.

She surrendered to tears then, but they did not cleanse her.

Odessa was reading aloud to Jessamine from a discarded *Post Dispatch* about two carriages that collided on Eads Bridge because of a high-spirited cat. Another article revealed that the symphony orchestra was performing Berlioz. While his eyes followed the print and his mouth said the words aloud, Odessa's mind, however, was envisioning grisly scenes of Genny being dragged into a dark alley, robbed of her four dollars and brutally assaulted. Why was she taking so long?

A black man in a white jacket pushed a creaking cart past where they sat, hawking, "Fresh apples and hot roasted peanuts. Hot peanuts here. Apple for you, mister? One for the lady?" His forehead was jeweled with sweat. "Lip-smackin' Romes," he tempted. "Picked 'em myself over on the east side."

"We'll take three of the apples," Odessa said.

It was as he was paring one of the Romes for Jessamine, a coil of crimson peel dangling between his knees, that Odessa spotted Genny.

The hair stiffened on the back of his neck. Sweet Jesus, he'd hardly recognized her. Sensing his alarm, Jessamine cocked her head. "Geneena has come back."

"Yes." Genny, Genny, what's happened to you?

Gone was Genny's fierce look of independence. Her movement was that of a grounded bird, and her slimness was frailty. Her feet moved as if they were weighted. She stumbled and covered her mouth for a brief moment, then searched in her bag for a handkerchief. Swabbing at her eyes, she tried to stand straight but couldn't. She sagged against a nearby pillar as if all her bones had suddenly stopped holding her together.

"Is she alone?" Jessamine asked.

He'd forgotten the old woman. "Yes."

Jessamine crossed herself. "He has failed her."

How many times, Odessa asked himself, had he heard his father say that to meddle into someone else's affairs was like grabbing a passing dog by the ears? This was the time, if he was smart, to bow gracefully out of these two women's lives. He could not help, and Genny would not thank him for witnessing her despair.

Even if she did turn to him, what would it mean? Nothing. Later, he would go his way and she would go hers. What was the point?

Jessamine was clucking to herself, trying to perceive the reason for her apprehension. "My dear Mr. MacGowan always warned me about men like Adam Worthington—always talking a good line, always charming, always brimming with big plans but never delivering. Or perhaps we're borrowing trouble, Mr. Gold?"

Odessa didn't think so. Rising, he kept his eyes riveted on Genny. "Stay here, Jessamine. I'll be right back."

Jessamine's acquiescence was a sigh. Where would she go? Genevieve Carlyle had been sent by heaven as a direct answer to her prayers. After burying three babies and a husband, she wasn't about to question Providence. There was no one who cared, no one except Geneena.

Odessa's boots clicked a litany of warning as he strode across the terminal to the woman who had unexpectedly come to occupy such an important place in his life. Like a boy, he took skidding shortcuts between rows of benches and hurdled a stack of luggage. By the time he reached Genny, his heart was thudding like a thresher.

"Genny?"

She looked up as if she had forgotten where she was, and her lips parted in a half-denial. She saw his hands reaching for her, and she held up her arms and shrank back, as if to touch him would be to consume her.

"I can't talk now, Mr. Gold," she choked.

"You don't have to talk, Genny," he said as he drew her, gently but firmly, into his arms and laid his head on top of hers. "It's all right. Whatever has happened, I'll help you."

She leaned her weight against him briefly, her palms spanning the front of his shirt and her forehead grazing his shoulder. But then she stepped back and touched a wondering fingertip to her temple. "I'm so sorry, I . . . I can't imagine . . ."

"Genny . . ."

Rattled, she hastily attempted to tuck her blouse into her skirt. She pulled her fingers through fallen ringlets and pushed them back, innocent of how provocatively her breasts strained against her blouse and how desirable her need had caused her to be.

"Sweetheart—"

"I can't imagine what came over me. This certainly isn't your concern, Mr. Gold. Not your worry, I mean."

Odessa felt as if he had unearthed a treasure, only to be brutally robbed of it. His hands balled into fists, and he said with cutting irony, "You'll forgive me, then, if I take a moment to stop the bleeding. I didn't realize you were armed."

Her lips trembled and she shook her head. "I didn't mean that I'm unappreciative." Wings of crimson sailed into her cheeks. "It's just that . . ."

"You don't trust me."

"It isn't you . . ."

"You don't trust men."

"Not exactly. I . . ."

"Speaking of the stronger sex, would it be out of line for me to inquire as to the whereabouts of our good Mr. Worthington?"

A dark, bitter anger snapped around her like steel armor. A single tear slid to the tip of an eyelash, and she brushed it bitterly away.

With a formality that Odessa found increasingly exasperating, she said, "I'm grateful to you for sitting with Jessamine, but I have everything under control now."

"You do, huh?"

She smiled stiffly. "We'll be just fine. Really. I wouldn't want to detain you any longer, Mr. Gold. I know you have troubles of your own."

Slap, slap! On both cheeks, as if he were a naughty child caught looking at pictures in a forbidden book. All he'd wanted to do was touch the quick of her, dammit, to be there for her.

Get out of here, Goldman. Cut your losses and fold. With a mocking salute from the brim of his hat, he pulled a grimace and took several steps backward.

"Why, you're just as right as rain, ma'am," he drawled nastily. "Guess I'll just git on mah horse and mosey off into the sunset. Got myself a lot of criminal duties to do, anyway. Banks gotta be robbed, you know, and trains held up. Women gotta be molested and citizens defrauded. Hell, if I didn't tend to it, no tellin' who would, just any ole Tom, Dick 'n' Harry. It's just work, work, work, from sunup to sundown. Nice talkin' to ya, though. Good luck with Mr. Worthington. I'm sure you'll both be very happy."

Odessa wheeled hard about, cursing himself bitterly. Why had he allowed the impassioned need of ten years to rise? Why had he indulged in such paralyzing hopes for the future? Thinking stupidly that he could enter the world Genny Carlyle lived in?

Her words followed him and struck him sharply between the shoulder blades. "You took my words the wrong way!"

He refused to give her the satisfaction of looking back. "You got it wrong, Genny, darlin'. I'm not takin' 'em any way at all."

"Odessa!"

When Odessa turned around, her hands were clapped over her mouth and her eyes swam with blurring misery. Her bosom was heaving and heartbreak was pulling at her shoulders.

In two strides he had caught her up in a desperate embrace. Her arms went frantically about his neck, and he held her off the floor, tightly, oh so tightly, and buried his face in the curve of her neck, rocking her back and forth.

"Oh, Genny, Genny. Don't cry, Genny, don't cry."

Her smallness, Odessa thought, was a surprise. Even though he'd done little besides imagine how she would feel in his arms, he was amazed at the fragility of her frame. Her breasts were ripe, yes; he had guessed that by just looking, but her back and hips and legs could have been those of a young boy. What kind of man would hurt someone as fine as Genny? Who was this Adam Worthington that he could bring such pain?

His hands filled with tangles of her hair. "I'm so sorry this happened to you, Genny," he whispered against her cheek. "I'm so very sorry."

"It was horrible." Her tears were staining his collar. "I was so ashamed. I *am* so ashamed. I wanted to die. I still—"

"Shhh." He kissed the capricious little curls that framed her ears, curls coyly unaware that their owner's heart was breaking. "You may want to die now, but you'll live to a ripe old age, I'm afraid. No matter how dark life gets, Genny, it's always worth having. Believe me. You're just going to have to back up and start over, sweetheart. We all do it many times in our lives."

With a sudden ferocity, she flung herself away and struck the space between them with her fists, as if it were the enemy.

"Start over?" she cried. "Start over with what? He took every last cent I had, Odessa! Except for that wretched four dollars, three dollars now, Jessamine and I don't have a dime to our names! So you tell me how to start over, Mr. Whatever-has-happened-I'll-help-you. I'm ruined. Jessamine is ruined because of me and my stupidity!"

Odessa had always known that his past would roll back upon him when he least expected it. It was the nature of a beast like his. He should have something to offer Genny now, and here he was standing before her, empty-handed.

God damn Eli Wright and C. E. McFee and Manville Platt!

Their tableau held for a moment longer, unconscious as they were of anything outside their own pathos. Neither realized when they slowly, mutually surrendered to the inevitable pull and moved toward each other. Odessa was enthralled by Genny's bravery and tear-weighted lashes, and she was mesmerized by his past and his gentleness.

Genny flicked her tongue across her lips. She wished he would hold her—closely, so she could feel another human being who was fighting for life. She wished he would share the harnessed strength of men that could perpetuate generations and build empires and defy the world. She wished he would envelop her, devour her, consume her until she disappeared.

Her harsh whisper came from a person who knew nothing of her heart's wishes. "I should be going now, Mr. Gold."

Hamstrung by his past, Odessa slowly closed his eyes. They were two children, tricked by life, whose innocence had been destroyed before it had a chance to fly.

"Go where?" he said sadly, tasting the salt of her tears.

Nothing remained in her voice now. No anger, no hope. "I don't know."

"Then we must go tell Jessamine."

Chapter Seven

"May Adam Worthington burn in hell," Jessamine said fervently, passing sentence to fit the crime.

Genny was recovered now, Odessa thought, as he sprawled wearily beside Jessamine. Like a tigress on the prowl, she paced in an attempt to collect her thoughts. Her skirt swished with a sleek grace, and her color was high. Glistening perspiration beaded her forehead. She was operating on the strength given by anger and panic and was capable of things she ordinarily would not have been. To him, she was the most intriguing, captivating woman he had ever seen.

"Adam told her he was going to Saratoga," she fumed and threw back her head in a caustic laugh that would have made him shiver had Adam been unfortunate enough to see her face. "Oh, it's exactly where he *would* go, isn't it? Now he'll no doubt ensnare some other innocent female and probably leave her with a fatherless baby, too. What a fool I was!"

Odessa wanted to nod his head yes, that she had been a fool to want any man but him.

"If I could get my hands on him," she seethed, "I'd drag him through the courts myself. I'd sue him for breach of promise. Then I'd sue him for robbing me of my life savings. I'd..., I'd..."

She shuddered in a way that made Odessa want to lunge to his feet and swoop her into his arms. But she dropped to her knees beside Jessamine and collapsed on the woman's lap as if she were coming down with a cold that would last forever.

The old woman opened her arms in the ageless comfort that women could share with each other. "Now, now, now..."

"We'll have to stay here for a while, Jessamine," Genny whispered, clinging. "Until I can make some money. But it won't be so bad, you'll see." She lifted her head. "We'll get a tiny flat like Mary Faye's. I'll buy you white bread and good books. You know the one you've been wanting to read, about the Rothschilds? And you can have a cat. We'll find a flat that gets the morning sun, and Tabby can nap in the window while I'm gone to work. Actually—" her lips trembled through her brave, false smile. "—St. Louis will be heaven compared to Wyoming. We're going to enjoy it here."

Slamming his feet to the floor, Odessa rose, his heart churning as if it had been put through a grinder. "I've had about all of this I can stand."

Blinking, her fury softening with gratitude for the solace he had offered, she thrust out her hand with a willing little formality that made Odessa want to scream.

"We owe you our thanks, Mr. Gold. And I really mean that. I've a feeling that we've inconvenienced your schedule and you're too polite to say so. If there's anything we can do to repay you..."

What did he hate most at this moment? he asked himself. Adam Worthington, or Genny's infernal determination to carry on no matter what?

He aimed a finger at her nose. "I've got something to say, Genny Carlyle, and you're going to listen. When I'm finished, you will not put on your rose-colored spectacles and say 'Thank you, God, for allowing my character to be tested.' You will not say, 'This is the way it was meant to be.' Is that understood?"

Surprise tinted her cheeks and Odessa grinned. "That's more like it. Now, I know Jessamine told you about my past. Don't bother denying it."

She shaped her lips into a little moue and smoothed the back of her hair. "She might have said something about you being in prison. I really can't remember."

"I served my sentence, Genny." Odessa wondered if he'd lost his mind, going through this thankless ordeal. "I don't have any warrants out for my arrest. I'm not wanted by the law."

"Amazing. Then why did the deputies stop the train?"

"Two men who were involved in the killing of my wife were never brought to justice. They have a lot to lose if I tell what I know."

"Would you tell?"

"That question seems to be on everyone's mind these days. Frankly, I've had enough violence to last me a lifetime."

He might want to avoid violence, Genny thought as she stared at his face, which was never quite at peace, even in repose, and at his limbs, which were like coiled springs. Violence lay beneath his surface like a volcano waiting to erupt.

"Why are you letting Adam Worthington do this to you?" he challenged as he moved closer and shut out the world with his bigness.

Genny was conscious of every pulse as his will forced past the locked doors of her heart. "Do what?"

"You actually would stay here in St. Louis and try to make up for what Worthington stole? Why do you lie down and play dead, Genny? Get your money back."

"Back!" His criticism had scoured her like sandpaper, leaving her raw. "Are you insane? I can't get my money back."

"Of course you can."

She stamped her foot on the floor. "He's gone to Saratoga Springs. What am I supposed to do? Reform him by long distance?"

"Go there."

Strength and virility were in his loins, enabling him. He had no idea what it was like to be a woman and have to fight for every precious inch. She wished she could set him back on his heels and wipe the male superiority off his face. "Just how many men have you killed, Mr. Gold?" she asked with deliberate venom.

His skin seemed to tighten and Genny cringed, wanting to place her hands on his chest and say she hadn't meant it.

"You press me hard, madam," he warned softly. "Be careful."

Genny groped behind her for Jessamine and reassured herself that the old woman was still there. "I don't know what to do," she whispered. "I honestly don't know."

As a younger man, Odessa had always believed that explanations belittled a person, but he wanted Genny to know the truth about his past.

"I wasn't always a convict," he said dully. "Before, I was an artist. I made my living illustrating books."

She took a moment to digest that surprising fact. "You could do it again."

His grimace was twisted with irony. "Unfortunately, there weren't many calls for painters in prison, so I was forced to cultivate other talents."

It was her turn to challenge him. "What other talents?"

In his mind, Odessa formed the words and tried them silently, not daring to say them aloud: It's fast, I know. I've always moved too fast. I want you in my life. Please say you'll be in my life. Let me fall in love with you.

"I learned to play cards," he said simply.

It was obvious that she placed the playing of cards with other sins of the flesh. She worried a stray curl that had crept across her cheek. "You're a cardplayer?"

"Yes."

Without warning, she laughed, and music seemed to fill the whole station—beautiful and lilting, resurrecting hope in the catacombs inside him.

"But, Odessa, are you any good?" she asked.

Odessa tipped back his head and laughed, too. "Yes, Genny," he said, nodding his congratulation of her finesse. "I'm very, very good."

"So now you're going to Saratoga Springs?"

"Mr. Worthington is in Saratoga, Geneena," Jessamine reminded her.

"I know that." Must the old woman put pressure on her, too? Genny thought resentfully. "*If* Adam was telling Mary Faye the truth," she said. "He hasn't been known lately for his honesty."

Genny plopped down on the bench beside Jessamine with a girlish abandon that made Odessa want to kiss her until she couldn't breathe. "We don't even have train fare left to get to Saratoga," she said to the old woman. "Don't even think it."

"That can be arranged," Odessa said.

"Now you're going to offer us money." She slanted him a look of suspicion. "Well, thank you, Mr. Gold, but we couldn't possibly accept a loan from you."

A dull flush of embarrassment crawled up Odessa's neck. He kept coming out on the short end with this woman.

"I wish I could loan the money, Genny, but the truth is, I'm down to my last two dollars. If you'll entrust your four, I mean, your three, dollars to me, I promise I can get you the fare to Saratoga."

Lightning wasn't supposed to strike twice in the same place. Trust me, Genny, give me your money. It was a law, lightning. Laws didn't change.

Genny blinked down at her dress and wouldn't have been surprised to find it smoking. Jessamine was drawing off her glasses and cleaning them with a vengeance. Odessa was not just looking at her, he was stepping inside, shar-

ing the shame and the misery of her life. He was offering
to help in the only way he knew how.

But she couldn't, she couldn't! Could he not see that?

He didn't misread her hesitation, though it wasn't more
than a second.

Without a word, he spun on his heel and walked swiftly
away, leaving her and her three dollars intact. Genny
watched the flexing strength of his stride as he crossed the
great expanse of Union Station. She wanted to run after
him, but her feet were nailed to the floor. She couldn't play
the fool again. She couldn't trust another man—this man,
this ex-convict, with his evil scar and beautiful hands.

She held her breath, waiting for him to look back, but
he didn't. He went to a window, spoke with a man there
and then fished a wallet from his hip pocket and drew out
some money.

The man said something, and Odessa pulled his watch
from his pocket. Opening it, he extended it to the man who
held it in his palm to admire it. Presently, the clerk laid it
on the counter and disappeared, returning to place the
money and the watch in an envelope. He wrote something
on a paper and stepped from behind his window to enter
an office several doors down.

It was as if she and Jessamine no longer existed for him,
and Genny wanted to scream, You can't come into my life
and then just stop being there, Odessa Gold! You can't
make me care, and then just . . . what? What came after
caring? Pain!

Returning, the man handed Odessa a piece of paper.
Odessa retraced his steps, and as he came nearer, Genny's
nerves danced along her flesh.

"He's coming back," she whispered raspily to Jessamine, and waited, wiping her palms on her skirt.

"I've made some arrangements for you," he said gruffly
when he walked up.

Genny shook her head in confusion. "Odessa, I—"

"You and Jessamine have a room on the third floor. For two nights only, I'm afraid, but it's the best I can do, considering."

Oh, she wanted to hit him for doing this. She wanted to scream, to weep, to claw his eyes and pull his hair. How could he go and do something so wonderful, so perfect, when she was drowning in her own morass of bitterness and self-recrimination? How could he make her want to trust him?

She gouged the front of his suit with her fingertip as her lips quivered and tears collected painfully behind her eyes. "You...you..."

"Genny—" he grasped her fingers "—accept the gesture in the spirit with which it was intended."

"We accept, Mr. Gold," Jessamine put in abruptly. "God bless you."

Genny shook her head. No, no! This wasn't right. It wasn't supposed to end like this!

Lifting her hands, Odessa pressed kisses into her palms and made tight fists of them. "Goodbye, Genny Carlyle," he said, and moving away, he touched his hat in a faintly self-mocking salute. "I wish you the best."

Genny was too stunned to move or speak. Jessamine didn't say a word, but the walls yelled their accusations: Fool, fool, fool, how could you let him leave? When in all your life have you known a man who could make you want to do something extraordinary? Have you ever known a man who made you feel things so deeply, made you look into yourself and almost like what you saw?

"Oh, Jessamine," she wailed, wringing her hands until they were bloodless.

"You must be the one to decide, Geneena," the old woman answered wisely, even before the question had been asked.

"You wouldn't think I was crazy?"

"One is never crazy to listen to their heart, child."

"But what if it's a mistake? I keep making these terrible mistakes."

"That only proves you're not God."

Odessa had already disappeared down the flight of stairs leading to the train shed. Gathering up her skirts, Genny flew after him, but when she reached the steps he was no-where in sight.

Her breaths were labored as she skittered down the stairs and darted out into the milling crowd. The noise was deafening as she searched up and down the tracks and slips and tried to see over heads that were higher than her own.

She rushed up to a redcap and took his arm.

He looked around in surprise. "Ma'am?"

"I'm looking for a tall man in a brown suit. He has a mustache and a scar." She pointed desperately to her own cheek and drew a line to her mouth.

"What's his destination, ma'am?"

"Ah, Saratoga. Yes, Saratoga Springs."

"Oh, that train left a long time ago, ma'am."

"Where did it leave from?"

"Gate seven, ma'am, but there ain't no train over there now..."

Genny nearly crashed into a dozen people as she raced toward gate seven. And there, to her sagging relief, was Odessa ambling wearily along a slip of unoccupied tracks, scuffing at the ground as if he were seriously considering hurling himself upon the tracks when the next train came in.

"Odessa!" she cried, but the scream of a whistle swallowed her shout.

She ran toward him, but stopped short when he, too, stopped in his tracks and turned, passing his hand before his eyes as if he could not believe he was actually seeing her.

A terrible urgency rose in her. She ran to Odessa and threw herself into his arms. His face pressed hard on the top of her head, and his arms tightened like a vise until she felt more of his body than she did of her own.

"Ah, Genny," he whispered and kissed her hair again and again.

She pushed back so she could gaze up into the storm clouds of his eyes. Please, please don't hurt me. I'll die if you hurt me.

"Would you need all three dollars?" she said.

Chapter Eight

"I declare, you're going to need new shoes, Geneena."

Jessamine was tucked in the big double bed of their hotel room, and her blind eyes were closed. Sleepiness had drugged her voice, but Genny was keeping her awake.

"What?" Distracted, Genny blinked at the woman.

"You're wearing out those soles with your pacing. The carpet, too. You shouldn't worry so, dear. Mr. Mac-Gowan always used to say, 'Worry will not add one inch to your stature.'"

"I think Jesus said that, Jessamine." Having to smile, Genny shook her head.

Their room was on the second floor—modest, clean and completely lacking in luxury. Genny was struggling to cope with the terrible risk she'd taken by giving Odessa Gold their last three dollars. Numb with misgivings, she'd walked Jessamine to the bathroom down the hall and given her a sponge bath and a liberal dusting of talc. By the time they returned to the room and she'd helped Jessamine into a worn cotton gown, brushed out her hair and gotten her into bed, worry had all her organs colliding painfully with each other.

If Odessa Gold was honorable, he would have returned by now. He wasn't coming back! Just as Amelia hadn't come back and Adam hadn't come back! Was it her destiny to be an eternal, doomed victim?

She kicked off her shoes, and they landed across the room. She felt a rush of nausea and, with only Jessamine's shawl covering her nakedness, hurried to the window and threw up the sash, leaning out into the foggy night to gulp great breaths of air.

Oh, God! Oh, God! Why hadn't she just gone somewhere and fallen off the edge of the earth? It would have been cleaner and infinitely quicker. How could she have done this to herself? How could she have let him do it to her?

Somewhere a clock struck eleven. Below, the street was quiet. The threat of rain burdened the night air, making everything move more slowly. In the distance, thunder rumbled, and periodic flashes of lightning zigzagged to the ground.

From far out on the river, the melancholy wail of a steamboat rolled in with the fog. The hansom cabs parked in front of the hotel were the only vehicles in sight, except for the ice wagon. The driver clucked and flicked the reins. The horse set off at a slow clip-clop, clip-clop.

Genny covered her face with her hands. "I never learn," she told the cabs and the ice man and the river.

At least her plans to meet Adam in St. Louis had gotten Jessamine and herself out of Wyoming. St. Louis was a big city. She could probably find another position teaching school. She might even find an older couple who needed a housekeeper. She could teach school during the day and clean house in the evening for their room and board.

"Please, please," she prayed. "If You'll give me another chance, Lord, I'll never be so gullible again."

Jessamine's slumbering breaths filled the small room. Peering between her fingers, Genny watched the fog curling and swirling at the end of the street, as if some predatory beast lay in wait in the alley, needing to feed.

She was too tired to wait up any longer. She began turning away, then whirled back, her pulse slamming violently in her temples.

A man! Odessa? It had to be Odessa! No one but him had that arrogant, lanky walk. No one but Odessa would be caught dead in that wilted hat!

"Oh!" She ran to the door and rotated in a confused circle. "Oh!" She raced back to dangle out the window again.

Had he won at cards? Was he bringing money? The jacket of his suit was open, and his necktie had been undone and was draped about his neck. A shock of hair fell across his forehead. A cheroot was clamped between his teeth.

Veering to the bed, Genny found Jessamine too deeply asleep to rouse. Stark naked, she snatched up a blouse and pulled it on. She had no time for buttons as she twirled her skirt into the air and let it drop down over her. With her hair tumbling about her face, she located her shoes and grabbed Jessamine's shawl, then slapped the tabletop for the key. Pocketing it, she slipped through the door and out into the hall, fighting with buttons as she ran.

Down the stairs she flew, her bare legs flashing and her skirt gathered in her hands. When she reached the landing, the man behind the desk looked up with surprise.

"Madam, may I help you?"

"No, thank you!" she said breathlessly and raced on. She dodged a group of men who were returning from a night of drinking. Their laughter was loud, and one called out, "Hey, wait up, darlin'."

Another man whistled. "Where're you goin' in such a hurry, sugar? Wait! I'll take you. We'll all take you!"

Horrid man!

Genny darted past the amazed doorman and into the street. Odessa was turning the corner where the sidewalk fronted the hotel. She skimmed along it, her gaze rushing on ahead, reaching for his face.

Seeing her almost immediately, he stopped where he was, and his smile made the tips of Genny's fingers grow hot, then cold.

Don't think he's the most wonderful thing you ever saw. Don't rely on him. Don't hope he came back with money. Don't hope anything!

But hope was a nightingale singing in her heart. She hardly felt her feet or the fringe of Jessamine's shawl dragging the sidewalk. She almost crashed into him.

Laughing, he caught her by the shoulders.

"My, my," he said and delved deeply into her eyes, then lifted his head to scan the street, making certain they were in no danger. "I have to say I question your judgment, pretty lady, running out into the night, but if you don't say you're glad to see me, I think I'll die right here."

"I'm glad to see you! I'm glad to see you!" She laughed and spread her hand on the front of his shirt, a gesture that seemed to please him. "What happened? Did you win?"

As deflating as it was to Odessa's ego to know that she was much more interested in his business than his feelings, he decided he would take her laughter however and whenever he could get it. She was bewitchingly lovely with her blouse open at her throat, looking absurdly like a child awaiting her present, her feet unable to keep still.

"Shame on you, Genny." He flicked his cheroot away and tapped the end of her freckled nose with a fingertip. "You thought I wasn't coming back, didn't you? You were worried, weren't you?"

The streetlights caught the subtleties of her flush. "Me? No, no." Giggling, she measured a tiny space between finger and thumb. "Well, maybe just a little concerned."

"Little, my foot." Odessa drew her into his side and realized she was wearing nothing beneath her skirt and blouse. Desire warmed his blood.

"For your refreshing streak of practicality, my sweet," he murmured, "I adore you. Where's Jessamine?"

He was deliberately drawing her into the shadows near the entrance of the alley that served the train depot. Genny caught a fleeting glimpse of two other people there, lolling against a wall, pressed together and kissing with gluttonous hunger, their heads moving and their hands seeking.

She stumbled into Odessa and coughed nervously. The sight of the couple was disturbingly erotic, reminding her vaguely of something she couldn't put her finger on.

She looked swiftly away. "I hated to wake her," she said quickly. "She was so tired."

She dared another glance. The man had his hands inside the woman's dress, fondling her. Genny's own breasts came throbbingly alive.

"You lost our money, didn't you?" she blurted. "You're trying to get up the courage to tell me."

Odessa busied himself with drawing the shawl more securely about Genny's shoulders. What he wished he did have the courage to say was how much he wanted her at this moment. She wore the night like velvet. The warm, humid breeze caught her skirt and tucked it between her legs, sculpting the slight curve of her belly and inviting him to spread his hand there, in the soft, feminine hollow.

"I did not lose," he said.

"You won?" Her lips parted with surprise and delight. "Really? You actually won?"

"I always win, Genny." Trembling raced through Odessa, as ragged as the summer lightning. "At cards, I always win." Not in other things, though.

Her shrug could have filled a book with meanings. "I thought you were just talking when you said that."

"I never just talk."

She was so close, he could take a deep breath and graze her side. He could move his arm an inch and brush the side of her breast.

She said, "How much did you win?"

"I don't really know. I haven't counted it."

Astonished, she stopped walking and brought her foot emphatically down upon the sidewalk. "Well, count it, you idiot! Do you want me to go mad?"

"That's what I like about you, Genny." He enjoyed laughing with her. "You're greedy. You can always trust a greedy person. They try hard."

Chuckling, he turned and walked her casually toward the cabs parked in front of the hotel. "What happens when you go mad, Genny Carlyle?"

"I grow fangs and froth at the mouth."

She was inching around him as they walked, plucking at his jacket pockets with the tips of her fingernails. Her dancing feet stopped, and she jerked up her head, bringing him to a standstill.

"There's money in there," she whispered in awe.

"I know." Grinning, he pretended to calmly straighten the collar of her blouse. His hands were shaking. Damn, Goldman, get a hold of yourself.

"Let's go somewhere and count it."

"My thoughts exactly."

Odessa stepped to the curb and gave a whistle that brought up the head of the lead cab driver. The reins flicked upon the back of the horse, and the carriage rolled toward them.

"Odessa, I—" Genny hadn't meant she wanted to go somewhere.

"We have to divide the spoils of war, don't we?" he challenged, wanting to get her alone and knowing it was the one bait she would not refuse.

The cab was large enough to accommodate four passengers. At first Genny was reluctant, but Odessa urged her up the step and she tumbled in.

Leaning to the driver's perch, he thrust several bills into the man's hand. "We'd like to see the river."

"Looks like rain," the man observed and doffed his stovepipe hat.

Odessa tossed another bill into the hat.

"A little wet never hurt anybody," the driver said and clapped the hat on his head. "Giddap."

Uncertain of what to do, Genny sat stiffly straight and folded her hands primly in her lap. She wished now she'd taken more time to dress. The way Odessa was lounging back and staring at her, she felt positively naked.

"I hope you don't freeze like that," he said mildly. "We'll have to have a closed casket at your burial."

The horse picked up speed, and Genny was thrown backward. Odessa laughed.

"That isn't funny," she snapped.

"No—" he leaned forward and pulled her knees apart "—but you are."

"Mr. Gold!" Genny gasped, wriggling.

"Hold out your skirt, Genny. And stop being so mistrustful of me. I have a fragile ego."

Smirking, Genny allowed him to spread her skirt like an apron. He emptied his pockets and heaped handfuls of crumpled bills into her lap, plus a healthy collection of coins that jingled like the most beautiful music she had ever heard.

She squealed with delight and clapped her hand over her mouth, bending low to peer at the numerals on the bills: ones and fives and tens.

She melted back against the seat in disbelief. "I've never had so much money in my hands at one time."

He dropped his sinfully long lashes in a wink. "If I'd foreseen that money could work this miracle," he drawled, "I would've stayed longer and won more."

"You're definitely not a nice man, Mr. Gold." She sniffed and giggled. "Let's count it."

She raked all the bills into a pile and proceeded to arrange them in numerical order. So inflammatory was her charm, Odessa wanted to pull her down and take her then and there.

She placed her stacks into diminishing order and grasped his hand, opening his fingers so she could count into his palm: "Sixty-six, sixty-seven, sixty-eight...."

Wide-eyed and infinitely kissable, she tipped up her face. "Sixty-nine dollars." She sucked pensively on her lip. "Too bad it's not an even seventy."

"Oh, what a poor spirit you have, Genny."

Flashing a smile, she grabbed the money and let it filter through her fingers back down to the skirt. Odessa saw his own face reflected in her eyes and wondered what she would do if he pulled her into his arms.

In a burst of exhilaration that caught him totally off guard, she leaned over and flung her arms about his neck. "We're rich! You're a genius, Odessa Gold! A genius if ever there was one! You know what I'm going to buy? Oranges, bananas and those wonderful little baby carrots. And melons!" She closed her eyes and drew a breath as if smelling the food already. "I'm going to eat and eat and eat. Ten melons all by myself! Hallelujah, we're rich!"

Genny knew that what happened next was her fault. She might have been an old maid, but she wasn't stupid. Odessa Gold was attracted to her, must have wanted her. The man had been in prison for ten years. Cinderella's stepsisters would have looked good.

Then why did she throw herself upon him as she did? What demons drove her to lean across the seat so that she was melting against him? When he reached behind his head and disengaged her arms, something deep inside her tore apart. Something fragile shattered into a thousand pieces. She went icy cold all over, and she watched, in horror, as a muscle tightened in his cheek and made the scar menacing.

He held her hands imprisoned in his big ones.

Embarrassment burned her skin like a poison, and she shrank back against her seat, acutely aware of everything . . . the clop of the horses' hooves, the wheels clattering on the cobbles, the sway of the cab, the thunder, the lightning, the boats on the river sounding their horns.

She wanted to throw open the cab door and hurl herself into the darkness. She wanted to hide.

"Genny," he said as he moved into the seat beside her and laid his arm on the cushions at her back. "Sweetheart—"

She lashed out at him. "Leave me alone!"

"Genny, I only wanted to talk to you before—"

"Before what?" Her eyes widened as she compre-
hended that the unhappiness in him was as real as her own.
With a frenzy, she began to rake the money from her skirt
as if it were tainted. "I don't want this. I don't want any
of it. I don't even know why I'm here. What am I doing
here? Oh, take it, take it!"

Money fell on the floor and scattered over the seat so
that he was forced to gather it up. She was wiping her
hands upon her skirt.

"Christ, Genny—"

Unshed tears dripped in her voice. "I'd like to go back
to the hotel, please."

The air inside the carriage was suddenly too close to be
borne. The sky flickered with lightning, making the street
lurid and the carriage stark with misery.

Meaning only to stop the lunacy before it got completely out of hand, Odessa took Genny's hands as he
would have taken hold of a stubborn child. To his dismay, she was anything but a child; she was amazingly
strong, and it took all his strength to prevent her from
striking him.

"Come on, Genny," he mocked around the desire that
was suddenly thick in his throat and forcing blood into his
head and his groin. "Don't be coy."

"Coy!" She freed a fist to swing at his head. "How dare
you, Odessa Gold! You, you—" She kicked viciously, and
her skirt rode high on her legs.

The flash of naked, cream-white thighs and thrusting
legs, the twinkle of coppery, tufted curls, were a spur in
Odessa, driving him to shove her back against the seat and
pin her with the weight of his body.

"Damn you!" she hissed, twisting her head from side to
side.

"For this," he gritted as he chased her mouth with his,
"I'm sure I will be."

If she had been honest with him, Genny would have admitted that she was not offended so much by his un-
leashed passion as by what had gone before. He knew he'd

hurt her, and now he thought she was so starved for love that if he kissed her, she would let it pass as nothing.

Her hair was a cloud between them, and he buried his face in her neck where her blouse had pulled apart. His mouth was hot and wet, and the scrape of his teeth along her skin was electrifying. Against her belly, he was hard and demanding.

"Genny." He spoke her name, half-groaning half-laughing. "Stop me before I do something really, really stupid."

But though laughter was couched in his words, he had no intentions of stopping, and Genny wasn't certain she wanted him to. Even now, as his hands were beneath her skirt, moving up her legs and cupping her bare hips, pulling her with ease closer to the unrelenting rhythm of his own, she wanted to go limp in his arms and end her innocence.

"If you think—" she managed to choke as she raked hair from her face.

But he smothered her words in a dizzying, unrelenting kiss. Genny's head whirled as if a swallow of whiskey had struck the bottom of her stomach and made her instantly drunk. His lips were parting hers and his tongue was exploring her mouth in a way Adam had never, never attempted.

Lightning illuminated the coach, and the horses whinnied. Genny wondered wildly if the storm had come inside, for she was surrendering to the most exquisite sensations she had ever known. Her skin was glowing and her skull tingling. His hands were moving possessively between them, unfastening her blouse so that his mouth, when it left hers, kissed the hollow at the base of her throat and shockingly swept lower to her naked breasts.

Her nipples leapt to him, and she tried to say his name, but she could only moan as if a terrible fever had her in its tormenting grip. She flicked her tongue over her lips. They were so dry! She couldn't keep still.

Were her hands free? Yes. When had he released them? When had he stopped forcing her and begun seducing her?

He was moving between her thighs, pressing and pressing the hard ridge against her, making her pool with silky wetness. Do it, a voice told her. Don't think about it. Let him do it.

And though madness was consuming her and she wanted most desperately this man whom she knew but did not know, the virgin beneath the passion was a very logical and very self-protective entity. Even as his fingers were discovering the secret of her desire, her innocence threw up a bulwark of such overpowering force that her head miraculously cleared.

"No," she whispered as his finger slipped with delirious sweetness inside her and his mouth fastened to hers so that she had to jerk her head away. "This is wrong, Odessa."

She battled his hands and his ravenous mouth. She wriggled and strained until he was jarred back to his senses.

He lay for a moment upon her, not saying a word as he battled to bring his breathing under some sort of control. He swore a terrible oath under his breath, and she felt the insanity drain from him, leaving in its wake an awful despair.

The part of her that loved him already made her place her hands upon the back of his head and stroke the damp tousled hair. "I'm sorry," she said, and truly meant it. "I've never. I mean, I haven't—"

"I know," he groaned. "God, I never meant to frighten you. I would never hurt you."

"It's all right, Odessa."

"No, it's not all right."

And it wasn't, but she'd never meant to cry about it. When he perceived the tears rolling down her cheeks, he raised up in disbelief at what he had done and what she had let him do.

Genny didn't know exactly what happened after that. As the cab took them back to the hotel, he held her, she knew, and he comforted her and told her things that didn't really matter and that she wouldn't remember. He walked her to her room, but she was so numb, she even forgot about the money. She was surprised when he kissed her and said he would give it to her at breakfast the next morning.

She was so tired, so tired. She wanted only to go to bed and sleep, but he caught her shoulder as she was preparing to slip inside the room. For long moments, he held her face between his hands, tracing the arch of her brows with his thumbs and touching her chafed lips, adoring her, worshiping her.

"Oh, Genny," he whispered and smiled unhappily, "you deserve so much more than this."

With a poignancy too eloquent for words, he gathered her into his arms and held her close.

As much as Genny knew it couldn't possibly have been so, she felt the muscles in his chest quiver as he buried his face in her hair, almost as if he were weeping. He held her with a fierce tenderness, as if he could not bring himself to let go.

If he had been weeping, if he really had been that soft and vulnerable inside, she would have said that of all the things they had done this night, perhaps of all the things she had known in her whole life, this sad final embrace was the most precious.

But of course he wasn't that sad. And with the dawn would come a moment of reckoning. Neither of them would get off so easily. She had learned that when she lived in the sassafras thickets of the Missouri River.

Chapter Nine

After his contemptible, despicable, cheap, scurvy, shabby, disgraceful and loathsome behavior with Genny Carlyle the night before, Odessa stared at his reflection in the hotel barbershop and wondered if he shouldn't take the razor and slit his throat.

"Are we unhappy with it, sir?" the barber inquired, tucking a dismayed chin beneath his stiff collar like a terrapin retreating into his shell.

Odessa eyed the razor with a bleak irony. He had vowed somewhere in the stranglehold of dawn that he would not draw Genny any deeper into his life. She must not be tainted by the forces that were chasing him. Not if he cared for her. And he cared more than he liked to think about.

"Perhaps if we shaved the beard, sir," the barber suggested hopefully.

Odessa needed the beard. If C. E. McFee and Manville Platt really were behind the search on the train, a beard could prove a useful camouflage. For a while.

"The beard stays," he said and picked up the mirror to examine the back of his head. His hair was cut neatly around his ears and barely touched the top of his snow-white collar. "It's fine. Everything is fine."

He fished out the appropriate coins and dropped them to the counter where they rolled against long-neck bottles filled with brightly colored toilet water and cologne.

The barber twitched away the cloth with the dexterity of a bullfighter, then brushed the back of Odessa's neck with talcum. Odessa had sent his suit out to be cleaned and pressed and his shirt laundered. Amazingly—hotel service had changed drastically in a decade—they had been returned an hour later, wrapped in tissue and fresh as daisies.

He rose from the chair and shrugged into his pressed jacket, making sure he had a cheroot in his inside breast pocket.

A bootblack asked from across the room, "Shoeshine, mistuh?"

With a grimace Odessa considered his boots and the bootblack, who had to be one of the most handsome black men he'd ever seen. Younger than himself, about the same height, the man's physique put his own to shame. His hips were trim and tight, and his shoulders strained against his crisp white jacket. His hands looked like a pianist's, long-fingered and powerful.

The man grinned and snapped his wrist, making his rag sing. Odessa chuckled, and the bootblack executed a few steps of soft-shoe and made an extravagant finale by dipping forward and tossing out his rag.

"Cost ya two bits," he said, jabbing a thumb toward the dais with its trio of chairs.

Odessa grinned back. "If I say no, you'll probably rip the base off the chair and twist it around my neck." Chuckling, he climbed onto the dais. "What do they call you? Samson?"

The young man drawled, "They calls me Buttercup, suh."

Laughter rolled richly from Odessa's chest. Buttercup turned up the cuff of Odessa's trousers and hesitated, angling his boot to scrutinize it. He drew a fingertip along the stitching of the sole. "I know these boots."

"What?" Odessa stopped in the process of clamping a cheroot between his teeth.

"I should say, I know the man who made them."

The Negro dialect had oddly disappeared, and the voice was now rich and cultured, threaded with an accent that Odessa surmised was a mixture of French and the King's English.

"I bought these boots in Paris," Odessa said.

"From Arnaud Duprée."

Odessa was amazed. "You know Duprée?"

"I knew of him, sir." An irreverent wiggle of brows accompanied his grin. "A bit before my time, but yes."

With astonishing skill, the bootblack laid cream to the cracked leather boots and worked it in. He positioned his rag across the instep and began to buff with snaps and swipes as artistic as a Gypsy making his violin weep.

"I used to live in Paris," he explained as his hands flew. "My mother was a ballet dancer and my father was a Frenchman. That was back when France was trying to figure out what they would do when they could no longer get Southern cotton."

Astonished, Odessa held out his hand to bring the ritual to a halt. "Your name's not Buttercup, is it?"

A guilty grin. "No, sir."

"What, then?"

"Angouleme Tulane, sir."

Odessa frowned. "Come again?"

Angouleme's laughter was as beautiful as he was. "My mother called me Angel, my father called me son, and everyone else called me nigger. You can suit yourself."

Odessa worried his beard. "Well, well, well. I think you've missed your calling, Angel Tulane. Tell me, what do you hope to accomplish with all the 'yassuhs' and 'nawsuhs'?"

"A man has to make a living, Mr. Gold. The white man is very keen on 'yassuhs' and 'nawsuhs.'"

Mr. Gold?

Angel finished polishing the boots and started packing up his equipment as Odessa removed a bill from his pocket. He felt again the fat envelope tucked into his inner pocket that contained fifty-five dollars, Genny's share, for he had kept out only enough for expenses to get to Saratoga.

He climbed down from the dais. "Now you can tell me how you know my name, Angel Tulane."

Beyond them, on the other side of the large streaked window where the red-and-white barber pole was turning, the street was filling with traffic. Inbound trains were shrilling and pulling into the shed. Late passengers were spilling out of hansom cabs and hurrying inside.

Angel watched the driver of a cab, a black man, lay down his reins and climb down to open the door for his passengers.

"I know your name, Mr. Gold, because I saw you play poker at Boone's Gaming House last night."

Odessa narrowed his eyes. Angel Tulane was not only handsome and smart, he was mysterious.

"Shining shoes is what I do for a living," Angel said, "but it's not who I am."

"And who are you?"

"I received my degree in engineering in Paris. I came to this country when I was twenty-one years old, full of dreams. I decided to make my fortune in New York where I thought people weren't so opinionated about the black man. That was when I learned about Harlem."

Odessa remembered Harlem well. He had often gone there to sketch. "I take it you didn't make your fortune in Harlem."

"Nawsuh, I sho didn't." Angel punctuated his dialect with a few steps of tap dance, then sighed with disillusionment. "But I did design a burglar alarm for a Fifth Avenue gentleman that cost over a million dollars to install. It was a work of art, if I do say so. A man could sit behind the desk in the main office, push one button, and every door in the building would lock. When I was done I took him my part of the bill."

"And?"

"He refused to pay."

"Did he give a reason?"

"He said the system had cost more than he'd counted on and had his white valet throw me out of the house."

Odessa turned the cheroot in his fingers. Placing it between his teeth unlit, he said around it, "Why didn't you sue?"

Angel's laughter filled the barbershop and drifted out into the noisy corridor. "A black man doesn't sue a white man, Mr. Gold. That's why I'm shining boots in St. Louis and doing a little soft shoe on the side."

Odessa felt for his watch and remembered that he had hocked it to the ticket agent to get the room for Genny and Jessamine.

The clock on the wall said he had three minutes to meet the women in the dining room. He still had no plan of what to say to Genny, not after last night. Maybe there wouldn't be a problem. She might refuse to speak to him at all.

He retrieved his hat from the coat tree. Shaping the crease without really thinking about what he was doing, he started to leave, but hesitated in the doorway.

Angel's next customer was climbing onto the dais. Returning, Odessa removed the cheroot from his mouth. "Ah, Angel . . ."

The man was waiting, and Odessa's gut felt the way it did when he held a winning hand. "I'm going to put a proposition to you, Angel Tulane."

Angel snapped his rag without comment.

"A person develops certain instincts, Angel. I'd like to offer you a job, if you're interested."

Angel returned to his customer and began to buff the polish. *Pop, pop.* Without looking up, he said, "I'm interested."

Odessa made a thoughtful sound between his teeth. "I'm on my way to Saratoga Springs."

A group of men entered the shop, bringing laughter and loud talk with them. Angel finished with his customer, and the man tossed him a tip.

"Thank ya, suh," Angel said, and gave a gallant bow.

"Saratoga Springs is where the rich people go to play, Angel." Odessa braced his hips against the dais and crossed his ankles as he struck a match on a screw holding down the chair. He cupped his hand about the dancing flame.

"I know Saratoga, Mr. Gold."

"I'm going to make myself a lot of money there, Angel."

"I believe you."

"But it would be a hell of a lot easier if I had someone to help me do it. Someone clever, someone with finesse." Odessa blew smoke at the ceiling.

Angel was packing up his tools.

"You would be paid well," Odessa said as he considered the white ash forming on the cheroot.

Angel's black eyes were quick and shrewd and calculating. "I don't doubt it."

"I'll be leaving in a few hours."

Settling his hat onto his head and making a final inspection in the mirror, Odessa didn't think he looked as if he'd just gotten out of prison.

Or did he? When he talked to Genny, he must remember prison and Eli Wright and McFee and Platt, not the tempting sweetness of her, not the honey of her mouth.

"I'll be ready," Angel said simply.

Odessa turned to face him. Angel understood the role he would play and would perform it magnificently, he knew. Grinning suddenly, he poked the cheroot into his mouth and thrust out his hand. Angel grasped it without hesitation.

"You'll be needing train fare," Odessa said and reached for his wallet.

Angel shook his head. "I'll provide my own ticket, Mr. Gold. I have some excess baggage I carry around, but it's necessary to me. I'll see to it."

What man didn't have excess baggage?

With a small salute, Odessa touched the brim of his hat. "All right. But the name isn't Gold. It's Goldman. Andrew Goldman. I'd rather you called me Odessa."

"Odessa it is."

"We'll make a good team, Angel."

The black man smiled his beautiful smile. "I know."

"Mademoiselle wishes a table for two?"

With the emergence of America's hotels as a social gathering place, and the dining room as test of sophistication and savoir faire, the hotel's maître d' considered himself to be, by the nature of his job, a flawless judge of character.

Philippe took one look at the two women who entered with the breakfast crowd and knew he would get little or no tip. He was never wrong in the matter of tips. The older woman was blind, and the younger...

The younger woman was one of the most attractive he'd seen in a long time, granted, with her height and her slimness, her green-and-white checked shirtwaist and oatmeal-colored duck skirt. But compared to the other ladies he had seated this morning, her sophistication left something to be desired. He was about to show her and her elderly companion to one of the tables he reserved for nontippers when she smiled.

Philippe shut his mouth with a snap.

"Please, no trouble," she said disarmingly and fixed him with lively green eyes. "Put us anywhere. We're meeting someone for breakfast." She glanced uncertainly around the large room. "He may be late."

Philippe found himself smiling back, something he hadn't done in years, and he bestowed upon her his ultimate compliment by guiding them to the best section of the room.

"Would mademoiselle like the morning room?" he offered generously. "There's a very nice view of the river."

"Jessamine," Genny whispered, suspicious of the generosity of strangers, "would you like to sit where we can see the river?"

The older woman moved her head as if straining to hear beauty in the ordinary sounds of people. "How delightful," she said to the maître d'. "Thank you, young man."

Feeling oddly naked before the old woman's blind eyes, Philippe bowed deeply. "This way, please. May I take your arm, madame?"

"Why, I think you're of the old school, sir," Jessamine said, and laid her fingers elegantly upon his cuff. "You remind me of my dear departed husband."

"And that's the highest compliment she can pay you," Genny mumbled, slipping into the depression that had crowded closer and closer since the crack of dawn.

She had dreamed of her mother. In the diaphanous haze, Amelia was lying in the meadow and holding up her arms to a man who knelt in the grass, a slash of sunlight on his face. Smells were vivid in the dream, and the grass had a summer fragrance, as if rinsed by a rain. She had seen the man's face as he knelt and the veins of his neck. His mouth was fixed with demand beneath his soft feathering of mustache. His face changed then, and became that of Odessa Gold. And the woman in the grass? The white shadow with flashing limbs? She wasn't Amelia at all, but her, Genny. She was beneath Odessa Gold, naked and writhing, arching up to draw him deeply inside and twining her arms about his neck. She had awakened, shivering and lost.

Now she looked quickly at the hotel's window where the Mississippi glinted, needle-bright, in the sunshine. "This is wonderful," she said to Philippe. "Thank you."

"My pleasure, mademoiselle." He bowed. "May I get you something while you wait?"

"We're fine, thank you."

He bowed again. "Very well."

Puzzled, Genny watched him walk away. "That man makes me nervous," she said to Jessamine. "I wonder what he wants."

Jessamine was making herself familiar with the table setting, touching the silver and locating her napkin, running a fingertip around the edge of her cup and saucer, smiling and smelling and savoring the sound of the silver upon the china plate.

"He wants nothing, Geneena. He knows. Or if he doesn't know, he senses."

"Senses what?" Feeling the need to hide before the old woman, Genny crossed her arms over her breasts. "You're talking in riddles this morning."

"Am I, now?"

More than a little irritated, Genny leaned over and tapped Jessamine's hand with a fingernail. "You don't have the faintest notion of what you're talking about, Jessamine. And if you're implying that something is wrong with me, forget it."

An understanding smile found its way into the deep lines of Jessamine's face. "Love has a force, Geneena, a radiance. It's like a circle of warmth, and when anyone steps into it, they feel it. It's very real. It cannot be contrived or faked. A woman has it for her children, a man for his beloved. Mr. MacGowan and I used to have it, they tell me. Now you have it."

Aghast, Genny sank back into her chair. "But nothing happened between us. Not really."

"Nothing has to happen dear."

Genny felt as if she were only now awakening from the dream, and that it hadn't been a dream at all. In her heart, she had given herself to Odessa Gold already. Whatever her body did from this point on would be an anticlimax.

"The sad part is—" Jessamine lifted her napkin, unfolded it and spread it lovingly in her lap "—if the love isn't nurtured, the radiance soon disappears. What color are the napkins, Geneena?"

"Pink," Genny numbly replied.

"I'm so hungry, I could take a bite of one. Don't they smell good?"

Genny glanced at the clock on the wall and said to Jessamine, "He may not come, you know. He may have changed his mind."

Jessamine lifted a glass of water to her lips. "The fires of hell could not keep Mr. Gold from coming to you, Geneena."

When Odessa caught sight of Genny framed by sunlight streaming through the dining-room window and setting her hair ablaze, his instincts told him to turn on his heel and never see her again.

"May I show you a table, sir?"

"What?" Odessa started, then scowled at the headwaiter and removed his hat. He reached into his pocket and took out an envelope and slapped it thoughtfully against the palm of his hand. He opened his mouth to speak, but the words were lost on his tongue.

He cleared his throat and said hoarsely, "Do you see that woman by the window?" He drew a line of direction with his nod.

"Would you like me to give her that?" Philippe nodded to the envelope.

Odessa tried to cauterize his feelings as he had done so often in the past. But he realized he could not bear not seeing her again, not hearing her voice one more time.

Despising his weakness, he shook his head. "I'll take it to her myself. Thanks."

"Very good, sir."

The maître d' let him find his own way to the table. With each step, Odessa swore he wasn't falling in love with Genny Carlyle. His long period of celibacy had stained his judgment, that was all. Genevieve Carlyle was not unique; she did not have the power he attributed to her. He wasn't going to hurt her, nor she him. This would end. Everything would be all right.

And then she looked up and a star rose inside him, burning the back of his eyes.

"Good morning," he said a bit too breathlessly as he walked up.

She had pleated her napkin into tight, severe creases. "Good morning."

He waited, his own victim. When she said nothing, he drew out a chair and sat. "Good morning, Jessamine. Have you been waiting long?"

"Yes!" Genny blurted, then shook her head. "I mean, no, we haven't been waiting long."

He was, Odessa thought, forming a habit of taking refuge in the old blind woman. Drawing his chair closer, he murmured naughtily, "You're looking absolutely radiant this morning, my dear Jessamine."

The word radiant made Genny flinch.

"And I'm much too old to fall for a silver tongue, Mr. Gold," Jessamine teased back. "I wasn't radiant when I was a young woman, and I'm certainly not now."

"We have only your word for that," he retorted, and signaled the waiter with a snap of fingers. "Besides, I'm not old. I'm young and sowing a few wild oats."

"I know wild oats when I see them." Jessamine laughed. "Or hear them, as the case may be. Having sowed a few of my own."

"I'm sure Mr. Gold isn't interested in your wild oats, Jessamine," Genny said unenthusiastically.

The awkward silence was relieved only by the waiter taking their order. Genny's long flirtation with starvation made her want to order one of everything. She asked the waiter to bring her an omelet with a sauce made of fresh herbs. Plus boiled potatoes with fish fresh from the Mississippi and slices of fried green tomatoes. And steaming hot biscuits with thick orange marmalade and coffee with heavy cream.

When the waiter left with the lengthy order, Odessa wryly observed, "The train for Saratoga leaves in two hours."

"We know," Genny said, not realizing he was teasing her about how long it would take her to eat.

Plucking a rose from the vase on the table, Odessa placed the envelope of money down and laid the rose on top. Genny stared for a moment and then, with a guilty glance, snatched it greedily into her lap and stuffed it into her bag.

When the food arrived, Genny sat for a moment just appreciating its beautiful arrangement on the platter. As the waiter hovered nearby, an expectant smile on his face, Philippe watched from a distance, approving of a woman who enjoyed her food.

Genny attacked her breakfast with a dainty yet eager gusto, savoring each bite and closing her eyes as she chewed. "Oh, my," she murmured and took another bite. "Oh, my."

Odessa ate very little, and when he finished and was sipping coffee, Genny broke one of the biscuits open and mopped each golden pearl of butter from her plate, then popped the crust into her mouth.

As if by magic, the waiter appeared with strawberries she hadn't ordered, and Odessa shrugged. "I thought you might enjoy them."

Genny's eyes widened. "They have whipped cream, Jessamine," she purred and dipped one succulent berry into the cream and held it to the blind woman's lips.

Watching Genny, Odessa thought, was more satisfying than a king's banquet. Around them, other diners had noticed her, too, and were smiling as Genny bit with strong white teeth into a last biscuit dripping with butter and marmalade.

"Divine," she sighed and washed it all down with rich, creamy coffee.

Odessa wouldn't have been surprised, when Genny finally blotted her mouth and laid the napkin gracefully beside her plate, if the entire restaurant had stood up and applauded.

When the dishes were cleared away, he leaned back in his chair and rolled a cigar between his fingers, breathing in the good smell of it.

"I've met a man," he said and proceeded to tell them about Angel Tulane.

Genny easily recognized in Odessa's voice the respect he held for the black man. "Why didn't he have breakfast with us?"

"He was finishing some things."

Genny shrugged, her thoughts on Saratoga Springs. Presently she asked him, "There are a lot of people in Saratoga during the season?"

"Thousands," Odessa said.

Genny wasn't sure why she said, "Maybe I can meet someone there." She hadn't consciously been thinking about meeting anyone, not in the romantic context that the chance remark implied. Perhaps she'd been feeling guilty over what had almost happened between Odessa and her the night before. Maybe she unconsciously needed some indication that their stolen intimacies would lead somewhere, that after she retrieved her money from Adam Worthington, her relationship with Odessa would not end.

But her mistake had the effect of Fourth of July fireworks. Odessa laid an arm along the back of his chair and crossed his knees. "What're you talking about, Genny?" He placed a small kick on each syllable.

Feeling unfairly attacked, she shrugged and picked up the rose and began plucking its petals, dropping them one by one upon the pink tablecloth.

"It was perfectly clear," she told him. "I said—"

"I heard what you said, I just can't believe it."

"What can't you believe?"

"That you want to find yourself a husband in Saratoga."

She felt as if she were standing in quicksand up to her shins. "I do have the future to think of. Jessamine and I can't keep rolling around like stones."

With a sharp sigh, he brought his elbow to the table and rested his head on his fingertips. "I can't believe this."

"People get lonely, Mr. Gold, and sometimes they would give a lot simply to have a pleasant companion. Who's to say there isn't a kind, upstanding older man somewhere who wouldn't mind in the least affording Jessamine and me a home."

"In exchange for what?" Odessa didn't cajole the answer from her. He pillaged with a blazing, destructive force. "Money?"

But Genny had been pillaged before, and she gave a shrug that could be taken a half-dozen ways. Why was he doing this? His need to hurt her showed in his face, and her protection of herself was as automatic as breathing.

She looked at Jessamine for help. Where is the radiance, Jessamine?

Leaning closer, she said with icy sweetness, "Haven't you ever done anything for money, Mr. Gold?"

His eyes were almost black. "No. I just kill people."

"I didn't say that!"

He rose harshly from the table and had to catch his chair to keep it from falling. Genny gazed down at the puddle of rose petals. Their beautiful breakfast was ruined, and it was her fault. Why had she said such a stupid, stupid thing? Husband hunting, for goodness's sake!

"Please," she whispered, coming quickly to her feet. "Sit down. Stay with Jessamine. Have some more coffee. I have to go back to the room, anyway."

She had to go because she wasn't sure how this man, this gambler, this mysterious ex-convict, made her want what she could not have. Why did it hurt so much? She had wanted things before.

She removed one of the bills from her purse and laid it upon the table. "This is for Jessamine's and my breakfast. Jessamine, I'll finish our packing. You and Mr. Gold enjoy yourselves."

A bitter taste filled Odessa's mouth as he watched Genny leave, and he didn't feel the least bit better when heads turned to admire her. Compared to the other women in the dining room, with their corsets and jewels and rouged cheeks and frizzed hair, Genny's grace was like a breath of fresh air.

But he wasn't concerned with that; he was concerned with the knowledge that her words, whether she had planned them or not, were perfectly true. She had no idea how easy it would be to find a good older man who would take care of her and Jessamine.

"Dammit," he said, then turned in a bleak apology to Jessamine who had yet to say her piece. "All right," he added glumly, "let's have it, Jessamine."

"I'm blind, Mr. Gold. How would I know what's going on between the two of you?"

She probably knew more than he did. "You remember what it was like when a man stuck his foot into his mouth, don't you?"

Jessamine's face was lined with deep affection as she felt around for her coffee cup and lifted it to her lips.

"I'll let you in on a little secret, Mr. Gold," she said with infinite tenderness. "Mr. MacGowan was an expert at it."

Before Odessa left the hotel, he performed two tasks. The first was to repay the ticket agent the loan against his watch—with interest—and put it safely back into his pocket. After that he met Angel Tulane and together they went to a notary.

While they waited, a secretary typed up a paper Odessa dictated. The contents resembled that of a will. In the event that anything should happen to him, Genevieve Carlyle and Jessamine MacGowan were to be provided for from the monies that lay in a New York bank—his Goldman inheritance that he hadn't touched since Anne's death.

"Angel," he said, "I'd like you to be the executor of this paper."

"Are you sure, Odessa?"

The secretary rolled the official paper from the type-writer and took the two men to the office of the notary. Before him, they both signed the document.

As they were leaving the office, Odessa stopped Angel. "There's something you should know. I didn't keep this from you purposely—I just didn't think of it at the time. If you want to change your mind about going with me, I'll understand."

He explained about C. E. McFee and Manville Platt and the governor of Wyoming. "It may come to nothing," he said with a shrug. "They may not be after me at all, but then again..."

Angel inclined his head, and the light glinted upon the sheen of his kinky black hair. "I understand completely, Odessa. But it doesn't change a thing."

As they were leaving the notary's office, Angel laughed and said, "Anyway, I have a feeling that we're about to experience a holiday that will go down in history as being outstanding."

Odessa thought of Genny being pursued by a half-dozen wealthy, respectable older men. "Heaven help you if you're right, Angel Tulane. Heaven help us both."

Chapter Ten

"What do you mean, you've changed your mind?"

They were waiting beneath the branches of an elm near the depot in Amsterdam, New York—Jessamine and Angel Tulane, Odessa and Genny. And Beggar; part of Angel's baggage, it turned out, was a sleek golden retriever whose deep brown eyes seemed to know the secrets of humans.

The storm that had drenched St. Louis two nights before had moved east, and the humidity had reached Amsterdam before the train and turned the industrial town into a steam bath. Leaves drooped in fatigue upon the trees. Houses on silent lawns were shuttered against the sun. Rocking chairs on the big porches were empty, and Chinese wind chimes dangling from the awning of a nearby shop blended in a delicate duet with a ponderous clopping of a horse on cobblestones.

The connection to Saratoga wasn't due to arrive for hours yet. Jessamine had spread her shawl in a dainty pallet and sat monotonously fanning herself with a folded newspaper: back and forth, back and forth. Doubled up Indian fashion beside her, Angel Tulane ceremoniously peeled an orange into a Limoges bread-and-butter plate.

A remarkably elegant man, Angel Tulane, Genny thought and understood perfectly why Odessa had hired him. The small picnic he had spread was elegant enough for the most fastidious gourmet, with its embroidered napkins and china and primrose bouquet.

He explained his penchant for luxury without abashment, joking that he carried his on his back in a large, brassbound trunk. "Like a tortoise. Take this knife, for instance," he said to Jessamine, extending it to her so that she could touch it. "My mother bought this knife in Albania. Excellent craftsmen, the Albanians. Known mostly for their stonework in this country, but still . . ."

The blade slipped with exquisite ease through the fragrant peel.

"What do you mean, you've changed your mind?" Genny directed her question at Odessa as he draped his jacket over a low-hanging bough and rolled up his sleeves.

She was acutely aware of his burnished biceps and the patches of sweat that stained his shirt. "We're nearly to Saratoga. It doesn't make sense to change your mind now."

His grin was appreciative of her own sweat-dampened blouse, and he clawed briefly at his beard. "I didn't say I'd changed my mind. I said we should change our plans."

"One and the same."

"Not at all."

Genny slapped petulantly at a mosquito that buzzed greedily away with some of her blood. Beggar looked up from his paws.

Odessa was hunkered down at the base of the tree where he removed a folded paper and the stub of a pencil from his shirt pocket. His perusal of her was unsettlingly thorough as he moved the pencil over the paper. Wilted, Genny blew down the front of her bodice.

"What are you doing?" she asked.

He didn't reply, and her pique grudgingly succumbed to curiosity. She craned to see. "Why, you're sketching me."

She maneuvered herself to his back and cast a look over his shoulder. Grinning, he shifted around the tree and effectively shut her out.

"You really love to rub me the wrong way, don't you?" she said peevishly, still chafed from their quarrel.

"I tried to rub you the right way, darling," he murmured wickedly as he continued drawing, "and you wouldn't let me."

Genny stalked ungracefully to Jessamine where she snatched a sliver of orange from the plate. Orange juice dribbled from her fingertips as she scowled murderously at Odessa. Ever since her ill-fated announcement at breakfast in St. Louis, tension had been burning between them like a fuse to dynamite.

Reaching the end of her endurance, Genny strode over and made a grab for the sketch, but he easily swished it out of reach.

"My, my, Miss Carlyle. Do I perceive a wee touch of vanity?"

"Even old maids don't want to look ugly, Mr. Gold."

"Your lack of trust cuts me to the bone, Genny. An artist captures the essence of his subject. The soul. If your soul is beautiful—" his mockery slid suggestively to her waist and drifted lower "—then *you're* beautiful. If not..."

He wanted a fight, she thought. He was itching to bring out the swords for a real duel.

She gave him ammunition. "What was wrong with the old plan?"

Finished, Odessa folded the sketch in half, creased it with his thumbnail and slipped it into his shirt pocket with a protective pat. He placed the pencil stub on the ledge of his ear, then, rising to his feet, he grabbed a tree bough and dropped his weight.

His shirt had pulled free of his trousers, and his pants shifted loosely about his waist. The dimple of his navel winked at her.

Genny looked in the opposite direction. Men!

"I've spent considerable time worrying about your best interests, Genny," he drawled. "My conclusion—should you wish to hear it—is that we make a detour to New York first."

"You," she spun back with a stabbing finger, "are *not* worried about my best interests, Odessa Gold, so don't pretend otherwise."

Pulling himself up so that he could hook both arms over the branch he cupped his hand about his mouth and bawled, "Hey, Angel, didn't I say that Genny should have a decent wardrobe before she tries to find some wealthy old coot to marry her?"

With her eyes raised to heaven, Genny ground her teeth, and Beggar whined and pulled up to his haunches. Jessamine coughed into her embroidered napkin, and Angel Tulane burst out laughing.

"I wouldn't touch that one with asbestos gloves," he told Odessa, but caught sight of Genny's glare and grew discreetly sober.

Odessa's smirk at Genny was guileless. He dropped his arms from the branch and walked in a slow, ceremonious circle around her. "Genny, Genny, Genny." He woefully shook his head. "If you want to attract a husband, you're definitely going to have to buy new clothes, show a bit of shoulder. You know, a little more..." He outlined a woman's figure with his hands. "Old men—"

She wanted to scream at him. She wanted to slap his sanctimonious face!

He bent his head in mock repentance. "Forgive me. I should have said 'gentlemen of a more genteel age.' Whatever, they tend to require a bit more stimulus than normal. If you want to be a blushing bride, my dear, a complete makeover is a must, head to toe."

If she'd had one of those swords handy, she would have run him through and laughed when he died. She was sensitive about her clothes, and he knew that. As for her remark, she would call back the words if she could. Thoughts of marrying for convenience galled her.

But they were said now, and Odessa Gold, if he had a single chivalrous bone in his entire body, would let the matter drop!

But no, he wanted her to publicly recant. Well, she wouldn't do it! She would drop dead in her tracks before she would take back a single syllable!

"Why, Mr. Gold," she purred with an evil smile, "I think that earns you the first invitation to my wedding. Don't you agree, Jessamine?"

Jessamine had the good sense to remain quiet and scratch Beggar's ears.

"How very thoughtful, Miss Carlyle." Odessa's expression darkened threateningly.

Genny showed her teeth. "I'm only thinking about your best interests, Mr. Gold."

His eyes narrowed to slits. "I'm much obliged, Miss Carlyle."

"You're welcome, Mr. Gold."

Enough!

Genny swept across the grass and snatched the sketch from Odessa's shirt pocket before he knew what she was about. Blocking him with her shoulder, she unfolded it with a snap, a scathing commentary ready and waiting on her tongue.

But her breath scattered, and her mouth shut. Odessa had sketched her from her breasts upward, a charming portrait of very few lines yet capturing her as perfectly as the snap of a shutter—her high cheekbones and thin straight nose, the length of her neck and her hair that refused to remain disciplined in its net. He had even managed to suggest her mannerism of tipping up her chin and slanting a look askance.

"Odessa," she breathed reverently as she drew her fingertips in awe over the skilled lines, "you should forget about gambling."

He did not reply, and Genny, looking up, felt as if she had literally stepped into the corridor of his past. Just as she was two women, one of whom she hardly knew, he was two utterly different men. He had been one of the chosen few, a man who took privilege for granted. The Wyoming State Prison had nothing to do with the man Andrew Goldman had been, and a few kisses on the seat of a hansom cab did not make her fit into Andrew Goldman's life any more than he could step into hers.

She could not prevent him from retrieving the sketch, crushing it into a ball and hurling it toward Angel.

"Don't do that!" she cried, and hurried to scoop up the crumpled drawing and smooth it against her skirt. "How dare you destroy something beautiful? What gives you the right?"

Angel and Jessamine didn't move from their tableau of shock, and Genny guessed that had she and Odessa not been distracted by the voices of three ragged youngsters, the moment would have ended in disaster.

The boys were pushing a rickety two-seater bicycle on the cobblestones fronting the depot. Beggar was instantly on his feet, trotting toward the children, his tail wagging.

They were a motley trio, all barked knees and hand-me-down pants, grime-smeared shirts with buttons missing, bare feet that danced around on the hot stones. None appeared older than five.

"If you don't git on, Joey," the one standing at the handlebars ordered with a series of pointed directions, "we're sendin' you home. I'm gettin' blisters on my feet."

"I'm tryin', I'm tryin'," poor Joey insisted. "Gimme a chance."

Joey, the runt of the pack, was gamely attempting to double with the third boy who was already balanced on the back seat. Despite the assistance he received by pulls at his shirt and breeches, plus shoves of his rump by the leader, he could not get his leg over the bar.

The bicycle wobbled fearfully. With whoops and warnings to "hang on" and "get outta the way," it crashed and sent all three youngsters spilling over the hot cobblestones.

Beggar skidded out of the way.

Up they came with a medley of blazing tempers. "I tole you! I tole you!"

"Lemme alone!" wailed Joey.

"Shut up and behave, or I'll punch ya. Yer too little. You couldn't reach the pedals iffen you could git up."

"You punch me, and I'll tell what you did behind the grocery store, Goober! I'll tell yer mama, and she'll whup ya."

"And I'll peel yer head off, you snotty little crawfish!"

Accustomed to such scuffling among young boys, Genny was much more entranced by the sight of Odessa watching them. He had not wanted to become caught up in their small drama, and had turned away at first, a slash between his brows and regret drawing his features.

Genny wanted to touch his sleeve, but he was pulling out his pocket watch, and frowning and squinting down the glistening tracks that led to Saratoga.

Without a word he scooped up his hat and jammed it on his head. Jacketless, shirttails flapping, he approached the boys.

"Hi," he said, pushing his fists deeply into his pockets, which stretched his trousers taut across his lean rump.

The leader of the gang exchanged a wary look with his cohorts. "Hullo."

"Nice bicycle you've got there." Stooping, Odessa brought his face to a level with the boy's and pushed his hat back from his forehead. "What's your name?"

"Eddy." The boy clutched the handlebars and gave Odessa a suspicious look. "You ain't gonna take it back, are ya? That yer dog?"

"It's his dog." Odessa stabbed a thumb over his shoulder at Angel.

One of the things he had hated most about prison was the absence of children in his life. His son, had he lived, would have been ten now.

"Where'd you get it?" Odessa asked, running his fingers along the spokes of the bicycle's rear wheel.

"We didn't steal it. We found it, leanin' against a wall by the laundry where they dump the water. An' that's the truth. You can ask anybody if we didn't find it."

"I don't doubt it for a minute, Eddy."

But the boys doubted *him*, Genny thought, smiling. Odessa hadn't taken the right tack. These boys had grown up on the streets and were accustomed to stealing just to keep alive.

When she moved to stand beside him, he rose and circled her waist with his arm as if their quarrel had never happened.

"They found it, Odessa," she chided gently. "It's plain to see that. They're just making sure it works properly before they return it to the laundry. Why, it's the only decent thing to do."

"That's exactly what we wuz doin'," the boy assured him, to the eager accompaniment of two other bobbing heads. "Makin' sure it works."

"Yeah," the one named Goober chimed in. Joey, who couldn't have been more than four, was unable to take his eyes off Genny's hair.

"How d'you get it that color, lady?" he lisped with a shy smile that revealed two missing upper teeth.

Genny braced her hands on her knees and whispered as if sharing a secret, "I eat lots of apples."

"Ohhh," all three said in a wisely informed unison.

Odessa, unfortunately, was presented with the other end of Genny, and as she bent, he stared at the pear-shaped slimness of her hips and opened and closed his hands and put them back into his pockets again.

She straightened, and he swiftly pasted an innocent smirk on his face. To the boys, he said, "Seeing as how you're returning the cycle in a few minutes, anyway, is it possible that you gentlemen would be amenable to a small business proposition?"

The boys blinked in apprehension.

"Uh-oh," Genny said with suspicion.

Odessa lifted his brows guilelessly. "Well, I was just wondering."

"Odessa..." she warned with a shake of her finger.

Eddy was shrewd enough to recognize opportunity when it knocked. "What's the deal?"

Genny stepped between Odessa and the boys. "Look, boys—"

"Don't listen to her," Odessa blithely retorted over her shoulder. "You'll be able to make a stop by the candy shop after you return the bicycle. What d'you say?"

Eddy thoughtfully scratched a chigger bite on the inside of his leg. "Lemme get this straight. You're wantin' to rent this here cycle?"

Odessa turned down the sides of his mouth in a negotiable way. "Could be, could be." He pursed his lips beneath the mustache. "But you hold me up on the price..." He mimed a slice to his throat and made a *phftt* sound.

"It'll cost ya two bits," Eddy said. "Take it or leave it."

Genny watched the bargaining with surprise. Odessa was a natural with children.

He was scratching his beard. "That's a pretty steep price, don't you think?"

"We-ell..."

"But I'll take it." He located a coin in his pocket and shook it in his fist like a die. "Tell you what. I don't have the correct change. Will this do?"

He flipped a shiny silver dollar into the air, and when it turned and twisted and sparkled on its way down, the boys let go of the bicycle in a mad scramble. Catching the machine before it crashed, Odessa set it upright and threw out his arm in an invitation for Genny to climb on.

"M'lady—" he bowed from his waist "—your chariot."

Disbelieving laughter bubbled from Genny. You do have a way about you, Odessa Gold, yes you do, yes you do.

"You're not serious," she said.

He laughingly crossed his heart.

She turned her head back and forth. "I can't."

"You mean you can't ride, either, Genny?" Sighing the weariness of one who has been much put upon, Odessa tossed one leg over the bar, straddled it and kept the bicycle balanced with the inside of his thighs. "You surely can't do very much, can you?"

"I can see through you!" she snapped hotly. Odessa took his teasing too far. "Don't think I can't do that!"

"Good." Laughter was smothered in his voice. "Now I don't have to suffer through all the malarkey of getting you alone for a few minutes. Hellfire, Genny, let's call a truce for the afternoon. Get on the bicycle."

Genny mutinously compressed her lips.

"My intentions are perfectly honorable," he assured, looking heavenward as if making a solemn vow. "I swear on a stack ... Well, take my word for it."

Not for a second did Genny believe him, but he was straddling the machine so brazenly, his hat cocked so brassily, he looked like a dry-docked pirate. What could it hurt? Riding a bicycle with the man wouldn't mean that she was admitting defeat.

With a brisk switch across the grass, she took hold of the rear handlebars, hiked up her duck skirt like a fishwife and swung a leg up and over with as little flash of stockinged leg as possible.

"Jessamine," she called, praying she would not live to regret this, "Mr. Gold is taking me for a ride."

"I might've put that a bit more delicately," Odessa dryly observed.

"Just don't fall down on your end of the deal." She stuffed as much skirt as possible between her legs as she found the pedals. "I don't relish having to pump both of us all the way back."

Chuckling, Odessa wondered just how many mistakes it was possible for a man to make with a woman. He had lost count of his list of crimes against Genny.

But she was tipping her face to the sky like a zestful young girl, and he could imagine her as a child—not in a

pretty bonnet and with bushels of flouncing petticoats such
as his sisters had worn, but as a freckle-faced imp with
braids sailing out behind her as she swung on a rope or
climbed to the top of a tree or leapt into a swimming hole
in her bloomers, squealing and holding her nose.

Thoughts of her enduring the clumsy pawings of an old
man made his blood thud heavily in his ears. "What you
need," he declared as he swiveled about on his seat, "is a
good hat."

He plopped his own upon her sunshiny curls and pushed
them off to a wobbly start.

The hat slid over Genny's eyebrows. "I used to have a
good hat," she reminded him and scrambled to find the
pedals and push up the hat at the same time.

He laughed as they weaved from side to side, and she
yanked vigorously the back of his shirt. "Slow down."

"A turtle moves faster than we're going," he retorted as
his cycling skills quickly returned. "And if you could re-
frain from permanently scarring my back, my love, I'd be
more than a little obliged."

Except for more smokestacks stabbing the skyline,
Odessa found Amsterdam very little changed from the
days when he'd come with his parents to visit his dreaded
Aunt Sophia on Canary Street and suffered through such
enormous Sunday dinners in the big dining room that
everyone was compelled to retire afterward to sleep off
their gluttony.

Amsterdam's carpet factories were still sluicing waste
down the Mohawk River, and the city streets were all
smells and noises, wagons jumping on the cobbles and
dray horses pulling cotton and wool and machinery. The
looms gobbled greedily and turned out miles and miles of
carpet every year.

For a time, Odessa and Genny pedaled in silence, being
passed occasionally by phaetons whose thick rubber wheels
skimmed over the streets with whispery ease. They soon

found themselves in a quiet residential district where sedate Victorian homes stood far back from the street.

Beautifully carpeted homes, probably, Odessa thought, like Aunt Sophia's. Here, manicured flower beds splashed the slopes. No screen doors slapped as children darted through them, and no dogs chased, barking. Here, hoses hissed. Gardeners sweated.

Higher and higher they rode until the town was beneath them and the river sparkled, snake-thin, as it meandered southward. When Genny could catch her breath, she saw they were surrounded by fields of vetch, that turned the hillsides a luscious purple.

"How're you doin' back there?" Odessa called when they crested the highest hill at last and he dragged his boot on the dusty road to bring them to a stop.

Genny would have suffered an heart attack before admitting she was exhausted. "I'm fine," she wheezed, and smiled brightly. "Why're you stopping? Need to rest?"

"What d'you mean, rest?" Laughing, he mopped his face with the crook of his sleeved arm.

"The way you were all bent over—" she collapsed on her handlebars, panting "—I thought you were tired."

"I've always been stooped this way. Haven't you noticed?"

She pulled a face at him beneath the brim of his hat. "Cheer up. It'll be a downhill coast all the way back, Odessa."

"Wicked child."

A tumbledown sign stood in the field beside them, listing on its four wobbly posts like a thumb in need of bandaging: Proctor's Custom Dyeing—a Rainbow of Colors. They climbed off the two-seater and walked it into the long reach of the sign's shadow, where Odessa leaned it against a post.

The wind was stronger here. Birds cheeped sleepily in the dusty trees, and industrious bees sipped honey from the vetch. Genny lifted her hair from her nape and searched out a clip in her pocket, then pinned the mass of it to the top of her head.

Odessa wished he'd had the foresight to bring paper and pencil. She was breathtakingly natural here, her beauty coming from somewhere inside as she rolled her sleeves to her elbows like a peasant. If he could capture her vigor, her wind-tossed freedom and at the same time her captivating femininity...

A challenge, for she was constantly changing.

"How far've we come?" she asked, totally innocent of how different she was from fashion-plate females.

"Far enough for you to sprout a dozen new freckles, beautiful," he said.

"I've burned?" Wailing, she cupped her hand over her sun-sensitive nose. "Oh, no."

Odessa leaned closer to inspect. "Mmm, well," he drawled as her fragrance went to his head, "perhaps only three. Or four. Oops, missed one there."

He pecked her cheek in a chaste kiss, then said with a recklessness he was certain to regret, "What I want to know, Genny Carlyle, is if you have such lovely freckles on the rest of you."

Time made one of its hairpin turns. Genny was hurled violently back to the moments when she'd been crushed by Adam's treachery and had reached out to Odessa. "If I weren't beginning to understand how your mind works, Mr. Gold," she said as she lowered her face into shadow, "I would be offended by that remark."

"I'm glad one of us understands it."

"Yes, well . . . we were married for ten minutes, you remember."

He braced a fist on the sign, directly beside her bent head, and Genny, by turning her face, could see the soft brown sheen of hair on the back of his hand, the whitened grooves of his knuckles. She could smell the sun's freshness in his hair, and the salty tang of his skin.

"I guess that means the honeymoon is over," he quipped, and she could think of nothing to say.

Neither of them had intended to engage in such a deadly flirtation, not after the disastrous breakfast, and Genny stooped to snap a bouquet of vetch blossoms growing at her feet. She stuffed her face into them, and when she peered through the lace of petals, he was peeling off his shirt and blotting his face.

His chest was lightly matted with silky whorls of hair, and long muscles roped his arms. He was darkly tanned, and there wasn't an ounce of fat on him anywhere.

"Don't you think we should be getting back now?" she said, and licked the beading of sweat that had sprung up on her lip.

Odessa paused to stare at her face. One would think that love would send out some signal when it was happening, reaching the point of no return. He'd been making tiny decisions about her all along, hour by hour, day by day. Now the thoughts of facing the rest of his life without her were hardly worth the trouble.

"In a minute," he said around a rasp in his throat.

"I understand," she mumbled to the blossoms in her hand.

But she couldn't possibly understand the sexual thrill that struck his groin and made him catch his breath as if a fist had plunged into his gut. "If you do," he mumbled, "my advice is to run like hell."

Slowly she faced him, and he closed his fingers about her wrist. She recoiled.

"I'm going to kiss you, Genny," he said, and refused to let her go, chasing her eyes until they stopped running from his. "I know the reasons I shouldn't, but I have to." He pulled her gently against him and bent his head. "So don't fight what has to be."

Part of Genny admitted that she had hoped something like this would happen. "You tried that already," she whispered in a desperate ploy for time.

"And it didn't take." He smiled. "I'm obliged to keep trying until it does."

His hands framed her face. With a kind of dragon-slayer's triumph, his lips reached for hers, and Genny knew a moment of swimming impressions as she battled to cope with her virgin's hunger.

She whispered hoarsely, "You don't want me, Odessa. You just need a woman. Any woman."

Before she could move or catch her breath, his mouth was claiming what it sought, and she was swept along on a dizzy current into a parched and hungry part of herself. He drank thirstily of her lips and tasted her brows, the smooth space at her temples, the hollows beneath her cheeks. Moaning, she closed her eyes and let her head fall back, offering him her throat.

"If you believed that," he grated against her parted lips, "we wouldn't be here."

If a fuse had burned between them before, now the combustion flashed—spontaneously, blazing out of control, so hot Genny could not breathe in the face of it and could not go on living. Her legs abruptly refused to hold her up any longer. From her center rose an expectancy that made her strain against him.

Was this the way it was supposed to happen? She, Amelia's daughter, who only a few days ago was engaged to be married? Had she no shame that she could hop so easily from one man to another? She pushed away from him, not really knowing why, and a covey of quails flew up from the grass, their wings a startling whir that made her gasp in surprise and clap her hands over her mouth.

He took her shoulder in an attempt to turn her back to him. "What is it? What's wrong?"

Perhaps it was part of the age-old battle between man and woman that prompted her to break and run. Heaven knew she wanted to run *toward* him, not away—to end it, to become like other women. But he didn't love her, and though she wanted him, she knew that she couldn't possibly love him. Love didn't happen that quickly. Love had to ripen and grow. Where was Prince Charming? Where was the dream?

She picked up her skirt and flew through the lacy purple fronds. Faster and faster she ran, away from Adam and her father and her mother and the emptiness of her life. She heard his steps behind her, stronger, faster.

"Genny!" He caught the back of her blouse and jerked her about. "Talk to me!" he ordered.

"Why, why?" she cried. "Why has this happened? Where will this end?"

Odessa wished to God he knew. But he could only take her into the waiting haven of his body and hold her close. "It's all right," he lied. "Everything will be all right."

But he didn't understand. She tried to explain, as they stood with such pathos in the middle of a field of vetch, about why her father had died and the look on Amelia's face, the horror she had felt when Mary Faye opened the door. But they were words. Having left their scars, they ceased to be.

"Tell me why you want this," she pleaded. "Make some sense of this. Why me?"

Never had Odessa felt so humble. She was close to fainting, and he scooped her up in his arms like a baby and took her to the shade of a nearby tree, where he dropped to his knees and held her, rocking as she wrapped her arms and legs around him and pressed her face into his neck and held on until the storm was passed. When she was quiet, he pressed his lips into the hair that veiled her ear.

He told her about his family, how his marriage was arranged and how he went along. His voice hoarsened as he spoke about Anne.

"I can't even remember what she looked like." He caressed the back of her head, over and over. "I know I loved her. Or I loved her as much as I was capable of at the time. But I can't bring back her face. I took her out to that wild country, and I was so full of myself I thought I could do anything. I never once considered what could happen. When those men dragged her off the train and she was screaming my name, I felt like one of those boys back at the depot."

The sun was dipping behind the clouds, and the breeze was cool. Genny was grateful for the hard security of his chest beneath her cheek and his powerful arms pinioned around her back. He was agonizing over his memories as she had agonized over hers, and she wondered if she weren't holding him more than he was holding her.

"They didn't want me to look at her after she was found," he whispered. "I thought I could handle myself. It was a boy. They'd lain out for more than a day, and the insects and the..."

His voice knotted. Pain slashed keenly through Genny.

"Her eyes wouldn't close." Grief clotted his voice. "I can't remember what she looked like, but I can still see her eyes that wouldn't close. I didn't care what they did to me after that. When I shot Eli Wright, I was hoping they'd hang me and put me out of my misery."

Now Genny's frustration at having no purpose in life seemed petty and childish. What did she know of grief, real grief? Leaning back so that their faces were on a level, she waited, no longer avoiding the truth, whatever it was.

"I want you," he told her gravely, "because you're the only one in the world I can tell this to. I want you because you can understand and accept me for what I am. I don't have to pretend with you, Genny. I've seen you at your worst, and you've seen me."

He tried to smile, but his mouth quivered, and his lashes, heavy with the weight of the past, could not remain open.

Genny understood what women had understood for centuries before her—that in the end theirs was the greater strength. Their giving was as much of an acceptance as an aggression, a sharing of secrets, a teaching. He was asking to be taught by her, and she was willing to learn from him.

She smoothed his hair back from his face and kissed his beard and, briefly, his lips. "Her eyes are closed now, Odessa. She doesn't blame you. No one blames you."

"I shut everyone out. I really didn't want to let them in, not even my family. I broke their hearts."

Genny lay in the soft bed of blooms and became the pillow for his head. She held him in the cradle of her arms. "Would they really kill you?" she asked, dreading his answer.

"McFee?"

"Whatever his name is. He and the other one."

"If they could find me, they might try."

He propped himself on an elbow so he could see her face. His lack of concern for his own life chilled Genny, but she also read his need as he mentally counted the buttons on her blouse.

"Why?" she asked again, and was certain he knew what she meant. "Why do you . . . ?"

"Want you?"

"Yes."

The desire was laid bare now, and he thoughtfully touched the very center of her breast where all the tiny nerves were connected to the deeper, more secret part of her womanhood.

"Because. . ."

A grim smile flickered across his face as he watched his fingers unfasten her blouse and fold back the sides, making it resemble the elaborate plunge of a splendid gown. "Because you're everything I'm not. You're honest and good and giving. You have good eyes, Genny, they don't lie. When you look at me, they make me want to believe again."

He savoured the valley between her breasts, the pale white skin and the curves that swelled. Before he dipped his head and pressed his lips into that hollowed place, Genny awakened to the emotions that were connected to her sexual hunger. She was pulsing with a thickness that was alive and needful, but she was incapable of coming so alive without love. With his hot mouth and his heat pulling at her, she knew there was no other way.

"I'm not good," she whispered as she closed her arms about his head. "I'm weak. I have terrible needs."

"I know."

He kissed her until she forgot where they were. His fingers moved beneath her skirt, and she no longer fought him with her knees. He drew in a sharp breath when he found the nested curls between her thighs.

"A hundred times I've seen myself doing this," he said gruffly against her ear as he searched and discovered that she was sleek and hot.

She closed her eyes as he pressed himself upon her and pushed aside her skirt, parting her legs with his knee.

"Don't close your eyes," he begged, and Genny looked up. "I need the truth of your eyes."

"Odessa." She stopped him abruptly. "I don't want to end up like Mary Faye."

He smiled, and she could see clearly as he freed himself from his clothes. She had never touched a man in that mysterious place, she had never seen a man naked. She could not remember now what she'd imagined a man was, but not this hardness, this satin as he grew against her thigh.

She drew back when he pressed himself there, but the act, once begun, must be played to its finish. He made a sound as if in pain and grasped her hand. Genny knew she must help him. She lifted herself in surrender, her body opening to him as naturally as the bloom seeking its sun.

"I hold you to nothing, Odessa Gold," she whispered.

Chapter Eleven

The building of hotels had become the favorite pastime of American millionaires.

For the wealthy, a hotel was immensely more satisfactory than a private banquet hall or restaurant. There were, after all, so many more opportunities to be seen than at a private party, and as the century drew to a close, being seen was what wealth was all about.

After the Waldorf-Astoria reared its head in Manhattan, less affluent hotels lagged behind in the Great Hotel Race. Nonetheless, the Jamison Hotel where Odessa registered them was pleasant. Like an aging but exquisitely mannered gentleman, it had installed one of the new steam-powered elevators to service its four stories. The Oriental carpets, though thinning, were impeccably clean. The rooms were lighted with gas and didn't have private baths with hot water, but they were large and gave an impression of luxury. Since Odessa required anonymity and Genny a time to rest from her ordeal with Adam, the Jamison suited both their needs perfectly.

"Two of your best rooms," Odessa told the concierge.

The small whiskery man cast a proprietary eye toward Angel Tulane and the golden retriever, that was sitting on its haunches and smiling up at him with disturbing omniscience.

"We do have a facility for animals, sir," he intoned. "Would you like a separate room for the colored man, as well?"

"Colored man?" Odessa did a double take. "Angel, are you a colored man?"

Angel smiled one of his incredibly handsome smiles, and the retriever showed his teeth. "Why, I dunno, Mr. Gold. I thought I was white."

Odessa smirked at the concierge. "Mr. Tulane happens to be white, and I would sooner manage without my right hand." He laid more money than was necessary on the desk. "We'll share a room."

The clerk tucked one of his three chins into his stiff collar. "Very good, sir."

"As for the ladies, whatever they need I would appreciate your seeing to it personally." Odessa added several bills to the growing pile and leaned so far across the desk, his face was almost touching that of the concierge. "I would appreciate it *very* much."

The concierge showed a set of teeth in which none, Odessa noted with relief, were missing.

"Absolutely, sir. Would you like the room, ah, adjoining that of the ladies?"

"That isn't necessary."

The man let out his breath in a whistle. "I understand, sir."

"I should hope so. Would you like to take the dog now?"

The concierge exchanged a doubtful look with the retriever and shuddered. He should have held out, he thought bleakly, for more money.

Sometime much later, very early in the morning, Genny was astonished to find her face wet with tears and Jessamine shaking her shoulder. "Geneena, child. What's wrong?"

"What?" Genny sat up in bed and swiped viciously at her cheeks, swallowing and praying that she hadn't been talking in her sleep. "What's the matter? Why did you wake me up?"

"You were crying, Geneena."

"Nonsense. Why should I be crying?"

"That was my question for you."

"You must have dreamed it," Genny said and flung herself facedown on the pillow. "Go back to sleep."

The old woman rolled obediently onto her side, and Genny, too, rolled over, awake now and staring at the cracks in the ceiling, stained by the night.

It was an airy room, pleasantly rambling with two large windows over which the curtains were drawn. The double bed, spread with a cream-colored counterpane, was pushed against a floral-papered wall. There were two stuffed chairs and a small, marble-topped commode that bore a ceramic pitcher and washbowl.

"Actually," she said as she sniffed and blotted tears from her voice, "I was thinking how far off course we've come, Jessamine."

"Off course?"

"Why did we leave Cheyenne in the first place?"

"Because we were starving. Because you were going to marry Adam Worthington."

"Now we're in an hotel in New York City, hell-bent for Saratoga with an ex-convict."

Jessamine rolled onto her side, and her old hands found Genny's hair.

"Mr. MacGowan, God rest his soul," she said quietly as she stroked it, "always used to say that no river ever ran in a straight line. We'll get it all done, Geneena, and in proper order. Faith, child. We must have faith and trust now. God works in mysterious ways, Mr. MacGowan always used to say."

Genny wondered what kind of girl Jessamine MacGowan had been before her marriage. "You must have taken one look at Mr. MacGowan, Jessamine, and known he was the man for you."

Jessamine was caught in an undertow of memories, and she didn't answer immediately. "When I married Mr. MacGowan, people shook their heads. I had married beneath myself, they said. I'd never have a thing. Six months they'd give me before I was back home with my mother."

The old woman laughed softly. "I remember thinking I should find someone else—someone safe, someone everyone approved of, someone dependable. But every time I told myself to find somebody else, I would wake up in the middle of the night and think about Mr. MacGowan. They were wrong about him, Geneena. I wound up with everything."

Genny was astonished. How could Jessamine believe that she had wound up with everything? Love was indeed blind.

"I know you did," she said dutifully and tried to imagine Jessamine making love with a faceless man. Her cheeks colored, and she moistened her lips. "Whenever you and he... I mean, the first time you and your husband... What I'm trying to say is..."

Jessamine's sleepy voice was heavy with the past. "He came to our house to borrow a pickax. I was sixteen—a late bloomer with big feet. I threw a rose from the upstairs window, and it struck him on the head. Two nights later, he climbed up to my window and asked if I'd sneak out and walk along the creek with him."

"Jessamine!" Genny was shocked.

"I didn't know what to expect. He wasn't a good-looking man, big and rawboned. But the feeling was there, and I wanted to know what everyone was talking about. Without saying a word, he was all over me, kissing me like a starved man."

Jessamine fell silent, and the sounds of the street drifted inside.

"Was it," Genny ventured, "what you thought it would be?"

The old woman chuckled. "It was the most disappointing thing I ever experienced. I was so sore, I couldn't walk for two days. He didn't know how to finesse me. It's often that way, Genny. The woman has to teach the man."

"I'm sure I wouldn't know how," Genny lied.

"In many ways, Mr. Gold is a lot like my dear Mr. MacGowan," the woman said as sleep dragged at her words. "He has more finesse, I think."

Genny was astonished at the woman's total lack of subtlety.

"Mr. Gold understands human nature," Jessamine intoned. "A prince..."

"I wouldn't endow him with *too* much royalty," Genny dryly retorted, but slumber, heavy-footed and certain, overtook the old woman.

Genny wanted to pound her pillow to death. A prince? Odessa Gold was a murderer, an ex-convict and a gambler. He was difficult and bitter and opinionated—and she was in love with him.

Ever so cautiously, she slid off the bed and moved to the dressing table to stare at her reflection in the mirror. As Jessamine's soft slumber filled the room, she drew her gown over her head and stared critically at her naked body. She pressed her palms to her breasts and felt mocked by the curls nesting between her legs. She wished Odessa were inside her now—moving deeper, deeper until the woman from Wyoming disappeared altogether.

"What am I going to do?" she asked the white-fleshed creature who stared back. "What will I do?"

In the darkness of the strange room, Angel was rudely awakened by a crash, an odd *ka-whump* and a curse he hadn't heard since his mother discovered his father in an unfortunate liaison with Mimi Gevaire on the Rue de la Paix. Bounding from his cot like a shot, he landed on the floor in a deep crouch, ready for battle, and snarled, "Who's there?"

"Who d'you think, Goliath?" Odessa sucked his breath harshly through his teeth.

Odessa, Angel perceived without the benefit of light, was apparently dancing around the room on one foot. The thumping was accompanied by a series of slaps and flailing.

"Shall I light a lamp?" Angel offered with more amusement than kindness.

"Not unless you want to see a grown man tune up and bawl." *Thump, thump.* "Judas priest, that hurts!"

"I think I'd better light a lamp, Odessa."

"I thought I'd seen a decanter on the dresser when we came in the room. Obviously I was wrong, which has probably cost me a broken toe."

"You mean, the empty decanter?" Angel laughed merrily.

"Where is the damn thing?"

Another crash. Angel heard the same oath repeated with embellishments, and he carefully felt his way through the darkness until he found the table, then the lamp, and finally the matches that were in a small cup.

The sulfury rasp sent grotesque devils cavorting through the room, and Angel burst out laughing at the sight of Odessa stark naked, balancing on one foot as he attempted to insert his unhurt foot into a leg of his pants.

Tossing a bleary look over his shoulder, Odessa said, "If a word of this ever gets back to me, I swear I'll take these confounded pants and hang you with 'em."

"I won't say a word," Angel gasped.

After several more colorful epithets, Odessa succeeded in getting his pants on and buttoned. He found the empty decanter, which had obviously been discarded by the last guest, and tilted it top to bottom.

He said with unflinching solemnity, "There's nothing to drink in this room, Angel."

Angel pulled on his own trousers, which he had neatly placed at the foot of his bed. "I didn't know you were a drinking man, Odessa."

"Don't you drink?"

"Not since two nights ago. And you?"

"1884."

Angel proceeded to dress, which for him, Odessa noted, was like preparing to attend a presidential summons. As he counted out the last of his St. Louis winnings, Angel lowered himself to mirror level and patted his glistening hair.

"Would it be out of order, Odessa," he inquired, "to ask what brought on this need for hard liquor?"

The brimming eyes of a fiery-haired young woman, Odessa thought, and wondered if Genny was asleep at this moment. He hoped she was suffering. As he was suffering.

"No," he replied, "it wouldn't be out of order."

A long, quizzing silence ensued.

Grinning, Angel bowed deeply from the waist. "I understand."

"For your great intelligence, you're to be commended." Odessa laid several coins on the table. "Did it ever occur to you, Angel, that the world would be a lot happier if there were no women in it?"

"Happier, possibly." Angel straightened his tie. "But it's my opinion that happiness makes a man die young."

Odessa snorted. "Then I should live to the age of Methuselah."

Chuckling, Angel walked to the door. He paused. "Do you have any preference in the brand of your suffering? Or is Miss Carlyle adequate to the occasion thereof?"

Odessa had opened the window and was bracing his hands upon the sill. "Since you know that much, I'll leave the brand of spirits up to you, Mr. Tulane."

"I'm a Frenchman who drinks Irish whiskey out of Baccarat crystal. Are you sure that's what you want?"

"If it's good enough for a cheeky black man, who am I to question it?"

Odessa did not turn from the window when Angel departed. He continued to lean, his eyes vacant and unseeing, his thoughts drifting again to Genny, to her innocence he had forgotten existed, to her ignorance of her own body

that refused to let his desire die a natural death so he could
move on.

And, like all innocents, she was hurtable. She *was* hurting. He could feel her hurt like a broken bone in his own
body. What if she fell in love with him? She mustn't. He
had loved his mother enough to keep out of her life. He
must love Genny that much. Did he have the strength of
character to do that, to put his own feelings aside? Could
he be her friend and not her lover? Help her do what she
had set out to do? Give her the things she needed, things
she had done without?

The kindest act would be to actually help her find an
older man, one who met his own standards—though he
wasn't sure such a man existed, including himself. Especially himself.

Damn it all to hell! His heart swelled to bursting, and he
turned from the window and ground the heels of his hands
into his temples.

When Angel returned a half hour later, he found Odessa
fully dressed. He had refreshed his suit and borrowed one
of Angel's own impeccable shirts, had shined himself,
combed himself, preened himself until he looked as good
as possible.

"You're dressed," Angel exclaimed, amazed. "I
thought you wanted to get drunk."

"Put your hat back on, Angel. I borrowed some of your
things, as you can see. I'm going out."

"At this hellish hour?"

"The good thing about poker, Angel, is that it never
sleeps."

When people called John Crichton a son of a bitch, they
did not smile.

John Crichton was the creator of American Steel, a bil-
lion-dollar monopoly, but steel wasn't what John wanted.
The one thing he really wanted—acceptance into the inner
circle of the old-money crowd—money could not buy. J.
P. Morgan and his friends—Frick, Guggenheim, Whit-

ney—loathed Crichton, and their wives never invited
Merilla to their afternoon teas nor his daughters to their
cotillions.

Crichton nursed his bruised feelings by purchasing a
twenty-thousand-dollar apartment at the Waldorf-Astoria
where he established a lavish gaming room—a gentlemen's club where every luxury was provided and late sup-
pers were created by a well-paid and cherished chef.

Though Morgan and Frick disliked him, they didn't let
that come between them and their love for gambling. Because they frequented his establishment, so did their affluent friends—a dubious irony, Crichton thought, the old-
money crowd coming to him.

At the Waldorf's Men's Bar, Odessa made inquiries.

"Crichton?" the bartender said. "Too rich for my
blood. A million dollars cross the tables in a night, they
say. Those clods never heard of a depression, did they?"

The bartender held up a finger to give pause and moved
to the opposite end of the bar. Odessa swirled the mineral
water in his glass, for he never drank when he played cards.
He paid little heed to the other customers as he imagined
Genny, sleeping, her hair spilling over her pillow like a
sunset and a gentle dew turning her porcelain skin to crystal.

He wasn't certain, as he mused about her, what made
the hair on the back of his neck rise, but in prison a man
survived by his instincts. He had learned to trust his own.

He searched the room for a reason and saw ordinary
people making ordinary, harmless conversation. At the
end of the bar, however, sat a tall, powerfully built man in
a tuxedo. Everyone here wore a tuxedo. He had never seen
the man before.

He looked closer and made note of the man's shabby
shoes and roughened hands. They didn't fit. The man was
transplanted, a rusty andiron in a cabinet filled with
Wedgwood china.

When the bartender returned, Odessa said casually,
"The fellow you just served, is he a regular?"

The bartender squinted at the man who had snapped down his shot of whiskey. "Red whiskers?"

"At the end of the bar."

"Never saw 'im before."

Odessa dropped tinkling coins on the bar and collected Angel's top hat and gloves. Leaving the bar, he walked outside and hesitated in the manner of a man who didn't want to return home.

His hackles continued to warn of danger. He was being followed. One of McFee's henchmen? One of the deputies on the train?

Angel was waiting at the cab when Odessa found him. With the wordless communication that was developing between them, Angel knew something was wrong. Abruptly he asked, "What's the problem?"

"I'm not sure yet. Be very careful returning to the hotel, Angel. Don't trust anyone. Keep your eyes open all the time. If anything happens to Genny . . ."

"You sound as if this could be dangerous."

"Just being alive is a dangerous business. Who would know that better than you?"

Putting a tight rein on his emotions, Odessa touched his cravat and returned to the steps of the Waldorf-Astoria with a calm, unhurried bearing. He was aware of everything, things he could not see or hear. He walked past the doorman and doffed his hat. Whoever was following was still there.

"Good evening, sir," the doorman said.

Watching Odessa's wariness but seeing nothing to justify it, Angel shrugged and began climbing into the cab. A movement caught his eye, and he focused on a man in a tuxedo heaving himself from the iron railing where he'd leaned to have a smoke—tall, built like an ox. As Odessa went through the door, the man tossed his smoke away in a rocket of red ash and followed.

Odessa paused to speak to the doorman, and the man slowed. When Odessa passed through into the hotel, the man climbed the steps after him.

"I'll be damned," Angel said, climbing into the cab. "The Jamison Hotel," he told the driver.

And be quick about it. I don't like this one bit.

It was an ancient and prestigious custom, the bribing of bell captains.

After insuring himself entrance into Crichton's game, Odessa moved with caution through the hotel. Even at this late hour, people still milled about the lobby. He weaved through them as ghosts marched through his mind, chains rattling. He was once again kneeling beside Anne and staring in horror at his baby, crusted with blood. Except that now he saw Genny, not Anne, as the victim. If this man had been following him long enough, he would know that Genny and he had been more than travelers passing in the night.

What he felt as he walked through the hotel was not anger. He was far beyond that. It was more like the deadly compulsion that had driven him to find Anne's killers. He wasn't even breathing hard by the time he turned the corner and entered a corridor and passed the elevator, hesitating as he pretended to consider catching it.

From the corner of his eye, he caught sight of a figure behind him.

With a cold, hard smile, Odessa moved to a door that opened onto the cobbled alley. Here, far from the glamorous, laughing people who filled the lobby, he stepped out into the humid night where the accumulated heat of the day still filled the street. Placing Angel's gloves into his hat, he sent it skimming safely away into the shadows, and then pressed himself flat against the stones so that the shadows dropped around him. With shallow breaths, he waited, so much a part of the night that a mouse crept from behind a can and sat, its whiskers quivering and nose twitching.

Presently the door opened, as Odessa had known it would. A spilling shaft of light sent the mouse scooting away.

Odessa kept his thoughts riveted, not on what the larger man could do to him but on protecting Genny. Come on, you son of a bitch. Closer, closer.

When the man drew even with him, Odessa's muscles twitched in galvanic response, and he moved as swiftly as a striking snake, closing his arms about the man's neck in a vise that could have snapped it.

What the man lacked in speed, he made up for in strength. He stiffened and threw himself backward with such force that Odessa was slammed against the building and pain went splintering into his skull.

But he hung on like a bulldog and dug his fingers into the man's windpipe. "Who are you?"

"No one!" the man wheezed as he staggered clumsily about in an attempt to free himself of the infernal creature that had him in his grip.

"Don't give me that! Who sent you?"

"Nobody!"

"Why're you following me?"

"I'm not, I'm not!"

The man was slowly strangling, weaving like a drunken sailor and gathering momentum to slam Odessa against the wall once more. Abruptly, Odessa let go and dropped to the street. The man crashed against the building with a dull thud and buckled to his knees.

Odessa threw himself on the man, but too late to avoid the glittering path of the drawn knife. Even as Odessa twisted to deflect the slash, the blade snagged his trousers and caught the inside of his thigh.

Warm blood streamed down his leg. Odessa sucked his breath between his teeth, spinning and bringing the side of his hand round so that it connected with a crunch to the bridge of the man's nose.

The man collapsed, moaning, and the knife clattered on the cobblestones. With his thigh streaming, Odessa scooped up the weapon, slicing the air, and faced the man.

"Now," he said as he shifted the knife to his other hand and gripped his thigh in an attempt to stay the flow of blood. "Now you'll tell me who sent you, or I'll gut you from stem to stern and hang you on a street lamp for the police to find."

The man whimpered as he rocked back and forth and cupped his broken nose. "Go to hell."

"I've been there. I didn't like it. Now are you going to talk, or shall I make some of this blood on the street yours? Talk to me, you bastard! A broken nose is better than no nose!"

The man still didn't believe him, and Odessa shoved him against the wall and pricked his bottom rib with the tip of the knife. His voice assumed an almost intimate softness. "Though I haven't done it myself, I've seen it often enough where I come from. Now tell me, who sent you?"

The man crumbled. "Nathan Hodges."

"Hodges!" Odessa was shocked. This wasn't the governor's style.

"He wants to know where you go. Somebody followed you to St. Louis, but they lost you."

"Who followed me?"

"I don't know. I was told to pick up your trail at Grand Central. Followed you and the colored. Saw you get rooms for the women. Then here. Please—"

"What's his name?"

"Whose name?"

"The black man."

The big man's brain was too dull to detect Odessa's backhanded strategy. He shook his head. "I dunno. What does it matter?"

"Who are the women?"

"Hell, man, I don't even know who *you* are."

For a moment Odessa was tempted to plunge the knife up to the hilt into the man. How dared Hodges commit this outrage? Of course. Where persuasion had failed in getting him to turn state's evidence, Hodges hoped that force would succeed.

But that didn't matter now. Only Genny mattered, and if his dreams of a future were fragile before, now they were shattered. Even if this man's silence was assured, he would eventually be found.

"I have no choice but to kill you," he said dully.

The man's eyes flared until the whites showed all around. His odor was that of true fear.

"No, no!" he pleaded. "I'm a plain man. I work the docks. I got a family. I swear I won't tell I found you. Lemme go, please. I was just trying' to pick up a dollar."

"I would've given you a dollar."

Odessa's leg was beginning to hurt like the devil. Inching back so the man could slip free, he pointed the knife at the man's face.

"If you tell anyone anything," he warned, "about the black man or the women, I'll hunt you down, I swear to heaven I will. Then I'll leave you for mortician's bait. If you think I won't, ask Hodges why he's looking for me."

The man could not escape quickly enough.

The way his luck was running, Odessa guessed he had made a mistake in letting him go. His first task, however, was to get his bleeding stopped and clean himself up. He had bought some time, yet it was imperative that he move Genny and Jessamine from the Jamison. He must get Genny out of his life as soon as possible. But to do that, he needed money. To get money, he had to win, wounded leg or not.

His muscles beginning to cramp and his ribs hurting with every breath, he drew out his handkerchief and wiped the knife blade clean and slipped it into his boot. Stooping, he retrieved Angel's hat and gloves and dusted them off.

He moved toward the front of the hotel, and when he was beneath a streetlight, he looked at the damage done him— Four inches long, but not too deep. By morning, it would hurt like hell.

He slipped back inside the hotel. It was time for another little bribe of the bell captain.

Chapter Twelve

"Attending to business, did you say?"

Genny was quizzing Angel Tulane from the doorway of her room when he came to take them to breakfast. Odessa, he said, had not returned yet. Genny was mildly disposed to being teased but not to being blatantly hornswoggled.

Wearing her best schoolmarm's frown, she continued to grill the black man. "Just what business did Odessa want you to tell me he was attending to, Angel?"

"Well, he wasn't too specific, Miss Genny." His grin was a twin to his perfectly pressed suit and mirror-bright shoes. "But since most business involves love or money, I think it's safe to say he's probably—" he turned up a pragmatic palm "—ahem, earning money."

"Gambling."

His shrug spoke volumes.

How Odessa made his money, Genny told herself, was none of her business. She was neither his wife nor his fiancée, nor sister nor nursemaid. She swept out her arm in an invitation for Angel to enter while she tried her own hand at hornswoggling.

"Can you imagine anyone wanting to cover these windows with such heavy draperies?" She gestured extravagantly at the windows. "No wonder the rooms are so stuffy and hot."

Jessamine was sitting on the side of the bed, lacing her boots. "One shuts the windows, Geneena, because it's better than smelling the city."

"Better smelling than roasting, I say."

"Air can be cooled now." Jessamine turned her black lenses on Angel Tulane.

Genny had begun to twist up her hair, and her mouth was full of hairpins. "It would cost a fortune," she mumbled around them. "*If* it can be done."

"Oh, it can be done, can't it, Mr. Tulane?" To Jessamine's mind, there was no greater authority than Angel Tulane.

"Absolutely." Angel laughed. "But it's costly, Miss Jessamine. Breakfast, on the other hand, is cheap. Shall we, ladies?"

Breakfast turned out to be an extremely depressing affair. Though Angel made a valiant attempt to keep their spirits buoyant, the more Genny pictured Odessa playing poker, the more withdrawn she became.

After breakfast, Angel and Jessamine took Beggar for a walk.

Genny found lunch without Odessa worse than breakfast.

Angel and Jessamine took Beggar for another walk.

Dinner was unbearable. For once, hunger did not drive Genny to eat. She couldn't choke down a bite of her aspic and paper-thin crepe. She wished she'd never met Odessa Gold. Even the heartbreaking truth about Adam wasn't as bad as Odessa's desertion. Why hadn't she been more careful? Placed a more vigilant guard upon her heart?

Angel and Jessamine walked the dog again. Genny huddled between her sheets while unhappiness clawed at her bones like a scavenger.

When Odessa had not returned by breakfast the next morning, Genny moved like someone coming down with a cold. She wondered if this was the way her father had felt when Amelia had gone away.

"Oh, Daddy," she whispered to the ghost that lingered in the corridors of her memory, "I'm sorry I didn't understand."

"Geneena, child," Jessamine said on the morning of the third day when Genny, dressed only in her wrapper, slowly lowered herself to the seat before the dressing table. "Are you ill?"

"I'm fine, Jessamine," Genny lied. "You worry too much."

The old woman glided across the room to place her hand upon Genny's forehead. "Tsk, tsk, tsk. I think we should call a doctor, Geneena."

"Nothing's wrong with me," Genny insisted, and removed Jessamine's hand, then kissed it in apology for her short temper. "I'm just a little tired. That's understandable, isn't it? All this business about Adam? Coming this far when we're not even certain we'll find him?"

"If not for me, you would be traveling twice as quickly."

"Nonsense."

"I should've stayed in Cheyenne with Betty Parson."

"Jessamine!" Exasperated, Genny buried her face in her hands. "If you weren't with me, I would be in St. Louis, too devastated to move."

Genny wrapped her arms about the blind woman's waist and pressed her face in the calico skirt. The tears she had forced back for three days cascaded down her face while Jessamine stroked the curls of the person she loved more than anyone on earth.

"Now, now, my sweet girl," she crooned. "We'll be fine, you and I. We'll do what has to be done. Here, dry your eyes on my hankie and turn around. I'll brush your hair. You know you love it when I brush your hair."

Snuffling obediently, Genny despaired of her reflection of red-rimmed eyes and puffy cheeks and a complexion that looked as if she had an incurable disease.

"I'm a mess," she groaned.

"The trouble with you, Geneena—" Jessamine drew the brush through the stormy curls "—is that you give too much. Mr. MacGowan always said a person has to be selfish sometimes, take time to heal. In Saratoga Springs, you must heal.''

In Saratoga Springs, Genny thought dismally, she would probably destroy herself.

The knock at the door was soft. Jessamine laid down the brush. ''That will be Mr. Tulane, coming to fetch us for breakfast.''

Genny sighed heavily. Another meal without Odessa. ''I'll get it.''

Opening the door, she was confronted by what appeared to be a free-floating stack of gift-wrapped boxes ascending dizzily to the ceiling: red boxes and blue-and-white striped ones, tissue-wrapped boxes with shiny pink ribbon, one of powder-blue tied with a great silver bow.

Beneath the boxes winked a pair of men's shoes. ''Angel Tulane,'' she scolded, ''are your feet in those shoes?''

The black man's laughter rang richly. ''Dey ain't King Tut's.''

Genny jerked the belt of her wrapper as if girding herself for war. ''What are these?''

''Boxes. May I come in?''

''I can see they're boxes, Angel. Who are they for? What's in them?''

''Well, I can't rightly say, Miss Genny. They were just delivered to the hotel, and the concierge sent a message to come get them. They're for room 306. That's you, isn't it? May I come in?''

Baffled, Genny checked the numerals on the door.

''Well—'' she shooed Angel emphatically back out into the hall ''—there's been a mistake. Return them to the concierge. All I need is a lawsuit for stealing someone's...what-have-you.''

Angel laughed. ''I'm afraid the concierge isn't in the what-have-you business.''

''Then take them to whoever they should be taken to, Angel.''

"Whomever, Genny," Odessa's deep voice corrected. "Whomever. I should think a schoolteacher would know that. Would you let the man inside?"

He could have swallowed the cage, as well as the canary, when he peeped around Angel. Genny went cold and her mouth fell open.

In a pearl-gray jacket and slim black trousers that made his lean legs seem to go on forever, he was the most handsome thing she'd ever seen. His shirt was stiff as cardboard and bibbed with rows of tiny snowy tucks, and in his cuffs, gold studs flashed. He'd had a manicure and a fresh trimming of his beard. In the loop of his left arm rested a gray silk hat into which had been tucked a pair of soft kid gloves.

Before she remembered all her resolutions about forgetting him, she went into his beckoning arm and pressed her cheek to his shoulder.

"You came back!" she said with a tiny cry of relief and echoed, whispering, "You came back."

In the flurry of their embrace, Odessa dropped his hat, but he tightened his arms about her and molded her against him as he pressed his face into her hair and squeezed his eyes shut. Oh, it felt so good to hold her again! How had he managed to stay away for three days? What would he do when he could no longer hold her?

"I don't know why you're always surprised to see me," he said with a secret fear of the future.

Sniffing, she beat his chest with her fists, realizing too late that she was practically naked, a fact he had not failed to appreciate; the tops of her breasts were winking brazenly from beneath the opening of her wrapper.

"I'm not surprised to see you," she fibbed with a comical huff.

Grinning, he retrieved his hat, and Genny wondered at the sudden spasm of a muscle in his jaw.

"It only goes to prove the old adage," he said tartly when he straightened, "that absence does make the heart grow fonder. Go on in the room, Angel. If we stay out here much longer, they'll rent out our room.''

The situation had gotten out of hand, as it always did whenever he breezed into her life and took over. Watching his back, Genny wanted to shout at both men, ''This is my life, mine and Jessamine's! Either get in it and stay or get out!''

She caught up with Odessa and lifted her shoulder in a grudging compliment. ''You look—'' she hesitated to call him handsome to his face ''—very nice.''

''Son of a gun.'' Laughter danced in his eyes. ''I'll bet that was hard to say.''

Genny gave him the benefit of her jutting chin. ''It wore me out, Odessa Gold.''

''Then shall we see what Santa Claus has brought?''

Before Genny could say that she had never believed in Santa Claus, not even as a child, he had drawn her hand through the loop of his arm and was escorting her ceremoniously to the boxes. He moved stiffly, she thought, and slowly.

''What's the matter, Odessa?'' she purred. ''Did three days and nights of debauchery prove to be too much?''

Scowling, he slapped the back of her hip, and she jumped. ''Be grateful, my darling—'' he kissed the curls framing her ear ''—that I wasn't debauching with you.''

She speared him with her elbow, and the sharpness of his breath gave her pause. Frowning, she stepped back to see the white ridges about his mouth, and the sheen of sweat across his forehead. He didn't look well, not well at all.

Angel had placed some of the parcels upon the bed and was stacking the last upon the chairs and dressing table. Genny stared at them until the truth finally dawned, and she picked up a box and shook it.

''You bought these for *us*?'' She looked from the boxes to Odessa, who had braced himself against the arm of a chair and crossed his ankles.

His grin was all the answer she needed, and she dropped the box as if it had burned her fingers. How many gifts did she accept from this man before she crossed the line?

"Genny—" he pinched the bridge of his nose "—you're the only woman I know who has to be forced to open a box from Simon's."

She walked around the bed and back again. Sighing, Odessa picked up the nearest box and began ripping off the tissue, plowing through a nest of rustling tissue.

"If a man wants anything done," he happily complained, "he has to do it himself."

Taking his cue, Angel guided Jessamine to a chair where he placed a box on her lap and her hand upon the ribbon. "Something lovely for a lovely lady, Miss Jessamine."

"Dear me," she said with a delight that made Genny want to shake her.

She swept across the room and gripped Jessamine's shoulder. "No Jessamine. You mustn't. We mustn't."

Odessa murmured to the ceiling, "Patience, Lord. All you've got to spare," and lifted out a skirt of cream-colored lawn that was so soft and feminine, it could have floated away in a cloud. Genny covered her mouth as he draped it against his own long legs, facetiously pretending to admire it.

Oh, he was ruthless! He was without shame! She could have snatched the skirt and drowned in its frothy, cream-soda depths.

"Dear me. Did I buy this?" He was burrowing through another box now, and bringing out a blouse of white linen with tiny red roses embroidered on the collar and cuffs.

"Of course, I had to guess the size." He made a prissy face as he held up the blouse and made a visual comparison of its shoulders to hers, its bust to hers. "Yes, I was right to keep with skirts and blouses. I imagine they'll tide you over until we can get to a proper dressmaker."

"A dressmaker? Have you lost your mind?"

Genny sank onto the bed, and Odessa laid the skirt and blouse in her lap. She was drowning. She was seeing Ame-

lia. She was seeing herself in a place where she had no right
to be. She wanted the clothes as she had wanted little in her
life, and she wanted to kiss him in gratitude for buying
them. But where was the end of this? How would she sur-
vive when he had gone his way and she had gone hers?

"Where did you get the money for all these, Odessa?"
she whispered and gestured at his own fine garments.

He had begun to unwrap another box. He didn't look at
her, but his voice was too tight and too edged with warning. "Where d'you think, Genny?"

The room seethed with tension. Genny and Odessa stood
like sparring opponents who had never intended to take the
fight seriously but who were now well into the third round.
He was stripping her to the bone. She was dredging up all
the reasons she wanted to despise him.

"We can't accept these things," she said on a ragged
breath. "I'm sorry, Odessa, we just...can't..."

Jessamine made a sound of anguish, and Genny turned
to her. "I tried to explain, Jessamine."

For once, Jessamine's spine was not straight. With tears
streaming down her face, she was clutching a pair of soft
button-up shoes with tiny feminine heels, and rocking.
Genny had never seen Jessamine weep so, not even at
Dwight Parson's funeral.

Hating herself and hating Odessa Gold more, she collected words in her mouth—hard words of protection and
self-preservation. She flung herself toward him, but with
two steps he thwarted her attack—a monarch who has
suddenly discovered the rebel in his camp.

"You mean, my darling," he said with a threat in each
word, "that because I didn't take up an offering at church
to buy these, Jessamine is to be deprived?"

"That's not fair!" she argued. "I don't approve of
gambling!"

His fists were braced on the sides of his beautiful pearl-
gray jacket, and his snowy-shirted chest was unyielding, his
thighs promising heaven knew what. Oh, he was tough, all

right, but a different kind of toughness than what her life had taught her.

"That point didn't seem to cause you too much pain before," he aridly reminded her. "When you needed train fare, it wasn't painful at all."

"That was different." Her temper flashed in her desperation to be right.

"Not so different."

Odessa tipped her chin up, seeing in the planes of her face the young girl she must have been, taking one disappointment after another and refusing to lie down for the count. She was, though she didn't know it, steadily chipping through the husk that protected him. Once that was gone he would be at the mercy of the world, at *her* mercy.

The throbbing in his leg reminded him of the lengths to which his enemies would go—Hodges wanting him to talk, McFee and Platt wanting to make sure he never talked. But he couldn't tell her the truth, so he turned away in defeat.

Feeling his rejection, Genny pushed him aside to reach Jessamine, and he stumbled with a sharp raspy hiss of pain. She spun around. He was ashen. His weight was thrown to one side, and he bent, favoring his left leg. Her eyes grew wide.

"What's wrong?"

"Nothing to raise a ruckus about," he said thinly.

"Really?" While Angel watched in silence, she deliberately touched the inside of his leg and watched Odessa swing out his arm in protest. "I'd raise a ruckus about that, I daresay. Angel, did you know about this?"

Before Angel could extricate himself from the boil of her wrath, Odessa said, "Jessamine, if you don't stop crying, I'm going to take those slippers back to the man and tell him they made you unhappy."

"Mr. Gold?" Jessamine clutched the gift to her bosom as if she would sooner part with her memories of Mr. MacGowan. "I'm not known as a violent person. But as God is my witness, if you should try to lay one finger on these shoes, I'll not be responsible for what happens."

"No one's going to take the shoes, Jessamine," Genny said and snapped her fingers. "Angel, I leave these boxes with you. Odessa and I have some, ah..."

"Yes?" The black man waited.

Genny realized she had just painted herself into a corner, a fact Odessa was apparently taking enormous pleasure in.

"Odessa and I have some business to attend to," she mumbled and dared Odessa to say a single word.

One of Angel's great talents was discretion. He scooped up several of the boxes and hurried after them, detaining Genny as she was pushing Odessa out the door.

He thrust the skirt and blouse and two smaller, flatter boxes at her. "You might find that the two smaller boxes will come in handy," he told her with a perfectly straight face. "After you've... attended to business."

Hardly were they in Odessa's room—Genny, still wearing her wrapper, having looked over her shoulder at every turn for fear she would be stopped and arrested for indecent exposure—than Odessa shut the door and leaned against it with an aha-I-have-you-now look.

"Don't get any rash ideas," she warned as she dumped the boxes onto a chair and prayed he could not hear the foolish thumping of her heart.

"I do believe Angel's having impure thoughts about your intentions toward me, my love," he drawled with a lewd grin.

"There's a lot of that going around. Have you checked your own temperature lately?"

Odessa laughed and dragged a straight-backed chair from beneath a table and straddled it. "At least you haven't caught the sickness, Genny. We can all praise the Lord for that."

"Odessa?" She jutted her weight to one hip and braced a fist on it. "I've been meaning to tell you for a long time that you have a very, very irritating streak of impertinence running through you. Sort of like the stripe down a skunk's back. You know?"

"Well—" his gray eyes were half teasing, half burning under his dark lashes "—at least you're on to me. I won't have to repent for having pulled the wool over your eyes, will I?"

No, what she had done had been with her eyes wide open, Genny thought, self-conscious now that she was in the midst of so many masculine things—half-smoked cigars and scattered pocket change, discarded shirt tissues, boot polish, toothbrushes. She nervously tightened her belt about her waist, as if that could protect her from his frank perusal.

"Pull down your pants," she ordered tartly.

"Gad, I thought I'd never live to hear you say those words!" He filled the room with thunderous laughter.

"You know what I mean." She blushed furiously. "So I can look at that leg."

He pretended to be deeply disappointed as he dragged himself from the chair and obligingly peeled off his jacket, handed it to her and flicked his belt loose from its clasp.

Genny placed his jacket upon the bed, determined that she would not be affected by his bold double entendres. But when he skinned down to his cotton drawers and she saw his leg, efficiency was forgotten.

"Good Lord!" The bandage was large and darkly stained with blood. "What did you do? Cheat?"

"I can do without that cruel wit of yours, woman," he growled and lowered himself to the chair, grateful that he no longer had to behave as if he were the big conquering hero come home from the wars. "The only cheating has been the hangman for the wretch who did this."

"And who was that?"

With a sharp upward glance as she knelt beside his feet, Genny saw he had no intention of telling her. Her hands shook as she unwound torn strips of a sheet.

Odessa no longer tried to prevent his hungry eyes from feasting on the sight of her as she worked over him. Her hands and her smile, even her merciless teasing were better than any medicine. There had to be a way out of his nightmare. Couldn't he do something? Pay someone off? Didn't he deserve a life with this woman without fear?

She probed gently around the slash. "There's some infection here, Odessa. You should've been stitched."

"It wasn't convenient, Miss Nightingale," he said, aching to hold her, to kiss her. "A fresh bandage, and it'll be all right."

"Have you put anything on it?"

"I'll get something later."

"Later?" Rising, she aimed a finger at his nose, and he captured it and placed a kiss on its tip. "You think you can ignore something like this and abracadabra, a miracle will happen? You need a doctor, Odessa."

"No, no doctor." Odessa didn't relish the questions a medical man might ask. One never knew how a chance remark from a total stranger could topple a whole chain of dominoes and cause lives to change. "Just help me with a clean bandage. I'll be fine. In prison, there were worse things, believe me, much worse."

She fetched water from the bowl on the stand and a fresh cloth. "What happened? How—"

"A mad dog bit me."

She flicked water into his face. "And I'm Queen Victoria." With deft ministrations, she cleaned the wound and tore up a pair of Angel's fresh underwear for bandage strips.

"Angel's going to be surprised," Odessa mused, then winced as Genny tied the outer strip with a brisk little tug. "Ouch. Be gentle, darling."

She made a survey of him from head to toe and said, "I'm going downstairs to see if the hotel has something for first aid."

"You're going like that?"

Genny had forgotten she was running around his room, half in the altogether. Her hand lifted automatically to her wrapper, pinching it closed as a flush sailed to her cheeks.

"Where do I change?" she asked at a loss and scooped up the clutter of bandaging and the clothes she'd brought.

She turned, searching for an alcove like the one in her own room.

He smiled happily at her dilemma. "Anywhere your sweet heart desires, pretty one."

"Lecher."

"I'll keep my eyes closed." He wiggled his brows in a dubious promise. "Word of honor."

She giggled. "Odessa, I trust your honor about as much as I trust..."

Though she didn't say Adam's name, it echoed through the room like the knelling of a bell, and Genny's breath fled. She swished behind his chair and, by a series of acrobatics that surprised even her, managed to pull on the skirt beneath the wrapper and fasten it about her waist. He had guessed her size exactly.

"If you look in the small boxes," he said, "you'll find a few other necessities."

One of the other "necessities," Genny blushingly discovered, was a delectable pair of champagne-colored bloomers trimmed with lace as delicate as a spider's web, together with a chemise of the same soft silk. She had never touched anything as beautiful, much less worn it, and thoughts of Odessa selecting such intimate apparel made the room suddenly smaller and infinitely warmer. She was breathing quickly by the time her wrapper whispered to the floor and she stepped in the dainty bloomers.

"You have excellent taste," she mumbled, then unthinkingly turned the chemise inside out to admire the exquisite handstitching. "This is beautiful."

"I agree."

Over her shoulder she found him devouring the sight of her naked back. Blood rushed to her head, and she pressed the silk to her breasts and glanced down to see them taunting her with bobbing pinkness.

"You gave me your word of honor," she accused.

"I have no honor, Genny. Not where you're concerned."

Trembling, Genny held out her hand in warning only to realize that she had exposed what she wanted to keep covered.

"Odessa," she reasoned sincerely, "we both know what would happen if this gets out of hand. It's not like we haven't had time to know where we went wrong before."

He came closer. "I've thought of nothing else, Genny. Hell, I've dreamed about it."

Her mouth was abruptly parched, and she licked her lips. "Then let's be sensible. I didn't come here for this—" she nibbled briefly on her lip "—and that's the truth."

Odessa felt his own resolutions streaming through his fingers like grains of sand. Was he so weak that he couldn't keep his hands off her, even this once, to protect her? Was he so low and unprincipled?

"What is truth, Genny?" Huskiness knotted his throat. "I can't find it. I'm not sure it exists."

Genny saw on Odessa's face the same bewilderment she was feeling, and his fingers were closing on the silk as his breaths begged for her willing surrender. Her own promises to herself were washing away like a child's drawing in the sand.

"Can you imagine," he said as he slowly drew the silk away, "can you imagine how hungry a man's eyes become in prison, Genny? A man would almost kill to see, for one moment, something as beautiful as you." A terrible smile touched his mouth. "It hurts me to look at you sometimes, I want you so much."

But she would be ugly if he would only love her! Could he not feel how deeply her love was embedded in her heart? Could he not sense her need for a life with him?

With an honesty she had never before felt, Genny stopped quibbling with his hands. Though she was unnerved and unsure of herself, she gazed down at her breasts, at their pink fullness.

She took his hands and placed them upon their curves. "This wasn't supposed to happen," she said on a dwindling thread of a sigh. "It wasn't supposed to happen."

"I know." His mouth was closing on the tiniest, most sensitive tip, and the impact rocked her until she feared she would faint.

"Odessa." She clung to his shoulders. She twined her arms about his head and wanted to smother him, to keep him trapped there forever. "Oh," she gasped. "Oh."

Her pleasure excited Odessa as nothing else could. He wanted only to tap her passion at its wellspring. He wanted to teach her ways of satisfaction that she carried deep inside her own femininity and did not yet know.

She was weaving dizzily, and her hair was swinging back with silky abandon. "What do you want, Genny Carlyle?" he whispered as his mouth swept to her waist and over her trembling, quivering sides.

Hardly a whisper came when she let him lay her down. "I want you."

He covered her with kisses that Genny knew would be different. He touched her in places she found embarrassing but infinitely fulfilling. He rubbed her, he stroked her and drove her to a frenzy with his breath and his tongue and the words he whispered in her ear.

She wasn't afraid to be loved by him now. His life had crossed her life, and it was right that she was filled with him, loving that she was loved.

But a disturbing independence came over her as he moved, and she turned her head from side to side. In a way she didn't understand, she wanted to wrest free and take some dangerous, exhausting journey on her own. She wanted to press herself into the center of his body, past the flesh and bone of mere mortality.

"I don't know..." she confessed and intuitively moved, searching.

But where she was ignorant, he seemed to be knowledgeable. He traced the shell of her ear with his tongue, and the excitement of his hands was like the symptom of pain. He put her above him so that she was like a cat, arching and stretching and purring. He was a fulcrum that she rode, and his flesh, so hot within, melted her shyness. Her lids fluttered like wings as he began to take her spiraling to a diadem, round and round, higher and higher, more and more golden. For once, she took more than she gave.

"Close your eyes," he whispered as his hands pressed her ever closer to the nameless pinnacle. "Love me, Genny. Love me."

From the tower of the ten-story Western Union building were strung dozens of wires, which crossed Broadway and Dey, cluttering the sky like coarse weaver's threads on a loom.

Not wishing to use the hotel's telegraph, for the fewer people who knew his identity, the better, Odessa decided to use the Western Union downtown.

The main floor was a beehive of activity when he entered—people rushing about and telephones shrilling.

He approached a counter where a man was busy writing messages, his half-dozen sprigs of white hair sprouting comically from his head. After he finished with the customer in front, Odessa stepped forward and leaned on a counter worn smooth by thousands of leanings.

"I'd like to send a telegram to Albany," he said.

The man reached for his pencil and dipped the point into his mouth. "Go ahead, sir."

"Send it to Morgan Goldman in Albany." Odessa gave the address.

"And the message?"

"Will be at the Waldorf-Astoria on Friday. Stop. Would like to see you. Stop."

"That's all?"

"That's all."

"How would you like it signed, sir?"

Sighing, Odessa pinched the bridge of his nose. Part of him ached to see his parents, but part was ashamed.

"Andrew," he said heavily. "Sign it Andrew."

"Yessir."

Paying the man, Odessa walked out onto Nassau Street. Now there was no turning back.

By the time Genny had her first glimpse of Fifth Avenue, Manhattan had been under the strict tutelage of Caroline Astor for a number of years.

Having inherited big bones and a plain face from the Dutch Schermerhorns, Caroline Astor's main problem, when she married William Backhouse Astor for his money, was that New York city boasted so many millionaires. Much of the nouveau riche blood was appallingly less than blue, however, a sore trial to the superlatively conventional Mrs. Astor. Keeping carriages, living above Bleeker, subscribing to the opera, going to Grace Church, having a town house and a country house and giving balls and parties did not a society make, according to Caroline Astor.

By an adroit manipulation of the press and the fortune of William Backhouse, Caroline came to be known in polite society as the American Queen. She controlled society with such a tyrannical velvet-gloved hand, everything from the specific use of a salt spoon and how much lace on a skirt to the exclusion of venerable Commodore Vanderbilt, J. P. Morgan and John D. Rockefeller in her circle. The two words "Mrs. Astor," came to be the definitive authority on all things social worldwide.

Life for Mrs. Astor's social milieu consisted of balls, dinners and Monday night Opera fetes with the traditional meal at Delmonico's afterward. If one was invited to one of Caroline's ten-course dinners where guests ate on gold service reputed to have cost four hundred dollars a piece—that it later turned out to be merely gold plated was of no consequence—all was good. If not, hearts were broken.

Genny knew no more about New York society than she had read. "When you're starving to death, Odessa, it really doesn't matter how many tines a fork has," she said.

Yet Genny's inquisitive mind commenced upon a crash course in Eastern society. She learned, for instance, that the streets from Washington Square to Madison Square, were where money was strutted. Tourists came from all over the world to admire the carved facades and ornate metalwork of the brownstone mansions. She peered through the windows of Tiffany's and other jewelers who did a booming business, what with Caroline Astor wearing hundreds of thousand dollars' worth of jewelry at a time.

She looked with secret longing at the Worth creations that clothed all well-cared-for female bodies. Odessa bought her roses from one of the countless florists who would retire wealthy unto the third and fourth generation.

Fifth Avenue was not to be believed. There, hackmen and pickpockets and brothel keepers and tourists mingled with gentlemen whose fortunes were measured in nine digits as they walked their showpiece women. One could see everything on the Avenue: white *peau de soie* hats trimmed with green ribbons and *paille de riz* bonnets with deep, ear-confining brims, fashionable Gimp, Leghorn, Coburg and Jenny Lind models, parasols of shot silk, cambric and muslin dresses with bishop sleeves.

"Jessamine," Genny said as she mentally evaluated how she fit into all this hubbub of activity, "in your wildest dreams..."

But Jessamine could feel the tremble of excitement as the four of them walked down the Avenue. It was in the sunshine and the wind and the smells. "Tell me what you see, Geneena," she said on a quivering breath. "Tell everything."

"I don't think I can." Genny shook her head from side to side. "Thousands of dollars' worth of lace being dragged in the streets, for one thing. There're enough diamonds here to feed the entire West forever."

Odessa sent Angel to find a cab, and as Odessa helped them inside, he dryly observed, "New York tends to lean to the extremes, my dear. We have Fifth Avenue, and then we have the rest of the world." We have the life you could have if you were to marry well, and then we have . . .

With Beggar sitting politely up front with the driver and Angel making certain Jessamine was comfortable, Genny leaned out to view the conspicuous carriages rolling past.

"Before Wyoming," she said to Odessa, not knowing exactly how to form her question, "did you live like this?"

"My family lived well." He smiled without rancor. "But the working class aren't allowed on the inside of the inside." To Angel, he said, "Have the driver take us down to Eighteenth, if he can get through this traffic."

Angel's brows drew together. "Eighteenth? Are you sure?"

"Eighteenth. I want Genny to see the other half."

In a matter of blocks, glamorous Camelot turned into a rotting sore. Here, the famous brownstones became shacks and lean-tos, where the walls crawled with vermin and the rats were plumper and livelier than the children who played with dogs in the streets. Now the extravagance of "gentle society" seemed even more of a crime, with John Jacob Astor heading the ranks with his infamous American Fur Company and his real-estate ventures.

Wyoming's innocence, Genny thought, suddenly didn't seem so bad, after all.

When Odessa had twelve pieces of exquisite matching luggage delivered, Genny knew better than to protest to the delivery man. She took the bill of lading and marched straight to Odessa's room and pounded upon the door with a force that would have roused Dwight Parsons.

"What's the meaning of this?" she demanded when he opened the door. She thrust the delivery ticket beneath his nose.

Odessa grinned one of his maddening grins. "Oh," he said. "It came."

"Twelve pieces. Not cheap pieces, either, Odessa Gold. What do you propose I put in twelve pieces of luggage?"

With a laughing gesture to Angel, Odessa left her simmering in the corridor as he fetched his jacket and hat.

"Come with me," he said.

Chapter Thirteen

There was no contest. Lanouette was the great costume maker of New York. Gossip had it that when Alva Vanderbilt gave her fancy-dress ball to spite Caroline Astor, Lanouette kept one hundred and fifty dressmakers working day and night to fill the orders.

Madame Louise Desmond knew she was as talented as Lanouette, and it was unfair, truly it was, that Lanouette was given favors by the Vanderbilts when she, Louise, worked just as tirelessly and well to achieve a fraction of Lanouette's formidable reputation.

What she needed was that magical someone, that once-in-a-lifetime client. Up to now that magical someone had remained hidden, but Louise was a woman of indefatigable optimism. She went courageously on, taking women whose figures resembled dry-docked battleships and turning them into creations of loveliness.

Outside the bay window of Madame's Dress Shoppe, Genny cupped her hands and peered through the showcase window.

The shop was designed to mirror the comfortable languor of a Paris sidewalk café. Brightly clothed tables flanked an oval rug in the center of the showroom, and at them sat a half-dozen women sipping Earl Grey tea and nibbling petits fours from delicate bone-china cups and plates.

Spilling over the tables were the latest Godey's magazines, and on the floor, wicker baskets overflowed with cunning laces and buttons and beading, everything in charming disorder, designed to dazzle and bedazzle.

"It's much too crowded," Genny told Odessa with emphatic finality and clasped his arm in an attempt to steer him down the sidewalk. "We should come another day. Besides, Beggar needs to be walked, and did you notice that Jessamine has used nearly all her blue yarn?"

Odessa thought he had never seen a woman so dedicated to remaining obscure. Grasping her shoulders, he all but planted her in the sidewalk.

"Genny! Listen to me!" When he had captured her stunned attention, he slid her a slow grin. "Have you forgotten Adam Worthington? Have you forgotten Mary Faye?"

Genny lowered her lashes to half-mast, "You're an evil man, Odessa. Evil to the bone."

He laughed. "I know. But until I go up in flames, think about working on your entrance, so that Worthington takes one look at you and goes out and shoots himself in the foot."

"That wouldn't be my choice of injuries," she wryly observed.

"Then, get your luscious rear..."

Genny sent him an arrowed glare, and Odessa made a point of clearing his throat while he grinned sheepishly.

"What I meant was, get your luscious, ah, self inside."

The past days, Odessa had been ruthlessly honest with himself, and as lovely as Genny was, she was nowhere ready to descend upon Saratoga.

Neither of them had ventured into the war zone of words again—her bluff of finding a kind older gentleman to marry and his changing his occupation from gambler to scholar and artist. But the possibilities hung above them like an overcast sky.

"Mademoiselle?" he teased and opened the shop door with exaggerated gallantry, then literally shoved Genny inside.

Over their heads, a silver bell merrily announced their arrival, and an half-dozen feminine heads lifted.

The silence was not unlike the horror of watching a priceless porcelain falling to a marble floor. China cups were lowered to saucers, and customers exchanged tacit looks.

The moment passed almost in the same instant it occurred. The murmurs resumed, but Genny was certain that she had been weighed in the scales of acceptance and found lacking. She was not their kind. She would not be allowed inside the circle.

"Please," she begged Odessa, capturing his eyes with a plea.

Odessa was a veteran of the rejection she was suffering, but this task could not be bypassed, not if she wanted some of the good things in life.

Under his breath, he whispered, "You're worth fifty of them. Head up, Genny. They're jealous. Don't give them anything of yourself."

But I'm not as strong as you are, Genny wanted to say. She would much rather let them have their place.

"Oh! *Ma petite!*"

The cry rang out through the small shop, and Genny, turning, watched a diminutive black-clad figure emerging from the back room and buzz toward them like a bee. Her round pudding face was wreathed in smiles and her bosom bounced as eagerly as her ample hips churned.

"*Entrez, entrez!*"

With her arms thrown wide, Madame Desmond waved Genny deeper into the shop. When Genny gave Odessa a shrug and ventured closer, Madame braced her fists on her waist—or where her waist should have been—and reared her head back to view Genny as a whole, much as an artist would step back to get a better perspective of the work at hand. "Why, look at you, *ma petite!*" She swept her hand from head to toe and back. "Where did you get such bones?"

"Hunger." Genny said, and Madame laughed, thinking she had made a joke.

Before Madame could gush one more time, however, two women rose and coolly murmured their excuses, scooped up their parasols, threw a parting dart of disgust at Genny for being such a commoner and swept out of the shop.

Genny hardly heard a word of Madame's gushing civilities as she watched them go. The dressmaker was introducing someone named Lady Eleanor Bentley, who was dressed completely in white and carried a white leather *Book of Common Prayer* with an embroidered gold ribbon to mark her place, as if her true home were heaven and she was merely visiting earth for a spell.

Also, a frightened mouse named Priscilla whom Genny might have liked had Lady Bentley not extended her pure, white-gloved hand to Odessa and cooed, "Such a pleasure to meet you, Mr. Gold. Are you saved?"

In the manner of the most nauseating kind of courtier, Odessa bent his head over the dainty glove. "I'm afraid I'm in dire need of saving, Lady Bentley," he murmured, including Priscilla Davenport in his gracious self-effacement. "Are you of the Harrold Davenports of New Haven, Miss Davenport?"

Priscilla assured him that she was not and rose hastily to see about a length of pink ribbon that Madame had been saving for her consideration. Lady Bentley, seeing the need for a missionary endeavor of grand proportions, girded herself to meet the devil in a battle to the death for Odessa's soul. She pressed a tiny card into his hand upon which was written a verse of Scripture.

"God bless you, sir," she said.

"I appreciate that, Lady Bentley," Odessa said with a deep bow.

Genny smiled in feeble apology at Louise Desmond. "We were just looking," she tried to say, but was drowned out by Madame's clap, clap, clap, and orders streaming in French. "Henrietta! Come, come! *A la hâte!*"

To Odessa, she gushed, "Oh, monsieur, you have come to the right place. I will make of her the rage. What skin, what bones! Don't you agree? Green, I think will be perfect, but black?" She kissed her fingertips and threw them wide. "And blue. Brown, *oui, oui!*" Then, nearing a screech, "Henrietta!"

What Genny did not know and Odessa could only faintly surmise was that Louise Desmond had taken one look at Genny and known with the instincts of a true artist that the subject she had waited for all her professional life had just walked into her shop off the street. If she never sewed another stitch for Eleanor Bentley or the fickle Tennessee MacFarland and her shrewish friend, Marie, the price of Genny would be worth the lost customers.

"Explain to her," Genny hissed at Odessa as Madame shoo-shooed them into a special niche reserved for her most important clients. Here, Irish-lace curtains afforded privacy from the rest of the shop.

"Sit, sit," Madame urged. "You monsieur, sit here. Henrietta, tea for our guests. And Madame Gold, do take this seat here beside your husband. I cannot tell you how beautiful I shall make you."

In horror, Genny realized the woman's mistake, and she gaped at Odessa who didn't say a word to set the dressmaker straight.

Swallowing, shaking her head, she mumbled, "Mr. Gold is not my husband."

Too late, Genny realized her blunder. Madame's brows rose ever so slightly, but in the matter of ambition, old-fashioned virtues didn't count. If a man must have a mistress, this man couldn't have chosen a more delectable one.

"*Certainement,*" Madame purred in her most worldly tone, breezing out of the dressing room and drawing the lace curtains more discreetly closed than before.

*   *   *

Over the next two and a half hours, Genny's modesty
was systematically demolished. Madame shut the front
door of the shop and posted a sign that said her establishment was closed for the afternoon. She then flew about the
shop, plucking bolts of cloth from her shelves, barking
commands to Henrietta and hurling out sails of fabric
across the rug, over the chairs, inside the private niche—
powder-blue brocade and ivory satin and pale peach
organza, a delicate piece of pink-sprigged lawn, and yards
and yards of green voile and the richest taffeta.

As Genny stood on Madame's footstool, stripped to her
underwear and measured in every way a woman's body
could be measured, Henrietta made quick but very poor
sketches of Madame's ideas. Odessa asked for paper and
pencil and drew his own sketches, sitting on a fragile chair,
the legs of which he'd tipped back toward the wall so that
Madame feared one wrong move would splinter her French
antique darling.

Sketch after sketch the drawings drifted to the floor like
leaves from a tree. Henrietta stooped curiously and
clapped her hand over her mouth.

Alerted, Madame turned to see, and the assistant thrust
a handful of drawings at her. *"Alors!"*

Drawn were likenesses of Genny in all the various cos-
tumes Madame had suggested—a tennis costume with a
large sailor's collar and a side sash of blue; a simple, almost stark skirt with a plain blouse and a man's tie, topped
with a studious little hat; an elaborate gown for the Opera
of flowered cretonne and a flamboyant leghorn that turned
sassily up on one side. He had sketched Genny in a riding
habit, too, and a swimming costume, then in morning
gowns with deep flounces of lace, and a breathtaking
traveling suit with a cunning shoulder cape. In all the cos-
tumes, Genny was slim and forthright, her hair a curling
crown of twists and braids or simply flowing down her
back.

Madame's gushing was hushed, and she looked from Genny to Odessa, back to Genny and to Odessa again. "My words are gone." She shook her head and flipped through the drawings again. "Might I keep these, monsieur? There are those who would love, who would be charmed—"

"I'm sorry," Odessa said with an abruptness that brought Genny's head sharply up.

He gentled his refusal with a typical artist's shyness. "It's just that I—"

Genny saved him. "Mr. Gold does not use his art professionally," she gently explained. "Only for his own pleasure."

Louise Desmond bowed her head in acquiescence. "I understand completely. You wouldn't mind if I kept them for my designs, would you? For a few days. They're so much better than Henrietta's."

The decision being his to make, Odessa grudgingly said that, yes, the woman could use them if they would help.

When eventually Genny and Odessa were back out on the street, Genny tried to bully her way past his artistic dogmatism.

"Do you have any idea of how many people work their whole lives to achieve what you were born with, Odessa Gold? You're always talking about crimes—well, that's a crime. Not to use a God-given talent."

Odessa could not share with Genny how wonderful it felt to draw her, or how frightening. He couldn't let himself hope to regain what he had once had. If he hoped for that, he would hope for her, and he would be more vulnerable to life than he had ever been before. And she...

Striding a few paces beyond him in her petulance, she waged a charming battle with the wind for her skirt.

"If you want to nag at me, my darling," he drawled to disguise the depth of his feelings, "I'm afraid you'll have to marry me."

Sharp-eyed and censuring, Genny had learned him too well. When Odessa talked of lasting things like marriage, he was making fun. When he talked of troublesome things, uncertainty and fear, he was serious.

Trembling, she retorted as flippantly as he, "And wreck my image of the kept woman? Never!"

From her shop, Louise Desmond watched the couple cross the street, then she flew about the room like a person possessed. Grabbing a portfolio and stuffing the drawings inside, she found her lace shawl and a magnificent hat she had designed herself, trimmed with ostrich feathers and twists of sheer voile.

Scooping up her parasol, she darted out of the shop and locked the door. She strode briskly down the street and headed straight for the offices of the *New York Times*. She had a good friend there.

Fifteen minutes later, after Mason Fleming had spread Odessa Gold's drawings over his desk, he exchanged a look of unadulterated greed with Louise Desmond.

"Well, well, Louise," he said, "I think your day may just have come at last. You have visions. I can see it in your eyes."

There was a fearful commotion in Louise's chest, making her so warm that she had to fan herself. "This has to count, Mason. I'll make a formidable enemy in this man when he learns what I've done, and I don't want you to publish a single drawing until I've clothed this woman and turned her into the creature you see here." She tapped the sheaves of drawings. "She will be this woman, I assure you. You should see her, Mason. She doesn't know what she is, and that is her enormous charm. See? He has captured it."

"You'll have women beating down your door, wanting to *be* this woman. I don't understand, Louise. These drawings will make this...Gold, whoever he is, famous. I guarantee it. Who wouldn't want that?"

"He will, once he's had a taste of it." Louise forgave herself everything in the interest of ambition. "He'll thank me, in the end. But now..."

Mason laughed and began to arrange the drawings in the order in which he wanted to publish them. "Get your money up front, that's all I can say."

"If I never get a penny, it will be worth it," the woman declared. "Lanouette, indeed!"

It seemed he was forever drawing her. Though he continued to disappear in the evenings, Odessa was invariably sketching her by noon—in the park, in their rooms, as they rode about the city.

Genny found herself blossoming beneath his constant attention, unfolding one petal at a time as she learned something new about herself or drifted off in a fresh dream of them together until the end of time. How natural it all felt, how poetic, and she wondered if he knew how much of the sensitive Andrew Goldman was emerging from beneath the tough Odessa Gold.

When he announced that they would be moving to the Waldorf-Astoria, however, her old concern with money brought her spinning around in disbelief.

"Have you lost your senses?" she scolded as they returned to the Jamison after walking with Beggar, who now trotted obediently between them, his beautiful head held high, his nose attuned to all the smells of the city. "Do you have any idea what that would cost?"

"Money is no object," he drawled.

"Maybe not to you. I'm indebted to you for an entire wardrobe as it is, Odessa. Now, you're wanting to move into the most expensive hotel in the country. No, no, no!"

"Oh, dear. I suppose I'm now obliged to start paying you by the hour."

Odessa stopped in the middle of the sidewalk, and the retriever politely plopped down beside his boots so that Genny very nearly tripped over him. Her whisper was sharp as acid. "Of all the cruel things you've ever said to me, Odessa Gold—"

Tipping back his head, he roared with laughter and infuriated her all the more by tweaking her righteously upturned nose. "Not for *that*, my darling. What do you take me for?"

"A beast! A nasty, lecherous beast!"

"True. But this would be a salary for posing. All artists pay their models, Genny. We'll enter into a business arrangement."

Blushing, though not entirely mollified, Genny sniffed with less suspicion. "We-e-ell . . . how much are you willing to pay?"

His grin was inflammatory, then more gentle, then wistful. "Whatever you want, Genny Carlyle," he said softly. "Whatever you want."

Of course, she could not say that the one thing she wanted he could not give, so she shrugged as if it were no consequence.

Presently he said, "Exactly how much do you know about Saratoga, Genny?"

Genny bent to scratch Beggar's golden ears. "I don't suppose it's too different from any other small town. Except the springs, of course. All that good health from drinking the water. Which probably tastes terrible. People are people the world over. Why?"

Odessa drew her arm through his and guided her across the street, Beggar trotting alongside. She was totally unaware of how passersby turned back to take a second look. Men were sending him envious messages. Genny made him feel good, as if his ten years in prison had never happened.

"Only a few people go to Saratoga to drink the water, Genny. The spas are just a good excuse to gamble and strut."

"I don't do either. So why am I going? Except to get my money back from Adam, of course. Anyway, I plan to be invisible."

Odessa laughed with genuine merriment. "Invisible is the last thing you'll be. They'll see you, Genny, and you'll see them."

"Adam's the only person I want to see."

"You'll see the big Eastern titans, the Western cattle kings..."

"I've seen enough cattle kings, thank you. Shooting at sheepmen over barbed wire."

"Nothing comes free. There'll be railroad tycoons, of course, and now that Gould's dead, Morgan's probably the top dog. But it's really a woman's town, Genny. The men come to gamble and show off their women, and the women come to be shown off while their men gamble."

Genny carefully picked up her skirt when they reached the curb, and took a firm grip on the leash. Recognizing the hotel a distance away, Beggar was anxious to return.

"At this very moment," he said, "thousands and thousands of women are climbing into their attics and dragging out the trunks. They're spending thousands of dollars to fill them. You think we spent money at Madame Desmond's? This is the time dressmakers live for."

Genny said in her most worldly tone, "It occurs to me, Odessa Gold, how extremely well-informed you are in the ways of women."

"I have a mother and four sisters, my darling. I was the one who got to pack all those ostrich tips and the tulle and bison serge and cashmere. Hats? Lord, you never saw the like. The boxes just to carry all their things took up an entire carriage. That doesn't begin to deal with gloves and embroidered handkerchiefs and jewels. Jewels, of course, are another science altogether. Tiffany's has a branch in Saratoga just to accommodate the tourist season."

Well, Genny thought with mounting depression as they approached the hotel, jewelry was one problem she didn't have. She nudged Beggar to a faster pace, and the dog, deciding he had earned himself a moment of abandon, ran in a happy circle about her feet, unwittingly wrapping the leash about her legs and necessitating that she spin in a circle to keep from toppling on her face.

Odessa lost his train of thought as her delight rippled musically on the warm evening air. She had clapped a hand to her head to prevent the wind from tossing her boater into the clouds, and dozens of wispy tendrils were set dancing. The leash grabbed her skirt just below her hips and molded their perfect curves. Her head, thrown back in laughter, exposed the gleaming ivory of her throat, and her teeth, sparkling and white as pearls, were parted so he could see the sweet pinkness of her tongue.

Beggar wagged a furious tail and wound the leash more tightly. From the passing carriages and the sidewalk and the steps of the Jamison, people were stopping to smile at her and each other.

Love for her broke his heart. "It's like the plague of locusts upon Egypt," he said quickly to keep his resolve from crumbling.

Her confusion showed in the arch of her brows. "Odessa, what're you talking about?"

"Saratoga, my love. What else? About the train coming into the station."

"What train?"

"*The* train. When it comes in, they sound the bell. The whole town turns out and descends like a horde of locusts. Hack drivers hawking for customers, and landaus, dogcarts, phaetons. It's at the station that one can tell the aristocracy from the lesser mortals."

Genny was beginning to be sorry that she had ever heard of Saratoga Springs. "Why couldn't Adam have gone to Philadelphia?" She sighed. "It's all so complicated."

"Not really."

"All right, I'll nibble. How do they tell the gods from the mortals?"

"My mother always used to say that luggage is the key. They take one look at luggage and know."

So, now they had luggage. But that posed yet another problem.

"And just what do you propose we put in all that luggage, Odessa Gold? Rocks? Your head?"

He grinned malevolently. "Your wonderful wardrobe, once it's done. Until then, we'll make do. Get your things together. I've also bought you a carriage."

"What?" This was going too far!

"Well, rented it, actually, along with a driver." He shrugged with that infuriating innocence men assume when they don't want to be cross-examined. "There's no help for it, I'm afraid. The Waldorf's expecting us this evening. You can't just up and make an entrance, Genny, not just like that. An entrance is a learned art. It takes practice and practice and more practice. The Waldorf will be your opening night, so to speak, so wear your prettiest frock. Half the people at the hotel will be at Saratoga in another two weeks."

Aghast, Genny barely managed to croak, "This is nothing but one big game to you, is it?"

He reached up to pull her boater low over her eyebrows so all that showed was the tip of her nose and her pouting lips.

"Life is a game, Genny. You win, you lose. It's all in the way you play."

She jerked off her hat and hit him on the shoulder with it, glaring. "Not *my* life. I'm a simple person. I don't know this game, and I don't think I want to play with you anymore!"

Dodging, he laughed and caught her so close that Genny shared the beating of his heart. Sweet mercy, she was falling more and more in love with him every day! What was going to happen to her?

"Have no fear, my love," he said, and studied her brows and her fretting pout with a growing despair. If she found herself a husband, he must be the best, the very best. "I excel at this game."

As Genny's wardrobe would not be finished for days, filling the new luggage for the move to another hotel was a problem that Odessa solved by packing box after box of books that Angel had found at a bargain price on lower Fifth Avenue, plus some old newspapers and tinned peaches and a really fine sidesaddle he'd won from a man from Ohio.

"This is horrible!" Genny railed throughout the entire procedure. "No bellboy at the Waldorf-Astoria is going to think these are clothes! They'll know we're frauds, and they'll dump us out onto the street in disgrace!"

Odessa hooked his thumbs in his pockets and paced. "The rich are an eccentric breed, Genny. Your first lesson in making an entrance—when we register—is to look like an aristocrat."

With a furious toss of her hair, Genny shoved her face beneath his. "And how, pray tell," she said between gritted white teeth, "does an aristocrat look?"

He playfully pecked her lips. "More disagreeable than that, I can assure you. One must learn disdain, Genny. And scathing looks of disgust."

"Scathing looks of disgust aren't in my repertoire."

"Pretend you're meeting Adam Worthington, and your money is sticking out of his pockets."

Genny chewed at the edge of her lips and considered just how far chasing her money had brought her.

"This is going to be a snap," she retorted and withered Odessa with a venomous look.

He grinned. "Now you've got the hang of it."

There would certainly be hell to pay, Genny thought as she arrived at the sinfully beautiful Waldorf-Astoria wearing the gray silk faille with an overskirt and basque trimmed in pink. It wasn't an elaborate costume, and at her throat was a simple black brooch; no jewels whatsoever were clipped to her ears or circling her fingers.

Yet she knew with an instinct that could never make a mistake in such matters that she and Odessa would somehow be esteemed as a couple of import. The worst part was that she hadn't been forced into this charade because of Adam Worthington's betrayal and desertion. She was doing it because she wanted to be a part of Odessa's life, any way she could be.

A battalion of bellboys whisked away the luggage without blinking an eye. Odessa and Angel crisscrossed the expanse of the lobby with an easy finesse and reached the registration desk just as the concierge was looking up from his newspaper and folding it. Pink-cheeked and innocent-looking, he made a ruthlessly thorough assessment of the tall, scarred man, as well as the black man who stood at stiff attention, slightly behind.

"We'd like rooms, please," said Odessa.

A dangerous sort, the concierge thought, letting his gaze drift to the blind woman who aroused his pity but did not change his decision about the scarred man. Then he saw the woman who waited a distance away.

She was looking about at the spaciousness, and something clicked in his mind. He frowned slightly.

"Would you excuse me a moment, sir?" he asked politely, then turned to pick up the newspaper he had just discarded.

There, in a small insert on page four—an advertisement for one of the local dress shops, and accompanying it was the very woman standing across the lobby. Oh, she was much better in the flesh! Who was she? Someone famous, certainly. Perhaps traveling incognito. Well, he was on to her.

Others in the lobby seemed to be preoccupied with the same question, and the concierge could feel them wondering if they knew of her. Some of them shrugged off the impression and moved on.

But he, shrewd judge of character that he was, returned to the scarred man and smiled. "Absolutely, sir. Do you have a preference?"

The man had removed his hat and was drawing off his glove, finger by finger. "Your best suite," he said in a voice that now reeked of impeccable breeding.

"That would be the Presidential Suite, sir," the concierge said and gave a snap of his fingers as he pushed the book forward.

As the name was scrawled on the line, he spun the book around and said to the bell captain, "See Mr. Gold and his party to the Presidential Suite."

The uniformed captain recognized urgency in the usually snobbish concierge, and he hurried for a cart and bowed politely to the lady as he loaded it and led the strange quartet past the hotel's famous staircase to the elevator.

The Presidential Suite was not one suite but two decadently lavish suites joined by means of a middle door with solid gold hardware on both sides.

It was said that the Waldorf-Astoria had been decorated with the Astors' cast-off furnishings—the needlepoint footstool, the Spitalfield silk chair, the goldbrocaded love seat and an Aubusson rug, the medallion of which was woven into a rose background, centered beneath the chandelier. The walls of both suites were covered with paper of a watery silk design, and the woodwork wasn't the old-fashioned darkly varnished kind, but an eggshell white that seemed to invite the sunlight through the gauzy lace curtains of the windows.

Genny remained coolly aloof until the door was shut safely behind the bellboys, then she almost collapsed with dithering excitement. With outflung arms, she whirled breathlessly through the rooms, crushing Jessamine in a hug and wanting to touch everything at once, each beautiful surface, each wonderful fabric.

Jessamine didn't need to be told that she was surrounded by beautiful things—she was learning with her fingertips.

Odessa unlocked the middle door and poked his head through the opening. "Ladies," he said with a laugh, "I trust this meets with your approval."

"Oh, yes!" Genny trilled and danced across the room toward him. "This is what heaven is, Odessa, I'm sure of it." She angled a look at his amusement. "With the exception of *that,* thank you very much."

With quick fingers, she robbed him of the key to the adjoining door and darted away. Too late, Odessa grabbed, but she coyly dropped the key into the neck of her basque and purringly struck a pose.

"Genny..." he warned, his brows drawing into a scowl as he took a step through the door toward her.

With a rising sense of feminine power, Genny pushed him back into his own side of the double suite and smiled at the dark color staining his cheeks.

"You're always pointing out how we should pretend not to know each other for my own safety. So now we don't know each other."

"Dammit, Genny!"

He made a wild grab for the key, but Genny deftly swept the door shut in his face and, with surprise in her favor, inserted the key and threw the bolt with a thud.

A moment of silence.

Then, "Genny, I demand you open the door this instant!"

"If you want to see me, Odessa—" was it possible to push him too far? "—you may knock on the front door like a proper gentleman."

He said some things she was positive she was better off not hearing.

Another heavy space of time. Genny warily pressed her ear against the door, not daring to breathe.

"I know you're over there, Genny Carlyle," he said presently, and she laid her hand upon her collar, just to make sure the key was still there. "But don't feel too safe. When I want to get to you, there isn't a door made that will stop me."

Chapter Fourteen

After sending a bellboy to their son's room with the message that they had arrived in response to his telegram, Felicia and Morgan Goldman joined Samuel Houseman in the richly populated lobby of the Waldorf-Astoria.

Surrounded on all sides by prodigious wealth, Samuel could remember sitting at a stark wooden table at the murder trial in Wyoming, where Andrew, the beloved son of his two dear friends, had sat with his attorney, Lucas Peevy. Morgan Goldman had paid the criminal lawyer a persuasive sum to get his son acquitted of murder.

Clean-shaven, deathly pale even beneath his wind-burned tan, Andrew had worn a brown suit that Felicia had brought with her from New York. His left arm was bandaged and cradled close to his side. His handsome face was haunted, gaunt.

Though Morgan and Samuel both pleaded, Felicia had refused to stay away from the courtroom. For long, wilting hours she kept vigil behind her son, her spine relentlessly straight as others sagged with fatigue and the dripping summer heat. She showed no emotion as terrible things were said about Andrew. She never moved and hardly seemed to breathe.

Checkers Peabody was a damaging witness. Called to the stand, he looked out over the crowd and wiped a dribble of tobacco juice from his half-toothless mouth onto his sleeve and said to Judge Atwell, who was leaning on one elbow and fanning himself with a newspaper, "I knew 'e was trouble the minute he walked in the door, Yer Honor." He stabbed a finger at Andrew. "You kin always tell when a man's trouble."

"I object, Your Honor," intoned Lucas Peevy with weary boredom. "This is a private assumption and totally unsubstantiated."

"Could you be more specific, Mr. Peabody?" The judge removed his gold-rimmed spectacles and cleaned them with his handkerchief.

The old-timer snorted resentfully at the Eastern attorney, whose stiff collar was cutting into his neck. "Well, I guess bein' from New York City with all them arist-o-crats, you don't know a man's ways like we do."

"Your Honor, ple-e-ease," Lucas Peevy protested.

"Do go on, Mr. Peabody."

Checkers smirked at Peevy. "Well, this here man, he made sure of 'is weapons then looked me square in the whites of the eyes and pulled out a drawin' of Dep'ty Wright. He says, 'Do you know this man?' I says I did. Next thing I knowed, Dep'ty Wright wuz dead. Is that specific enough for ya, Mr. New York City?"

Lucas Peevy rose and hooked his thumbs in the pockets of his wine-colored vest. He gave the courtroom the full force of his impressive defense-attorney persona. "Did you actually see Mr. Goldman shoot the deputy, Mr. Peabody?"

"Ever'body seen him."

Behind his spectacles which he carefully adjusted about his ears, Judge Atwell was sympathetic to the brooding, bandaged man. Andrew Goldman claimed to have done no more than extract the Biblical "eye for an eye." But not a shred of evidence had come out to support his claim that Eli Wright was the train robber who had caused the death of Anne Goldman.

Andrew Goldman was called again to the stand.

"Earlier, you testified, sir," the prosecuting attorney, Jason Beane, recalled over the scrape of chairs and hacking coughs, "that Eli Wright was one of three men."

"Yes, I did."

"And you're telling this court that you would know these three men again if you saw them again?"

"Absolutely."

"Can you describe them to us now?"

"No, Mr. Beane, I cannot."

"You mean, you will not."

"I showed drawings of them all over the territory of Wyoming."

"Then show them to us."

"I cannot."

"Why not, sir?"

"Because I destroyed the drawings."

A gasp of disbelief rippled through the room as fans stopped waving and people leaned forward.

"Destroyed!" Beane exclaimed. "But they were evidence, sir!"

As he glimpsed the mockery staining Andrew's face, Samuel wanted to lunge to his feet and shout, "If you won't save yourself, why don't you think of her, your mother? Look at her!"

"I don't know why, sir," Andrew snapped icily to the prosecuting attorney. "You don't believe I correctly identified Eli Wright or that I saw the men's faces. Why would you believe what I drew?"

Beane's color was florid, and his eyes bulged as he shouted, "Do you know who the men are now, Mr. Goldman? Can you tell this court, without the drawings you claim to have possessed, who the two other men were who robbed the train?"

A shutter snapped down upon Andrew's face, and he was no longer a part of the court.

"Is that a no, Mr. Goldman?"

"That is a no."

With hands thrown to the ceiling, the attorney appealed to the judge. "Your Honor, this man has maliciously, and with foresight, shot down a man of the law. It is our belief that he will, given the opportunity, do it to anyone else he assumes is guilty of his wife's unfortunate death. In all due respect, Your Honor, and in consideration of Mr. Goldman's understandable grief, we cannot allow him to walk the streets any longer. The prosecution rests, Your Honor."

"Silence, silence!" the judge shouted. "Silence, or I'll clear this courtroom!"

The gavel cracked sharply upon the crude judicial bench, and Atwell gazed over the observers who had filled the sweltering courtroom to hear the trial—the uniformed, sweating soldiers from the fort, the spurred ranchers, the merchants.

Judge Atwell fanned himself briefly before spreading his arms and gripping the sides of his desk.

"Mr. Goldman," he said to the defendant, who had slumped low in his chair, brooding, "may I remind you that you have killed a man in front of witnesses. We have heard your testimony of why you did what you did. I must ask you again, sir, have you seen the two other men who robbed the train and abducted your wife, the men you claim made such an impact on you that you can identify them after all this time?"

Only to Samuel had Andrew confided the truth. The evening he had learned from Checkers that Eli Wright was a deputy marshall, he had sought out the lawman and found him in the dining hall of the Sweet Charity Hotel. There was no mistake.

Not quite certain of how one went about accusing a lawman of robbery and murder, Andrew lay upon his hotel bed and faced the truth. No one would believe him about Eli Wright. No matter what he said, no one would help bring a deputy marshall to justice. He had to be his own justice.

By eleven o'clock the next day, heat had wilted Laramie. The leaves on trees hung straight down, and the sky was the color of brass. A few exhausted clouds floated by giving momentary relief, but soldiers trotted up and down the street on horseback, cursing the sun as their hooves stirred up dust in the street.

From the town's two saloons, piano music jingled off-key. The windmill that pumped water into the storage tank beside the depot creaked on every turn like a strange, grieving rooster. If not for the gold expected to arrive at the Wells Fargo office at noon, no one would have been out.

In the darkened saloon Andrew sat pondering his dilemma. It was then he perceived a horrible truth; in all his practice of shooting, he'd neglected to realize that firing at a target of wood or glass wasn't the same as shooting a man.

When the Wells Fargo wagon clattered into town, Andrew moved onto the sidewalk with everyone else and tugged at the brim of his hat. A guard sat perched on the seat beside the driver, a shotgun across his lap.

The clatter of the wagon brought Union-clad soldiers out to stand guard along with the Wells Fargo officers. Men pushed through the swinging doors of the saloon and ladies stepped out of the shops, their petticoats dragging in the dust. The horses tethered to the hitching posts skittered, and the loafers, hunkered against the buildings, talking and smoking, came to their feet.

Andrew crossed the street and entered the Sweet Charity Hotel.

"Checkers," he said to the proprietor, "I'd like the Colt, please."

When Checkers pushed him the handgun, Andrew buckled it about his waist. "Now, the Winchester."

The man's eyes widened with surprise. "Why, yer goin' to hold up Wells Fargo, as I live an' breathe!"

Andrew pulled a sour grimace. "You know, Checkers, your mistrustful attitude isn't very attractive. You really should give some thought to changing it."

Walking out into the street, Andrew moved beneath the overhang of Bartlett's Dry Goods store and watched Eli Wright leave the jail to help oversee the safety of the shipment.

Even if Eli Wright hadn't been a thief and a murderer, he wouldn't have been a likable man. He was tough and crude. Turning, he called to two men who had also come out of the jail and were bringing up his rear.

When he saw Wright's companions, Andrew's heart turned to stone. One was a heavy bulldoglike man with tiny close-set eyes, and the hair that showed beneath his hat was silver. Beside him walked a taller, thinner man with a nose as sharply beaked as a vulture. His hair was tricolored— red, yellow and brown. Both wore badges.

Andrew wasn't aware of thinking or feeling anything as he stepped into the dusty street. He was in a dream. He was kneeling over Anne. He was picking up the object that would have been their son and wrapping it in a blanket. He was roaring with pain.

The three deputies reached the center of the street where they met the Wells Fargo officials. Andrew brought the Winchester to his shoulder and fixed Eli Wright in his sights. He didn't think about it. He simply fired.

Hardly had his shoulder absorbed the kick than bedlam exploded on the street. The deputies scattered and returned his fire. Andrew spun with the force of the bullet that struck him.

"Watch out!" someone screamed as horses reared and thrashed against their traces.

"Edwin, get out of the street!" a mother shrieked to her child.

Hardly hearing the shouting or seeing the people running in all directions, Andrew brought his mind to focus on the one thing that had driven him for so long. Dragging himself up from where he'd fallen, he fired again. Eli

Wright dropped to his knees in the street, surprise staining his features before he toppled, facedown.

In the cell with Andrew, Samuel had begged for the names of the two other men responsible for his daughter's death.

A sad smile found Andrew's lips as he rose and laid his hands gently upon Samuel's shoulders. "Sir, I don't know you well enough to get you killed."

"You think I care about my life?" Samuel had raged. "I've buried the two people I loved the most!"

"And I have the living to consider, sir. Have you forgotten my parents have come to my trial? These men are here. Now they know who you are and who my parents are. Forget about Anne's killers, Mr. Houseman. With all due respect, sir, enough blood has been shed. Nothing will bring her back."

But Samuel had thought of nothing else for ten long years.

As Genny brushed her hair dry, she was roused by a sudden and thunderous attack upon the door that separated the two suites.

"Genny!" Odessa roared as he pounded with both fists in a deafening percussion, "if you don't open this damned door, so help me heaven, I'll kick it in!"

"Oh dear, oh dear, oh dear," Jessamine said as she sat up in her chair with a start from her catnap. "Has it begun to storm?"

"Not as much as it's going to," Genny quipped as she fetched the key and strode through the suite to fit it into the lock. She hesitated before turning it. "Odessa?"

"No, it's J. Pierpont Morgan. Of course it's me. Open this door, Genny."

Genny's opportunities for winning with Odessa were too few and far between to let this one go by. She smiled with an impish satisfaction. "What d'you want, Odessa?"

"I don't think you really want me to say it out loud, do you?"

Her amusement evaporating, Genny stiffened and said peevishly, "You already have a long list of sins to atone for, Odessa. I wouldn't go adding any."

From the opposite side came a strenuous oath and a splintering kick at the bottom of the door. The door handle rattled meaningfully.

"Madam, if this door isn't open in the next three seconds..." A hesitation, then a sigh. At last, more solemnly, "Genny..."

Something was different, Genny knew, and she fumbled with the key, threw the deadbolt with a *thunk* and swung the door open.

He was standing on the opposite side, flushed and tousled in a pale blue alpaca summer suit, his blue-and-white striped shirt buttoned at the collar but loose and flapping at the cuffs. A tie was looped about his neck, obviously having refused to be tied. In the gray of his eyes was not the steely gambler nor the embittered man, but a sweet, wistful boy who has just realized that he's unprepared for a crisis he's had ample time to prepare for and hasn't.

Genny thought she loved him more in that moment than she ever had in the past, and she was suddenly shy and unsure of herself.

"Oh, dear," she said, fluffing her damp curls. "Are you having a bit of difficulty?"

Distracted by her dishevelment, he moved his inspection thoroughly over her sleeves, which were rolled to her elbows, and her shirtwaist, which had been unbuttoned to her breasts, its collar turned inward to avoid wetting during her shampoo.

"Not nearly as much as I was," he drawled, grinning.

Set suddenly adrift by his tone and his look, Genny wet her lips and eyed him speculatively. "Wh-what did you want?"

She gestured at the door, and he gently plucked the key from her fingers and dropped it into the deep point of the V of her neckline. The metal was cool between her breasts, and he watched the brass disappear into the lace placket of her camisole.

"What?" he eventually replied and drew a deep breath through his nostrils.

Genny blinked. "What?"

He lifted his flapping cuffs and then began to pat his pocket for the studs. "I, uh..."

He moved back into his own rooms, and Genny, as if connected by a length of silver cord, followed. Angel had gone out. The wardrobe that held their clothes was thrown wide, and jackets and trousers had been removed and tossed haphazardly on the bed. Bureau drawers were open, spilling socks and undergarments. A half-smoked cigar was drizzling smoke toward the ceiling.

As she was taking in the disorder, that was so unlike Angel and Odessa, he said with endearing helplessness, "My mother and father are downstairs."

Caution settled like a glaze over Genny's mind. She said warily, "How did they know you were here?"

He explained about his telegram. He had made an attempt to reinstate himself into his family, Genny thought, but now he was regretful and ashamed. She wanted to take him into her arms and stroke the back of his head, to tell him not to have regrets. Family was everything.

She removed a cuff link from his long beautiful fingers. "You did the right thing," she said as she deftly folded back a cuff and inserted the stud.

They were both acutely aware of the ways in which they touched. Yet another crisis had arisen, and they were dealing with it, only this time she was *his* support.

"You think so?" he asked with childlike sincerity.

Genny looked up. "Of course." A grin played about her lips. "As the venerable Mr. MacGowan would say..."

They both laughed, and their mutual warmth was like wine. But it wouldn't do to become drunk just now, and they pushed apart.

"They must have been something," he mused. "A perfect marriage. I wish I could've seen it."

"No." Genny shook her head and slipped the remaining stud into its holes. "Amazingly, it wasn't a perfect marriage." Shocked at her audacity to speak of something as dangerous as marriage, she added with a shrug, "They didn't expect perfection, apparently. They just took the good they had and worked around the rest. Anyone could do it. In fact, I doubt that a perfect marriage has ever existed. Oh, Adam and Eve, maybe."

"Not for long."

She giggled, and Odessa thought as he stretched his neck against the strangling collar that she was perfect. To him, she was. She proceeded to tie his tie and stood back to inspect the final product. Did he perceive a slight quiver of her lips? Or was his own guilt coloring his vision?

"Now *you're* perfect," she said, but did not smile.

"Funny," he said, "I was thinking the same thing about you."

She had started back to her own room where Jessamine sat rocking before a sunshiny window. Unable to bear the sight of her back, Odessa stepped behind her and wrapped her in his arms and pulled her against his body, his mouth finding her ear beneath the damp curls. "I need you . . ."

Confused, she shoved against his crisp shirt. "This is the wrong time, Odessa."

" . . . to go with me. I need you to be with me when I face them."

Despite the thrills that always attacked her when he was so near, she pushed him away and backed warily from the room. She couldn't allow herself to get that close to a family. She wouldn't be able to climb over her need and escape before they rejected her.

With swimming eyes, she shook her head. "No, no. You're not doing this to me, Odessa. You can't. It's not fair. You don't want—"

"I do want. You have to, Genny."

She opened her mouth as she groped for a fresh batch of excuses. She licked her lips and lifted her hands to her frenzy of hair. "I just washed my hair."

"I just washed my hair," he mimicked so perfectly that she wanted, suddenly, to punch his face. He was suddenly grave and very, very honest. "It'll be all right, sweetheart. I promise."

Morgan Goldman was not as tall as his wife, but he gave the impression of being larger.

He was a devoted father, a considerate husband and had worked long and tirelessly to provide his family with everything good. When his son went to prison, his heart had been broken. Now he had a tendency to look upon members of his family with an overprotective eye. With a pervading dread of disaster, he watched Felicia pacing—as much as Felicia ever paced!—the veranda of the hotel.

Without making an issue of it, for Felicia hated making issues of anything, she kept the lobby within her field of vision. Her beautiful gray eyes moved from her husband's worried frown to the staircase that swept down from the second-floor mezzanine, back to his frown, then back to the staircase.

"Darling," he said, and pressed her hands with a sincerity that did not console, "we've waited this long, we can wait a few minutes more. Everything's going to be all right, you'll see."

"I'm afraid to hope that," she said in her cultured-pearl voice.

"I know."

Hardly were the words out of his mouth than Felicia gave a small startled gasp. Morgan followed her stare while, behind them, Samuel gazed, not at the stairs where a tall, striking slim man was descending with one of the most beautiful young women on his arm since his own lovely Anne, but at Felicia.

Felicia was unaware that heads were turning as she lifted her voluminous skirts and skimmed through the open door and across the teeming lobby. Silent stares followed her, and Morgan was unable to keep up. Elegance forgotten, Felicia was openly weeping as people made way for her.

They saw the handsome man stop before he reached the landing of the stairs. He spoke, Samuel saw, to the young woman on his arm.

Then, disengaging himself, he took the last steps two at a time. Guests of the hotel stood with their hands covering their own quivering mouths as the beautiful mother went into the arms of the son and laid her head into the curve of his neck. With the scar and stern tanned looks, one could easily assume he was a soldier.

And in a way, Samuel thought, Andrew *was* a warrior. He had waged a one-man crusade and lost. As Felicia now received her warrior-son to her bosom, Samuel was overcome by a wave of anger. Andrew was home, but Anne would never come home.

Gutted, broken, his big body wanting to come apart at its hinges, Samuel was about to turn away in despair when he sensed another's despair.

Over the heads of the reunited family, as Morgan wrapped his arms about his wife and son together and the hotel's guests resumed their lives and moved on, Samuel watched the young woman who had descended the stairs with Andrew. She had placed her hand upon the banister and was holding on, as if weakened, making her way down one hesitant step at a time.

Then amazingly, as if Samuel's great loneliness and heartbreak touched some resonant chord in her soul, she lifted her head and found him in the crowd without hesitation. In her brimming green eyes, Samuel saw a mirrored heartbreak—that of being on the outside looking in. He saw a history of her as she waited while someone else was chosen.

Andrew, from his family's embrace, was searching for the woman, and Samuel drew near enough to hear him say, "Mother, Dad, there's someone I want you to meet."

He motioned for the woman on the stairs, and when she shyly joined him, Andrew said. "This is Genevieve Carlyle. She's traveling with Jessamine MacGowan from Cheyenne. If not for Genny . . ."

He left the sentence unfinished, and Felicia opened her mouth to speak but did not.

"Genny, these are my parents, Felicia and Morgan Goldman."

With throbbing gratitude, Morgan Goldman took Genny's hand and kissed it. "My dear, we're so happy to meet you."

"And that big tall gentleman standing behind them—" Andrew signaled toward him "—who is much too well-mannered to come forward, is Anne's father, Samuel Houseman."

When Samuel bent politely over Genevieve Carlyle's hand, he wasn't surprised when she gripped his hand with a forthright strength.

"I'm very happy to meet you, Mr. Houseman," she said and tipped up her head to smile.

Again the deep understanding.

A tiny dam of pent-up tenderness burst inside Samuel, and he feared he would make a fool of himself by bursting into tears. He closed his other hand over hers. Anne was gone, but he had made a new friend. His happiness was sweet.

They had a picnic in Central Park. From the hotel, Odessa purchased two large hampers packed to the brim with cold fried chicken and Scottish beef and stuffed crab, with boats of potato salad and spears of pickles, tiny individual loaves of fresh bread and wedges of cold melon. Wrapped in cool, checkered cloths were two bottles of champagne, and tucked between the napkins, glasses.

The Park was crowded with picnickers, aswirl with the laughter of scampering children as they flew kites and played tag. Genny gazed longingly after them and across the carpet of emerald grass to the graceful sweep of women's flowered hats, and lovers migrating to pools of shade beneath the trees.

Jessamine and Angel had come, too, and Beggar was loping over the grass, his tail wagging so jubilantly she feared he would wag it off.

Odessa carried one basket and Morgan Goldman the other. Genny tried to make small talk with Felicia as they passed the menagerie where men in Panama hats had lined up to view the animals and mothers were pushing prams as elaborate as phaetons.

In a gondola being poled out on the lake, a fashionable young woman leaned back on the cushions and trailed her fingers in the water while her foppish young man laughed and serenaded her with a Stephen Foster ballad.

"Isn't she pretty?" she said and smiled as Felicia watched from beneath her lacy parasol.

Felicia's own beauty was undiminished, though she had to be about fifty-five. Tall and slender and dressed as fashionably as a duchess, her greater beauty was her breeding. Felicia rarely spoke of herself and was not often heard speaking ill of anyone. Her daughters found her standard of excellence inimitable and had despaired early on of ever pleasing her.

But it wasn't Felicia's desire to be distant. She was happy to see that Odessa had found someone who could ease the pain of his past. She wanted Genevieve Carlyle to understand that she accepted her as part of Odessa's life, no matter what her background. Perhaps, if she had not been so insistent upon Odessa marrying Anne Houseman, things would have turned out differently.

"Miss Carlyle," she began awkwardly, "I've been trying to think of a way to make you feel welcome, and I'm not quite sure how to go about it."

Puzzled, Genny met the woman's eyes with an open frankness. "I don't understand, Mrs. Goldman."

"I don't want you to feel that we would try in any way to interfere with your... friendship."

"Ma'am?"

Felicia felt foolish and wished she'd held her tongue. Now she had offended the young woman, and that had been the last thing she'd wanted to do. She lifted perfectly manicured fingers to touch one well-kept temple where gray was only beginning to show.

"Please forgive me," she said, lowering her eyes in apology. "I wanted to put you at ease. I didn't want you to feel that we resented...I mean, because of Anne..."

Genny again felt the sting of the dead woman. She was tempted to let Felicia work her own way out of her dilemma, but Odessa loved his mother very much, and because she loved Odessa, Genny loved Felicia, too.

Though she was aware of Felicia's reserve, and though her own shyness made the gesture difficult, her rougher, working hands an embarrassment, she reached out and grasped Felicia's silky fingers.

She looked the older woman full in the face. "Mrs. Goldman, please believe that you have nothing to fear from me."

"Miss Carlyle—"

"I met your son under very humiliating circumstances. I was jilted and robbed, and I had—still have—the responsibility of a blind woman. Odessa, I mean Andrew, and I have a business arrangement, that's all, until I get back what was taken. I don't say that to elicit your pity. I wouldn't do anything to prevent Odessa from taking up his life as it was before. I think he should. But, of course, it's his decision, isn't it?"

Relief flooded Felicia, and she felt near to tears. "Miss Carlyle, I've never met a woman quite like you before."

Genny laughed. "What a relief. I was hoping there weren't too many of me around."

For the first time in many years, Felicia laughed without fear that she would pay for being happy. She could see, now, what Andrew saw in the young woman—a refreshing ability to cut through all the layers of pretense and accept reality.

Slowly, guessing that Genny Carlyle understood without further words, she nodded and pressed the fingers that lightly held her own. "Then we'll keep this little secret to ourselves," she said softly.

Through her smile, Genny wanted to say, You'll do all in your power to reinstate Odessa into New York's fashionable society, but what about me? Why can't someone want something good for me?

But she said brightly, "I choose to call it discretion, Mrs. Goldman. And a woman can never have too much of that, can she?"

When Genny said later that she thought she would stroll over to the lake and feed the ducks, she was actually saying that she had to get away from the Goldman wealth for a moment and get a fresh hold on her perspective.

Felicia quickly searched for bread crumbs. "Ah," she said with a silvery laugh that made Morgan feel gratitude toward Genny Carlyle, "what have we found?"

Armed with a small loaf of bread, Genny scooped up the hem of her skirt and trekked to the lake.

If you can't stand this gentle difference between you and the blue bloods, her logic scolded, why are you going to Saratoga at all?

To get my money back from Adam. Not to find a wealthy husband, and I certainly don't expect anything from Odessa Gold, if that's what you mean.

Then, what are you so upset about? Because you aren't Anne Houseman?

Absolutely not. I'm just tired of being such a misfit.

You're lying to yourself.

That hardly matters now, does it? He's back with his family again.

The ducks, being in a much better frame of mind than she, gathered along the shore and bobbed and dipped beneath the surface, scrabbling like children.

"My Anne was fond of ducks," Samuel Houseman said as he appeared at her side, his hands stuffed in his pockets and the summer wind ruffling his jacket. "Fond of everything, actually. One could hardly walk through the house when she was a child, for fear of stepping on a kitten or a puppy.''

''I would like to have known your Anne,'' she said honestly. ''She was very lucky to have someone to love her so much.''

''Lucky? I was her father. Fathers love their daughters.''

Genny could see Raymond drinking himself to death upon the front porch. A sad smile found her lips, and it was, she thought, the first time she had been able to think about the episode without anger or grief.

She shook her head and shaded her eyes against the sunlight. ''Not all, Mr. Houseman. Not all.''

Slowly, in his big loose-jointed way, he began to walk, drawing her along with him, though he did not touch her arm or offer an invitation.

For some time they walked in silence, watching the children romp and tumble on the grass like puppies. Presently he said, ''You've known Andrew for a long time? Pardon me, I mean Odessa. He says we must call him Odessa, not Andrew.''

''Has he told you what he does now?''

''In a manner of speaking, yes.''

She shrugged.

''I don't think Odessa realizes how old I'm getting,'' Samuel said with a laughing shrug.

Before Genny could protest that he wasn't getting old, he waved her words away. ''No, no, indulge an old man, my dear, and let me speak before we return to the others. I've been watching you all day, Miss Carlyle. You're different from us, and I think you must be telling yourself that this difference is bad. I saw what you did with Felicia. She really means well, you know. She's simply had her heart broken once too often. She doesn't mean not to accept you.''

''Acceptance, sir, is not exactly—''

''Forgive me. I move too quickly. It's a failing of mine. What I really wanted to say is that I think it's good Andrew isn't using his name. He isn't the same man who married my Anne. He's much stronger now. He's a different man."

"I wouldn't know about that."

"Miss Carlyle, let me assure you that what I'm about to say is not meant to put any pressure on you, but I'm wondering if you'd consider speaking to Odessa on my behalf."

Confused, Genny stopped walking. Though he didn't realize it showed, she could see a strong, determined man beneath the broken outer surface.

"You're the only one I can talk to about this," he said. "I can't go to Morgan or Felicia. I want badly to know, Miss Carlyle, before I die, who the other two men were who murdered my Anne. Odessa owes me the truth. In time he'll come to see that, but I might be dead by then. Could you, *would* you, speak to him about it? He cares deeply for you. If you were to ask him..."

Genny opened her mouth to protest, but he shushed her with a finger on his lips. "We both know he loves you. And if you don't know, trust an old man on this. If anyone can convince Odessa to confide in me, you can. Would you do that for me, Miss Carlyle?"

As quickly as a summer squall, Genny breathlessly replied, "Yes, if you'll do something for me, sir."

She couldn't believe what she was saying, and her plans evolved even as she spoke. Samuel Houseman hunched forward, his big shoulders curving and his shrewdness glimmering through the perpetual unhappiness.

"You have only to ask, madam. I'm at your service."

Genny nervously moistened her lips and looked back at the picnic where Odessa was sprawled on the grass, chewing a twig as he chatted with his parents. As if he felt the birth of her idea, his gaze moved over the space between them and found her.

She smiled, and he, sensing something afoot, removed the twig from between his teeth.

Quickly, Genny said as she shifted her attention to Samuel, "Odessa has a collection of drawings, Mr. Houseman. They're of me, but it really doesn't matter who the model is. They're very, very good." She gulped a deep breath. "You're a publisher. I think you should publish them."

Samuel sucked in his breath and also pondered Odessa who had now come up to a sitting position. The air seemed charged with wordless messages back and forth. "Have you talked about this with Andrew? Odessa?"

Genny shook her head. "But I don't think he'll object."

Samuel was reminded of another contract he'd had with the son of Felicia and Morgan Goldman. But that was another time....

He smiled in approval. "I perceive a good business head on your shoulders, Miss Carlyle. Yes, if Andrew agrees that I can consider his drawings, of course I'll do what I can."

Chapter Fifteen

Their first quarrel approached Armageddon. Felicia and Morgan had returned to Albany when the opening shots were fired, and the reverberations prompted Angel to tactfully whisk Jessamine downstairs while Odessa stormed through Genny's suite.

"You went behind my back to speak to Samuel about the drawings?" he thundered. "You asked him to publish them in a book? I can't believe it. I can't flaming believe it!"

"It was only a suggestion, Odessa."

"And he suggested—again—that I give him the names of Anne's killers. Pretty strong suggestions, Genny, pretty strong."

Genny mildly tied up her hair in a blue ribbon and poked among the ruins of the picnic baskets where she salvaged two drumsticks, a dish of potato salad and six ripe olives along with two half-empty champagne bottles that were still wrapped in checkered napkins.

"Your fangs are showing, Odessa," she said as she tore off a bite of chicken with her teeth and shook the drumstick at him. "It isn't very becoming." She chewed with customary relish. "So don't expect me to offer my neck."

"Your neck!" he growled. "I should wring your beautiful neck, my sweet, and put us all out of our misery."

Genny skewered him with a heavy-lashed weariness. "You're the only one who's miserable around here,

Odessa. Samuel Houseman thought it was an excellent idea, and for your information it wasn't something I planned in advance. It felt right at the time, so that's what I did. Would you rather I'd walked over and asked your permission in front of your parents? Here, have some leftover champagne.''

The bottle had gone flat, but Odessa snatched it from her anyway and tipped back his head and let the vintage sluice down his gullet.

He wiped his mustache with the back of his hand and reached up to strip loose his tie, leaving it draped across the back of his neck. Fighting was hard work.

"I've gone ten years without telling Samuel about McFee and Platt. Primarily because Sam's no match for them. Hell, I'm no match for them. And you—" he aimed the champagne bottle at her and bared his teeth "—you wouldn't stand a chance."

"It's his choice to make, Odessa." Genny popped a ripe olive into her mouth. "He *was* her father, after all."

"Yes, and I was her husband!"

Genny had not forgotten that fact, and she carried the dish of potato salad to the silk-covered chair, plopped down on the rug before it and stabbed the salad with a fork.

"Well—" she took a monstrous bite "—that was ten years ago."

Screwing up his face as he struggled to decipher what she'd said, he leaned over and twitched the ribbon from her hair and flung it petulantly behind the chair.

"I knew you wouldn't understand," he accused.

Genny thoughtfully laid her hand where her hair ribbon had been and ripped off another bite of fried chicken with her teeth. "I understand perfectly." Rising, she chewed, then swallowed. "Lovers and business partners aren't allowed to have a say over what affects them."

He watched her pink tongue come out to find and lick a crumb of crust from her upper lip. He gazed up and down her reed-thin figure. "You're not going to get fat on me, are you?"

To Genny, it didn't matter at all that he was assuming they had a future together, for *he* was the one who didn't understand about the times she had gone hungry. She had a right to eat whatever she chose and whenever she chose, and she impulsively threw the chicken bone at his head.

Which he deftly dodged. "Temper, temper, Genny," he mocked, and wagged his finger before her face.

Genny consoled herself by dragging out the other half-empty bottle of champagne and taking a long swig.

"Get fat?" she echoed as she blotted her mouth on her sleeve. "I don't think I'll live long enough to get fat, Odessa. To hear you tell it, Samuel and I won't last out the week. So why not eat, drink and be merry?"

She made a toast with the bottle and took another lusty guzzle of flat champagne, adding, "You know it occurs to me that these two men afford you with no end of reasons for not resuming your life like a normal man."

His scar thinned as he drew his lips back from his teeth. "Normal? Did you say normal?"

Reeling slightly, Genny ripped his tie from around his neck and threw it behind the chair with her hair ribbon. "You heard what I said."

The corners of his mouth tilted nastily downward. To get even, he reached over to rip open the top three buttons of her dress. "That hurts my feelings, Genny. It really does."

Glaring, Genny snatched his blue-and-white shirt free of his trousers.

He took the bottle from her hand, sniffed it suspiciously, then banged it on a nearby table.

"I'm beginning to believe that you want them to get me," he said. "I can see it all now." He sketched headlines in the air. "'Ex-Convict Publishes Drawings and Is Gunned Down in Street Like a Mad Dog.' It wouldn't hurt your reputation very much, either, would it, Genny? You might just turn out to be famous."

His eyes narrowed and he proceeded to jerk her shirt-waist from her skirt, and Genny took a cockeyed swing at his head and missed. As she spun around, he laughed and dragged his belt from his pants and stood slapping it against the palm of his hand.

Not certain if he was seriously considering using it on her backside, Genny thought it only made good sense to get in her licks before she was completely incapacitated. She staggered over to the champagne bottle and held it up to the light to assure herself that there was, in fact, a good half-cup remaining. With a blissful smile, she poured that same half-cup upon the toes of his new boots.

"Aggh!" Odessa lunged and Genny skittered, adroitly she thought, beyond his grasp.

But Genny hadn't counted on snagging the tail of her skirt on a splinter of the woven picnic basket, and before she could free herself from the hateful thing, he had swatted her soundly on the rear.

"Oh!" she yelled, coming around with her nails clawing. "That isn't nice, Odessa!"

"I told you I wasn't a nice man."

"Now I believe you!" She lunged at his face and missed, but he did not. He caught her wrist and swung her around to fling her down into the chair. There, he braced a hand on each arm and leaned over until his face was scant inches above hers.

"Let me give you some advice, Genny," he rumbled. "Don't try to con a con man. You'll lose every time. Meanwhile, I've had about all the well-meaning interference I can stand for one day. When you're ready to apologize, I'll consider Samuel's request."

He sauntered infuriatingly to the open door that separated the suites. Genny leapt from the chair, tripped on her own feet and half-fell, half-swam toward him.

"Apologize? I haven't done anything to apologize for, you idiot! You'll apologize to me, mister! You really take first prize for lunacy, Odessa Gold. Did anyone ever tell you that?"

"Many times." Turning, he smiled sweetly and kissed her on the lips. "Good night, my darling. I don't envy you the headache you're going to have when you wake up in the morning."

Genny didn't wake up. She didn't go to sleep. As the night pearled heavily with dew and moths careened about the streetlights on the corner, she didn't even close her eyes.

Jessamine had been slumbering for hours. Yet Genny tossed and turned and rehearsed the pros and cons of apologizing to Odessa. Why should she? He was in the wrong. Samuel Houseman had the right to know who had killed his daughter. Odessa was just being mule-headed.

Rising, she considered getting dressed and going outside, but Fifth Avenue wasn't Wyoming. One didn't just wander out beneath the stars and listen to the coyotes playing in the foothills. And she couldn't ask Angel to go with her, for he'd gone out again, as if he'd had his fill of quarrels and chose another brand of trouble. A woman, more than likely.

In the darkness, Genny weaved unsteadily through the maze of the Astors' cast-off furniture and slammed her foot against the foot of the Spitalfield chair.

"Damn!" she groaned, and sank to the rug and drew her foot into her lap, rocking her bruised toes as her heart began to break and tears skidded down her cheeks.

She didn't want to be angry at Odessa, and she didn't want to love him anymore. Loving someone was worse than the hunger and old-maid jokes.

It wasn't as if he were such a prize catch, either. She could count on both hands the things wrong with him. But who wanted a saint?

Knowing what she must do, she pushed up to her feet and found the key to the door, winking at her from the top of the bureau like the apple on the tree. Well, she was a willing Eve, wasn't she?

She turned the key and the dead bolt slid back with a thud as startling as the fire of a gun. Holding her heart to prevent it from leaping completely from her breast, she waited for wrath to pour down from heaven and consume her.

Amazingly it didn't. With a shallow uncertain breath, she stepped gingerly into Odessa's darkened rooms, her bare feet peeking whitely from beneath her gown.

The draperies were drawn, and the room was very dark, and when something cold and wet touched her hand, she gasped loudly and clapped her hands over her mouth.

Beggar happily wagged his tail, proud of having protected Odessa from harm. Genny collapsed on him and laughed soundlessly.

"You...you beggar you!" She ruffled the dog's fur and rested her head upon his. "If that didn't give me an heart attack, nothing will."

"That's good. The last thing I need is a dead woman in my room."

Genny felt rooted to the floor, and her heart seemed to fall to her feet. "Oh, murder," she wailed softly.

"A rather strange choice of words," he blandly observed, removing the key from the door and pushing it shut. "Considering that I almost mistook you for a burglar and did exactly that. Go, Beggar. Sit somewhere, and don't look at me with those eyes."

As silence unspooled between them, Genny looked up to find a rumpled half-naked savage staring down at her, his trousers unbuttoned and his hair sticking out in all directions.

She held the apology in her mouth as long as possible, shaping it on her tongue. As she started to speak, he spoke at the same time.

"I'm sorry."

"I'm sorry."

They laughed sheepishly, and Odessa shook his head. "I was standing at the door, about ready to start pounding on it when you came through. I really am sorry, Genny."

"And I'm sorry, too. Really."

She went into his arms, and as he held her, Odessa squeezed his eyes tightly shut. But presently she detached herself, mumbling, "I have to go. I just...I just wanted you to know how I felt."

"You can't go yet," he said thickly. "We haven't talked about Samuel."

"We can talk about Samuel another day."

"But you just got here. Look, Beggar doesn't want you to go, either. See, he's hiding his face in grief. Stop wagging your tail, you dumb dog." Quickly, before she could escape, he caught her face and caressed her features with his fingertips.

He whispered, "All right, *I* don't want you to go. Every time you go, Genny, a little part of me dies."

Tears collected in her eyes, sparkling like tiny jewels. "Don't say sweet things to me, Odessa. You know I'll believe you."

Even as Odessa's lips were reaching desperately for hers, Genny was spearing her hands through his hair and pulling his head down with a hunger that sent thrill after thrill jolting through him. Raw, urgent sounds came from her throat, and her fingers moved impatiently over his head and his face until the muscles inside his thighs were jerking and trembling.

"Odessa," she choked as he slipped between to seek her breast, "I love you."

Odessa knew she did. And he knew she wanted him to say the words back. Her hunger could not begin to equal that which gnawed inside him like some insatiable creature living inside his skin. But he was no more sure of his ability to protect her than he was before. Less, in fact.

"Oh, Genny..."

He was failing her again, and she was trembling. He scored the side of her neck with his teeth, and she dropped her head back, groaning, then lifted her leg and hooked it wantonly about his waist, climbing him blindly, clawing his arms and his back.

Odessa feared he could not last, and he cursed his guilty hands as he dragged her gown over her arms and kicked at his own hampering clothes.

"Take me to bed, Odessa. Take me . . ."

But he pushed her against the wall, kissing, caressing, until Genny forgot the words she'd said or he hadn't said, her eyes, her cheeks, her nose and her throat, her breasts. Did she say his name as he rose up in her like a spear and she writhed until she was as taut as the wires connected to her brain?

"Say my name again," he mumbled into her open mouth. "Say again that you love me."

"No." She held tightly to him, for he was making her move with what he did, making her forget everything except the center of herself. "You never say it. You never tell me."

Suddenly a shock went through Genny, and she jerked against him, and tried to speak but couldn't. She scraped her teeth against his ear and wished she could draw the life from him, but she could only shudder as the life poured out of her into some empty, foreign place.

She collapsed, and he moved with a powerful strength, slamming her against the wall and going more deeply than she thought it was possible to go. Again the spearing thrill made her gasp, and again and again until she could no longer hold on. Only then did he wrap her legs about his waist and carry her to bed.

"I'm branding you, Genny Carlyle," he said as he laid her back and bit her shoulder and thrust deep enough to touch that secret woman no one ever saw. "Now you're mine . . ."

Guilt convulsed Odessa. He buried his face in the forgiveness of her neck and wanted to die when she said, "Then why don't you marry me?"

He knew then that he had done the unforgivable. He had sold them both to the devil. Now would come the hurting part.

* * *

Neither of them talked about it afterward. With the dawning of the new day, they silently agreed to back away from the question. Like locking a room in the attic on a secret.

Genny took some of the hotel stationery and posted a letter to Samuel Houseman. She gave him the names of C. E. McFee and Manville Platt and explained that the two men were now wealthy cattle barons.

> It is with great misgiving that I tell you this, sir. According to Odessa (Andrew), the governor wants him to turn state's evidence against McFee and the other man. Hodges wants to reopen the case, but Odessa has refused, fearing that hurt will come to his family if he does.
>
> Though I can understand the grief you have suffered, having watched my own father die of grief, I cannot explain to you enough how seriously Odessa takes these men, sir. They are truly evil, and their present standing in their respective communities has only increased the amount they have to lose if the truth comes out.
>
> Be very careful, Mr. Houseman. There has been enough tragedy in this matter. Notwithstanding, I am enclosing the men's full names, but Odessa has no knowledge of their whereabouts. That, I expect, must come from the governor himself.

Genny read the letter aloud to Jessamine. "What d'you think?"

The old woman removed her black glasses and folded them in her lap. "Mr. MacGowan always said that vengeance belongs to God. But I'm not sure that Mr. Houseman believes that. Lord have mercy upon him."

* * *

In Cheyenne, a message came over Nathan Hodges's teletype machine. From his desk opposite the governor's, Lewis rose to read the message.

The governor was talking on his new telephoning machine. After he replaced the earpiece into its bracket and reverently pushed the instrument to the center of his desk, he leaned back in his chair and laced his fingers over his girth.

"One tends to wonder," he said in awe of modern science, "how one ever did without it." He smiled at Lewis. "Do you want to hear something funny?"

Lewis had already heard a lot of funny things, some of them at the governor's mansion. He wasn't sure anything could impress him ever again.

"Of course, Your Honor," he said.

"The first time I ever used that thing—" Hodges indicated the telephone "—I was afraid I would get electrocuted."

Lewis assuaged Nathan Hodges's ego by laughing and waited a respectful moment before proffering the telegraph message that had come.

"What's this?" Hodges asked, then read Samuel Houseman's submission of the names of the two men involved in the train robbery and death of Anne Houseman. "'Respond,'" he dictated the final lines aloud to Lewis. "'Saratoga during August. Stop.'"

He smiled, then laughed, then leaned back with a sigh. "So Andrew Goldman has broken his silence at last, has he? Well, well, well, Lewis. I've waited a long time for this. Justice may yet be served, and I . . . well, I might get a few things I've wanted for a long time."

"Yessir," Lewis said obligingly.

"I have to send a few telegrams of my own, Lewis. Why don't you inform Mrs. Hodges that we will be leaving day after tomorrow for Saratoga Springs?"

Lewis felt the tingle of lust in his groin. Beatrice would be in bed by now. But the governor knew that. Hodges always knew.

"Very good, sir."

"I've been needing a vacation." Nathan Hodges removed his glasses and held them to the light in search of a smudge. "We'll combine business with pleasure."

"Absolutely, sir."

"That'll be all for tonight, Lewis. But be down first thing in the morning, will you? We have a lot of preparations to make."

Lewis grinned. He would have a whole night with Beatrice, uninterrupted. He swiftly gathered an armful of paperwork he was certain didn't deceive Nathan Hodges but was all part of the strange game they played.

"I'll be down early," he promised. "Good night, sir."

"Good night, Lewis."

When his secretary shut the office door behind him, Nathan Hodges smiled and muttered to himself, "And tell my darling wife good night too, Lewis."

Chapter Sixteen

Spring was the signal for the spiritual guardians of Saratoga to arm themselves for a vigilant, unflagging war against Sin.

For three terrible months the natives fought Satan, but it invariably proved to be a losing battle. No place could swagger and glut and gamble and race horses in the style of Saratoga. The registers of Saratoga's hotels, notably those of the Grand Union and the newly rebuilt United States, read like the most recent printing of *Who's Who*. The possession of a mere million dollars was nothing. Not when John Jack Astor III and William B. Astor, Jr., had both inherited two hundred million from their fathers.

William Vanderbilt's mere ninety millions were looked upon by the Old Guard as vulgar. Mrs. Astor had been heard to remark pontifically that Commodore Vanderbilt had "manipulated railroad stock" to get his money, and she had never admitted him into her circle.

After the excesses of Fifth Avenue, Genny believed she was prepared for anything, but when her carriage turned onto Saratoga's Broadway, she leaned forward in disbelief.

For 450 feet, the Grand Union Hotel fronted Broadway, and swept back in two splendid wings for a quarter-mile each. Between the wings, eight hundred guests could walk its twelve acres of carpets and a full acre of tiled lobby. If guests wished and could afford them, cottage suites were available. The dining room of the Grand Union could seat 1400 guests beneath its crystal chandeliers, and at dinner, 250 Negro waiters rushed about serving eight-course dinners.

But it was the mile-long piazzas that truly staggered the mind. There, men in white hats tilted back in their chairs and angled their cigars toward their faces. In outrageous gowns and jewelry, their wives ogled each other's jewelry. Diamonds were *the* badge of distinction in Saratoga.

The United States Hotel was somewhat smaller than the Grand Union, boasting only a thousand guests at meals and wings that stretched back for only an eighth of a mile. They serviced only 768 guests with rooms and suites.

But the United States, where Odessa and Angel had gone ahead to take rooms and discreetly reserve a suite for Genny, had one thing that the Grand Union did not—the North Piazza. Here was the true retreat of the infinitely rich—the holy of holies.

Odessa should've been on top of the world. He had just come from a rousing meeting with Richard Canfield who owned the Saratoga Casino where he had spent his past several evenings so profitably. Canfield had proved to be both challenging and stimulating—a felon like himself but a gentleman, a student of art and literature and, so the grapevine said, a discriminating collector.

But Odessa had no desire to either contribute to Canfield's collection or admire it. He wanted only to win some of the man's money. Meeting the man had been no small feat. He had discovered that Canfield's daily habit was to stroll to his broker's branch office after breakfast and play the market. The day before, he had made certain he was in the vicinity of the brokerage house and had casually struck up a conversation.

"I pride myself on providing my guests with the best, Mr. Gold," Canfield said as they walked along Broadway and cut across Congress Park. "What you see here is only the beginning. I plan to completely refurbish the Casino.

When I'm finished, it will be the most spectacular gambling house in the country.''

Canfield had taken him on a private tour of the building that was already richly appointed with mirrors on all walls, glittering chandeliers dropping from the ceiling, a rug from Scotland which was the largest ever woven in one piece and valued at $10,000.

"Quite a place you have here," Odessa casually observed.

Canfield smiled. "A touch of beauty consoles my guests when they lose."

"But what if they win?"

"All gamblers lose. It's the nature of the business. It's my job to make sure they can afford to lose. Can you afford to, Mr. Gold?"

"I wouldn't be here if I couldn't." Grinning, Odessa removed a cheroot from his pocket, drew it beneath his nose and rolled it lovingly between his fingers.

"Good." Canfield's hands gestured as they walked. "Here, the downstairs is for the public. Faro, roulette, whatever you want. White chips are a dollar, the red five, blue ten, yellow a hundred, and brown a thousand. The heavy hitters who favor a more escalated stake go upstairs. There, white chips are one hundred dollars and the brown, one hundred *thousand*."

Odessa had the good taste not to declare himself a heavy hitter. With a gentlemanly bow, Canfield extended his hand and said as Odessa shook it, "I wish you the best of luck, sir."

"A fickle lady, sir," Odessa said around his cigar. "I confess to not depending on her."

"Wise, indeed, Mr. Gold. I'm at your service."

As he left, Odessa made note of the private detectives who were scattered strategically throughout the establishment. They had him memorized by now, down to his formal dress that Canfield insisted upon in his establishment.

Now, as he was returning to the hotel, Angel had appeared out of nowhere and fell into step beside him.

"Canfield has acquired a French chef," he said, laughing. "Jean Columbin. They say he travels in Europe during the off-season seeking ideas for new concoctions."

Odessa took out his watch and stared at the futile sweep of the hand. Genny should have arrived by now.

"You might make more money working as a waiter for Canfield, Angel," he quipped to the handsome black man who was dressed completely in white. "They earn fifty dollars a day in tips alone."

Angel grinned. "I'll valet for you, and you win ten percent for me. We'll both retire wealthy."

The park behind the United States was filled with couples, women in veiled hats and men in fawn-colored coats and carrying gold-tipped walking canes. The fretwork of branches overhead allowed sunshine to dribble through like raindrops. Marble benches offered rest in the cool shade.

"Good God!"

Odessa spun hard on his heel and walked swiftly in the opposite direction, the skirt of his jacket sailing out behind him. Startled, Angel Tulane did likewise, keeping his head discreetly bent as he matched his strides to the longer ones of Odessa.

The question didn't need to be posed between the two men. Hardly a day had passed that they hadn't discussed the possibility of danger.

"On the bench," Odessa said tightly.

"McFee?" Angel said.

"And Platt, too. Both of them—murdering sons of bitches! With Genny arriving any minute! Angel, I'm a fool, a blithering, piss-for-brains fool."

All twelve pieces of the new luggage were now filled with Madame's lovingly crafted gowns and were riding safely in a second carriage behind the smart Victoria in which Genny and Jessamine arrived at Saratoga. In the luggage were silk parasols to match the dresses and eight pairs of slippers. In one bag were cosmetics and creams and perfumes.

In the carriage with them, however, was the quaint enameled jewel case that Odessa had found during one of his excursions. It was all for show, for Genny had almost started a revolution when he suggested placing some of the Goldman jewelry inside.

As they rolled to a stop, it seemed that all the people on all the piazzas looked up and said her name.

"This was the worst idea I ever had," she said to Jessamine.

As Jessamine's eyes were not bedazzled by the splendor, she sensed the undercurrents of electricity more than Genny. She knew of the hardness and tenacity that produced great wealth and that Astor himself had been a notorious slumlord.

"The talent of the rich is to spot those who aren't one of them. Be yourself, Geneena."

"I'm not sure I even know who that is anymore."

"Do you see Mr. Gold, dear?"

"No, but you can be sure he's here. Goodness, is there anywhere that he *isn't?* The important question is, is Adam here?"

"Indeed. I would like to have a few words with that young gentleman myself."

Before the eyes of the whole world, Genny stepped onto a street that vied with the Prater of Vienna and the Champs-Élysées of Paris.

The thoroughfare was teaming with landaus and phaetons and barouches. Whiskered gentlemen in summer suits walked ladies in Parisian silks and satins. She prayed that their arrival would go unnoticed, but a bevy of hotel staff swarmed out to help her with Jessamine.

"She's accustomed to me," she told them and promptly forgot herself as she assisted the blind woman.

The bellboys scooped up boxes and cases and trunks and rushed them into the lobby. Since Genny did not know that she was supposed to put up her parasol and wait prettily to be screened by the opinion of those who watched, she began guiding Jessamine up the steps.

She walked past the Negro doorman.

"Ma'am!" he exclaimed, shocked when she actually took hold of the door to open it herself.

Turning, Genny said, "Hello. What's your name?"

The doorman blinked at her in surprise. "Marvin, ma'am."

She smiled. "Thank you, Marvin. My name is Genny Carlyle. Jessamine, this is Marvin. If Jessamine should ever need to go out onto the veranda, Marvin, and I'm not here, could you help her find her way?"

Accustomed to being passed over as if he did not exist, Marvin moved an experienced eye over the young woman and her aging blind friend. The young woman possessed a pleasant, friendly way that he didn't encounter too often among white people. She wasn't constantly looking over her shoulder to see if anyone was watching. And she had asked his name. He rather liked that she hadn't tried to purchase his courtesy with money.

Smiling, he inclined his head. "I'd be much obliged to assist Miz Jessamine, ma'am. And yourself. Anytime."

Jessamine smiled politely in the direction of the voice. "Thank you, Mr. Marvin."

The man laughed. "Jus' Marvin, ma'am, jus' Marvin."

As they moved through the doors into the lobby, Genny whispered to Jessamine, "Do you have this awful feeling that the world's going to come to an end while we're here, and they'll find our bodies later and list us among the dead? Two frauds from Wyoming?"

The old woman chuckled into her staid collar. "We *are* frauds from Wyoming. Try to think about the stairs to the pearly gates, Geneena."

"I'm reminded more of the road to hell. This one is just as wide and many there are who've taken it."

Saratoga was in the midst of change. The Gay Nineties were in their autumn years, and as the century drew to a close, a new strain was finding its way to the Springs.

Especially the independent-minded young ladies who were
not starving for the crumbs of society icons like Caroline
Schermerhorn Astor and her newest, most powerful lady-
in-waiting, Ava Vanderbilt.

Lady Eleanor Bentley had arrived only the day before
with her friend, Priscilla Davenport, and had just paid
court to the powerful Ava Vanderbilt. Mrs. Astor, it
seemed, was in Newport this season.

As Genny alighted from her carriage, the dowager
placed her dewy glass upon the white-clad waiter's tray.
When she picked up a pair of gold opera glasses set with
diamonds and her initials interlaced in pearls, and said in
her lusty, country-bred voice, "Who, pray tell, is that?"
the query had much the same effect as the proverbial shot
heard round the world.

The entire North Piazza fell silent. Waiters who were
milling about exchanged wordless looks. Every eye was
riveted to the entrance of the United States, and by night-
fall the town would have not only repeated the question a
dozen times but would have described in meticulous detail
every distinguishing trait of the carriage from which the
young lady had alighted.

"It's her," someone said.

"You mean . . ."

"Do you think I'm blind? She's the woman in the
Times."

Though many of the ladies on the piazza would refuse
to admit it, the drawings had caught their fancies during
their lengthy preparations for the season. Some of them
had discreetly deserted their usual dressmakers and had
found their way to Madame Desmond's dress shop. The
miracle was that neither Genny nor Odessa had noticed the
small advertisements. Not even Angel had chanced upon
them, and he was a devout reader of everything he could
get his hands on.

But one saw what one looked for, and Genny's fashion
needs were not uppermost. Not so with the shrewd females on the North Piazza, however, and one could liter-

ally hear ice melting in the glasses as the slim young redhead stepped out of a carriage that Lucky Baldwin himself would have envied.

"Good-looking horse flesh," Sir Walter Reynard observed, who, being a Wall Street banker of long standing, considered himself something of an expert on the matter of horses.

"But she's traveling alone!" someone exclaimed. "Or she might as well be."

Rising from his table, Sir Walter walked with the aid of his gold-tipped cane to the edge of the piazza. An owlish-looking, middle-aged little man, he perched his pince-nez upon his prim nose.

"Unmarried women quite often travel alone," he said. "My mother is quite fond of doing it."

"She looks like a suffragette," someone else chimed in.

"Perhaps, perhaps," Reynard agreed, rather liking the philosophy of suffragettes.

"Well, it is very chic, don't you think? So...twentieth-century. I mean, inheritance is all well and good, but..."

Reynard peered through his pince-nez at Jason Montague whose reputation for squandering his family's wealth at the poker tables was legendary. He and Jason had been playing whist before the mysterious woman's arrival.

"There's no call for vulgarity, Jason," he said. "Inheritance is what separates the beasts from the savages."

Eleanor Bentley paled when Ava Vanderbilt lifted her legendary glasses. She would have given anything for the woman to take a second look at her, and once she recognized the newcomer as the woman in Madame Desmond's dress shop, she clutched her prayer book and whispered loudly to Priscilla, "My God! She actually had the nerve to come!"

Jason Montague looked up from his cards to the woman with whom he had just ended a torrid affair. Eleanor Bentley, beneath her pious exterior and staid little prayer book, was a rabid lover. Frankly, he hadn't been able to stand the pain.

"Oh, don't begin something without finishing it, Eleanor." His voice had a mean edge to it. "Do you know something juicy or not?"

Shooting him a vicious look, Eleanor threw back her head and pressed her prayer book to her breast. "I really shouldn't."

"Oh-h-h," Jason drawled. "Don't tell me she's someone's, ahem, niece?"

"More's the point," another guffawed, "who is the lucky uncle?"

Sir Walter was highly uncomfortable with such talk, and he disapproved of Ava Vanderbilt's allowing it to go on. Caroline Astor would never have tolerated such gossip in her presence.

Those days, alas, were gone forever, and everyone knew about the scandalous liaisons that distinguished gentlemen engaged in nowadays, disdaining to visit the local brothels and boldly bringing their "ladies" with them under the guise of niece or sister or secretary. The hotel cottages were not bound by the eleven o'clock lockup, nor the sharp eye of the detectives, and some philanderers paid a hefty hundred twenty-five dollars a day for the freedom.

Not that he had ever paid it. Nor would he ever!

Priscilla Davenport said quietly to the group, "Eleanor and I met the woman in Madame Desmond's. Would you all excuse me? I seem to have developed the most frightful headache."

Ava Vanderbilt gave the shy creature a nod of dismissal. "You will be missed, dear."

"Thank you." To Eleanor, Priscilla gave a pleading look to please be kind.

When the young woman had entered the hotel, Eleanor smiled. "Well, I'll tell you what I know," she said, "which isn't much. She appears to be the mistress of a marvelously wicked man named Gold." Eleanor arched a meaningful brow at Jason. "A *real* man."

"How romantic. Having drawings of herself in all the papers and now a passionate love affair!"

"Gold?" snorted Reynard, disliking the man already. "Whoever heard of Gold?"

Jason Montague threw down his cards. "I have. The deuced fellow beat me out of a thousand dollars last night. Comes from out West, they say. A real talent for blood-letting."

"Well, find out who she is," Ava Vanderbilt ordered imperially. "Perhaps I should wire Louise Desmond."

Fans fluttered fiercely, and no one spoke as they waited for a decision of the Vanderbilt thumb as to whether this woman was to be accepted by them or scorned.

Sir Walter was touched by the sight of a young woman being so selflessly concerned with someone of advanced age, and blind at that. He was of the old school himself, and at sixty-one, he was wondering if he hadn't made a slight mistake in remaining a bachelor.

"Perhaps it's a fashion in the making," the Vanderbilt verdict came down with a knowing eye for Reynard's interest, Reynard being one of her favorite courtiers. "Madame always did have an unerring sense of the extraordinary. Not that I go to her myself, you understand. Of course, the woman isn't wearing jewels, but trends are changing, and her skirt is obviously of the best China silk. Rather charming, I think."

Genny became an instant enemy of every woman on the North Piazza.

Chapter Seventeen

Angel Tulane was uneasy with Odessa's extravagant hatred. When a man could not control his hates, he could hurt those he cared about. It was understandable but dangerous.

"Did they see you?" he grilled as they walked quickly away from McFee and Platt, unaware of the stir on the North Piazza.

"I don't think so," Odessa said.

"Ten years is a long time."

"I sure as hell knew who they were."

"But you have a keen eye for such things, Odessa, and you've been looking. They're not looking."

"Don't kid yourself. Why else would they be here?"

"Easy, easy." Angel had to acquaint himself with these two murderers. If not for his own protection, certainly for Odessa's.

They were halfway across the courtyard of the hotel now, slowing down to linger in a niche of elm trees.

"Wait," he told Odessa, and moved his gaze over the strolling guests and those who were seated upon the marble benches scattered amid beds of peonies and poppies and petunias. "Point them out to me from here."

Odessa patted his pockets for a cheroot and lit one, puffing for a moment before he picked McFee out in the crowd. He blew a spiral of smoke at the sky. "D'you see

the woman spilling out of her yellow dress? Sitting beside
the marble Cupid?''

Angel took one look and laughed. ''The whore?'' He
bent his head in chagrin. ''I beg your pardon, Odessa.
That was uncalled-for.''

''Because she's white?'' Odessa shook his head. ''That's
what she is.''

McFee had grown heavier in the past decade, Odessa
saw. His eyes had sunk into heavy folds of cheek and his
body was so bloated he looked as if he'd float to the top of
a scummy pond. He had grown bushy muttonchop whiskers, too, one of which he was busily exploring with the tip
of a forefinger. Finding nothing, he folded his arms across
the shelf of his stomach.

''That's McFee beside her. And the one behind him who
looks as if someone should have put him in a coffin years
ago,'' Odessa said as a tiny tremor attacked the flesh
around his scar, ''is Manville Platt.''

Platt's thin gray face was made even more unattractive
by his prominent beak of a nose and strange-looking head
of hair.

Angel was more concerned with the two men who were
talking to Platt; they were built like mastiffs. ''Bodyguards,'' he said succinctly.

''That would be my guess.'' Odessa frowned heavily and
considered the white ash of his cigar. ''I need to warn
Genny, get her away from here immediately.''

''Not so fast. How would they even recognize you?
You've changed, too. You're older. You have a beard.'' He
laughed. ''We can borrow Jessamine's dark glasses and
find you a walking stick.''

''Wiseacre.'' Odessa's stomach was churning. He could
see Genny lying in a deserted place, surrounded by blood.

He hurled his smoke to the ground and trod on it. He
adjusted the knot of his tie and his cuff links. He buttoned the coat of his suit and drew a long breath.

"You want to know if they recognize me?" he challenged. "Well—" he jutted his chin against his collar "—here goes."

"Wait a minute!" Angel was amazed at the gambler's nerve. "I didn't mean—"

"There's only one way to do it." Bluffing was Odessa's best suit. "Come on."

Slowly, without speaking, Odessa and Angel walked back to where the two Wyoming men were talking. Odessa kept his gaze fixed upon the two murderers, and Angel watched the faces of their hired men.

"My family's arriving in two days," they heard McFee telling the woman. "You can stay in the cottage till then. After that, you'll have to meet me."

The prostitute fluttered her lashes and poked out her lip in a pout. "I was hopin' I'd have you the whole time to myself, darlin'," she purred, then puckered her scarlet lips as she crossed her legs so that she could stroke the side of McFee's shoe with her own.

The cattleman glanced around them, and he moved his gaze over Odessa who was hardly twenty feet away. Nothing aroused his alarm, and he draped his fleshy arm about the woman's shoulders.

"There's plenty to go round. If I win at the Casino, I'll bring baby a bauble."

Gurgling, the woman snuggled beneath one of McFee's drooping chins. "You cuddly old bear."

"Just don't you forget it," McFee chortled as he grew redder.

"Can you give me just a little bit of spendin' money till then, sugar lump?"

"Damn, woman, I just gave you money."

"A girl has expenses, daddy-poo. Just a eensy, weensy?"

The big man swore, and Odessa, still unsatisfied, stepped onto the sidewalk and removed a fresh cigar from his pocket. He caught Angel's eye and pretended to jerk a book of matches from the black man's hand.

"You clumsy ape," he snarled. "Can't you do anything right?"

His sharp censure drew several people's attention, along with that of the hulking hired men. While Angel meekly hung his head, Odessa made a production of lighting his smoke and waving out the match. McFee glanced idly at him and was distracted by the prostitute's finger circling his ear, and Platt, after looking Odessa up and down, snorted and returned to his bodyguards.

"Guess that answers that, doesn't it?" Odessa said with a sigh.

"It buys a little time, at any rate."

With a muttered grumble that Genny had had enough time, Odessa struck out for the hotel. If she hadn't arrived by now, he was sending out a search party.

Angel warned as he fell into step, "Now, don't go getting cocky, Odessa."

"Me? Cocky?" Odessa lifted a calculating brow and twirled the tip of handlebars that his mustache didn't possess. "Humility is my middle name, Mr. Tulane."

Unfortunately for Genny, Horace Winnows, the assistant manager, did not read the *Times* with any regularity, and he was as fervent in his guardianship of the United States as the religious advocates were for the purity of their own.

During his six years beneath the eagle eye of Percy Van Yarborough, the manager, Horace had seen countless men who called themselves decent and upstanding attempt to smuggle mistresses into the hotel under the guise of being sisters or nieces or secretaries. One railroad tycoon who had arrived with six "secretaries," ensconced them in an adjoining suite, and so enflamed the locals that the *New York Herald* sent a reporter to do a piece on the depraved morality of Saratoga, calling the United States a "high-class brothel." It had taken years for the talk to die down!

Horace was patiently biding his time. Van Yarborough would pass into the great beyond someday, and he meant to have the man's job. Meanwhile, he was fastidious in his scrutiny of all guests whom he did not know personally or by reputation. The young woman with hair the color of strawberries, for instance, who walked across the lobby without deferring to anyone or anything and calmly announced that a suite had been reserved for her, was a fraud if ever there was one.

"Your name, Madam?" he said with his most worldly disdain when she stepped to the desk, just so she would know who was who and what was what.

"Genevieve Carlyle," she said without any to-do.

Horace ran an expert finger down the list of reservations, and sure enough, clipped to the page where her name was entered, was a telegram from the Waldorf-Astoria. He had opened the wire himself, but upon reading it he had envisioned Miss Carlyle's arrival to be more traditional, one containing the usual retinue of maid, butler, and perhaps a private physician and a traveling companion of some social standing.

He did admit that she possessed impressive luggage, but her clothes were merely adequate—a sea-green skirt that was quite apt for her hair and a boater that was banded with an excellent sea-green tulle and floated airily down her back. But her blouse was extremely mannish, and she wore no jewelry at all except a small plain brooch at her collar. Any genuine lady would have dripped diamonds. Who did she think she was fooling?

"Ah, madam," he said, and touched his cardboard-stiff collar as he frowned at the registration book. "I do indeed realize that a suite has been reserved for you." He looked over his shoulder for Van Yarborough and, not seeing him, lowered his voice to a murmur. "Might I perhaps make a suggestion to madam and mention that we have accommodations on the east side that catch the very best of the sun. A delightful room that, ah, madam might find more to her, ah, liking."

Though Genny's courage was slowly fading she gave the prissy little man a cold smile. If he thought she would crumble after surviving Adam Worthington, he had mis-judged her.

"Are you suggesting that there has been a mistake?" she asked icily.

Horace took a short, nervous breath. "Absolutely not, madam."

"Might I have a look at your register?"

"Oh, madam, I assure you that the reservation has been made. I'm not suggesting that at all."

He swirled the large book around on the desk, and Genny bent over it, pretending to search for her own name, though she was actually looking for Adam's. There! So, he *was* here, the thief! He had taken a room on the third floor. A single. She hoped nothing happened to him before she could get her hands on his throat!

The clerk tapped her name with an impatient mani-cured fingernail.

His voice was syrupy sweet. "The reservation is per-fectly in order, madam. It's just that this is a ground suite, and the cost—" he underscored his meaning with arched brows "—is perhaps more than madam had anticipated."

So that was it, Genny thought. Money! Everything boiled down to money. Odessa had been right. Romans liked other Romans, and she was a foreigner. If she'd worn his family's diamonds, the man would be fawning.

"I had been led to believe that the United States was a hospitable establishment," she said coolly, and began to turn away.

"Oh, madam . . ."

With a touch of fingers upon Genny's sleeve, Jessa-mine said prudently, "Geneena, I think we should tell the gentleman that a room on the east would be perfect."

And after all her promises that she would never be vic-timized again! She wasn't her father's daughter for noth-ing, was she?

"Very well," she said, giving a sigh of resignation rather than creating a scene with the man. "We'll take this won-derful room on the east."

Watching from a distance as rage washed around his ankles and, in seconds, was closing over his head, choking him, Odessa started across the hotel lobby in seven-league strides.

"Why, that little dried-up rooster," he muttered as he envisioned the satisfaction he would feel grabbing the man by the collar and dragging him over the desk and slamming him to the floor.

Angel's grip was one of patience and not impulse. Which was why Odessa paid him so well.

"Protect your flank," he advised and flicked his gaze to the opposite side of the lobby where McFee, minus the company of his lady friend, was entering with Manville Platt, followed by the two bodyguards who tried unsuccessfully to look like guests who were in Saratoga to take the waters.

"Angel," Odessa said in the arid, toneless voice that Warden Potanski had been on intimate terms with, "would you mind walking over to the desk and fetching me a pen and paper?"

When the black man returned, Odessa scribbled a note, folded it and placed it in his hand. "Give this to our Mr. Winnows, Angel. Quickly, before Genny reaches the elevator."

The assistant manager paled slightly when he read the note, and he gave one look at Angel and brought his hand smartly down on a bell. When he didn't receive an immediate response, he rang it as if summoning a fire wagon.

Percy Van Yarborough emerged from his office, a slight, bespectacled man who had no chin at all but several folds of skin where it should have been. He didn't walk to the desk, he glided, and Odessa shifted his weight as Winnows explained the arrival of Genny and the ensuing note.

A dark look of displeasure passed over Van Yarborough's face, and he slipped from behind the desk and glided with extraordinary rapidity to where the bellboys were preparing to place Miss Genevieve Carlyle's and

Jessamine MacGowan's luggage on the elevator bound for the third floor.

"Miss Carlyle," he called, stopping her just as the door was opening. "Miss Carlyle, please wait!"

Keeping a cautious eye on the whereabouts of McFee, Odessa moved within hearing of Genny and the manager. The man snapped his fingers and directed the bellboys to please take the luggage of Miss Carlyle and party to the downstairs suite.

The bellboys obeyed with smart promptness, and Genny, her lips parting in surprise, looked around to see the cause of such courteous attention. When she spotted Odessa and Angel, Odessa's heart lurched.

Smiling, she turned as if to walk toward him, and Odessa gave an imperceptible shake of his head.

Van Yarborough was waiting to accompany her to the suite personally. Realizing this, Genny rubbed at a muscle in the back of her neck and shook her head. "But I don't understand, Mr. Van Yarborough."

With more snaps of his fingers, the manager summoned Horace Winnows. "Miss Carlyle, I do regret that I wasn't at the desk when you arrived. This unfortunate misunderstanding would not have occurred. Your suite has been made ready, and we wouldn't hear of you and Mrs. MacGowan occupying anything else. Mr. Winnows—" Horace had hurried over and was now pinned by managerial displeasure "—did not understand, I'm afraid. Did you, Mr. Winnows?"

"Oh, no, madam." Winnows made an obsequious bow. "I didn't understand at all, Miss Carlyle. Please accept my deepest, deepest apology. If there is anything that madam requires during her stay here, anything at all, you have only to tell me. Again, my apologies, both to you and Mrs. MacGowan."

"Thank you," Genny said lamely and cast Odessa a frown as she was escorted into the elevator by the manager of the hotel. What was happening?

The proximity of the two men who wanted him dead to the object of his heart's most tender dreams caused Odessa to feel the beating of wings of something dark and sinister. His selfish need for Genny was costing a price that even he was not prepared to pay. He wouldn't be able to go on living if anything happened to her.

With eyes that craved absolution, he said, as much to himself as to Angel, "This is insanity. I have to end this. One way or another, it must end."

Not for a moment did Angel believe he could talk Odessa out of his decision. He had seen the look before. It had been on his own face often enough.

"Miss Carlyle might have a few opinions about leaving," he warned. If Odessa could not see how deeply the woman loved him, *he* was the one who was blind, not Jessamine.

A cutting smile flashed briefly on Odessa's face.

He clipped off orders as swiftly as his mind made them. "Arrange for her carriage to be brought round in two hours. Get a message to her that she's to drive west of town. I'll meet her there."

Swiveling, Odessa considered the famous front desk as tiny flames of intensity licked at his nerves. "I guess I'd better ensure that little weasel's silence, too."

He waited for Winnows to finish with a guest, and then he stepped forward, painted the assistant with a long, menacing survey, leaned an elbow on the polished surface of the desk and slouched as if he had no intention of leaving anytime soon.

Winnows swallowed and touched his collar. "Ah, Mr. Gold, is it?" He knew full well who the man was. Who could forget such a scar? "What may I do for you, sir?"

With an arch of brows that made Winnows abnormally uncomfortable, Odessa Gold picked up the registration book, slipped something inside and closed it. He gave it back to Winnows who, frowning, promptly opened it, saw the two one-hundred-dollar bills and snapped it shut the same as he would had a scorpion attempted to crawl from between the pages.

"What's that for?" he asked as sweat dampened his collar.

"You received a note a few minutes ago, Mr. Winnows."

This was a stated fact, not a question, and the man considered his fingernails with an idleness that didn't deceive Winnows for an instant.

Licking his lips, Winnows said, "Yes, sir."

"I'd like it back."

"Oh, but it's the property of the manager, sir."

"It was sent to you, Winnows." The explosive gray eyes whipped around. "You only *gave* it to the manager."

That information, Winnows quickly digested. "Remain here, sir."

"Oh, I intend to."

Winnows returned and proffered the note with shaking fingers, holding it by the smallest corner. Odessa took the paper and slipped it into his inside pocket.

He clapped Winnows rousingly on the back of one shoulder. "I don't expect you to ever mention this to anyone, Mr. Winnows."

Winnows bobbed his head and compressed his lips so tightly shut, nothing could have pried them open.

"I expect you'll know how to handle any future situation should it arise," the tall man said. "And Winnows, perhaps if you loosened the collar a bit, life might run a little smoother."

Another bobbing of Winnows's head.

Smiling, Odessa walked away. The minute he was out of sight, Winnows collapsed on his stool and laid his head upon the desk.

When Angel returned to the room, he heard a strange noise coming from Odessa's side of the door. Opening it, he found Odessa, stripped down to his cotton underwear, stretched out on the carpet, doing knuckle push-ups. He did not pause when Angel entered but said through his teeth, "Eighty-five, eighty-six, eighty-seven..."

Sweat was pouring off his sides as muscles the color of molten copper flexed and rippled. His belly was hard and ribbed, and his hair was soaked and clinging to his scalp. Beneath his drawers, his buttocks were tight.

Angel could almost feel the adrenaline of rage flowing through his friend. Removing his own jacket, he rolled up his sleeves and laid out a fresh shirt for Odessa and gave his gray suit a sound brushing. When Odessa was finished and had rolled onto his back with a groan, he flung a sweaty arm across his eyes and lay gasping.

Angel moved to the washstand and ran a glass of water. "Want me to send for ice?"

"Water," Odessa gasped and, sitting up, guzzled the water in one huge swig.

After he caught the towel Angel tossed him, Angel dropped to the floor and sat cross-legged.

"Did you give her the message?" Odessa asked.

"I'll pick her up and drive her there myself in one hour."

"Good." Odessa heaved himself to his feet and walked to the washstand where he turned a spigot and filled the sink with cold water. He splashed his face and dried it, then wet the towel and wringing it, proceeded to scrub his chest and beneath his arms, rinsing and wringing and wiping down his legs.

After brushing his teeth, he studied the dark reflection in the mirror and didn't like what he saw. He leaned closer and began to trim his mustache with scissors.

"Odessa?"

"Hmm?"

"I learned something else."

From old and intuitive habit, Odessa halted the scissors and watched Angel's quick hands as they found the proper tie and laid it out.

"Your governor friend," the black man said without looking up. "Hodges?"

Odessa heard a crack inside his head.

Angel dropped cuff links on the white shirt. "He was checking into the hotel. With him was a woman I assume was his wife—she looked as if she was suffering from a hell of a hangover. And some prissy twit who, by the way he looked at the woman, may or may not have caused the hangover. Just thought you'd want to know."

Odessa drew on fresh trousers and clean socks. He could not believe that it was coincidence that Hodges was at the same hotel as McFee and Platt, and he now had a pretty good idea of how the two murderers had found out so quickly about his release.

Angel was helping him shrug into his shirt, and when he said, "I want you to leave when Genny does, Angel," the black man stopped cold, his handsome features blank.

"I don't want to hear that kind of talk, Odessa."

"Dammit, man!" Odessa dropped to a chair and began pulling on a boot. "The connection between Genny and me is fragile enough, but between you and me? I can't have blood on my hands again, Angel. I'll pay you twice what we agreed, but I want you out of here tonight. Are you listening to me?"

Odessa's voice had risen to nearly a shout, but Angel's was low and icy calm. "I hear you. But I'm not going."

Picking up his remaining boot, Odessa threw it at the man, and Angel, catching it, grinned.

"You're a gambler, Odessa. The best I've ever seen. You've got nerves like steel. I'm not worried."

"Yeah," Odessa muttered, "nerves like steel."

When he was done dressing, Angel playfully licked his finger and rubbed a scuff from the toe of Odessa's boot, then did a soft-shoe on the rug.

Grinning sheepishly, Odessa waved his hand in acquiescence. "With luck, maybe they'll be gambling men." He dumped change into his pockets and picked up his watch.

He held up a reminding finger before walking out the door. "But Genny goes."

* * *

Horsemanship had never been Odessa's strong point. As he rode out of town, his mount periodically rolled an eye back at his rider in the interest of self-preservation.

Once one left the commercial aspects of Saratoga behind, houses and gardens soon gave way to fenced farmland. Saratoga was a beautiful place, and the countryside smelled of summer flowers and mown hay. Stretches of uncultivated woods jutted up between the farms, and roads struck out to first one farm, then another. Presently Odessa dismounted not far from a stream and drew out his watch, but the hand traced its pattern much too slowly.

He squinted down the dusty road, lit a cheroot and blew smoke into sun that beat in and out of the trees.

"This is what happens when a man falls in love," he told the horse. "He'll devour anything that stands between him and what he wants. He's blind and confused and thinks he's God."

The horse snuffled sympathetically, and Odessa leaned against a tree and listened to the saw of insects, the wind sighing in the boughs. He was considering going into a deep depression when the faraway clatter of a carriage quickened his pulse, and he extinguished his smoke and, like a boy on a first date, sleeked back his hair and replaced his hat.

By the time Angel reined in the horse, Genny was already climbing down and falling into Odessa's arms.

"I thought you'd never come," he said as he laughed into her hair and swung her in the air. "God, I've missed you!"

"It's only been a few days, Odessa," she said demurely, her cheek pressed to the front of his shirt.

Over her head, Odessa met Angel's amusement with a surprising inhibition. "I've known decades that passed faster," he murmured. "I'd forgotten how good you smell."

Angel climbed down from his perch. He would ride Odessa's horse back to town and leave the rig for them. "I'd best be getting back," he said, not expecting an argument, nor did he get one. "A basket of food's in the rig. Shall I check in on Miss Jessamine when I return?"

"Would you mind?" Genny said.

"I'd be delighted."

Odessa shook Angel's hand in thanks. "Keep your ear to the ground, Angel," he warned softly, out of Genny's hearing. "And be careful."

Angel swung up into the saddle of Odessa's horse and laid the reins against the beast's neck, bringing him round. He touched his hat in a jaunty promise. "As if I were handling dynamite, gambling man."

Odessa stood holding the basket as he watched Angel grow smaller upon the road. "You are, my friend," he said softly as the dust settled behind Angel. "You are."

Chapter Eighteen

"You're in an awful hurry to get undressed," Odessa couldn't resist teasing.

He had turned from the rig to find Genny in a pool of shade that matched her eyes, removing her hat and shaking her hair so that it fell in a cascade of curls down her back.

He held up his hands. "A very bad joke. There's a lake on the fringe of Judge Wharton's property, Genny, through those hills over there."

"What hills?"

With pleasure he fastened himself to her back and turned her head and pointed. "I had the idea we could trespass and go wading," he said and breathed in the scent of her sun-warmed hair. "If you can climb a fence in that getup, that is."

She gave his hand a sound slap and twirled away, with a sniff. "You don't like my hat."

Madame Desmond's genius had produced a filmy concoction of layer upon layer of voile and white silk flowers banded about with narrow ribbons that twisted with ropes of small white beads. When Angel had brought her the message from Odessa, she had dived into the trunk and brought out her most revealing, low-neck blouse and tucked it into her green skirt. Now she wanted to throw caution to the wind.

"I love your hat," he growled and nursed his hand. "Damn, Genny, that hurt."

"After that remark about undressing, I wouldn't go if you *ate* my hat."

"You can't resist." Grinning, he held the picnic basket at arm's length over her head. "*I* have the food. Unless, of course, you'd rather eat your hat."

She giggled. "But *I*—" she playfully flexed her muscles "—have the good news." She walked to the rig and swung herself in like a farm woman. "Adam's registered at the hotel. I checked. First thing tomorrow, bright and early, I'm going to present myself at his door and demand my money back. He's in for a surprise, don't you think?"

"Whoa!"

Odessa climbed in beside her, though he had difficulty thinking about Adam Worthington when the tops of her breasts were nested so bewitchingly in the lace of her bodice. And all those tiny buttons marching from the low, rounded neck to her waist would provide a considerable deterrent, even to his quick fingers.

"In all the excitement, I forgot about that invertebrate," he muttered. "And yes, if he doesn't have an heart attack, he'll be lucky. But don't go to his door, Genny, not if you want to really skewer the slug."

She wanted to skewer Adam in the worst way, and she paused in the process of making room for the basket at her feet. "You have a better strategy?"

"Your way doesn't have enough pain."

Genny laughed. "I want a lot of pain."

Shaking his head, Odessa slapped the reins on the back of the horse. "Genny, remind me never to get on your bad side. Now, if you want to make Worthington pay, do it in style. Else you might end up with nothing more than a hangdog apology."

Sucking on her lip, Genny sprawled on the seat and plucked her buttons in consternation. "I think you just want to be in on it."

"Darling—" he leaned over and pecked her cheek "—it's what I've lived for."

They talked nonstop as the rig jounced along the country road—about his parents, about Samuel, about Richard Canfield's casino and how Odessa, in a few days, had achieved the reputation as the biggest winner around. Every man who gambled was itching to take him on. The real stakes, however, took place on the North Piazza, where a chance word could be felt on Wall Street the following day and a fortune could be made or lost.

The only thing they didn't talk about was their future—as if by tacit agreement this afternoon was a no-man's-land where nothing except their pleasure in one another was allowed.

When they reached Judge Wharton's property with its white rail fence protecting three Kentucky-bred race horses that had won consistently at the Saratoga tracks—the judicial fortune had been earned much more in racing than in the hallowed halls of justice—Odessa unhitched the horse to let him graze.

They took a quilt from the rig and the basket of food and engaged in the more enjoyable aspects of getting across the fence while falling over each other and rolling in the tall, soft grass until they were filled with laughter and a gentle, seductive reminder of why they were here.

Genny had never known the pure sensuality of touching a man without guilt. She had never reveled in a man's worship of her body. With something akin to fear, she wanted to fix in her mind every texture of Odessa, every aroma, every articulated muscle and bone while she could. She wanted to hold this day in suspension against the time when she might not have him, and drain it of everything good. She would not think about tomorrow, she promised herself. Today she was luxuriously alive and with the man she loved.

"Now I know why you wanted to do this," she sighed when Odessa lay back in total disregard for his suit and drew her into his arms and pulled her on top of him. "Food is the last thing on your mind."

"How would you know what's on my mind?" Odessa moved so she could feel his desire pressed between them.

"Because—" she smiled and traced the ragged shape of his scar with a tenderness that made the matter of McFee and Platt more grievous to Odessa than ever "—I know you, Odessa Gold. You're keeping a secret, and I want to know!"

Odessa could not bear for anything to mar her perfect allure for him. He trapped her bright innocent face between his hands. "The secret is how much I love the smell of soap on your skin."

She smiled again, but the sparkle in her eyes softened, and she smoothed his beard and his hair and his brows.

"The secret is," he said, "I love the way your hair tangles in the wind, the way it feels between my fingers, the wonderful way you have of smiling when I least expect it, all the little freckles on your shoulders, the way you crinkle your nose when you eat strawberries, the slimness of your pretty feet." He sighed. "And a host of other things too numerous to mention."

She was no longer smiling. Mist had blurred her eyes, and her lips quivered so that she had to bite them. Ever so tenderly she kissed his ear. "I have never been as happy as I am with you."

Odessa could not tell her yet that she must go away. Later, after he had filled himself up with watching her, after he had stored up all the sweetness, maybe then.

They spread their picnic and ate, and afterward, as the sun was dropping, they held hands and walked over the meadow and peered in Wharton's barn. A mother cat was there with round-tummied kittens, and she stropped their legs when Genny knelt to cuddle her babies.

When they returned to the pond, neither of them wanted to wade, and Odessa couldn't bring himself to make love to her and then crush her with the news. She seemed to sense his heavy dread and pulled off his tie and unbuttoned his shirt. She kissed a tiny curl on his chest, and then kissed his lips and moved her hands boldly over him. She knelt beside his waist so that her breasts were an invitation to his hungry eyes, and, loosening the tiny buttons, she let them spill from their nest of lace and moved them against his lips.

It was she who drew him into the hollow of her arms. She was not shy. She unfastened his belt and slipped inside to find him and curl about him and seek the ridges and roundness. She wanted him with her eyes, as well as with her hands. She aroused him as he had never been aroused before, and when he wanted to turn her and end it, she would not, but loved him with the hot sleek wetness of her tongue. Then she was the yielding one, surrendering the treasures hidden beneath the volumes of filmy skirt, showing him the way and never flinching, never looking away as he spilled himself into her and became that most vulnerable of all creatures, a man who loves.

When it was done, the ritual that had to be, Odessa gathered her into his arms and told her the truth, that she must go because he could not protect her here.

"No," she said all the way back to the hotel. "I won't do it. I won't go. I don't care if the governor himself is involved. No."

Darkness had fallen now. They had agreed they would part at the livery stable.

"I won't do it," she told him again, so loudly and so sharply that Odessa was certain the owner thought he was abusing her.

He smiled thinly at the man and tipped him generously.

"No," Genny said as she gathered up her hat and stuffed her hair beneath it and straightened her clothes. "I've come too far. No."

"She has a mind of her own," Odessa lamely explained as they collected their quilt and basket.

The man from whom they had rented the rig felt a certain sympathy for the tall, scarred man, but he would have died happy with such problems.

"Be sensible, Genny," Odessa ordered as he walked her toward the hotel. "This is not a game. These men won't be the least bit charmed by a pretty young schoolmarm who believes that anything can be negotiated in a logical fashion.

"I never said they would be," she retorted, thrusting her nose into the air and lifting the hem of her skirt as they reached Broadway. "I have no intentions of negotiating, but neither am I running away. No, Odessa, and that's final. No."

Odessa supposed, as he watched her strong, energetic walk taking her farther and farther from him and finally climbing the steps of the hotel amid the piazza strollers, that her rebellion had been inevitable. She spoke to Marvin and disappeared without looking back once. What a mess!

One would have thought that spotting Adam Worthington in a dining hall so vast that it required twenty chandeliers to light it would have been difficult.

It wasn't. Genny found Adam as easily as tripping on a rug.

Two days had passed since she and Odessa had gone to the country. Her pique had abated only slightly. She considered skipping dinner; even with her healthy palate she didn't relish searching for Odessa among so many people—though he seemed to have no difficulty finding her.

She saw him now, sidestepping waiters and the slow-moving stampede of people. When he was sure he had her eye, he flashed her a shrewd grin, pulled out a chair from the third table from the door—everyone knew that only Morgans occupied the third table!—and sank into it.

Those who were already seated looked up in fascinated horror. No one dared ask him to move.

All of which would have been amusing had not Genny been knee-deep in troubles of her own.

And people were turning to stare. She had grown accustomed to the puzzling way men watched her lately and women lifted their fans to whisper when she walked past. She had no way of knowing that she was something of a celebrity, and considered that her Wyoming unsophistication somehow showed beneath Madame's lovely clothes. She ignored them as she sent Odessa a series of agitated signals, deflecting his attention to Adam.

On Adam's arm was a rigidly corseted, comically overdressed woman twice his age. Her gown was obviously designed by Worth, but its satin skirt was too heavily embroidered with pearls to be proper for dining, and the bodice and train were of sweltering brocade. On her pompadour was perched a diamond tiara, and her throat was circled by triple strands of diamonds. Another cluster of diamonds formed her brooch, and a spray of flowerettes was pinned to her shoulder. Her wrists and fingers and ears were dripping with stones.

"I'll be switched," Genny breathed. "Jessamine!" She plucked at the woman's sleeve. "It's Adam. And he's with a woman. Don't look, don't look."

"I won't, I promise," the blind woman quipped, but obediently shielded her face. "Dear me, Geneena. What do you intend to do?"

Genny swung her attention to Odessa whose amusement had solidified on his face, making the scar across his cheek into a livid weal.

That's the son of a bitch? his frown asked.

That's the son of a bitch, she signaled back, drooping.

Go to your room. I'll come there.

"I think we should go, Jessamine," Genny whispered and kept her head angled away, lest Adam recognize her.

But the son of a bitch wouldn't have seen anything, for he was too busy drooling and fawning over the woman hanging on his arm. Genny wouldn't have been surprised if the imbecile had dropped to his knees in the middle of the dining room and licked the woman's shoes.

She waved the waiter away when he offered to help them find a seat.

"How could he?" she wailed as they left. "After leaving me, and leaving Mary Faye Spender, how could he? I'd like to wring his cursed neck."

Odessa's plan was better. With another outlay of Genny's precious money the next day—she nearly burst into tears when he'd suggested paying for it himself—they sent train fare to Mary Faye who was, beyond a doubt, still waiting trustfully on Hollybrook Street in St. Louis for Adam to come home.

The wire read: "Come at once to Saratoga. Adam needs you."

"That isn't exactly true," Genny said as she counted out her money, bill by laborious bill.

"Don't worry, my pet." Smiling, Odessa slipped his arm about her lovely waist. "It soon will be."

Samuel Houseman arrived in Saratoga during the adagio movement of Vivaldi's Concerto in A, just as the solo violinist's embellishments of the melody reached their particularly long-breathed and elaborate expression.

"Why, Miss Carlyle!"

Genny had brought Jessamine out for the morning concert, and at the sound of Samuel's voice, her spirits sang with more quickness than she had ever felt for her own father.

"Why, it's Mr. Houseman," she exclaimed to Jessamine, and she turned delightedly to search for the big, lumbering man.

Luckily, they had found seats near the outer fringe of guests who collected each day in Congress Spring Park. Clutching his silk hat, the tails of his morning jacket catching on ladies' skirts and parasols and chair backs, Samuel was having some difficulty maneuvering his frame through the listeners, who were crowded around tables or sitting on quilts, but he plowed bravely on and arrived to clasp Genny's hands with an eager paternal affection.

"How good to see you," he said, adding, "and it's a pleasure as always, Mrs. MacGowan." Over and over he pressed Genny's hands. "I had to come tell you in person how grateful I was to receive your letter, my dear."

Genny's heart swelled for the kind man. Rising, she laid her hand on his arm. "Odessa was worried about your having them. You will be careful, won't you?"

From behind them came a loud clearing of a throat; they were interfering with someone's pleasure.

"Of course," Samuel said, awkwardly seeking a place to sit and finding none. "But life has purpose once again, Miss Carlyle. That's very precious. One must guard it carefully."

Apprehension settled like a glaze over Genny's mood, yet she said brightly, "Did you just get here? Have you seen Odessa? He's around." She pulled a face. "He's always around. Sometimes when you don't want him to be. Why don't you call me Genny?"

With a *ha-rumph* appropriate for her dowager status at the springs, Clementine Morgan leaned from her table and rapped Samuel's hat soundly with her walking stick.

"Mind your manners, young man," she said in a loud voice, "and save your talking until after the concert. A body can't hear the soloist."

Genny giggled. "Why don't we take a walk, Mr. Houseman?"

The big man laughed. "I was about to suggest that very thing. Vivaldi gives me a pain." He whispered, "I tend to lean to the Russian composers, myself."

Fetching her parasol, Genny bent to Jessamine. "I'll come for you when the concert's finished."

"Take all the time you need, dear," Jessamine said cheerfully. "I've heard that our soloist does Boccherini for an encore. You know how I adore Boccherini."

"I used to enjoy Boccherini when I was a young man," Samuel mused.

"You're still a young man." Even now, Genny's smile gave way to her automatic search for Odessa.

"You remind me so of my dear Anne."

"I'm glad."

He walked her a distance from the concert, then stopped in the walk to remove his hat. Frowning, he turned it round and over and upside down. "I do believe that Morgan magpie has ruined my new hat."

When Genny saw Odessa and Eleanor Bentley beneath the Congress Spring pavilion, her first thought was they were not together. But then Eleanor Bentley laughed up at him, and Genny's heart somersaulted. She stumbled slightly on the walk, and Samuel turned to give a teasing support to her elbow. Not wanting the man to perceive her rush of jealousy, she touched her fingers to her forehead. Beneath her palm, her eyes again sought Odessa.

He was waiting for her to look at him. As if he had planned to be seen with the Manhattan socialite, he did not flinch. Eleanor was carrying the same white prayer book as in Madame Desmond's shop, and she remarked upon some detail of the pavilion, tipping her face to his with angelic devotion.

Witch!

As if she had shouted the word, Eleanor turned and fixed her gaze on Genny.

"Miss Carlyle?" Samuel said. "Genny?"

Genny jerked her startled focus back to Samuel and tried to arrange a passable smile. "Forgive me. I'm perfectly fine. I just..." She laughed breathlessly. "I don't know."

Samuel looked from Genny's disturbance to the pristine blonde to Andrew Goldman. "I understand," he said, and took her hand again.

Odessa was playing one of his charades, Genny fumed as they climbed the wide steps approaching the pavilion. Some conniving purpose, no doubt—his being with Eleanor Bentley. Connected with Richard Canfield's gambling casino or some of the powerful men he spent his evenings with. She couldn't be mistaken about his feelings for her. She couldn't be that wrong. But she'd been wrong with Adam, hadn't she? Eleanor Bentley, in her fervently pure gown with its yards and yards of white lace, making her look as if she could float away to heaven, laid her immaculate gloved hand on Odessa's sleeve.

Some sort of hubbub occurred at the spring, and Eleanor laughed and reached up to blot a droplet of water from Odessa's beard with her spotless handkerchief. To Genny's dismay, the woman looked her way again and nodded to Samuel and herself. So. She did remember that morning in Madame Desmond's shop!

"If you'd rather go somewhere private, Genny dear," Samuel suggested, "we can talk about the drawings."

Genny was briefly distracted. "I beg your pardon?"

"You remember we spoke about my publishing them?"

"Oh, that. Well, Odessa wouldn't hear of it. He's so touchy, you know, about keeping that part of his past separate, as if he's forfeited it or something. Personally, I think it's a terrible waste, but..." She shrugged. "They are his drawings, after all."

"Then I don't understand."

"Sir?"

"That's what I wanted to ask you about. Why did Andrew, Odessa, I mean, sell the drawings to the *Times*? I would have done much better by him, and he would have had nationwide circulation. Not that I'm offended, I'm just puzzled."

An alarm shrilled in Genny's head, and her jaw sagged in confusion. She leaned more heavily on Samuel's arm. "Sold the drawings? To the *Times*? You mean, you've seen them?"

Samuel laughed his broad publisher's laugh. "Everyone's seen them, Miss Carlyle. People have been talking of them for days, wondering who this new captivating creature is. The dressmakers, I've been told, are being deluged with orders for clothes like the ones Andrew drew. Everyone wants to be you, my dear."

Never in her life had Genny fainted or come close to fainting, but a drowning wave of blackness swirled about her feet and threatened to pull her under. Samuel thrust out his arm to keep her from toppling forward, and he looked up in time to see Odessa striding toward him, coattails flapping about his legs.

"I insisted that Mr. Gold bring me over," Eleanor was cooing as she thrust out a snowily gloved hand to Genny. "I'm not sure you remember me, Miss Carlyle, but we met at Louise Desmond's. I've just been explaining to Mr. Gold that you've become an overnight sensation in New York. I beg of you to tell me who the artist is for the drawings that the *Times* has been running. I will pay absolutely any price he asks, no matter how great, to have a series done of me."

After Odessa's feelings on the matter of Louise Desmond's blatant betrayal had been made perfectly clear to everyone, especially to Genny, Eleanor Bentley stuck to him like a wild-clover burr. Genny was torn in all directions. The stares and whispers made sense now, but the frightening part was that she would end up making Odessa's identity and whereabouts impossible to keep secret. She would, just by being seen with him, end up hurting him. If she truly loved Odessa, she would find her own life, apart from his.

Deeply depressed, she took Samuel aside so that even Odessa's sharp ears could not overhear, "I have a question to ask you, Mr. Houseman."

The man dusted a park bench with his handkerchief and invited her to sit. "You have but to ask, my dear."

Genny sat beside him, snapped her parasol shut and mauled the toe of one shoe with its point. "You might have figured out by now that I've depended fairly heavily on Odessa. Financially, I mean. But that isn't the way I want things. I've never depended on anyone for anything. I guess what I'm trying to say is that I could use a job." She slid him a look askance. "You have a publishing business. I'm an intelligent woman. I've taught school a number of years. I wouldn't let you down, Mr. Houseman."

Tipping back his head to the sun and thanking God for
sending him someone after all these years to take Anne's
place, Samuel Houseman let out his breath in a deep, satisfied sigh.

Taking her hand in his large one, he laid it on his cheek.
"I would be honored to give you a job, my dear. Deeply
honored. Why don't you come to my cottage for dinner?
I'll send a telegram to my office and give you something
definite. And then—" he winked "—we'll eat until we
can't move."

If Saratoga wouldn't have been gossiping about it by
dusk, Genny would've thrown her arms around the man's
neck in a whooping hug and covered his dear face with
kisses.

She restrained herself to a squeeze of his hand. "If it's
all right with you," she said with a ripple of happy laughter, "I'd like to bring Odessa. I have a terrible need to rub
it in. Just a little."

"I was about to insist on it," Samuel said and nodded.
It was good, very good.

Chapter Nineteen

A messenger brought a stiff white envelope to Genny's door on a silver tray. Inside was a card written in Samuel's hand requesting the "pleasure of her company."

Genny's head was already swirling with visions of candles on a perfectly laid table, succulent dishes of boned goose with aspic, and Newburg lobster, watercress salad and wonderful little sponge cakes trembling on a sea of tutti-frutti pudding. The coffee would be served in china cups that would make a rich, decisive clink upon the saucers.

"I think I'll wear the India silk," she told Jessamine, then paraded before the mirror to admire the cream-colored gown with its low scooping neck and black velvet bows, the lush leghorn hat trimmed with lace and yellow roses, the way the narrow waist flared into the skirt.

"It looks lovely on you," Jessamine said.

Genny laughed. By the time she was ready to leave, butterflies were swarming in her stomach. A real job in an Eastern city! Not bad for a Missouri River girl grown up in the sassafras thickets. Despite her feelings of guilt about the drawings having placed Odessa where he did not want to be, she was looking forward to setting him back on his heels. She wanted to be absolutely beautiful!

Satisfied, she kissed Jessamine goodbye, took up her parasol and breezed through the lobby. Now that she

understood why the stares followed her, she rather enjoyed her small celebrity status.

When she passed Ava Vanderbilt on her way to the dining hall, terribly overdressed for such a hot evening in her
high-necked, long-sleeved black satin and weighed down
with a diamond necklace, bracelets, rings, brooch and
earrings, she inclined her head in a jaunty nod.

"Good evening, Mrs. Vanderbilt," she said airily.

To her surprise, the woman lifted her lorgnette as if she
approved of young women with the courage to defy con-
vention. "Good evening, Miss Carlyle."

Genny swept down the steps and tossed a gay good-
evening to Marvin as if she were off to play tennis. She
hoped Odessa was waiting on the veranda that ran the
length of cottage row. He had lectured her about en-
trances. She would make an entrance.

He didn't disappoint her. From a distance she spotted
him—propped on the railing of the veranda with his white
tails fluttering free, his fashionable Panama hat perched
debonairly, and the smoke of his cheroot curling up in a
thin pale thread.

When he spied her swinging briskly along the walk, his
grin was a flash of white. He detached himself from the
railing and skittered lightly down the steps.

Genny held her head high, her uncorseted body lithe-
some and supple and her parasol tucked beneath her arm
like a general's quirt. Her gown showed a bit of shoulder
and bosom, and she didn't mar it with so much as a locket
about her throat.

Smiling at Odessa's bold approval, she reached up to
push aside her hat's veil that was fluttering about her face.

"Why, Miss Carlyle," he drawled as he bowed and lifted
her gloved hand to his lips, "if you looked any better,
darlin' I'd have to shoot myself in the foot."

"After Eleanor Bentley, that would definitely not be my
first choice of anatomy, Mr. Gold."

How wonderful his laughter was, rolling richly into the
evening air. "After a morning with Eleanor Bentley, I

really don't care. There isn't a subtle bone in that woman's body."

"Yes, but it's sure to go to heaven," she retorted wickedly, then changed the subject. "I trust you brought a healthy appetite."

He made sure she blushed beneath his lusty appraisal. "You'll never know how healthy, Miss Carlyle."

"Then I think it's time to tell you."

He was handing her up the steps to Samuel's cottage door, and he reared back, giving her one of his oh-no looks, eyes narrowed and warning. "Why do I get this bad feeling in my stomach every time you make one of those remarks, Genny Carlyle?"

"Don't be such a stick, Odessa. Mr. Houseman is giving me a job at his publishing house in Albany. We're making the arrangements after dinner. And stop scowling." She reached up playfully to tug on his earlobe. "We'll have to have a closed coffin at your funeral."

"Son of a gun, Genny—" he shoved his hat farther back on his head "—why'd you go and do a dang-fool thing like that?"

"What do you suggest I do?" She stabbed him less playfully with her parasol. "I owe you a lot of money. This way I can pay you back. You do want to be paid back, don't you?"

Certain the evening had just taken a drastic turn for the worse, Odessa was dragging his feet by the time he knocked on Samuel's door. When Samuel didn't answer immediately, he was of a mind to say they should forget the whole thing. He felt like going to his room and sulking.

But the waiter was speeding down the veranda, a huge tray held high above his head and covered with a freshly ironed cloth and sending out a perfume of smells that made Genny's mouth water.

"I see our dinner has arrived," Odessa said with a sour smile for the waiter. He knocked again, more sharply. "Samuel? Samuel, your guests will be skin and bones if you don't hurry up and open this door."

"Perhaps he had to go out," Genny suggested. "Try the door."

Odessa turned the heavy knob and was surprised when the door opened and afforded a view of the darkened interior. With a puzzled lift of brows, he motioned for both Genny and the waiter to wait while he stepped inside.

The lamps had not been lighted. The windows were closed, giving the room a tight, cloistered stuffiness. The quietness possessed an unreality that prompted Odessa to remove his hat and place it on the table, his cigar into an ashtray.

He moved through the suite to the bedroom, his gambler's instincts making the hair stiffen on the back of his neck. Something was wrong here. Opening the bedroom door, he peered inside.

Samuel Houseman was stretched upon his unmade bed, turned on his side in a posture of sleep. Odessa's first impulse was to smile, but the room had a troubling feel—tiny details that hardly registered and innocent in themselves but somehow disturbing.

He sniffed. Gunpowder. He could never mistake that smell. He grasped the older man's shoulder and turned him over to see the blood matted on his temple. A deafening roar rose up in him, and thoughts slammed into his mind in quick succession: Samuel's having known McFee's name, McFee in Saratoga, Samuel's turning up dead and . . . and Genny having been seen with Samuel at Congress Springs all morning!

He spun around, his only concern now to protect Genny.

She was standing in the doorway, her hat dangling from her fingers and her parasol dropping to the floor in a clatter. "Oh, no," she whimpered and stumbled forward, bumping into a small table and knocking a lamp to the floor. "No, no. Is he . . . ?"

"Yes."

Odessa pushed past her and caught the waiter before he could leave. "Quickly! A man's been shot. Get the police. After you do that—" he fished paper and pen from an inside pocket and scribbled Angel's name on it "—find this man and tell him to come immediately."

The black man's face was wide with shock. "Yassuh," he said, and laid down his tray to bound over the veranda's hurdle and dash across the manicured lawns to the hotel.

Genny hardly felt anything at all. Numbness had set in. In Samuel Houseman, her heart had found a drop of healing, and she must hold tightly to that.

Odessa was not numb, though he wished he were. Passionate fury roiled up in him for the moment his enemies would discern that Odessa Gold was Andrew Goldman. What did it take to justify his existence? He was out of prison and finding a new life. His scarred heart was softening beneath Genny's sun until he thought maybe, just maybe, he could be the man he once had been.

But the past was a scavenger. It skulked behind a person's back, letting them have a taste of the good in life, then bam! It hit you from behind, so that you toppled and fell.

Saratoga, for all its boasts of being so deliciously wicked, was rocked on its heels by the death of Samuel Houseman. The police were accustomed to dealing with harlots frequenting the hotel or troublemakers who had imbibed too much at the Casino. They were slow to deduce what had happened to Samuel Houseman.

Odessa knew exactly what had happened, and he ordered Genny, after she had told the authorities what she knew, to go to her room and stay there. She should take meals there and pack. Angel was to go on watching McFee and Platt and Hodges.

Odessa wired his parents. They helped make arrangements for Samuel to be buried in Albany. Odessa argued that Genny should leave Saratoga, but she refused. When he argued, she wept that she loved him and she wasn't going.

Cursing himself for having brought her to Saratoga in the first place, he began solving his problems the only way he knew how. For four nights, Manville Platt had been winning heavily at the poker tables. It was time, Odessa thought, to put one of his enemies underground.

Ruining Platt would not be easy. Night after night Odessa had been observing the man as he gambled. Platt was a shrewd and careful card player. He sent his opponents mercilessly from the tables with bleeding wounds. But he had one great strike against him. He was ill.

Angel, spying on the Wyoming rancher, had seen him slipping from the tables to take medicine. "Digitalis would be my guess," he said.

With a self-discipline that had been whetted to a point as sharp as one of Genny's hat pins, Odessa forced back his passionate hatred. He pushed from his mind the sight of Samuel lying dead. He would not think of Genny, nor would he think of McFee, whom he was certain had had Samuel killed.

The police were calling it a robbery. No one had seen anything or heard anything. Most of Saratoga had been attending a concert in the Grand Union courtyard.

Wearing his usual formal dress of white cravat, cream-satin vest and black tails, with an unobtrusive diamond ring on his finger, Odessa left Angel to guard Genny and drifted through the Casino for the early part of the evening.

Most of the men present knew of his prowess with cards, but Odessa made it his habit to occasionally lose; it whetted the appetites of those who envisioned themselves beating him.

Eventually Platt and his bodyguards moved upstairs where the stakes were higher. Odessa, seemingly off his usual pace, took a seat opposite Platt. It didn't take long until the table had become the one where the action was.

For two hours Odessa played modestly, winning only enough to attract Platt's interest. Gradually the game was reduced to three players. Most of the chips were stacked before Manville Platt who, concentrating hard on his cards, had hardly glanced at Odessa except to take note of what he drank and how much.

The third man who had survived the initial weeding-out was a railroad tycoon from Rhode Island, Sturdevant Irish, a man with money to lose. Again and again Odessa folded when he had winning cards in his hand. The only time he allowed himself to win was when he was certain it would annoy Platt.

The night wore on. Food was brought in. Those of short wind returned to their rooms, and those who stayed kept the waiters busy bringing drinks from the bar. Platt did not drink when he played. Neither did Odessa. He lit a fresh cheroot.

With the passing of hours, Manville Platt began to study the tall, scarred younger man. He tried to pick up the tiny quirks that would enable him to get an edge, but the only thing he received was a mocking silence.

Sturdevant Irish was showing distinct signs of wearying. If Odessa had not been in the game, Platt would have finished Irish off quickly and left the Casino with a handsome bulge in his purse. But Odessa kept forcing the winnings to be divided and kept Irish in the game.

By now a sizable crowd had gathered to watch, mostly diehard players who had the stamina for the big game but not the money.

Odessa began to win. For the next two hours, he chipped away at Platt's confidence. Now the pile before Odessa was worth in the neighborhood of $250,000.

Platt's color, already like that of a corpse, worsened. Twice he left the table, and Odessa was positive he'd gone to take medicine.

"One card," Odessa told the dealer at half-past one in the morning, and he let a certain cockiness show for a flickering moment before shuttering it with his facade. In his hand were two deuces, nothing more.

"One card for the gentleman," the dealer said.

Odessa slipped a trey beneath the two deuces and discarded a six and pretended to be struggling with a smile.

He could smell the nearness of the kill. The dealer quizzed Manville Platt with a wrinkled brow, and the cadaverous-looking man eyed Odessa with suspicion.

An unsettling twitch in Odessa's stomach warned him to play the less experienced gambler pitted against a veteran. All the while he could feel the man's memory thrashing, trying to connect something for which he had no name.

"One card," Platt said and showed yellow teeth in a smile, for he was looking at two fours and two tens.

Manville quivered when he turned up a third four, but his face showed nothing; he made certain of that. He could not lose, and now he was going to show the cocky gambler a thing or two.

"Ten thousand," Odessa said with a twinkle that lasted an instant too long.

Platt studied his opponent and studied the table. "Excuse me," he said and motioned his guards to accompany him to the men's privy where he took a strong dose of digitalis and removed his last twenty thousand dollars in cash from the money belt circling his skinny waist.

Returning to the table, he cracked a grin. "I'll match you, sir, and raise you ten."

With a lift of brows that appeared respectful, Odessa looked at his cards again, as if he weren't quite sure he wanted to continue.

Before the game, Odessa had purchased two 500-thousand-dollar chips, which represented his banked winnings. In his pocket, he also had twenty thousand dollars in cash. If he had to, he would use it all to break this man.

He sat a moment, licking his lips as if in a deep quandary. "What the hell," he huffed at last and laughed. "Let's cut to the finish. I meet you and raise another ten."

For long irritated minutes, Platt did not move, and neither did anyone else in the room.

Presently Odessa leaned back in his chair and hooted with laughter. "You folding, old man?"

Odessa made as if to gather the pile of money and, reddened to the roots of his tricolored hair, Platt held up his hand.

"Not so fast." He removed his handkerchief and blotted his motley skin. His hands were shaking. One of his men detached himself from the wall where he'd been slouching and came to stand solicitously at the back of Platt's chair.

"I'm all right, I'm all right," he told them and again considered his cards.

It was a winning hand, he knew, and this damn fool puppy was yipping and snapping around his feet when he, with one sound blow, could send him yelping away, his tail tucked between his legs. A hard lesson, but a good one.

He leaned forward and tugged at his beaked nose. "Let me give you some advice, young man. Don't try too hard to teach an old dog. Now, just to show you how bad you can get burned, I'm going to put up my Wyoming ranch and call your hand. Ten thousand acres of the best grassland in the state. It's worth four of what's on this table. With your permission..."

Platt snapped his thin fingers for a pen and paper, which was quickly produced by one of his guards. He wrote out an IOU, using his ten-thousand-acre ranch as collateral.

Smiling triumphantly, he slid the paper to the center of the table. "Now, *you* fold."

Odessa spent a moment pretending to mull over the cards in his hands. With a sigh, he took out his two 500-thousand-dollar chips and laid them meticulously on top of Platt's IOU. "Sorry, can't do that."

If it were possible, Manville Platt's corpse-gray face turned paler. He had nothing left to play, unless he borrowed. And McFee, even if he could find him, would never fork over enough to stop this maggot.

A muscle in his neck knotted, and a pain shot down his left arm. He sagged heavily in his chair and tried to breathe. A terrible battering ram was striking his chest, and he could not move.

His men were at his side, instantly. Onlookers fell deathly silent. Platt worked his mouth in an attempt to plead with his opponent.

Odessa's grin was without mercy. He now allowed himself to think about Anne. And Genny. And Samuel. In a voice cold as a dagger of ice, he said, "Ante up or lay down your cards, Mr. Platt. I've come a long, long way to break your back."

The bitter note in his voice set off an alarm in Manville Platt's head, and suddenly he clawed at his shirt where it was strangling him. His eyes bulged from their sockets.

"Who...?" he croaked.

Calmly, as an entire room of people looked on, Odessa gathered the winnings from the table and began putting them into his pockets. When the table was clean, he stood and braced his hands on it and leaned over until his face was inches from Platt's.

The man was going into cardiac arrest, and Odessa knew it. "Don't you recognize me, Mr. Deputy Marshall?" he asked with a low, silky threat. "You should. You saw me get this scar."

Manville Platt's mouth dropped open, and his eyes moved wildly. In a child's whisper, as he relived the past, he said. "I always knew this day would come."

A murmur ran through the gaming room. Platt fell facedown on the table. One of his bodyguards lunged for him and the other started toward Odessa.

With lightning reflexes, Odessa was in a stance of self-defense, his lips drawn back over his teeth. "Don't even think it," he warned.

Wisely, the man backed off, and Odessa knew a moment of pity for the dying Platt. But then he remembered his son, and Anne's eyes that wouldn't close. With a flick of his fingers, he peeled off a one-hundred-dollar bill and tossed it on the table.

"A man shouldn't die broke," he said, but he didn't think Platt heard him.

* * *

Light from a single gas lamp was flitting about Genny's suite like a will-o'-the-wisp when Odessa returned there and laid his hand on Angel's shoulder in gratitude for having kept a vigil.

Jessamine should have been sleeping at this hour, but she sat in a winged chair with her feet up, dozing. She started at the sound of Odessa's voice. "Mr. Gold?"

"Don't get up, Jessamine," he said. "I'm sending Angel home, that's all."

"What happened?" Angel quizzed softly. He drew Odessa to one side, by the opening to the bedroom where Genny lay sleeping on the ornate bed.

Odessa's mouth twisted bitterly. "Platt has had a bit of physical difficulties. You made yourself a considerable percentage tonight, Angel. How's Genny been?"

"She's had a rather bad time of it," the black man said, "but she finally went to sleep. I was beginning to worry about you."

Dead on his feet, Odessa passed his hand over his face. "Things are happening too quickly. If McFee doesn't know who I am, he soon will. This is all coming apart, Angel. I'm afraid for her."

Angel laid his hand upon his friend's shoulder. "We talked a long time about her leaving, and she's right about this, Odessa—leaving now would be like putting up a sign. It would be better for her to remain here and keep out of sight."

Odessa gouged his fingers into the corners of his eyes. He had already come to that conclusion himself, though it chafed him sorely to be trapped so by circumstance.

"Hell, go get some sleep. Tomorrow's a new day."

"Yeah." Angel laughed. "We can have some real trouble tomorrow."

When the door closed soundlessly, Odessa walked with equal softness into the bedroom and stood over Genny, gazing tenderly down at her red hair spilling over the pillow like a sunset. His love for her had brought him more happiness than he could ever have hoped for, but also more heartache.

Genny, Genny, how can I do it differently? Don't hate me.

Her lips were parted slightly, and she moved in her sleep, moaning softly as if some level of her had heard his tormented thought. The fanciful wisp of lace that Louise Desmond had designed hardly covered her breasts. A strap had fallen low so that one nipple winked coyly at him. Her hand was curled beside her cheek, and Odessa stooped, feeling as if his entire existence lay within the small, satin hollow of her palm.

Many years had passed since he had prayed, and Odessa wasn't sure what he believed anymore. But if there was a God in heaven, he had to protect this woman. She had done no wrong, yet she had been wronged, badly. She mustn't follow the same violent path as Samuel.

"If someone has to fall—" he squeezed his eyes tightly shut "—let it be me."

Not wishing to awaken her but needing the reassurance of her in his arms, he lay on the bed and gathered her to him.

She roused to murmur, "Odessa?"

"I'm here, darling. Everything is all right."

"Samuel's dead."

"I know, sweetheart."

She smelled wonderfully of flowers and soap, and she clung to him willingly, tucking her head beneath his chin and wrapping her arms about his waist. Odessa brushed her hair aside and kissed the high, porcelain brow. He fit his palm to her cheek and tilted her face to his. She kissed him, and he felt the lick of heat deep in his belly.

As they held each other in the darkness, a knock made Odessa jerk.

Twisting, he caused Genny to scramble around on the bed, wide awake. "Shhh. Easy."

"What time is it?" she whispered.

"Three o'clock."

"Who could that be?"

"Angel, maybe." He came to his feet and the creak of the bed was like a rifle shot.

"No, let me open it."

She was pulling on her wrapper, and before Odessa could catch her, she was sweeping through the sitting room and hurrying to the door.

Odessa had a ghastly vision of her being shot down the moment she opened the door. A roar formed in his chest and was boiling up in his throat when he heard a woman's husky voice say, "Are you Miss Carlyle?"

Don't answer! Odessa wanted to shout, but another instinct kept him where he was, hidden in the shadows of the bedroom.

"Yes," Genny said cautiously.

"I'm Beatrice Hodges. My, uh... my husband's the governor of Wyoming. I really have to talk to you, Miss Carlyle. Please, may I come in?"

Chapter Twenty

To Odessa, it was perfectly sensible that the particulars of his existence should have been played out so perfectly between three women in a small sitting room in Saratoga Springs. It was no more bizarre than the events that had led him here.

With smooth, catlike grace, he slid down the wall to hunch just inside the open door of Genny's bedroom and listen as Beatrice Hodges was seated and Jessamine roused and the introductions made.

"Could I get you something, Mrs. Hodges?" Genny offered as she lit another gas lamp.

"Do you have anything to drink?" the woman asked.

"We have water, but no ice, I'm afraid."

Beatrice made a small sound of disappointment. "That will be fine, thanks. I won't take up much of your time."

"It's quite all right. Jessamine, would you like a drink?"

"If you don't mind, Geneena."

Odessa heard the sound of water filling two glasses, then Genny's soft step on the rug. "How do you know my name, Mrs. Hodges?"

"I saw you at Congress Springs with Mr. Houseman."

"You know Samuel?"

"Only through my husband, Miss Carlyle. Mr. House-man sent Nathan many telegrams, wrote many letters over the years, begging to know the name of the man responsible for his daughter's death, you understand. That's what I wanted to talk to you about.''

"I'm afraid I don't understand.''

Beatrice sucked in a sharp, nervous breath. "This is difficult for me.''

An edginess was in Genny's tone. "You have information about Samuel's death?''

"Not exactly.'' An ironic laugh. "And my life wouldn't be worth much to some people if they knew I was here telling you this. You must be discreet, Miss Carlyle. This was not a simple grudge killing.''

"What a horrible way to put it. Samuel Houseman was a decent human being. He never hurt anyone. Mrs. Hodges—''

"Hear me out, please. Nathan wanted very much to re-open the Andrew Goldman case, for political reasons, you see. For the publicity the case would receive, primarily. He is honest in wanting the men responsible brought to justice, even if it is for the wrong reasons.''

As exhausted as Odessa was, he began to shake with a rush of adrenaline.

"Pray go on, Mrs. Hodges.''

"Nathan tried everything to get the convicted man, this Andrew Goldman, to turn state's evidence against Mr. McFee and Mr. Platt. But the man refused, and so Nathan and Lewis—''

"Who is Lewis?''

"My . . . Nathan's secretary.'' Beatrice Hodges's voice abruptly assumed the harshness of a rusty blade. "Lewis is very clever. He came up with the idea that McFee and Platt could be caught in the act of trying to get to this Andrew Goldman—their hands in the till, so to speak. When Nathan learned that Mr. Houseman was coming to Saratoga this month, he informed Mr. McFee and Mr. Platt. They all came here in the hope of learning from Mr. Houseman the whereabouts of this Goldman person.''

"My God!'' Genny gasped.

Odessa's heart ached to go to Genny. He ground his teeth until his jaws ached.

"That is barbaric," Genny said. "Unbelievable."

"My husband can be a barbaric man."

A silence filled the room.

Presently, Genny cleared her throat and asked, "Have they…I mean, has your husband or this… What did you say his name was, MacFee?"

Odessa had to smile. You're quite the little con artist yourself, Genny Carlyle.

"Yes, McFee. Mr. Platt's heart attack has alerted them, Miss Carlyle. The bodyguards—Mr. Platt's bodyguards, not my husband's—believe the man who played poker with Mr. Platt tonight could conceivably be Mr. Goldman. That's what I came to ask you, Miss Carlyle. You were Mr. Houseman's friend. If you know who Andrew Goldman is, you must warn him that my husband is going to instigate a full-scale search for him first thing tomorrow."

The silence was long and uneasy. Odessa heard Genny rise and pace the floor for a time, no sound of her feet but a whisper.

"Mrs. Hodges, forgive me if I sound rude, for I certainly have no reason to mistrust you. You have been extraordinarily frank by coming here tonight, I grant you. It's that frankness I'm wondering about. Why would you, the wife of the governor of Wyoming, tell me all this? How did you find out? I'm forced to wonder if this isn't some clever trap."

Odessa heard Beatrice sigh and set down her glass, clinking it gently against a lamp. Her voice was weighted with an underlying emotion that Odessa recognized easily as hatred.

"As to how I know all this, Miss Carlyle, Lewis told me. Lewis is…an ambitious man."

"The governor's secretary? But why would he tell you?"

"Why do you think, Miss Carlyle? You look like a woman of some sophistication."

Jessamine made one of her *tsk, tsk, tsk* commentaries, and Genny murmured something that Odessa did not hear. Then: "Well, Mrs. Hodges, I can only tell you this. I don't know Andrew Goldman personally."

"But—"

"*But,* if I did know the man personally, I would surely give him this information. And I am sure, if I did know him personally, that he would extend you his heartfelt thanks."

The silence closed avenues and doors, but the understanding between the two women couldn't have been clearer. Beatrice Hodges rose, and Odessa was certain she extended her hand.

"I appreciate your hearing me out, Miss Carlyle. Please, I'm afraid, very afraid that Mr. McFee is in some way responsible for the death of that poor man. I can't prove it, but if he is, then Nathan and Lewis could both be guilty of conspiracy. I can't go to the authorities—surely you can see that. I'm risking my life just telling you this much."

Genny hesitated, and when she spoke, her voice was compassionate and gentle.

"I admire you for your bravery, Mrs. Hodges. You're an honorable woman. Somehow I don't think that Governor Hodges knows exactly what he has in you."

Did he hear a sob? Odessa wondered, straining to listen.

"God bless you, Miss Carlyle." Beatrice blew her nose. "God bless you."

A moment passed, and after the door of the suite clicked shut, Odessa rose, his joints aching and stiff. When he turned, Genny was standing in the doorway, her beloved face streaming tears that broke his heart.

"I'm so afraid," she said as he crushed her in his arms.

Sir Walter had made inquiries about Genevieve Carlyle. Other than her place of origin being Wyoming, however, he had been unable to learn much. When he first saw her with the older gentleman whom he learned later was

Samuel Houseman, the publisher, he assumed they were together. But he soon realized that they were simply friends.

Reynard wanted an introduction to Miss Genevieve Carlyle, but being a shy man, he didn't know exactly how to go about getting one with finesse—her being so young and such an unknown.

Upon learning about the unfortunate demise of Mr. Houseman and imagining how terribly the young woman must feel, he saw his excuse, and decided to invite her to the Wednesday night cotillion. A courtesy to cheer her up.

But he must first find someone to introduce them. And he must find *her*.

Friday he watched for her without success. And Saturday. None of his friends on the North Piazza had seen the woman whose reputation was now a dual one—the young woman of fashion and the one who had been with Samuel Houseman the day he was killed. Where was Genevieve Carlyle?

For two days Genny stayed in her suite, petrified with fear. Manville Platt's heart attack blessedly attracted little notice, but if Beatrice Hodges had seen her with Samuel and guessed she had a connection with Odessa, what would keep her husband from doing the same? And C. E. McFee?

But wouldn't hibernating give the same impression, only more strongly? She must make herself seen, behaving as if she hadn't a care in the world. With any luck, she could flaunt herself before the governor himself until he would have to conclude that she would never lead him to Andrew Goldman.

She laid out a number of Madame's clothes on the bed. Selecting a plain linen skirt, she topped it with a trim tucked shirtwaist and a patent-leather belt. Around the collar, she knotted a mannish tie and drew on a vest, which she left unbuttoned. Knotting her hair on the crown of her head, she held it down with her straw boater, which she pinned securely.

After making a thorough inspection of herself in the mirror, Genny left Odessa and Angel holed up in their room trying to devise a way of stopping McFee's deadly vendetta. Without saying a word to them, she took Jessamine and a great gulp of courage and breezed into the lobby of the hotel.

People turned to stare. With pretty bobbing nods, she spoke to everyone. Wincing, but determined to give them something to talk about besides Samuel Houseman or Manville Platt, she purchased a drawing of the hotel that could be sent through the mail. She glanced through a *Harper's* magazine. She bought Jessamine some candy.

The ladies in their ruffles and laces and diamonds and silk flowers were pretending not to look, but Genny knew they were secretly devouring her.

"Let's sit on the piazza, Jessamine," she suggested, "and get some of the morning sun. I haven't seen anyone who looks remotely like the governor of Wyoming."

Just as Genny was considering giving it all up and having the carriage brought round, Reynard was returning to his room. His heart made a twisting leap at the sight of her, and his pince-nez slid off his nose.

"My word," he said to himself and quickly perched the spectacles back into the permanent groove on the bridge of his nose. "It's her."

With brisk clicks of his walking stick, he advanced upon the desk where Horace Winnows had just come from delivering a personal message and was hopping around like a jay.

"Sir Walter," the man said and predictably began to fawn. "What a charming surprise to find you up and about so early, sir. And may I say how well you're looking. I heard from Mrs. Vanderbilt that you were feeling poorly last evening. I do trust that it was the water, nothing more serious?"

"Put your worries away, Mr. Winnows. If I weren't in the pink, I wouldn't be here. I came to beg a favor."

"Oh, absolutely, sir, absolutely. You have but to ask."

"I'd like you to introduce me to a young woman."

"But, of course, sir. Just tell me who."

"Miss Carlyle."

Winnows blanched as visions of Odessa Gold's scarred face rose in his mind; yet he dared not refuse the titled man. Oh dear, oh dear.

"I, ahem, trust that you prefer this to appear as if it were an impromptu meeting, do you not?"

Reynard tucked a prim smile into his collar. "I was certain I had chosen well, Mr. Winnows."

"Then follow me, sir. I have the perfect plan."

"I'm in your debt, sir."

As he walked out onto the piazza, making sure that the part of his hair was absolutely flawless, Winnows called, "Oh, Miss Carlyle, Miss Carlyle."

Genny turned to find Winnows prancing toward her, his hands aflutter. "Yes?"

"How fortunate to see you, Miss Carlyle. You might be interested to know that I've placed a message in your box. A telegram, actually, from St. Louis, I believe."

Mary Faye!

Genny smiled pleasantly. "Thank you very much, Mr. Winnows. I'll see to it first thing."

"Very good, madam." Reynard stepped to his elbow. "Pray, forgive my rudeness. Have you met Sir Walter Reynard? A guest of long standing at the hotel, I assure you, and a dear friend of Judge Hargreaves and Ava Vanderbilt."

Genny looked at Sir Walter and saw a much more effective deterrent for Governor Hodges. A twinge of guilt gave her pause, but to insure Odessa's safety, she would have ingratiated herself to McFee himself.

Sir Walter didn't appear to be a bad sort, though she could imagine him bending to thump the edges of folded shirts in his drawer until they were perfectly aligned and buttering his toast to the very edge of the crust.

''Miss Genevieve Carlyle from Wyoming,'' Winnows said, finishing his duty with thoroughness.

Reynard, had anyone asked him, would have sworn on his sainted mother's grave that he was beyond blushing, but as he lifted Genevieve Carlyle's slim fingers to his lips, his face flooded with color.

''My dear Miss Carlyle,'' he murmured as his pince-nez slid over her sleeve and into a pocket of her delightful little vest, ''it is an honor and a privilege. I've been deeply interested in the drawings that have been appearing in the *Times*. They are of you, are they not? You must tell me, my dear, about this remarkable artist. The man's a genius. But then, he has such a magnificent model.''

With considerable awkwardness, Genny fished his spectacles from her pocket and put them back in his hand. After that, things became easier.

Over the next two days, on the arm of Sir Walter, she was taken places she could never have gone alone. Or even with Odessa. Saratoga couldn't stop talking about the young woman of the *New York Times* who breakfasted with Sir Walter in the garden with the Vanderbilts and strolled through the elm-shaded gardens with the nephew of Jay Gould.

Genny and Reynard attended concerts with the Coventrys, and then ambled down to Reynard's brokerage branch on the ground floor of the United States. In her simple attire, her pleasant skirts and pretty blouses and light, airy hats, sometimes with only a parasol and her hair sailing free, she could be seen reading to him on the piazza. Often he would doze off, and she would gently place a light quilt over his knees and lift his pince-nez from his nose and slide them into the pocket of his blazer.

Then she would sit beside him, rocking with a faraway sadness on her face that only made her more beautiful. It was deeply romantic and infinitely touching. Anyone could see that she was grieving for her friend, the publisher who had met such an unfortunate end. And wasn't it sweet that in her grief she had turned to Sir Walter who occupied such a special place in their hearts? Jason Montague went so far as to make a wager with Eleanor Bentley that Sir Walter would propose before the week was out.

Jessamine was not given to scolding, but she did take Genny to task for leading poor Sir Walter on—though she understood perfectly why Genny was doing it. And, she reflected, if Mr. MacGowan's life had been at stake, she would probably have done the same.

What with Geneena sacrificing herself to Sir Walter most of the day, and not wishing to call upon Angel Tulane every time she wanted to walk, Jessamine laboriously worked out her own navigation.

From the door of their downstairs suite, it was exactly fifty-six steps to the turn in the corridor. Another two hundred steps brought her to the desk beneath the stairs. Usually she detoured for forty-eight steps to rest where the ferns grew so tall they drooped on her head when she sat beneath them.

Today, Jessamine sat beneath the ferns and fanned herself, content in the knowledge that she was totally invisible, out of everyone's way and more or less capable of striking out on her own—though she wished she'd worn a more lightweight dress. The warmth's seduction was well-nigh irresistible, and she found herself dozing more than fanning, and more than once had to snatch up her head, blinking in an effort to come fully awake.

But the sleep she had lost the past few days lay like weights upon Jessamine's eyelids. Her blind eyes closed and her head dropped to her chest. Exactly how long she remained in that position beneath the ferns, Jessamine had no idea, but the men's voices that woke her were quite close and the parties had obviously been speaking for some time.

She came awake with a start and groped for her collar, making sure it was buttoned. The voices grew distressingly audible, and her fastidious manners forbade her to eavesdrop.

Taking hold of her walking stick, meaning to clear her throat loudly and rise and finish her journey to the piazza, to wait there until Genny came to fetch her for luncheon, Jessamine started to rise.

"You cannot do that, goddammit!" a voice hissed somewhere in the vicinity of her right shoulder. "I've got my reputation to think of. Years and years of work, and a future that could take me straight to the White House. What do you think I am? A fool? I won't hear of it. I'm ordering you to stop this insanity right now!"

"You shoulda thought about your future 'fore you tole me to come. It's gone too far. You're in this up t'your honorable neck."

"I'm telling you to let it drop. A man's dead."

"Two men are dead."

Jessamine clapped her hand over her mouth in shock. "Well, one of them won't be any great loss to the planet. Listen to me. If you don't undo what you've done, I'll have you arrested for murder in the first degree."

The second man's raucous, gravelly laughter made Jessamine cringe, and a rigor of fear sent gooseflesh over her body. Too much had been said by Beatrice Hodges that night for her to be mistaken about what was being discussed now almost under her nose. Didn't they see her? Did they think she was mentally incapacitated just because she was blind?

"You do that, your lordship," the man mocked and struck a match, sending the acrid smell of cigar smoke right into Jessamine's nostrils and making her terrified she would succumb to a coughing fit. "And I'll testify that you've been neck deep in this muck from the very beginning. I ain't goin' down alone, no sirree."

"Oh, listen to reason. You've passed over the line."

Jessamine tried not to breathe the smoke.

"I ain't the only one. Now the deed's done. The doer is comin' and by Wednesday night it'll be over. So, set tight and don't get no ideas about goin' off half-cocked. It ain't like you never got your hands dirty now, is it? You're no better'n the rest of us, when it comes t'that."

Jessamine didn't dare move. Nathan Hodges, it could be no other. And the second man? McFee, surely.

Nathan Hodges shifted in his chair as if preparing to leave. Before he did, he asked, as if he didn't really want to know, "Would it be asking too much to know the identity of this... doer?"

"Lillian Cavendish."

"A woman! My God!"

"Ain't it a gasser? And they call 'em the gentle sex. I'm tellin' you, Gov, there ain't anything more cruel than a woman. You take them Apaches? An Apache squaw would do things that'd turn your stomach inside out, and that's no lie."

"My God!"

"She don't know who th'mark is, so don't worry, there ain't no way this could leak out, even if she made a mistake. She'll check into the hotel, and I'll have instructions waitin' in her box. But no names, mind you. Ain't that coverin' all the bases? That way, she'll never know, and she'll never talk. Durin' the big dance? Wham! It's over and you and we're home free. Now, that's all you need t'know, Gov. Which, by the way, is enough to insure you keep your tongue in your mouth where it oughtta be. Get my drift?"

As a stir told Jessamine the men were leaving, she dropped her head to her chest and let her lips fall apart— the ultimate sacrifice, for she had a horror of someone seeing her asleep with her mouth open.

The men moved on without giving her a second look— at least she assumed there was no second look. She was truly too numb and too appalled and too frightened to move, and it took her a good half hour to collect herself enough to get to her feet.

She thought, as she considered calling Marvin to help her to the front piazza, that she would have given a year off her life for the use of her eyes for just ten minutes to find Geneena. How could she keep this terrible secret until luncheon?

Chapter Twenty-one

On Wednesday, Genny asked Sir Walter if he would accompany her to the station to meet Mary Faye's train.

She explained what Adam Worthington had done to both of them. Reynard was appalled at such goings-on, but Genny's mind was so burdened with Jessamine's information, not even Mary Faye's arrival could excite her.

She had told Odessa about McFee's plot with a sense of drowning, but he had received the news with an infuriating lack of alarm, brushing it off as nothing. They had quarreled terribly, ending with his threat to pick her up bodily and carry her to a train if she didn't leave Saratoga.

Then McFee would most assuredly know who she was, she'd countered in blistering fury. She was in this now. If Odessa died at the hands of McFee, of what use was life to her?

He was not going to be killed, Odessa had stormed, making her feel foolish. "You've attracted your rich older man, Genny. Give me some peace of mind by going after him."

She had slapped his impertinent face—the first time she had ever lifted her hand in anger against anyone in her life—and then collapsed in a frightful fit of weeping that left her exhausted.

Waiting for Sir Walter now, she was as nervous as a hummingbird, twittering at every sound, unable to keep still or concentrate. Her skin crawled as if she were being watched by McFee himself. She looked at the clock. Sir Walter was late.

She passed the desk and quickly, before she talked herself out of it, she stepped up to Winnows, stood paralyzed for a moment, then asked if her dear friend, Lillian Cavendish, had arrived yet.

Winnows checked his book. "I'm sorry, Miss Carlyle. Not yet."

Her heart thundered in her ears. "Will she be staying on the ground floor?"

Winnows told her that nothing on the ground floor was available, not at this late date. "But Miss Cavendish will be occupying very nice quarters on the fourth floor—room 402, as a matter of fact. It's the best we could do."

Genny smiled lamely. "I'm sure she'll be pleased." She actually simpered! "Lillian is such a dear, sweet-natured thing."

By the time Sir Walter, in his impeccable blue suit and pince-nez, arrived and helped her into his carriage and drove them to the station, she was on the verge of collapse. Apologies kept bubbling past her lips. Poor dear, he said, and kept reassuring and patting her hand with promises that she was doing the right thing.

The arrival of a train in Saratoga was exactly what Odessa had described it as being. The bell rang, and hordes of bored hotel guests stampeded down to see who was arriving for the last ball of the season.

Sir Walter braved the bedlam of porters and hacks and carriages and parked as best he could to fetch the dazed pregnant woman.

The return trip was awkward, as Genny explained to Mary Faye about Adam's newest "friend." Sir Walter snorted with disgust, and Mary Faye, after having shown such courage in St. Louis, burst into heart-wrenching sobs.

"There, there, my dear," Reynard consoled and said to Genny, "I think I should retain Miss Spender a good attorney before she confronts this godless scalawag. Don't you agree, Miss Carlyle?''

It was the best suggestion Genny had heard in days.

The afternoon called for one of the most nerve-racking performances Genny had ever given.

After dragging Jessamine down to the lobby and planting her beneath the ferns, prompting the blind woman to say that one of the maids would probably water her if she didn't find somewhere else to sit, Genny was confronted with finding a reason for being in the lobby. She was driven to keep vigil over the tiny cubicle behind Winnow's head, and she felt as if she were the target of a thousand raised lorgnettes.

"He said he would put instructions in her box," she fretted as she rose and stared out at the piazza, then walked to a window to stare up Broadway. "There's nothing in her box. Maybe something has happened. Maybe she's not coming.''

"I'm sure I wouldn't know, Geneena," Jessamine said in a valiant attempt to be patient. "I think we should have told Mr. Gold about this.''

"And Mr. Gold would just tell me to mind my own business! That's what Mr. Gold would say.''

Jessamine's sigh said that perhaps Mr. Gold would have been right.

The hotel, however, proved to be in such a furor in preparations for the ball, their presence in the lobby couldn't have gone less noticed. Which didn't help Genny's feeling very much; she feared being seen by Odessa almost as much as being discovered by McFee.

"McFee knew it would be this way, the slime!" Genny wailed in a harsh whisper, having resorted to nibbling on her nails so Jessamine could hardly understand a word she said. "In this crowd, the woman will come and go and I won't get a look at her. The next thing we know, Odessa will be dead, and then what will I do?''

"Hush, now!" Jessamine was as frightened as the younger woman, but she possessed far less energy in which to go to pieces. "The question is, what will you do if you get a look at this Lillian Cavendish? Mr. MacGowan always said, 'Turn your eyes from blood.'"

Genny thought if Jessamine mentioned Mr. MacGowan's name one more time, she wouldn't be responsible for her actions.

"I don't know!" she said and crossed and uncrossed her legs and began chewing her nails again. "Wait!"

Genny grabbed Jessamine's arm with unintentional force. "There he is! McFee. Oh, Jessamine, he's going to the desk. He's . . . he's giving Winnows an envelope. Odessa's death warrant, Jessamine! Oh, Lord, help me to be strong, just this once. Help me know what to do."

McFee was leaning his fleshy hulk against the desk, and Genny watched him reconnoiter the lobby before reaching into his pocket and removing a bill. Winnows was cautious about receiving McFee's bribe; Van Yarborough, in this hectic time, was also working the desk, and the manager would have undoubtedly fired his assistant on the spot if he'd known.

"What would Odessa do if he was waiting here and McFee was about to have *me* killed?" Genny debated and knew with crystal clarity before the words were out of her mouth exactly what Odessa would have done.

Her voice lost its desperate quiver, and she was resilient with resolve. "Winnows is putting the message in the box, just as you said he would," she reported with toneless calm. "I believe it's written on hotel stationery. Stay here, Jessamine. Don't move a muscle."

Jessamine couldn't have moved even if she'd been of a mind to.

With her attention spattered on a dozen things at once—who was where, new faces, old faces, the layers of noise—Genny walked with her head held high to where paper and pens had been laid out for guests. The two men, Winnows and Van Yarborough, were systematically dealing with first one emergency, then another.

A memory of Amelia flashed through Genny's mind as she took a piece of stationery and dipped the pen into a well of ink. One does what one has to do, eh, mother?

With clear, decisive strokes, she wrote, "His name is McFee—fleshy, white hair with muttonchop whiskers. Take care. Very dangerous." She debated about adding some bluff about a money settlement, but decided against it and blotted the paper. The woman wouldn't have agreed to come if money had not been discussed already.

A thrashing heart was her only symptom of nerves as she placed the note into an envelope and sealed it. She waited until Winnows was caught up in a complaint about the capricious electrical wiring that was one of the new attractions for the ball, then she walked quickly to the desk.

"Mr. Van Yarborough?" she said in a sweet voice.

The older man turned, remembering her well. "Oh, Miss Carlyle, what may we do for you today?"

She lifted her shoulders in a girlish self-effacement. Please, please make this work. "The most stupid thing, I'm afraid. My friend, Miss Cavendish—Lillian Cavendish—is arriving shortly, and I must go out. I've left her a note, but I'm afraid I made a mistake. Would you mind terribly handing me down my first note and putting this one in its place?"

The older man scratched his temple. "Let's see... Cavendish is..."

"Room 402," she supplied helpfully.

"Oh, yes. Certainly, I'll be happy to, Miss Carlyle." This was the simplest thing Van Yarborough had been asked to do all day. "We'll just put this one in... Ah, shall we throw this one away?"

Genny smiled as her stomach rolled over. "That's all right, I'll take it."

He smiled as he placed McFee's note in her palm. "Anything else we can do for you, Miss Carlyle?"

Bile as bitter as vinegar rose in Genny's stomach. The deed was done. *I had to do this, Odessa. I had to do something.*

"No, thank you. I must hurry now. I'm afraid I have to work extra hard to be beautiful for the ball tonight."

"Now, now," he chided with a wagging finger as she turned to fetch Jessamine. "True beauty is on the inside."

"Yes, but I'd like a little of mine to show."

He was chuckling as she left, and no sooner had they returned to their suite than Genny raced for the bidet and dropped to her knees and retched until she couldn't breathe.

By eight-thirty, in the courtyard of the hotel, paper lanterns glowed beneath the trees like exotic birds, as if they'd swooped down from heaven to watch nearly a thousand people go through the motions of having a good time.

The ballroom was filled with guests, and every gas jet in the brass chandelier flared as the fifty-four-piece orchestra warmed up and began to play. In a gathering of such swarming size, even a dowager as prestigious as Ava Vanderbilt had difficulty holding court. She wore her most costly diamonds, and the moment she was seated in her special chair across from the orchestra platform, she briskly requested them to play "My Wild Irish Rose."

Eleanor Bentley and Priscilla Davenport arrived in a party of twenty mutual friends. Jason Montague, who had been drinking since two o'clock that afternoon, was already so drunk that he was considering enticing Eleanor to his room after the dance. Florenz Ziegfeld was accompanied by naughty Anne Held who attributed her great beauty to a daily bath in a tub of milk.

Nathan Hodges was stroking his bald spot and fighting a losing battle of nerves by the time he and Beatrice arrived. Beatrice, strangely, was not drinking, and that threw the governor more off balance than the sure, certain knowledge that tonight McFee's dreadful assassination would take place. He had instructed his bodyguards, with the exception of McPherson, to remain outside the ball-room. At the first sign of Andrew Goldman, however, he was to be notified.

Hodges immediately spotted McFee standing just in-side the ballroom door and wondered vaguely if he had to have his clothes specially made. Appalling how a man let himself get into such a condition.

McFee was keeping a vigil on the desk in the lobby, and they exchanged wordless messages. When Lillian Caven-dish arrived, McFee would signal him.

"This wretched thing will probably last the duration," he complained to Beatrice as they plowed through the throng of people, and he took out his watch for the ump-teenth time.

Beatrice, wearing gray tulle, eyed her husband with cold dispassion. "Sit down, Nathan. Let's have something to drink."

Distractedly he said, "All right, what're you having?"

"I'm having lemonade, Nathan."

Hodges experienced a tiny snapping of nerves at the base of his skull, and he slid his wife a hard, puzzled look. How strange she was tonight. How very strange.

"Lewis—" he snapped his fingers "—fetch Mrs. Hodges some lemonade."

"Yessir."

Genny arrived on Sir Walter's arm, though she hadn't planned to attend the ball with anyone. Despite Odessa's repeated insistence that they not be seen in public to-gether, she had been certain he would come and she wanted to be especially pretty, to lure him to her side and keep him there, safe.

But he had been gone from his room all afternoon. Had something gone wrong? Had Lillian gotten another mes-sage from McFee, after all? Was Odessa lying dead some-where at this very moment? She swayed lightly against Sir Walter and searched face after face as it came through the ballroom door.

"You look especially lovely tonight, Miss Carlyle."

Genny was distracted and blinked at him.

Reynard, in flawless formal dress, adjusted his pince-nez with an indulgent smile and walked her across the huge room to peer out at the new electric light that was creating a sensation in the center of the garden, drawing as many oohs and aahs as it did June bugs and flitting moths.

"Thank you, sir." She dipped in a curtsy.

Did she? Was she? Genny could hardly remember getting dressed, though she obviously had, for she was wearing Madame's most splendid gown with its off-the-shoulder ruffling that dipped scandalously low in the back, the yards and yards of susurrus tulle that made her feel as if she could float away. Her white gloves reached to her elbows, and a small, glittering evening bag was tucked beneath her arm.

With Reynard had come Clinton Amesbury, a local attorney he had retained for Mary Faye and who was, he had been quick to assure her, utterly discreet and trustworthy.

Amesbury trailed along behind them now like a shrewd little ferret with his nose constantly twitching. He and Mary Faye had spent the afternoon cloistered in Reynard's room, and the plan was for Mary Faye and Genny to confront Adam together.

If Adam attended. And *if* they found him among this volcano of overdressed people.

Reynard found them a dinner table and graciously held her chair. He smiled and said, "Where is your friend, Miss Spender? I assumed she would join us."

"Oh!" Genny exclaimed and leapt on the excuse. "Stay right here, I'll go fetch her. Isn't this madness? She was probably afraid to come by herself. How thoughtless of me!"

Not allowing Reynard time to protest and not looking back, Genny clutched her small evening bag and jumped from the table to work her way harriedly against the surging grain of incoming guests.

As she approached the door, however, she spotted C. E. McFee, and she began to weave on her feet. The knowledge of the evil McFee had done to others was suddenly not enough to justify what her own hand had done to him. How much easier it would have been to have simply taken a gun and shot him.

She hurried past and raced down the corridor and into the empty lobby. Her eyes flew to the pigeonhole for room 402 behind the desk. God help her, it was empty!

On the road leading south to Albany, two miles out of town, Odessa and Angel Tulane reined in their horses in a cloud of dust and dismounted with a creak of saddle leather and a jangle of trappings.

"What time is it?" Odessa asked as he shuffled about on the tufted grass and stretched and dusted his dark trousers and removed his hat to comb his hair with his fingers. "They're very late."

"They'll be here, Odessa," Angel reassured him and, ever the valet, reached up to brush dust from Odessa's shoulders. "It's not even forty miles to Albany. And you've sent them three telegrams."

"But they could've been delayed."

"I'm sure they weren't. Your father said they would start immediately. The two attorneys were ready. All this you know. Be brave, little buckaroo."

Odessa inspected his hat and slapped sprigs of debris from its crown, then turned to listen for the sound of an approaching carriage. "Genny will have gone to that damned thingamajig by now, I suppose. She's probably half out of her mind wondering where I am."

Angel shrugged his agreement. "You did the best you could do. We were three hours at Judge Wharton's just making your statement and drawing up the necessary papers." He chuckled. "The law moves slowly, my friend."

"I should've turned state's evidence when they wanted me to. Genny wouldn't have had to go through all this. Samuel would probably still be alive."

Angel pointed with a jut of his chin to the now-distinct sound of thundering hooves and the rattles of carriages. He flung his arm about his friend. "If you'd turned state's evidence, you wouldn't have met your pretty lady."

As weary and as hungry and worried as he was, Odessa grinned. "That's true."

"And Samuel's life is and always was in the hands of God. Not your hands, Odessa."

Odessa rubbed his eyes and pressed his palms to his tired face. Straightening, he lit a cheroot and ground the toe of his boot on the match.

"I guess this means you'll have to start calling me Andrew," he said as the smoke bit the night air.

The twinkle of running lights of two carriages came into view, winking in the distant darkness like flirtatious fireflies. Odessa felt an excitement at seeing his parents that he'd not felt before. He would be Andrew Goldman again, a flawed Andrew, yes, but the man he had been born. He would bring to Felicia and Morgan his bride, and he would make a good life for Genny.

If she would still have him after today. He just wanted to collect her and Jessamine and get out of Saratoga.

Angel was laughing. "At least I'll be a rich man when I call you Andrew. Ten thousand acres of Wyoming grassland ain't bad for a cheeky nigguh. Nawsuh, it sho ain't."

With a relief that was a surprise after such harried weeks, Odessa threw back his head and let his laughter pour out over the warm summer evening.

"You're right, Angel, it sho ain't."

Genny stood for some moments gaping at the empty pigeonhole, and the cold truth settled in her stomach like a stone. Why did you have to do this, Mr. McFee? Why did you put me in this position? Why . . . ?

Picking up her skirts, she skimmed to the front piazza where Jessamine sat in one of the thousand wicker rocking chairs, creaking back and forth, back and forth. She dropped to the floor at Jessamine's feet and laid her gloved hands urgently on the woman's knee.

"Jessamine, have you seen Odessa?" she whispered.

The rocking stopped. The black lenses turned, and Jessamine reached out, finding Genny's bare shoulder. "Isn't he at the ball?"

Tears were dammed painfully behind Genny's eyes, threatening to burst with a force that would surely kill her this time. "No, no, he isn't. Oh, Jessamine, what if that wicked man has changed his plan? What if Odessa's dead somewhere—"

"Stop it! Stop it this instant! Now, get ahold of yourself, child. Have you been to his room?"

"Yes, yes. But I'll go again."

"Check at the desk. Maybe he left you a message."

"All right. I'll do it."

Lunging to her feet, Genny raced frantically to the desk, but Van Yarborough shook his head; there were no messages. Genny sped to Odessa's room, terror snapping at her heels, and banged desperately on the door. "Odessa, it's me, Genny. Open the door. Please, open the door. It's me, oh, it's me."

She sank against the wall in defeat. He was dead. She knew it. She had lost Odessa just as she had lost her father and Samuel. "No, no, no."

With the steps of an old woman, she made her way to her room and turned the corner to find Odessa standing in front of the door, his fist raised.

"Oh!" she cried. "Oh!" Gathering her froth of skirts, she sped down the hall and hurled herself into his arms. "Thank you, thank you," she wept and pressed her face deeply into his lapels and savored his strong, hard arms and back that could fend off the world.

She didn't know half the words that rushed in a tangle past her lips as he kissed them and drank her tears until they were wrapped in each other, and her fears became a dream.

"Darling, darling," he said as he rocked her in the fullness of his love. "It's all right."

"You were gone. I thought you were dead."

Odessa laughed into her glorious, tumbling hair. "I told you McFee wasn't going to get me." He tipped up her face and blotted her tears with his fingers. "Listen to me, Genny. I've spent all afternoon with Judge Wharton. We're going to trial. My parents have just arrived with attorneys. Everything's going to be all right, Genny. Genny, look at me. Will you marry me, sweetheart? Will you marry Andrew Goldman? Be my wife?"

Despite the nightmare of the past hours, or maybe because of it, Genny leaned back in his arms, safe in the knowledge of his strength. "For the next ten minutes?" she said with a wicked, teary grin.

For the next ten minutes, neither of them could say anything. And then, as they made their way slowly along the corridor's turns to the hotel lobby where his family was waiting, Genny told him about Lillian Cavendish and what she'd done.

"She's here, Odessa," Genny finished. "Somewhere in this hotel. My note was gone."

When C. E. McFee signaled that the time had come, Nathan Hodges didn't waste his time contemplating the events that had brought him to this moment. This night had not burst upon him because of one decisive choice— to give up or make a pact with the devil. His life had been a succession of choices, moment by moment, day by day. He couldn't remember when he had gone past the point of no return.

Without a qualm, he flicked his fingers in a signal to McPherson to follow the rancher.

Without hesitation, the bodyguard made his way through the throng. When it was over, he would bring McFee to Hodges so that the governor could have words with him, to insure the integrity and power of the office.

*   *   *

Genny and Odessa indulged in the luxury of returning slowly to the mainstream of their lives. Every few steps they paused in the muted corridor, as if by some tacit consent they wanted to put off the moment when, by a connecting of eyes and smiles and hands to the generation that had gone before, they would pick up their lives in a much different place from the spinning fairy tale of the past.

Genny was nurtured by Odessa's arms moving gently around her, holding her in the leashed passion of his love, yet she knew a moment of fear that she could never fit into his life. The future seemed a succession of pretenses. Could she exist in such a world?

Yes, for Odessa, she could do anything. And even if she failed, it would have been worth it.

He drew her into a doorway and kissed her, his tongue playing around her lips until they opened. "I love you, Genny Carlyle," he whispered, and was comforted by her smile.

"I know you do." She drew his head down to hers, stroking the powerful column of his neck and touching his lips. "I'll make you proud of me, Odessa."

"Shhh. Don't change for me."

Genny would wonder later how long McFee had been waiting for them at the end of the corridor. Had he been watching them all along? Had he seen them kissing and heard their intimate declarations of love?

She thought, as Odessa reacted with a quick deadly speed of something more animal than human, that he must have smelled the man long before he looked up and saw McFee rolling his hulk toward them. He was tense as a spear, hardly breathing, his lips curled back over his teeth.

The fleshy man's face was florid with hatred. Genny saw Odessa leaving her, moving toward the man, and in a ghastly sudden presentiment of the future, she saw herself losing it all before she had ever held it in her hands.

"No!" she heard herself scream as the two men were separated only by feet, then inches. She threw herself at them.

But her cry was drowned by a shot that came from nowhere. In a fraction of a second, a falling star, a flash of lightning, McFee stopped in his tracks. His knees buckled, and his great walrus bulk dropped to its knees and weaved before it fell facedown to the floor and spread there like melting lard.

Stunned, Genny clapped her hands on her mouth to stifle another scream as Odessa bent over the man in dazed disbelief.

"You stupid bitch!" a man screamed. "You killed the wrong one!"

But the corridor was empty, as if a ghost had passed through. Except for the man who now faced Odessa with the expression of one who has just been diagnosed with a fatal disease. He stared blankly at Odessa and moved his lips as if trying to speak, but no sound came, and he spun on his heel and disappeared.

Odessa's boots were thunderous and swift as he sprinted after the man. Genny raced behind him, running, stumbling, weeping, teetering on the brink of hysteria.

It was Felicia Goldman who intercepted her in the lobby and, catching her short, folded her into her arms.

"Miss Carlyle. Be still now, dear. Genny?" Finally Genny looked at the woman. Felicia touched Genny's cheek as if she had found something she'd lost and said, "Thank you for my son, dear girl. Thank you. Everything will be all right now. You saved his life, Genny. Can you hear me? You saved Andrew's life. Morgan, could you get Genny some water to wash her face? We're going to take you home now, Genny."

But not yet, not yet, Genny thought. Jessamine's stitches still to be caught up. Breathing deeply, she steadied herself and laid her hand upon Felicia Goldman's thin wrist. Odessa was heading for the ballroom.

"I have to be with him," she protested. "Don't you understand?"

Felicia smiled. "Yes. Yes, of course I do."

Pivoting, Odessa looked back for her and held out his hand. "Genny?"

She ran to him.

With a retinue of lawyers, along with Judge Wharton who had arrived only moments before, they moved into the ballroom, led by a much-distressed Percy Van Yarborough.

Saratoga's guests were celebrating the end of a wonderful and glorious season. Nathan Hodges was dancing with Beatrice and Eleanor Bentley and Sir Walter were making a toast. Ava Vanderbilt was holding court and Mary Faye was shrinking against a distant wall, lost and full of her unborn child as she searched the crowd for the face of the man who had started it all, Adam Worthington. The orchestra was playing "Beautiful Dreamer."

Van Yarborough hurried to the conductor and motioned him to lend his ear. The baton lowered, and the music stopped. Whispering rippled through the crowd, and scores of faces turned to see the reason.

McPherson had been speaking to Governor Hodges, and the balding man swept his bespectacled gaze to the door where he found Odessa waiting.

The hush that fell over the room was absolute. Even the small precise steps of Van Yarborough were audible as he came forward to motion Judge Wharton to approach with the group of lawyers.

"Odessa," whispered Genny, clutching his fingers, "don't go. Let them do it."

Laughter, deep and bitter, rumbled in Odessa's chest. "He can't hurt us now, Genny."

"You said that before."

"But this time it's true."

Like the Red Sea, the crowd parted for the phalanx of men. When they stopped before Nathan Hodges, Genny was certain that she glimpsed a small smile on Beatrice's face.

It wasn't necessary to inform the governor what had happened. When Judge Wharton said, "You'll have to come with us, sir," Hodges didn't blink an eye but fetched his hat and turned briefly to his wife. Without a word, he and McPherson and Lewis stepped out and were immediately surrounded by men who would take them to the authorities.

Snap, snap, went Van Yarborough's fingers. The conductor lifted his baton. It lowered, and the strains of a waltz spun through the room. People exchanged quizzing looks but were soon consumed with their own lives again. Time moved on. The interruption would be gossiped about, but its cause soon forgotten. Such were the ways of the world.

Genny felt strangely adrift. Odessa surprised her by kissing her hard and quickly on her lips. "I believe our business among the good folk of Saratoga Springs is finished, my love," he said, and drew a deep draft of air into his lungs and smiled over her head at his father.

Spying Mary Faye making her way laboriously toward them, Genny shook her head. "Not quite, Odessa."

"Genny? Genny?" The male voice that accosted Genny came from out of the past—not loudly, not rudely, but almost lost.

If she had been of a mind, Genny could have kept on walking and no one would have known or cared. But for Mary Faye's unborn child, she could not. She pressed her bag securely beneath her arm and drew her gloves reassuringly higher on her arms. Her turn was swift, and she scoured the room for the man who had spoken her name.

Adam Worthington was a distance away, midway from his chair to his feet. A napkin was clutched in his hand. His table was tucked among fifty other tables just like it, and sitting with him was the older woman, weighted even more heavily with diamonds than before. Expensive wines cluttered the table, and gourmet delicacies. Adam was wearing a tuxedo. Diamond studs sparkled in his cuffs.

"A moment," Genny said to Odessa as Adam took in her clothes and the people who waited just behind her. "Unfinished business."

A dazed, sheepish smile was briefly on Adam's lips, then gone. It had been a terrible mistake. If she had not already seen him, he would have turned away, Genny knew.

With an odd sense of emptiness, she approached his table while the orchestra played and the dance floor was a kaleidoscope of couples. How often had she relished vengeance on this man, wanting him to suffer mercilessly? But she had seen too much of real suffering lately, and suddenly Adam Worthington wasn't worth the trouble.

With a half laugh of disbelief, she stopped where she was. Over her shoulder, she found the watchful, loving eyes of Odessa, and she turned up a gloved palm as if to say, He's not worth it.

But Mary Faye, with a hand upon her burgeoning belly, drew near, and Genny, smiling, motioned the woman on. Looping her arm through Mary Faye's, she escorted her to the table. Adam's face blanched and he stumbled, crashing into the table and knocking over the glasses of wine, bringing a bevy of waiters to clean up the mess.

The bejeweled older woman drew Genny's vague pity. "Adam," Genny said with a bright, cutting smile, urging Mary Faye forward. "Mary Faye and I came to see you."

In horror, Adam looked at his lady friend, then at Odessa, then at Mary Faye who made a sound of disgust deep in her throat. He swallowed convulsively, and his Adam's apple bobbed against his collar.

"Mary, darlin'—"

Before Mary Faye's anger could erupt, Genny purred, "I believe you know everyone, Adam. With the exception of Odessa. Oh, you haven't met Mr. Amesbury, have you? The gentleman coming toward us is Clinton Amesbury,

Mary Faye's attorney. I'm sure you and he will have much to talk about.''

Adam dropped to his chair as if all the bones in his body had come apart at their joints. He buried his handsome head in his hands.

A rage rose in Genny, and she took several more steps to the table. To the woman, she said, ''I don't believe we've been introduced. You must be Adam's mother.''

''Oh!'' the woman choked, clutching her bosom with mortification and then striking at Adam's shoulder with a diamond-covered fist. ''What is the meaning of this?''

''And this is Mary Faye Spender.'' Genny showed her teeth. ''She's carrying your child, Adam. We're hoping for a boy.''

Odessa, hearing this exchange, could hardly believe the venom of his wife-to-be. But he wouldn't have stopped her if the walls of the United States Hotel had come crashing down around them. He only hoped Worthington didn't have a cardiac arrest before he suffered his comeuppance.

''I'd like my money now, Adam,'' Genny demanded in a whipping, cutting tone.

The beaten man lifted his head, imploring her to have mercy. ''Genny,'' he wheezed, ''I don't have any money.''

Genny's eyes were merciless. ''Of course you don't. Ask your mother for it!'' She arranged a smile at the dumbstruck older woman. ''He never has any money.''

With a snap of the clasp on her purse, Genny opened it and reached her gloved finger inside to find the bills Odessa had won gambling in St. Louis. She had hoarded each single dollar, measuring out the pennies in dread of some future hungry day. This money was her final break with the past.

She leaned forward and stuffed the bills into Adam's pocket. ''On second thought,'' she said, retrieving them and giving them to Mary Faye with a smile, ''you take care of them, Mary Faye. Mr. Amesbury, I leave her in your capable hands.''

The attorney narrowed his ferretlike eyes and snapped his heels together. Behind him, removing his pince-nez, Sir Walter was smiling.

Dear Sir Walter, Genny thought with her only pang of regret. Dear, kind Sir Walter.

Pressing her lips together, she walked over to the elderly man and rose on her toes to place a kiss on his cheek. "You've been very kind to me, sir. I never meant—"

The old gentleman placed a finger on her lips with a boldness that made him flush. "My dear, don't say a word. Your radiance speaks for itself. I understand completely. Be very happy, Miss Carlyle. I don't expect I'll be seeing you again."

She shook her head, happy and sad at the same time. "I'll be leaving tonight with my fiancé. He's very talented, you know. A great artist."

"I know."

Reaching around her, Reynard shook hands with Odessa, then indicated Felicia and Morgan with a nod of his head. "Your family?"

"Yes, sir," Odessa replied.

"Then I'm sure Miss Carlyle is in good hands."

Odessa drew Genny to his side and into a life that would be new for both of them. Angel was busy making preparations to leave. The carriages were being loaded, and the hotel bills were being paid. Jessamine was being seen to, and his family was waiting to take them to Albany. With a smile that was as much of a promise as a kiss, he tipped Genny's beautiful, shimmering face up to his.

"The very best of hands," he said to Reynard as he adored her. And to her, with a tender, poignant catch in his voice, he said, "It's time for us, Genevieve Carlyle. It's time to take you home."

"Yes," she said breathlessly and pressed his hands as the orchestra reached a new crescendo and the whole world seemed filled with music and laughter. "Oh, yes."

*   *   *   *   *

**THIS JULY, HARLEQUIN OFFERS YOU
THE PERFECT SUMMER READ!**

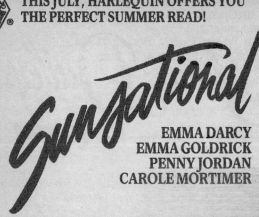

**EMMA DARCY
EMMA GOLDRICK
PENNY JORDAN
CAROLE MORTIMER**

From top authors of Harlequin Presents comes
HARLEQUIN SUNSATIONAL, a four-stories-in-one
book with 768 pages of romantic reading.

Written by such prolific Harlequin authors as Emma Darcy,
Emma Goldrick, Penny Jordan and Carole Mortimer,
HARLEQUIN SUNSATIONAL is the perfect summer
companion to take along to the beach, cottage, on your
dream destination or just for reading at home in the warm
sunshine!

Don't miss this unique reading opportunity.

Available wherever Harlequin books are sold.

Back by Popular Demand

Janet Dailey
Americana

A romantic tour of America through fifty favorite Harlequin Presents, each set in a different state researched by Janet and her husband, Bill. A journey of a lifetime in one cherished collection.

In July, don't miss the exciting states featured in:

Title #11 — HAWAII
       Kona Winds

  #12 — IDAHO
        The Travelling Kind

Available wherever
Harlequin books are sold.

Coming soon
to an easy chair near you.

FIRST CLASS is Harlequin's armchair travel plan for the incurably romantic. You'll visit a different dreamy destination every month from January through December without ever packing a bag. No jet lag, no expensive air fares and *no* lost luggage. Just First Class Harlequin Romance reading, featuring exotic settings from Tasmania to Thailand, from Egypt to Australia, and more.

FIRST CLASS romantic excursions guaranteed! Start your world tour in January. Look for the special **FIRST CLASS** destination on selected Harlequin Romance titles—there's a new one every month.

NEXT DESTINATION:
FLORENCE, ITALY

 Harlequin Books

JTR7

HARLEQUIN
American Romance®

From the Alaskan wilderness to sultry New Orleans . . . from New England seashores to the rugged Rockies . . . American Romance brings you the best of America. And with each trip, you'll find the best in romance.

Each month, American Romance brings you the magic of falling in love with that special American man. Whether an untamed cowboy or a polished executive, he has that sensuality, that special spark sure to capture your heart.

For stories of today, with women just like you and the men they dream about, read American Romance. Four new titles each month.

HARLEQUIN AMERICAN ROMANCE—the love stories you can believe in.

AMERICAN

Take 4 bestselling love stories FREE
Plus get a FREE surprise gift!

This August, don't miss an exclusive
two-in-one collection of earlier love stories

MAN
WITH A PAST

T R U E   C O L O R S
by one of today's hottest
romance authors,

Now, two of Jayne Ann Krentz's most loved books are
available together in this special edition that new and
longtime fans will want to add to their bookshelves.

Let Jayne Ann Krentz capture your hearts with the love
stories, MAN WITH A PAST and TRUE COLORS.

And in October, watch for the second two-in-one
collection by Barbara Delinsky!

Available wherever Harlequin books are sold.